The Best
AMERICAN
SHORT
STORIES
1981

The Best
AMERICAN
SHORT
STORIES
1981

Selected from
U.S. and Canadian Magazines
by Hortense Calisher
with Shannon Ravenel

With an Introduction by Hortense Calisher

1981

Houghton Mifflin Company Boston

Copyright © 1981 by Houghton Mifflin Company

Library of Congress Catalog Card Number: 80-679
ISBN: 0-395-31259-0

Printed in the United States of America

V 10 9 8 7 6 5 4 3 2 1

"The Idea of Switzerland" by Walter Abish. First published in *The Partisan Review*.
Copyright © 1980 by Walter Abish.

"Small Island Republics" by Max Apple. First published in *The Kenyon Review*.
Copyright © 1980 by Max Apple.

"Winter: 1978" by Ann Beattie. First published in *Carolina Quarterly*. Copyright
© 1980 by Ann Beattie.

"A Working Day" by Robert Coover. First published in *The Iowa Review*. Copyright © 1980 by Robert Coover.

"The Moth and the Primrose" by Vincent G. Dethier. First published in *The
Massachusetts Review*. Copyright © 1980 by Vincent G. Dethier.

"The Winter Father" by Andre Dubus. First published in *The Sewanee Review*.
Copyright © 1980 by Andre Dubus.

"The Assembly" by Mavis Gallant. First published in *Harper's*. Copyright © 1980
by Mavis Gallant.

"The Bookseller" by Elizabeth Hardwick. First published in *The New Yorker*. Copyright © 1980 by Elizabeth Hardwick.

"Shiloh" by Bobbie Ann Mason. First published in *The New Yorker*. Copyright ©
1980 by Bobbie Ann Mason.

"The Future" by Joseph McElroy. First published in *The New Yorker*. Copyright
© 1980 by Joseph McElroy.

"Fogbound in Avalon" by Elizabeth McGrath. First published in *The New Yorker*.
Copyright © 1980 by The New Yorker Magazine, Inc.

"The Mountains Where Cithaeron Is" by Amelia Moseley. First published in *The
Massachusetts Review*. Copyright © 1980 by Amelia Moseley.

"Wood" by Alice Munro. First published in *The New Yorker*. Copyright © 1980 by
Alice Munro.

"Presque Isle" by Joyce Carol Oates. First published in *The Agni Review*. Copyright
© 1980 by Joyce Carol Oates, Inc.

"The Shawl" by Cynthia Ozick. First published in *The New Yorker*. Copyright ©
1980 by The New Yorker Magazine, Inc.

Contents

Introduction

IF POETRY has the direct line to the highest laurel — or the noblest life — and the novel is sometimes cock-of-the-walk conversationally, then the short story, somehow frozen or immured between them, is everybody's prize orphan, of whom one speaks tenderly, if not for long. It's the chamber music of literature and has the same kind of devotee. Besides, it doesn't sell. There's often that confusion between the commercial fact and the Parnassian one.

Sometimes I think that the salvation of literature in this country is that we haven't yet got used to it. For while Europe for centuries has regarded the *conte*, the tale, not as a mere bypass to longer works and greater career but as one of the natural paths of a writer's way through the world, it is the United States that for the past fifty or sixty years has most seemed to harbor the short story and to sustain it. Possibly the deepest causes of this aren't literary per se, but political, regional, or financial. We still had great new regions to contend with — in that period, our West and our South — and this always both stirs the urge to recount and gives it new furnishment, as is happening now in South America and also in Canada, as we will see in this volume. We had newer responses to war, to the rise of great cities and their conflict with the provinces, and to rising generally; and we were nouveau riche in the power of print. We still felicitated ourselves on our libraries. Poe and Hawthorne are often regarded as the shapers of the modern short story — in its incarnation as a moment in experience, as against the traditional tale, which rambled in the "folk" or the picaresque consciousness.

Whatever, we've most surely had our story renaissances, and this collection is related, though perhaps deviously, to the latest of them — or to what I heard referred to at the University of East Anglia as "your American Workshoppe." Without arguing the pros and cons of whether one can make writers by the atelier method, it's fair to observe that in a country huge as ours, where once a writer who wanted confreres or even publication might well have to migrate, the university has willy-nilly become the café, whatever that does or doesn't do for the writer of talent. However, a writer is tied to experience in a special way, though not always a literal one, and certainly a great many are spending a large portion of the most important postgraduate life at school, an enclosure, no matter what one does there. If one teaches and writes there as well, the effect of immersion in talk about "techniques" may also enter in. Subtlest of all influences or hazards for the silent persona of a writer may be the constant verbalization of energies and meditations better saved for the page. Since so much of writing-school study does concentrate on the short story, does the reading of 120 published during a year suggest any conclusions on the above? Of course, but not without examining, as another part of the creative-writing phenomenon, the magazine outlets for the literary story — much decreased in the public sector, but much increased in the government-grant-sustained little magazines, some of the best of which are attached to universities.

There is now an enormous literacy at loose in the land of the short story. Many more people seem able to give fairly well-wrought accounts of experience, and in good language — much as the products of good British schools were often able to do en masse. But what once would have been nonfiction memoir or essay is now attempted as art. I've no doubt that the writing courses, graduate or undergraduate, so many of them focused on the short story, have much to do with this — along with the more general rush of youth into the arts. But the hazards of art remain as usual, as do the effects of coterie. The strong will either make good use of such derivations or escape them. Less so the weak. I can't guess how many of the stories I read emerged from such influences, except now and then where they seemed to me to fail.

There were a goodly number of stories set in academia, often obviously authored by its denizens, or the wives of denizens, who either were or were not themselves professionals. Some stories betrayed their origins at once, either by the language itself, of a sort not to resist words like *eidolon,* or by that crabbed self-commentary where the critique is more antic than the action. Some ached only from the enclosure itself — an honest enough subject — but suffered too much from the effects of it: I couldn't include one witty, vivid story soured by sheer invidiousness.

Yet there is one story here whose subject is academia bung on, and comes naturally out of the riches possible from any milieu when not theorized over in concert but caught by the singular pen. I was understandably cheered when I saw it, since, some time back, defending the university as milieu and not merely classroom, I'd written: "Fashionably considered, the university is not a part of going 'life' at all, as against the pursuit of homosexuality in Algiers, or strong drink in Connecticut. But I find it impossible to exclude from at least tentative reality any place where so many people are."

When stories are in a sense needed or bespoke by the life around us, writers write them, and readers recognize them, as sharing the same lights and darks. For some time American writers, and readers along with them, have seemed more than usually troubled about the means of narration. I'm not speaking of the real innovators, whose method is almost always innate, but of otherwise conventional stories and novels compelled to excuse their reason for being; the teller is talking to a psychiatrist or a tape, or can't rest until "things are sorted out" — just as in earlier times a man might talk at his club, or to his priest. Nothing new except in the recording devices, but the token use of such interlocutors, or of any, can convey the writer's own unease with "story." There's also a more febrile use of the present tense, as if to make reality more immediate, or — by scrapping flashback — young. Quote marks are dispensed with, in one more effort to rid the writer of that ever-present monkey-on-the-back, typography. All writers, possibly all artists, at times feel an impatience with the physical limitations of their own media. Literature's two classic answers are in opposition: elaborate the page or typeface, as in medieval illumination, Victorian illustration pursued even to the three-dimensional, or Wyndham Lewis-style *BLAST* (which last may have had its influence on comic books); or — scrap everything but ink, down to the last Dada word. Neither answer can be permanent, nor can one ever satisfactorily enlist another art, though I've in the past received desperate manuscripts with disc attached. And we all know about danced poems. Music, especially, can make a writer jealous of its closeness to the ineffable. We are artists of the effable. There's no cure for that but the daily one: to write what even Beethoven, with all the chromatics pushing heavenward, could not have said.

Among the stories considered, some do seem to have lost confidence in the medium itself, expending their main juice in antic buzzing between "fact" and "fiction," this posed as a dilemma of technique rather than as one of the complex and fruitful obscurities of life. The current fashion is to throw that "dilemma" straight into the lap of the hopefully dissective reader, who may not thank you for it unless he or she has been eating the same dogma as you. Much of twentieth-century art does of course subtly plead "Help me with the technique of this," but in the spirit of play, or intimate connection, or a joint truth-seeking in which the artist asks participation in a discovery — not out of any implication that the pursuit itself is suspect.

There is perhaps a deeper question and dismay. Surely, though fiction has often before nuzzled close to history or journalism or current events, Dickens, George Eliot, Tolstoi, and legions of others even to today seem not to have worried over the categories, or had any gnawings over whether art can sustain its own tragicomedy in face of the terrible or absurd facts. Nowadays some writers do. There's no answer to that except the personal one. Writers plug on out of obsession, nerve, exaltation, agog at what happens in the world or what does not, forever entranced at the power of the word to present it.

Here are twenty of those short stories published during 1980. They have been chosen in turn by three successive tastes, the magazine editor or editors having first go. These editors wield the ultimate power — the power of print. Can one be assured that their choice is in all respects right and representative? They would more likely be among the first to say not, making the decisions as they do among the many, and within the terms of available space, special audience, literary preference, and sheer accident. Not all good stories get published, I fear, and many that eventually do must wait beyond their time.

The second taste is that of the *Best American Short Stories* annual editor, Shannon Ravenel, who scanned approximately 1250 stories published within the calendar year by nationally distributed American and Canadian periodicals, then read carefully the 900 stories which merited that. Except in rare and exceptional cases, stories may not be translations, must show evidence of having been written as complete stories, not as excerpts, and authors must be citizens or permanent residents of either the United States or Canada. Of the stories that qualified, the 120 I was sent were garnered from 151 periodicals, of which the selected stories represent 11, the magazine represented by most stories being *The New Yorker* with 9. Shannon Ravenel further reports: "The American short story abounds. Most of those I read are literate and technically adequate. But filling the 120 slots with outstanding stories is not as easy a job as the large numbers above might have us guess. Nevertheless, the overall quality is, I think, high, and I find the state of the American short story in 1980 to be good."

From this group I was asked to choose the top twenty. Several stood out immediately as ones I had previously read and remembered as exceptional. After that the choice was harder, there being at least thirty all told I could wish to single out. There are, I see, ten men and ten women; this was not intentional. About half are from *The New Yorker,* which publishes fifty-two issues per year and a major portion of the country's short fiction, and will naturally get first look at much of the best of it. I have chosen without stricture as to subject, geography, periodical, or indeed author, where that is humanly possible. Where an author is already known and the body of already read work stands behind the specific story, I have considered that. I've also considered my prejudices — those known to me — though without much hope of conversion. I will accept any convention or breakdown of language if it is alive, obviously willed by the author rather than fortuitously dripped, and if it unites with its subject in the extra skin that language can give. The supreme story seems to me one so knitted that we cannot extract its single theme. As in life.

I'll discuss the following in that technique known as the "alphabetical."

Walter Abish's novels are often called avant-garde. They seem to me not to have enough linguistic or other shock for that, perhaps because in these days of laissez faire it's harder to be in the rear than in the front. "The Idea of Switzerland" is certainly less formalized than his other work, though it has a faint trace of his rhythmic repetitions, which when less constant seem to add more, indeed real cogency and movement. Did I choose it in part because it reminded me pleasantly of the European short story? Indeed. It has the reek of history, of politics and of people who sweat out the past in dark brown corners long given over to that. Its worldly taint reminds one how so much of the American short story even now concerns itself with domestic family relations, and how often we still seem to go to foreign fiction for the world view.

Some American writers become hybrid through travel, while others are able to draw on that view while seeming not to leave home. "Inudo was probably the world's tallest Japanese-American," Max Apple's "Small Island Republics" begins. Inudo is also the only "ethnic" in this collection, and since his great-grandfather was born in California he not unsurprisingly spends his time trying to make his Americanism stick. Though this is a story that hops over the years, it has the sprightly brevity of an anecdote. Satire does that to our writers more than to most — unless they write novels, in which case they often overpay their dues. Apple is one of our few real satirists: I can't think of another like him. We have many jokesters. Some bog in heavy literary parody, some in their own plaintive antihero egos; most write for a constituency. The real mark of a satirist is in his or her choice of subject. The initial impulse, as in Swift and Orwell, is often as slender as a gag. The risk is topicality, and Apple's story has perhaps too much for what could be a cleaner scenario. But the choice of subject is a nourishingly eccentric one, and there is wit along the way. There's no telling what Apple, no mere humorist, may do. He should be watched.

Ann Beattie's people lead what used to be called amoral lives, while their whole preoccupation is moral, if narrowly so. Indeed, they are religious fanatics preoccupied with the sin of unhappiness. The guilt of drifting is upon them; though the malaise of drugging is the official symptom, that other unease lies heavy. In her earlier stories the narrative method drifted also, in counterpoint to the characters, as if only interminably unresolved length could uphold their rhythms and no story they inhabited could dare to make up its mind. In "Winter: 1978" this has focused and sharpened. Beattie has ever surer grasp of her world, and of course its conventions have become clearer to us. Her people know the terms of their own appeal — the wastrel glow of an intellectually fashionable hell to which the stupid or the poor need not apply. Or, until recently, the old. Whether or not their hell is sufficient only to the day, and not yet imperial enough for greedier literary hopes, there have always been people like them, and Beattie's precision fascinates.

Is Robert Coover's "A Working Day" a send-up of the sad and hilarious yet sometimes exquisite repetitiousness of porn, here marvelously united with the perfect stylistic instrument, the ditto, ditto, yet ditto repetitiousness of the once nouvelle *nouvelle vague?* If you have seen Forty-second Street pornshop paperbacks or have read *The Story of O,* you may agree on the porn. If you recall how Robbe-Grillet's cinematic stop-time inches forward and retreats down a page, relentlessly engaging the metronome moment in a battle against too much meaning, you'll see the resemblance. Perhaps Coover, going Robbe-Grillet one better and exceeding his own intention (though I doubt this), has written an extraordinary exercise on the demonstrable connections between sadism and humility, torture and saintliness, authority and helplessness — and on perhaps half a dozen other paradoxes — yet in so doing, he has created, inch by rigorous inch, two characters who have turned, if in bas-relief, into real people, in a bedroom carved by these progressions into forever's brilliant "still."

If Vincent G. Dethier's "The Moth and the Primrose" had left out old Prout and the parson, a human framework whose presence I half resented on behalf of the flora and fauna, we might have had only a fine piece of what we have come to call nature writing, a genre I find too exclusionary for comfort and at the same time too loose in its metaphors. (Can we really trust wind, sea, and stars, plants and rocks, our own soma *and* molecular biology, when they all sing together similarly corybant, though under such diverse orchestrators as Loren Eiseley, Henry Beetle Hough, Lewis Thomas, and Henry David Thoreau?) This story reminds us of how seldom the anti-anthropomorphic emotion enters our serious imaginative work — or our lives? Perhaps we have relegated it to the galaxies, where it is not yet serious. Good to see it grounded, and several evolutionary steps below even James Agee's cows in "A Mother's Tale." The curiously healing pleasure is to find, as I do here, that it is an emotion.

"The Winter Father." Andre Dubus has found a fell phrase. Two stories about the new generation of divorced fathers appear in this collection, culled from among several more. Stories on this

subject were among the most affecting of the domestic tales, perhaps because vulnerable children were usually present. The pain
seemed fresher than some, and the men so clumsily lorn. Yet we
have had all that before, and in a great story, Fitzgerald's "Babylon
Revisited." It took me a while to identify what was really new.
There is a word that used to be applied to delicate feeling delicately responded to. Applied to women, and to modes of writing
presumed to come out of the female situation, it came to be a
pejorative. I don't use it so. But men are now writing — from the
sensibility. "The Winter Father" is as masculine as need be. But the
sensitively harbored details of an enforced domestic pattern are
what you learn to watch.

Remember the "short short"? Some magazines and newspapers
still run them; others scorn them as tricks. They are. But when the
sleight of hand comes from a master — I believe Tolstoi wrote one
once — it can be as satisfying as a final gambit. Mavis Gallant's
"The Assembly" is a dialogue short enough to poise on the point
of the mythical pin, though it contains no angels. You may have to
diagram it for full savor — or even read it aloud with the aid of
friends. It doesn't take long. "The Assembly" is like a Simenon too
soon read on a long journey. Too short only for us.

Elizabeth Hardwick's "The Bookseller" is privileged reading, of
a kind rare now that the journal, which in other times has had
many guises — a daily gallery crowded with portraits, a religious
meditation, even an art form — is much perceived as mere back-
door revelation or psychic relief. She has time for conning the
alphabet of sensation, time for recording it, and for here revisiting
that happy, scruffy place in which the best books reside and the
people have the peculiar durability of the transiently seen. They
are presented as having already passed through the narrator's
sieve, and we accept that, in the contemplative ease which the good
journal provides. We travel the prose as nabobs once toured Europe, in the hands of a sturdy and elegant guide. The very pace of
her prose is a reminder not of old times but of the continuous
presence of literature in life.

Leroy and Norma Jean in "Shiloh" belong to those inarticulates
necessarily distanced from any writer by gaps of education and/or
intelligence. The genre's a hard one, its worst hazard being any
hint of patronizing. In our generation, Flannery O'Connor
bridged the gap best, perhaps because hellfire in one's cosmos

likely equalizes all. Humor helps but is dangerous. Language must synchronize but not be sacrificed. Bobbie Ann Mason does well in a natural, forthright way. I'd read it before. One remembers its small progressions. The ambiguity of the ending? Perhaps somewhat handled. One hopes that it was not edited.

I often think that Joseph McElroy ("The Future") wills his indirections toward us as poets do their private metaphors: it's up to us. Here the method very much matches the subject — what a mother and a twelve-year-old son, living together apart from the father, hide from one another. Davey belongs somewhere in that legion of "divorced" children, but is himself, a hypersmart boarding-school kid, almost fatherly. The story is the harder to follow because the pair speak in the lingua franca of their own reticences. The "event" — a restaurant robbery at which they are present — is more baldly told, but the complexity is the more seductive side of the story.

Elizabeth McGrath's "Fogbound in Avalon" is a stunner. I use that word because it is how one might describe the narrator, a woman academic breaking with marriage and much else to return to her home town, St. John's, Newfoundland, to wrest with old friends, old house, and old wanderings. Wry, fierce, tough, she at times calls to mind those heroines of Christina Stead who arrive in this or that environs, to start the conquering or begin anew. There is the same bitterly intimate energy in the conversational tone of more than one of these colonials; one mulls its sources, finding it tonic, salutary. Perhaps we were such colonials, once.

I asked for help on Amelia Moseley's "The Mountains Where Cithaeron Is." (Cithaeron is where Oedipus as a babe was exposed to die, with a spike in him, and Pentheus in Euripides' *Bacchae* is destroyed by the women for watching their mystic worship.) I distrust stories, or novels, that depend on preliminary quotes. This one is surely out of many recent isms, from fem to veg, yet it has its own dogged assurance, and, maybe, mandala, along with that commanding strictness in the narration which is always bracing for fantasy. It takes on much, and perhaps the boundaries aren't clear, but as we discussed it we found it more and more discussable, as I hope you will.

Alice Munro is a superb writer. Book after book arrives *live*. Her sagas are smaller than some from writers whom Canada more commonly regards as its major ones; but I've long since thought of her work as part of world literature. "Wood," one of her best, I admire very much. Use the concrete, yes, but how many can, like this? How plain the language is, and how eventful. On second reading it delighted me more, a story one hopes will widen her American audience. When one has enough "wood," one can do anything.

Joyce Carol Oates's "Presque Isle," as the title indicates, is a story of milieu, one that we feel we almost already know ("the wealthy Scudders," "the camp"), as we also almost know this mother with her alcoholic "queen-bee" confusions, this daughter with her resultant ones, and even the husband, the disaffected James, who from a distance supplies the only "moral" stance the story will get — except from the reader. In this broken-down Sodom the flash of the two gays "going at it" confirms rather than surprises. All the conventions by which the daughter comes to be what she is are now here. Technically the story is almost rushed off its feet by the novelistic wisdom behind it; the economy is almost shorthand. The short stories of novelists are different; the pen becomes farsighted, or bifocal, rather than near. The stance widens, even in a shorter work. In "Presque Isle," if the people are inarticulate in their own way they have none of the winsomeness of the underdeveloped; each is a concept clearly preconceived. What illumines is the author's own romantic spirit, that of the true storyteller whom nothing amazes, to whom everything is new.

"The Shawl" is a long story, profoundly short. In it we walk with three victims of the Holocaust: Rose, who has the nipple and the shawl; Magda, the suckling; and Stella, the fourteen-year-old girl. Many have written of the Holocaust, never quite freeing themselves from reverential agony for the past. Cynthia Ozick invades it with intensity; it is her present. In a most remarkable evocation, it becomes ours.

Poets often keep the prose they write politely quiet, undemonstrative; the poems of a novelist may do the same — as if the real arena is elsewhere. "The St. Anthony Chorale," by Louis D. Rubin, Jr., is written with an "old-fashioned" ambling integrity; earlytwentieth-century memoirs of the Lincoln Steffens era come to mind. The mode, of course, is sempiternal, but in these flashy times we don't see much of it. Here the setting — the South — may account for some of the moseying, in fine tune with the subject, a young man's undercurrents of inner change. The story's lack of posturing is a joy. If the ending epiphany has just a touch of it, well, that's music for you.

"Wissler Remembers" is the teacher's story, anointed, as the best of these are, by love. Yes, the academic life can isolate the educated, the expressive, in a world of peers whose destinies are for the most part so similar and fixed that demiurges often do ply; but Richard Stern's windows are wide open, as Lionel Trilling's were in "Of This Time, Of That Place." He knows that, as R. V. Cassill phrased it, "Larchmoor is not the world." If it is a harder literary task to create interesting good people than bad ones, it is just as hard for the critic to characterize a story in which love outreaches sentiment. Richard Stern will show you how it's done.

Elizabeth Tallent's "Ice" is a story I myself asked to be added to the list sent me, having come upon it in my own reading. It remained in my mind. During that period, a person whose taste I respect — though it often differs from mine — asked, "Did you by any chance read —?" There is a suspending magic about it, which haunted us both.

Perhaps this is a good place to talk about the "typical" *New Yorker* short story, since the proportion of my inclusions from that magazine will give pain to some. There is no typical one, really, but I can describe what people think it is: a story of suburbia or other middle-class to "upper" milieu, which exists to record the delicate observation of the small fauna, terrors, and fatuities of domestic existence, sometimes leveled in with a larger terror — a death, say, or a mortal disease — so that we may respond to the seamlessness of life, and of the recorder's style. To move on casually from these stories, as we often do, is a guilt, since they are as often, if subduedly, about the guilt of moving on. Muted response is the virtue. Never break out. *The New Yorker* does publish such — and beautifully done, some of them are — but never exclusively. "Ice" is not one of them. Rather, it is made of shards stuck together like charms to keep down the violence, to close out the hidden knowledge. And the bear-dance, on what note did that tease me? The sound of the voice in Cocteau's film *Beauty and the Beast:* "*Bête. Bête.*"

John Updike's language seeks commonplace bases as steel filings seek iron. Where does feeling creep in, while one is watching? Gratefully, one can't quite say. A divorced father, his former wife, and their two sons are exercising their disposal rites on the attic stuff of their former house, now to be sold. The wife's new husband "had been off in his old town, visiting his teen-age twins." The emotions are almost the ordinary ones that attach to objects in most people's lives; we may have had them or be on our way to them. What takes place here, in the small actions and judgments, may be more coherent than we could manage on our lonesome, but the language, however just, never exceeds. It is all arrestedly clear here, recognizable, though the relief may hurt. Art is not disturbing these people. "Still of Some Use" has it, though, in abiding resonance.

"Change" has the fierce humility of a man so close to his feelings he has to be humble about them. The words *shaky, shaken, shaking* are used over and over again, to disarm maybe us, maybe God, but Larry Woiwode's story centers in, on the neighbors, the narrator's wife, daughter, and newborn son, the city, with power sufficient to each, and a religious grace, shaky too, which will save us all from the lightning, if it can. A beautiful story indeed.

•

I should mark what I do not see among the total 120. There are fewer city-focused stories; these have perhaps temporarily disappeared into television sociology. Though fields and barns abound, the husbandry is not always of the highest, though the ethic is. I saw not one story of black life, which in view of black theater, novels, poetry, and open black expression in all the arts, astounds me. I can scarcely believe either that no one is writing them or that none is publishable, so responsibility must rest with the magazines on which this book is built. I see also, as I do in private reading, that the level of respectable communicators all but brims over. As the books press toward the desk, one is stunned at how many people can now construct bright, representative, and coherent studies of life. It is clearly that way now in the story. However, my guess is that, down the ages, the incidence of true artists remains about the same.

These twenty are the real report. The short story marches as writers do — singly. The shape of the short story? There are these shapes. Nothing gives me more heart.

Hortense Calisher

WALTER ABISH

The Idea of Switzerland

(FROM PARTISAN REVIEW)

I

A GLORIOUS German summer.
Oh, absolutely.
Easily the most glorious summer of the past thirty-three years.
Thirty-three years? Oh, I agree.

•

When my father Ulrich von Hargenau was executed by a firing squad in 1944, his last words were: Long live Germany. At least, that's what I have been told by my family. He was killed in July 1944. What was the summer of 1944 like? Active. Certainly, active.

•

One runs little or no danger in speaking of the weather, or writing about the weather, or in repeating what others may have said on that subject. It is safe to conclude that people discussing the weather may be doing so in order to avoid a more controversial subject, one that might irritate, annoy, or even anger someone, anyone, within earshot. I am past avoiding risks. Just a few weeks after my return from Paris I narrowly avoided being killed on a deserted street by the driver of a yellow Porsche. It was a beautiful summer's day, and I was thinking of getting started on my new book, the one that is based on my stay in Paris. I am convinced that the driver of the Porsche had intended to kill or maim me for life. Yes, definitely. I was going to be put out of action. There's little risk in writing this. I did not recognize the driver, whose face I saw for only a split second. It was not an unattractive face. It was a German face, like mine. A determined and somewhat obdurate face, a face that Dürer might have taken a fancy to, and painted or sketched. Consider yourself lucky, said a passerby, after having helped me to my feet. He took it for granted that I spoke German. He also, I assume, took it for granted that it was all an accident, just as I took it for granted that it was not.

You really ought to take greater precautions, said my brother Helmut, when I mentioned the incident. And why on earth did you decide to return to Würtenburg, in the first place?

Because I was tired of hearing everyone around me speak only in French, I replied flippantly.

Well, try not to take too many risks.

The Hargenaus are not known for their humor. But then my brother might say: What's so funny about getting your head smashed in.

II

What is my brother saying?

You should never have married Paula.

I was crazy about her.

If our father wasn't a bloody hero, and your name wasn't Hargenau, you'd be doing ten to fifteen behind bars. Maybe they'd permit you to have a typewriter, he added as an afterthought.

•

My brother has not yet had an opportunity to design a house of detention, as it is now called euphemistically, be he has designed a large assembly plant for Druck Electronics, an airport in München, a library and civic center in Heilbronn, another factory for Stüppen Plumbing, and at least half a dozen apartment buildings and three or four office buildings in addition to the new police station and post office in Würtenburg. He has also designed the house in the country where he and his family spend most of their weekends and their vacation each summer. I admit he works harder than I do. He works incessantly, spending at least a quarter of his work day on the phone. He never loses his temper. He is never impatient. He takes after my father.

•

As I was leaving my brother after spending a weekend with him and his family, he said: we must get together, you and I. We really must sit down and discuss things. I didn't have the heart to tell him that there wasn't anything left to discuss. At one time, years ago, we had our differences; now they hardly matter. I don't even remember what they were. Perhaps I had been envious of the success that he took for granted. He expected it. He was a Hargenau. He confided to me that if our father hadn't been such a complacent and self-assured aristocrat, he might have made a better conspirator. At least he was shot, instead of being left to dangle from a meat hook in front of a film crew recording the event.

•

Helmut rises each morning at 6:30. By 7:10 the entire family is at the table having breakfast. No one is ever late for breakfast. The children watch my brother intently. They wait for him to signal what kind of a day they can expect. He looks at his watch and purses his lips. He has two important business meetings first thing in the morning. He confides everything to Maria. She is blonde and blue-eyed like him. She faces him squarely across the table. She informs him how she intends to spend the day. Nothing is too trivial to be omitted. The children listen intently. They are seeing at first hand the life of an adult world unfold. It is a real world. Each day their father contributes something tangible to the world. Each day several buildings all over Germany rise by another few feet and come closer to the completion that initially had its roots, so to speak, in his brain. By now, the entire Hargenau family knows their architectural history, backward and forward. They know how an architect must proceed with his work by cajoling, reasoning, and reassuring his uneasy and nervous clients. The children gaze into Helmut's blue eyes and are reassured. The English suit speaks for itself. At quarter to eight he's at the wheel of his car. The children admire him. His wife admires him. His secretary admires him. His colleagues admire him grudgingly. His draftsmen admire him. His clients more than admire him, they attempt to emulate his relaxed approach to anything that may come up. What they all see is a tall, blond, blue-eyed man wearing a well-tailored English suit, preferably a plaid suit, and a solid-colored knit tie that is several shades darker than the button-down shirt. He shakes hands with a firm dry grip. He never perspires. Not even on TV with the bright floodlights focused on him. Perfectly at ease, he addresses the TV audience, the vast German audience, discussing his favorite subject, architecture. The splendid history of architecture. Greece, Rome, Byzantium, a slow parade of architectural achievement culminating in the new police station in Würtenburg. Most of Würtenburg tunes in to listen to my brother, amazed at the riches he presents for their appreciation, the architectural riches in their immediate vicinity, the riches of genius. Helmut Hargenau, he's something else, they say, shaking their heads in amazement.

And his brother Ulrich?

Best not talk about him. One never knows who may be listening.

III

On my desk is a small framed photograph of my father, taken in his study. In the background hangs a drawing by Dürer. In the lapel of his jacket is a tiny swastika. The photograph was taken in the summer of 1941, a good summer for Germany. Next to the photograph of my father is one of Paula, my former wife, Paula who calmly informed me that some of our friends had stashed a couple of cases of World War II hand grenades in the cellar. She said it quite casually, as if they were cases of champagne. I in turn admired her incredible coolness and courage. Like my father who removed the swastika in 1942, she believed in causes, and temporary solutions.

Now that I know where she is, why don't I make an effort to get in touch with her?

Answer.

Answer immediately.

IV

A glorious summer. A glorious German summer.

Repeat.

Sometimes I feel as if the brain has become addicted to repetitions, needing to hear everything repeated once, then twice, in order to be certain that the statement is not false or misleading. I find myself repeating to myself what I intend to do next, even though I would be the first to acknowledge that repetition precludes the attainment of perfection, or, as the American philosopher Whitehead puts it: Perfection does not invite repetition.

My brain says: repeat.

The summer this year is really quite exceptional. It is almost (take note of the *almost*) perfect. Not too hot during the daytime, and not too cool at night. I may be imagining this, but the satisfied looks on the faces of the people I see daily must reflect, I am convinced, their contentedness with the weather and, in turn, with their pleasant and harmonious surroundings and, in turn, with their more or less amiable friends and relatives and in turn, with the intimate affairs that are now and then bound to occur, particularly when the person in question is not overly hampered by discontent, or some emotional disturbance, something that might impair his or her ability to judge people, and, among other things, to respond correctly to a sexual overture when it is made.

•

I met Paula in the Englischer Garten in Munich. I was bleeding slightly from a cut I had received when a policeman punched me in the face at the public rally in which a group of my friends and I had participated. Have you ever felt the temptation to blow up a police station, she asked me. I just laughed at the time.

You've taken leave of your senses, said Helmut in his pompous and condescending manner, when I mentioned that I intended to marry Paula. Father would have admired her guts, I said. He had a lot of guts, but little else, said Helmut, otherwise he would have headed for Switzerland. Helmut had met Paula only for several hours. What was it that he could discern in her that I failed to see?

Answer.

Answer immediately.

•

The characters in my books can be said to be free of emotional disturbances, free of emotional impairments. They meet here and there, in parks or public rallies and, without spending too much time analyzing their own needs, allow their brains a brief respite, as they embrace each other in bed. You're a pretty good lover, but are you able to blow up a police station, asked Paula.

•

What constitutes an emotional impairment?

•

An inner turmoil, an absence of serenity, an unresolved entanglement, self-doubt, self-hatred may be due to nothing more serious than a person's inability to appreciate the idyllic weather.

•

In this instance it is the perfect weather in Würtenburg and its immediate surroundings. Now, at this moment, along with the entire population of Würtenburg (approximately 125,968 according to the latest census), I am experiencing the fine weather. I am completely relaxed and have nothing but the weather on my mind. I do not expect ever to hear from Marie-Jean Filebra, or from my former wife, Paula Hargenau, the one, I assume, still in Paris, the other now free to go wherever she chooses.

Repeat.

The brain keeps persisting that it can survive on images alone.

•

Helmut, on meeting me at the airport on my return from Paris, promptly informed me that Paula was living in Geneva. He seemed put out when I burst into laughter, uncontrollable laughter. Geneva? What is she doing in Geneva? He smiled awkwardly, then shrugged his shoulders. I guess she's fond of the place.

Paula. In Geneva. Impossible.

•

Apparently I was mistaken. I still don't know what she's up to in Geneva, and have no intention of inquiring. I wouldn't want to embarrass her with my questions, my interest, or my presence. I am happy that she is free.

•

I am not hiding in Würtenburg. I am listed in the phone directory. If my former friends wish to locate me they can easily do so. Each morning I go out for the paper. In the afternoon, around four, I take a walk. Each morning, each afternoon, more or less at the same time. In that respect I present no problem for anyone who would wish to kill me. The man in the Porsche could give it another try.

•

Frequently, two or three times a week, I receive a letter from some anonymous person who appears to hate me with a greater passion and intensity than I have ever been able to hate anyone. Are all these letters written by lunatics? I could, I suppose, hand them over to the police; instead I toss them into a drawer of my desk.

Maria, my sister-in-law, calls me every three or four days. She asks me how my work is progressing. She tries to elicit from me what I am writing. Is it autobiographical? she asks.

Existence does not take place within the skin, I reply, quoting Klude.

Nonsense.

Only Maria is able to put me on the defensive by saying: nonsense.

It's true.

Repeat.

I am telling you the absolute truth.

V

A young earnest-faced woman moved into the empty apartment
on the floor above mine. I helped her carry a few heavy cartons of
books to the elevator, since the doorman was on his lunch hour.
Würtenburg is gradually emerging from its medieval past to which
we are still so attached . . . the medieval past that is etched on so
many of the faces of the people who live here. My brother and I
are no exception. I gravely stare at my face in the mirror and see
Germany's entire past.

•

A stranger, a young earnest-faced American, for instance, cannot
help when visiting Würtenburg but see the world of Albrecht
Dürer come to life. Dürer becomes his or her point of reference,
or perhaps even guide, as he or she takes a leisurely walk down the
main street past the cathedral designed by Müse-Haft Toll, with its
frescoes by Alfredo Igloria Grobart and stained glass windows by
Nacklewitz Jahn and then past the World War I monument on the
left, a bronze riderless horse rearing up on its hind legs, the four
metal tables on its granite base bearing the names of those killed
in action. There are at least six Hargenaus, all officers, who died
in World War I, and another half a dozen (my father's name not
included) whose names are carved into the large slab of marble
now standing, after a heated public debate, behind the Schotten-
dorferkirche, a somewhat out-of-the-way part of the city, considered at the time by many as a more suitable spot for a World
War II monument. After turning right at the public library it is
only a five-minute brisk walk to the University where old Klude is
still teaching philosophy. Or, should one say, is once again teaching philosophy after an enforced period of idleness, the result of
too many reckless speeches in the thirties and early forties,
speeches that dealt with the citizen's responsibilities to the New
Order. Poor Klude. Once he stopped dealing with abstract theo-
ries and was able to make himself understood to one overcrowded
gymnasium of students after another, the ideas he expressed were

reinforced by statements such as: We have completely broken with a landless and powerless thinking. But by now Klude's former platitudinous speeches have been forgotten. His students swear by him, and his classes are always crowded. Sometimes as many as 400 sit in a large drafty auditorium, listening attentively to Klude as he lectures on the meaning of a thing. What is a thing? he asks rhetorically. Klude is not referring to a particular thing. He is not, for instance, referring to a modern apartment building, or a metal frame window, or an English lesson, but the *thingliness* that is intrinsic to all things, regardless of their merit, their usefulness, and the degree of their perfection. I mention the latter only because the mind is so created that it habitually sets up standards of perfection for everything: for marriage and for driving, for love affairs and for garden furniture, for table tennis and for gas ovens, for faces and even for something as petty as the weather, and then, having established these standards, it sets up standards of comparison which serve, if nothing else, to confirm in our minds that a great many things are less than perfect.

VI

My brain relies on words to describe my promising future. A future filled with expectation. A future built on the words I manage to put on paper. The words in themselves would not necessarily bewilder the doorman who daily greets me with: Looks like another fine day.

    Repeat.

•

For all I know the doorman may have been one of the squad who shot my father. It is highly unlikely. And if he had, he was under orders. If you're part of an execution squad, you can't pick the people you want to shoot. Or can you?

•

It is a glorious day, and I wouldn't want to be anywhere else in the world.

•

I am convinced that my feelings are echoed by the people now casually walking down the Hauptstrasse, stopping now and then to gaze briefly into a shop window, looking at the things that are on display, sometimes peering into the interior of the store to see if

9

they can spot a familiar face, no doubt a German face, a Dürer-like face of an acquaintance or friend.

•

Daphne, the earnest-faced American woman, was walking back to the apartment building, her arms wrapped around a large shopping bag filled with groceries, when I ran into her. I offered to help, but she wouldn't hear of it. I then suggested that we have dinner together. She allowed a few seconds to spell out the silence of rejection. She was too busy, she explained. She was trying to put her place into some kind of order.

Well, yes, I nodded sympathetically. How about joining me for a walk this afternoon. I was afraid that I was about to burden her with the responsibility of having to reject my second invitation. But she accepted.

•

Why on earth should I wish to spend an hour or two together with this earnest-faced young woman. Is it because I desperately need someone to talk to, someone who does not instantaneously recognize the name Hargenau. Ulrich von Hargenau, the elder, executed after an ill-fated attempt to kill the Führer, and Ulrich Hargenau, the younger, witness for the defense in the recent conspiracy trial of the Einzig Gruppe. Why doesn't someone ask me what I think of the Einzig Gruppe.

Assholes. A bunch of assholes with hand grenades that had been stored in the cellar of the house where Paula and I lived, until we went our separate ways.

•

What do you really want? Paula had once asked me.
Redistribution of wealth, I said instantaneously.
No. What do you really want?
Success, I said cautiously.
No. Not success. What do you really really want?
Why not success?
You're terribly devious, did you know that.
No.
If only I knew what you really wanted I would be able to trust you, she said.
You can trust me.
No.

VII

By now I like to think that most people in Würtenburg have put
me out of their minds. My somewhat inept performance in court
as reported widely in all the papers and on TV and radio has
fortunately been superseded by more recent events. An earthquake in Chile, a famine in Ethiopia, a coup d'état in Tanzania,
widespread use of torture in Latin America and Greece. Once in a
while, one of my wife's former friends, a fellow activist, now serving ten to twenty, or was it fifteen to thirty years for a long list of
alleged crimes, including: arson, assault, kidnapping, armed robbery, and second degree murder, will go on a hunger strike and
receive mention in the papers. But no one is really interested in
my whereabouts. No one could possibly care what I plan to write
next. I expect that a number of people familiar with my work
expect to find in my next book some kind of explanation of my
obviously, to them, aberrant behavior . . . an explanation that
strikes me as being totally redundant. I have been led to believe
that a great many of my acquaintances were convinced that I lied
to the Police and in court in order to extricate Paula and myself
from the mess we were in. I didn't. I merely told the truth to save
our skin. It wasn't necessary to fabricate anything. I didn't have to
worry about being caught telling a lie. I didn't have to worry about
contradicting myself. Still, it comes to the same thing. What I had
to say enabled the Ministry of Justice to convict eight people who
had frequently eaten at my table and, for reasons I still cannot
explain, entrusted me with their idiotic plans. After all, Ulrich von
Hargenau, the elder, had died without divulging to the *Sicherheits-*
dienst the names of his fellow conspirators. So why shouldn't Ulrich
Hargenau, the younger, be expected to do the same. The police
knew that Paula had been the chief strategist, the planner, the
brain behind so many of the Einzig "wargames," just as she must
have known that I, or rather our hallowed name Hargenau would
pull her out of the mess.

And it did. A few hasty telephone calls, a few conferences, a few
tears, a few negotiations, a few promises, and the Ministry of Justice was prepared to overlook, this once, our indiscretions. The
day after the trial, the newspapers quoted Paula as saying point-
edly that she and her group had been betrayed. No, she said. She
would prefer not to name names. Well, she had said rather smugly

when we met briefly in our house, this affair can't have hurt the sale of your books, or has it?

VIII

What are you working on, my publisher asked me when we met shortly after my return to Germany. Something quite intriguing, I said. A love affair in Paris. He looked relieved. So much has already been written about your past political involvement, he commented tactfully. Still, I was under the impression that you might wish to add your . . . recollections.

Had he been about to say, your version?

I still receive a good deal of hate mail, I said after one of our customary prolonged silences.

We must have you over for dinner soon, he said politely. He had known my father quite well. It was an impossible situation, he had once told me, referring to my father. As a man of honor, he had no other option.

IX

I told the young American woman who had moved in upstairs that on my mother's side I was a distant relative of Albrecht Dürer. I said this without the slightest desire to impress her. I would not have brought up the subject had I not run into her in the university bookstore holding a book on Dürer. She greeted my statement with an appropriate skepticism, staring at me as if trying to gage my intentions. My mother's maiden name is Dürer, I explained. Her family moved to Würtenburg in 1803. At one time my family owned six drawings by Dürer, but now we are down to one. For lack of anything else to say I kept on talking about Dürer. I described one of the drawings that had been in my family's possession. It was one of his last drawings, the *Double Goblet*. As the title indicated it offered the viewer a view of the two ornate goblets, one balanced on top of the other, as well as revealing upon closer scrutiny an entirely different picture, one that disclosed an explicit sexual content.

You like that, don't you, she said, challenging me.

What? The sexual content?

No, the duality in the picture. Seeing something that others may have overlooked.

She looked startled when I said: Why are you attacking me?

•

Later that afternoon in a bar frequented mainly by students, she told me that she had been in Würtenburg a little over six months. Tired of sharing a place with another American student, she had looked around for an apartment and found one in the building where I was staying. To support herself she gave English lessons to young German business executives, most of whom expected to be sent by their firms to America for a year or two.

Teaching beginners must be a bore, I said sympathetically.

Oh no, she said. I enjoy it. They're all extremely eager to learn English, in addition to being so very . . . Here she paused briefly, evidently searching for the right word.

Understanding.

Understanding?

I was puzzled by the word. What did she mean. Why should her German students show understanding for anything other than the information she was imparting to them. Understanding. I think that word, more than anything else she may have said, served to arouse my curiosity. It is quite conceivable that had I not been so involved in writing about Paula Hargenau, my former wife, and Marie-Jean Filebra, my former mistress (to use an old-fashioned description), I might have paid closer attention to Daphne. From her appearance and her surname I assumed that she was of German extraction. I admit that I found her serious face, her measured and frequently humorless responses to what I said, not unattractive. I don't know why. Perhaps because she gave me the appearance of someone in need of protection, although I felt convinced that she would not permit herself to accept it, if it were offered. I had not spoken of my work to her and had no reason to believe that she knew what I did or, for that matter, who I was. She did not ask questions, and I did not offer any information. I was not in the least attracted to her sexually, and for some inexplicable reason wanted to communicate this fact to her, as if feeling the need to reassure her of my intentions, as if to indicate that she could allow herself to relax in my presence. No, that is patently untrue. At this time the burden of another intimate relationship would have been more than I could handle. If anything, I was signaling to her my own unavailability.

It was a glorious summer day. Daphne and I were seated at a sidewalk table drinking beer and observing the people passing.

She mentioned that she was studying philosophy under Klude. An American studying Klude and seeing us, as only strangers can see us, with a mixture of envy and a certain disdain.

•

We Germans like to draw attention to our most conspicuous flaws, since the uncertainty and doubt we arouse in strangers saves us from being inundated by a deluge of uncritical admiration.
     Did I say this? If I did I retract it immediately.
     What does Daphne think of me?

x

Daphne moved into the building less than three months ago. She had found her apartment the way I had, by looking at the real estate pages of the *Würtenburger Neue Zeit*. She spoke a fluent German and had no difficulty in following the lectures at the Würtenburger University, a university, incidentally, with a reputation second to none in ancient and medieval history, the history of religion, and philosophy. She had studied German in America. Why not French or Italian. I wanted to study under Klude, she admitted shyly. Was he the principal reason why she had chosen German, I asked with what must have been a look of astonishment. She laughed. No, she had been exaggerating slightly. By the time she came across the work of Klude, she had already been taking German at college. Her father, she added, had a great many friends in Germany. He had been there during the occupation. It was he who encouraged her to study German. When I inquired if he was connected to a university, she responded with a curt no.

•

When Daphne moved into her apartment she found an attractive armchair, a large bed, and a chest of drawers the former tenant had left behind. There may have been a few other things, but the super and the doorman always had first picking. I was surprised that they had not taken the armchair or the chest of drawers. They wouldn't have been difficult to move. I too have discarded a great many things, yet I continue to cling to so much that has clearly outlived its usefulness.

•

Where did you live before you moved into this building, asked Daphne.
     I was deliberately vague. Oh, here and there. I chose this place

because I wanted some privacy. I didn't want to run into people I knew everytime I stepped out of the front entrance. When Daphne discovered that I had been a former student of Klude she danced a little jig, which I took to be an American way of expressing enthusiasm. I wasn't a particularly successful student, I hastened to tell her. I don't believe that Professor Klude ever paid the slightest attention to me. All the same, I have sent him a copy of every book I have published. Once or twice, despite his heavy schedule, he was kind enough to send me a note thanking me for the book. He greatly looked forward to reading the work of one of his former pupils, he wrote, something I had every reason to doubt.

•

I didn't mention this to Daphne. I didn't want her to think of me as discontent with the notes I received from Klude. Naturally, as soon as she had discovered that I was a writer she felt impelled or obliged to buy several of my books, which is more than I can say for most of my friends and acquaintances, who expect free signed copies which they do not read. Having completed or partially completed one of my books, Daphne felt compelled to say something about the work, and, being straightforward and candid, as well as a student of philosophy, she couldn't, I recognized, simply say, I enjoyed it, and let it go at that. She had to say something that would express on her part a recognition of what I had attempted to achieve, or what she thought I had tried to achieve. Obviously she tried to like the books because she liked me, or was prepared to like me or, possibly, because she wanted to like me, but no matter how hard she tried, the work was somehow inaccessible to her. That is hardly surprising in someone who admitted that she found the exploration or probing of a relationship between two or more people as something somewhat distasteful. She felt that the writer was trespassing, and I have to admit that writing is a form of trespassing. Instead of reading on and on about the tenuousness or uncertainty of someone's feelings, she preferred to question the meaning of a thing, or the meaning of a thought, preferably raising the question in German, a foreign or at any rate adopted language that enabled her to reduce these crucial questions to pure signs, since in German the word *thing* and the word *thought* did not immediately evoke in her brain the multitudinous response it did in English, where the words, those everyday words, conjured up an entire panorama of familiar associations that blunted the preciseness needed in order to bring her philosophical investigation to a satisfactory conclusion. Could this be the reason why she came to Germany? To think in German, to question herself in a foreign language?

•

Has she ever slept with a German?
   She must have, I tell myself.
   Why this curious constraint on my part.
   Answer.
   Answer immediately.

XI

The police in our precinct have moved into their new quarters with a great deal of fanfare. My brother's photograph is in all the papers. All along he had been convinced that his design for the police station would be selected out of the nineteen or twenty that had been submitted. There had been a good many insinuations that he had won only because he also happened to be the son-in-law of the police chief of Würtenburg. Perhaps it did influence the jury's unanimous decision. I still recall urging him to abstain from participating for that very reason. If you win, they'll say it is because of your father-in-law. He called me naive. Christmas, he told me gleefully, he had sent the policemen at the old station a case of Piper Heitzig. Prost. Of course the newspapers did not neglect to state that the architect Hargenau was the brother of Ulrich Hargenau, the author who had admitted to being a political activist in the Einzig Gruppe. I suppose I could sue, but it would simply focus more attention on me. Attention is the last thing I need. Let Helmut get the attention.

XII

My brother takes me on a tour of the new police station. Why had I agreed to come? Immaculate corridors, large well lit offices with plate glass windows, white formica-topped desks, everything gleaming and new, and everyone, in and out of uniform, smiling broadly at us. It's like a circus. Everyone beaming their approval of my brother who is, let me not forget to add, the son-in-law of the chief of police. Helmut introduces me with a special flourish to everyone he meets. He keeps saying: This is my radical brother. Ulrich Hargenau, the writer. You may have read some of his work.

To my surprise quite a number of policemen say yes. They all smile at each other as if sharing a huge joke. Any questions? my brother asks me in front of a group of senior police officers, all with glasses of champagne in their hands, all a bit red in their faces and a slight bit unsteady on their feet.

Yes. Is the young American woman on the floor above mine a radical?

I can easily find out for you, says the chief of police, smiling, feeling proud of the Hargenaus. Old, old family with a castle somewhere in East Germany. Pity that they decided to drop the *von*.

I return the chief of police's smile. A brief sense of camaraderie. My period of irresponsibility is past. I have become respectable again. When it came to the crunch, I did the right thing. I swallowed my medicine, and now I am back again, free to do what I want, to go where I wish.

My brother is working on another book, says my brother.

This time, be sure to make it a best seller, says the chief of police, and they all roar with laughter.

XIII

You spend an awful lot of your time sleeping, don't you? said Daphne, wrinkling her nose critically. How do you manage to get any work done?

I work late at night.

Did she look skeptical.

•

At the university library I looked up her father in the *International Who's Who*. Mortimer S. Hasendruck. b. Debunk, Illinois 1920. M.I.T. 1941. Dept. of Defense. 1944. Founder and President of Dust Industries. m. June G. Steinholf, 1946. s. Mark D. Hasendruck 1949. d. Daphne S. Hasendruck 1952. Address: Edea, Illinois.

•

What? said my brother, you mean you've never heard of Dust Industries. He seemed incredulous at my ignorance. What kind of an activist were you? Dust is one of America's largest armament manufacturers. They produced most of the advanced equipment used in Vietnam.

I guess, I said, that's why Daphne doesn't wish to speak about her father.

•

We must have her over for dinner, said Maria.
  Sure.

XIV

Today I received a note in the mail. It was brief and to the point. We know where you are. Did you expect to hide from us? Because of you Ilse, Adalbert, Jürgen, Heinz, Helga, Assif, Lerner, and Mausi are rotting in jail. Do you really expect to get off scot-free? We intend to get you. If not tomorrow then the day after, if not the day after then next week, or next month. Soon. We promise.
  I didn't destroy the unsigned note. I can't bear to throw anything away. I can't even bear to discard old magazines. It is not the first note I have received. Did they really believe that I moved here to escape from them.

•

Sometimes I really can't understand the Germans, said Daphne. I speak the language. I read Klude, yet . . . despairingly she shook her head . . . I can't make you out. Is this the new Germany? she asked mockingly.

•

My brother Helmut studied architecture at M.I.T. He likes to wear button-down shirts. One day he hopes to design a sixty-story office with an underground garage in Detroit. I guess he's the new Germany.

•

But what about you?

XV

In addition to killing two postal workers, the explosion of at least twelve to sixteen sticks of dynamite at the new post office designed by Helmut also totally destroyed four recently acquired sorting machines, as well as two dozen large sacks of unsorted first-class mail. Had the explosion taken place an hour earlier, a great many more people might have been killed. As it was, the damage to the building was considerable. Half an hour after the explosion, a woman called a local radio station and announced that the newly formed Seventeenth of August Liberation Group took full respon-

sibility for the action, which had been designed to draw attention
to the plight of the eight imprisoned members of the Einzig
Gruppe, all sentenced to long jail terms on the seventeenth of
August, one year ago. So a year had passed. I had just reached
page 134 of a manuscript that was entirely based on events that
had occurred since then. Until the explosion had destroyed the
new post office I felt pretty confident that nothing would interrupt
my work. I would go on writing the book until I was ready to
submit it to my publisher, and then I would take a brief vacation,
after which I would start thinking of the next book. Now I was no
longer certain.

•

With one explosion the name Hargenau was in all the papers
again. Great outrage at the senseless killings and at the mutilation
of thousands of letters. Those letters would never reach their destination. Naturally there was also some speculation as to the identity of the members of the recently formed Seventeenth of August
Group. My wife's name kept cropping up. She could be behind it
all. But why pick on the post office? Why mutilate and destroy
innocent first-class letters that may have been carrying checks to
war widows and other people in need.

•

On the evening of the thirteenth I had dinner with Daphne in my
apartment. We listened to the news. We ate sauerbraten. That's
the way it reads in my diary. Dinner with Daphne. I don't keep a
journal. I just jot things down in an office diary. Dinner with
Daphne seemed adequate for my purposes. Explosion at post office, two dead, *Seventeenth of August Group* accepts responsibility.
Did not call off dinner with Daphne. Watch news. Make love.

•

Do you still love her, Daphne asked.
  Who?
  Paula, your wife.
  What made you ask me that question?

XVI

The first thing Daphne said to me the next morning when I
opened my eyes was, I know nothing about you . . . absolutely
nothing.

•

You'll find everything in my books.
  Is that true?
  No.

•

Daphne dressed in front of me and then walked to the door of my apartment.

•

I retain in my mind a picture of her standing at the door. Before leaving, she turned to look at me, at my possessions, at my apartment to which she now had a key. As far as I was concerned, everything was at a complete standstill, as the brain, feeding on the present, made room for Daphne, naked, legs parted, absorbing the image with the same ease as it had absorbed and incorporated the images I had formed of the explosion at the post office. The image of the explosion and my making love to Daphne were linked or connected by the date on which they had taken place, and possibly by a conviction I have always had that nothing is what it first appears to be.

XVII

The following Sunday Daphne and I visited my brother Helmut and his family at their house in the country. Helmut was in a great mood. He dismissed the bombing, saying that he had never been quite satisfied with the design of the post office and secretly had always wanted another go at it. Of course, it was too bad about the two men who died, and all that mail. God knows how much of it was intended for him. Before dinner we all dutifully posed for Helmut who took our photographs on the wide terrace overlooking the dense forest in the distance where Klude spends his summer months in a small house in a clearing deep inside the wood. Helmut offered to drive Daphne to see the house the next day. Knowing that she was American he spoke at great length of his stay in America and how much he enjoyed living in Boston. He kept on about his visits to Montana and Wyoming, Arkansas and Southern California, one amusing anecdote after another, then, when she least expected it, he began to question her about herself and her family. Helmut was smiling at her as she described the town in Illinois where she had grown up, her friends, her decision to come to Germany after a year in Geneva.
  Geneva? I said.

Yes, she had a number of friends in Geneva. She also gave English lessons in Geneva.

My brother interrupted her. To get back to your father.

I left the room.

•

Could she conceivably have met Paula?

•

One has so little control over the irresponsible meandering of one's brain, over the improbable connections that are activated as thoughts by impulses from the brain, although, occasionally, these remote farfetched hypothetical links have a way of coming true. Almost anything the brain can conjure up is plausible.

•

Daphne living in Geneva.

Daphne moving into the building where I live.

Why that particular building.

Because it had been advertised in the local paper.

But had it?

XVIII

On Tuesday afternoon, when I returned from the library, the doorman informed me that Daphne had moved out of her apartment during my absence. She had not given any notice and therefore was forfeiting one month's rent. Apparently a young man in a station wagon had helped her move some of her belongings. Speechless, I looked at the doorman, then walked to the elevator. No one answered when I rang her doorbell. On Sunday she had promised me a key to her apartment. She intended to have a duplicate made that morning. Her letter to me was slipped under my door. It was addressed to Ulrich von Hargenau. It was in her handwriting, a handwriting that was still unfamiliar.

Why the *von?*

What was she trying to say?

Dear Ulrich,

I am returning to America, in part because I do not wish to become emotionally entangled with you at this time. I do not feel happy in a role that is so devoid of any certitude. I do not like to feel that I am depending on another person. Please feel free to take anything I have left behind in

the apartment. I may continue my studies in America. I wish you had
not taken me to visit your brother and his family. Daphne.

XIX

I am the first to admit that I don't know Daphne. I think I know
what she thinks of Klude and of Germany in a vague sort of way.
To some extent I knew her taste in furniture, in music, in books,
in clothes. If I know little else, it is because I failed to show much
interest in her initially and did not engage her in conversations
like my brother did in order to elicit from her why, precisely why
she was in Germany, and what she felt about her father. That is
not to say that I had ruled out ever asking her any of these questions, but until I received her letter, I had felt quite content to
leave things as they were. I was content with our new relationship,
content to sit back and muse over Daphne, the young earnest-
faced American in Germany who never once asked me a single
question regarding my dead father or my own somewhat dubious
role at the Einzig trial.

XX

The doorman took a certain pleasure in telling me that Daphne
had left. He had watched my face to see how I would receive the
news. I turned and stiffly walked to the elevator, pressed the up
button, entered the elevator, and pressed the button to the seventh
floor under the stern unforgiving gaze of the doorman.

XXI

I took a taxi to the airport which is on the outskirts of Würtenburg,
and checked with a number of airlines if anyone by the name of
Daphne Hasendruck had booked a flight to America. She had not,
at least not under her own name. Wishing to be thorough, I inquired at Lufthansa if a Miss Daphne Hasendruck had booked a
flight to Geneva that morning. Trying to sound as diffident as
possible, I mentioned that my niece, Daphne Hasendruck, was to
call me on her arrival in Geneva. Since I hadn't heard from her, I
was inquiring if, in fact, she had left for Geneva. I don't think that
the clerk believed my story, but she did inform me — after checking a list — that a Miss Hasendruck had taken the afternoon flight

to Geneva. It was not a direct flight, but her destination was Geneva.

•

Did she fly there to join Paula? Or did she fly there for another reason?

•

My brother Helmut did his best to talk me out of flying to Geneva. Whatever it is, you don't want it. Whatever it is, you don't need it. You're free. You're in the clear. She may not know Paula, he argued. She may just be drawn to the Alps, or the abundance of chocolate.

•

I left for Geneva the next day. As I expected, my wife was not listed in the telephone book. I had been to Geneva several times before and without giving it much thought checked into a hotel where Paula and I had once stayed for a couple of nights. It was conveniently located near the Quai du Mont-Blanc. The first thing next day I purchased a ream of paper and a map of the city. As I rather aimlessly walked around the downtown area in the vicinity of the Jardin Anglais I kept asking myself if I was in Geneva in order to locate Daphne, or my former wife, or if I was simply collecting fresh material for my next book. On the third day I found a small decent restaurant. I also found a store where the *Würtenburger Neue Zeit* was sold. I was still in Geneva when another bomb went off in Würtenburg. This one destroyed an entire floor in the fingerprint section in the new police station. When I spoke to Helmut on the phone he, in a weary voice, suggested that I remain in Geneva for the time being, adding his cautionary: Please don't fuck up . . . do you understand what I am saying. I know it's your specialty, but try not to this time.

•

In my hotel room I was prepared for every eventuality. I had a ream of typewriting paper and a portable Hermes, but I couldn't write a line. My brain, my body, had stopped functioning. Everything around me seemed at a standstill. On one of my walks I had picked up Victor Segalen's *Rene Leys*. I began reading the book one afternoon in a cafe on the rue de Rhone. Somehow, it seemed to me that the narrator in the book, a Frenchman living in Peking in 1911, was contemplating an action that in many respects paralleled or, at any rate, appeared analogous to my own endeavor in Ge-

neva. At a time when the Forbidden City was still closed to all
foreigners, the Frenchman's one overwhelming desire — in order
to understand what he kept referring to as the "Within" of the
Chinese Empire — was to enter (penetrate would be the right
term) the Imperial Palace and see what had been withheld from
him all along. Clearly, in my case, the city of Geneva did not
withhold anything as tangible as the Imperial Chinese Palace,
something one could assess from the outside. No. By drawing this
somewhat specious comparison to the Frenchman in *Rene Leys* I
was simply indulging in a favorite habit of mine — namely, attempting to view and place my personal affairs in a literary context, as if this would endow them with a clearer and richer
meaning.

•

But why had Daphne left for Geneva?

XXII

The day Klude died it was in all the French, Swiss, and German
newspapers. Lengthy obituaries. Germany's greatest thinker since
Hegel. Photographs of Klude in his log cabin that was only a
twenty-minute drive from the country house my brother had designed for himself. An entire page listing Klude's philosophical
achievements. To my surprise the editors had not omitted mention
of Klude's somewhat ridiculous role during the coming to power
of the Nazis. Later that day, in a quarter of Geneva I didn't know,
I spotted a small bookstore. I was pleased to discover that they had
several of Klude's books in French and German. After some hesitation I chose *Jetzt Zum Letzten Mahl* and *Ohne Grund,* an early work
written in 1936. Upon leaving the store I caught a brief but unmistakable glimpse of Daphne in the passenger seat of a passing
bright yellow Porsche. I called out, shouted her name at the top of
my lungs, frantically waving my hand as I ran after the car, but
probably she did not see me. Hours later, when I returned to my
hotel, the desk clerk handed me a note that had been left for me.
It was from Paula. It simply stated: You have taken enough. Leave
us alone.

•

Leave us alone.
  Us? Us? Who is us?

XXIII

The interviewer arrives punctually at three. He has a foreign-sounding name which I do not catch. He is in his twenties, wearing a very worn-looking tweed jacket. I have no reason to feel distrustful of him. I've been through too many interviews. I smile at him, aware all the time of his thick spectacles, his disconcerting stare, his tape recorder dangling from one shoulder, all weapons that I wish to disarm with my cordiality and candor. From the very start the difficulty lies in trying to establish who exactly is interviewing whom. The tape recorder, set on the table, records a trite meaningless exchange. He looks around the room, recording in his brain my few visible possessions: the Hermes typewriter, a ream of paper, a small pile of books, underwear drying on a back of a chair, shoes, a guidebook. I offer him a glass of wine, but he declines. This makes it difficult for me. I could order tea or coffee, but he says that he has just eaten. He is not rude, at least not intentionally rude. I smoke, sip wine, and stare out of the window. I also inquire how he had managed to find out that I was staying in Geneva.

It's such a small city. Someone from the magazine recognized you on the street and passed on the information to me. I called a few hotels. I tried some of the more luxurious ones first and then worked my way down . . .

There are a lot of hotels in Geneva, I remark.

I was lucky.

It's very gratifying that you would wish to interview me. As I mentioned to you on the phone, I hope to have a book out at the end of the year.

Have you completed it.

No, I am just putting the finishing touches to it.

You're not using Geneva in the novel, by any chance.

I find it difficult if not impossible to write about a city I happen to be in, although Segalen, who I have just been reading, managed to write an extraordinary novel set in Peking, while staying in that city.

Segalen? Swiss?

No, French.

He jots the name down on a small yellow pad, then, avoiding my eyes, remarks that he had been informed that Paula was currently living in Geneva. Is that the reason why you are here? And have you been in touch with her?

I take a puff on my cigarette. I feel strangely lightheaded. I feel comfortably relaxed in my chair. From where I am sitting, I can see the street below. Looking down at it, I am reminded of Tanner, since it is the kind of street that frequently can be seen in his films. Tanner provided me with my first real glimpse of Switzerland.

No, I reply. My wife and I are separated. I don't even know where she is staying. I'm not even certain that she is in Geneva at this time. We have not seen each other since the Einzig trial.

Does she blame you for the excessively long sentences handed out to the Gruppe?

You'll have to ask her.

As the only writer in the Gruppe, did you ever feel tempted to keep a diary or journal during the period of time you were . . . associated with them?

Quite candidly, I see no point in discussing the Gruppe. They belong to the past. Moreover, my and Paula's decision to separate had nothing to do with the Einzig Gruppe, or the outcome of the trial. Most political trials, I have come to realize, are badly in need of some sort of scapegoat to deflect questions that try to probe a little deeper . . . This trial was no exception. What I had to say at the trial was not said under any duress, contrary to what most people seem to believe. I was never an actual participant or member of the Gruppe. True, some of them had been friends, and I helped them because they were friends. Admittedly, I got a slight kick out of helping the so-called conspirators, not because I believed for one moment in their methods or in what they were hoping to achieve, but simply because I tend to dislike bureaucrats in positions of power. I didn't mind giving them a kick in the ass.

Would you consider what happened recently in Würtenburg as a kick in the ass?

No, that was very unfortunate.

Is it a coincidence that the two public buildings recently blown up by the Seventeenth of August Group, or whatever they call themselves, had been designed by a Hargenau?

I doubt that the action was aimed at him or me. It certainly wasn't aimed at my late father, who is something of a hero in Germany.

To return to you. Do you intend to finish your book in Geneva? And why Geneva?

I hope to complete the book here. As to why Geneva. I like being a stranger in a city . . . I like being anonymous. Incidentally, Paula and I stayed in this hotel several years ago. I remember feeling pleased when I discovered that Musil had stayed here briefly upon his arrival in 1940.

What is the title of your forthcoming book.

The English Lesson.

It's not a German lesson, I see.

No. We've had enough German lessons to last us for several generations.

A number of critics have referred to the element of ambiguity that permeates much of your work. One reads your books, always feeling as if some vital piece of information is being withheld.

I'm not sure how I can respond to that. If someone withholds information, surely it is not merely for the sake of withholding information. All the same, characters, like people, frequently misread each other's intentions. In *The English Lesson* a man follows a woman who left him to Geneva.

So Geneva does play a part in your novel.

Only a minor one. Almost a negligible one.

Does he locate her?

Who?

The character in your novel.

That remains to be seen.

Why Geneva?

I picked Geneva because of the image Switzerland evokes in people. A kind of controlled neutrality, a somewhat antiseptic tranquillity that I find soothing. I may also have been influenced by the films of Tanner.

But Tanner is fundamentally a politically oriented filmmaker. His films are never devoid of a political content . . .

Well, yes. In *The English Lesson* the unexplained departure of the young American woman who supports herself in Germany by giving English lessons, hence the title, from a man ten or twelve years her senior, a man who might be labeled a political reactionary, could be viewed in a political context.

What kind of a political statement are you making in your book?

I'm sorry, my mind was on something else. What did you say?

What kind of a political statement are you making in your book?

A novel is not a process of rebellion. Just as it validates and makes acceptable forms of human conduct, it also validates and makes acceptable societal institutions.

Does that trouble you?

Not at all.

When are you planning to return to Germany?

As soon as I complete the novel. I am, you might say, searching for an appropriate conclusion. In yesterday's paper there was mention of a young woman who jumped from the fourteenth story of an office building only a few blocks from this hotel. I mention this only because in life, jumping out of a window is an end, whereas in a novel, where suicide occurs all too frequently, it becomes an explanation.

I'm terribly sorry. The interviewer looks at me apologetically. I forgot to press the record button. This has never happened to me before. Could we possibly go over the interview again. Just briefly . . .

Yes, why not, I reply.

•

An hour later, after the interviewer has left, the phone rings, and when I pick up the receiver, ready to welcome any interruption, any small diversion, anything that will keep me from sitting down and trying to write, my brother Helmut on the other end of the line, at that hour, I presume, still in his office, calmly says: I thought you might want to know that your Daphne Hasendruck is not Daphne Hasendruck.

Of course she is.

The real Daphne Hasendruck is married to the head of Dust Enterprises in Spain. They live in Madrid. They have two children. Her name, should you wish to contact her, is Daphne Wheelock.

You spoke to her?

I was just being thorough.

Then who is our Daphne?

I haven't the foggiest idea.

Did you mention this to your father-in-law?

Do you take me for an ass?

You spotted her that weekend. You saw through her. Was that the reason for all those questions?

No. I'm just thorough. I don't want you to fuck up. It takes too much of my time.

By the way, I'm sorry about the police station.

We'll patch it up. But I've been told they lost all their files, including the one on you.

•

This is Switzerland, I say to myself, as I set out for a stroll later that afternoon. This is the place where Musil died, where Rilke died, where Gottfried Keller lived and died, where Jean-Jacques Rousseau was born, and where Nabokov lived, as much a prisoner of the past as I am a prisoner of the present.

•

Geneva 1977.

MAX APPLE

Small Island Republics

(FROM THE KENYON REVIEW)

INUDO WAS PROBABLY the world's tallest Japanese-American. Six-five-and-a-half barefoot, he also had extra measures of Oriental cunning and agility. He was good at basketball and paper folding. He honored his parents and got all A's at Harvard where he majored in American history. He was twice voted the Japanese-American teenager of the year and went around the country giving after-dinner speeches to fourteen-year-olds who wanted, someday, to be like him. Young Japanese girls swooned as if he were Mick Jagger when he told them that their parents had been put in prison camps in California. They admired his silky complexion and his deep rich voice reading racist tracts of the '30s and '40s in which San Fernando Valley farmers accused the Japanese of pissing on their lettuce.

"You've got to be aware of the fact that some of your neighbors still think of you as the yellow menace," he told the youngsters. They took notes and asked for his autograph.

It bothered young Inudo to hear Japanese-Americans talk about "the homeland." "My homeland is California, U.S.A.," he said. He rode along the scenic U.S. 1 on his two-cycle Suzuki with a short throw engine. In polished knee length boots, leather jacket, and cycling helmet Inudo looked like a Kamikaze pilot. He liked to talk in generalizations. Hannibal of Carthage was his hero. The Japanese-American Citizens League voted him a trip to Japan including a ceremonial meeting with the prime minister.

Inudo refused the trip. "When will you start believing that you're full American citizens?" he bellowed to his young audiences. "When will you stop thinking that it's kind of our hosts to keep us here? My great-grandfather was born in California and they still imprisoned my father during the war in case he was an alien spy."

"Forget the war," his father told him. "I forgot, the Japanese forgot, the Germans forgot. You weren't even born until 1956. If you want to talk about old wars stick with your Hannibal and the Romans."

Inudo's mother wanted him to be a senator. Even a state senator would do. "Look at B. S. Hirahimo," she urged him, "Daniel Iawahara, Victor Benawara . . ." She knew the names of Japanese elected personages down to the county level. "You could be a justice of the peace next week," she said, "if you'd just stop talking silliness." Senator Hirahimo himself nominated Inudo to be a page in the U.S. Senate.

"Let them use computers more effectively," he said turning down the job. "The hand carried message is as obsolete as the Morse code."

He liked to gun his Suzuki through downtown San Jose. The wind in his wake lifted skirts. People watched the tall handsome Oriental vanish uphill, his chrome tailpipes smoking.

"A year out of Harvard and still nothing," his mother complained. "You turn down what others dream about." Gradually, and much less radically than other Americans his age, Slim Inudo stopped honoring his parents.

"Why do I have to be something?" he asked. "Why can't I be Slim Inudo of San Jose and work for one of the local conglomerates? Why in the hell don't you get off my back?"

"Stress," the senior Inudos thought. "Too many A's, too much of an idol. Who at fifteen and sixteen should be held up as an example to strangers?" "I'm sorry," Mrs. Inudo moaned to her husband, "that I taught him the Gettysburg Address at age three. I trained him to be a credit to his people and he was. And now at twenty-two he's retired."

Inudo began dating a Caucasian coed from San Jose State. She could be seen clutching him from behind astride the Suzuki. She studied journalism and wanted someday to edit the newspaper in her Iowa hometown. She had light brown curls and kept a stenographer's notebook tucked in her jacket. She met Inudo when she interviewed him for the college newspaper. She admired his honesty in the face of journalistic pressure.

"I don't like it," Mrs. Inudo said, "a Caucasian girl, a Jane Some-body from Iowa. I was sure he would marry one of our own."

"Jesus Christ," Inudo said, "she is our own. My grandparents were in California when hers were still in Ireland."

"Look, Mr. Historian," the senior Inudo said, "we know the facts too. I don't want you to talk that way to your mother."

Inudo apologized. "The world is in turmoil," he said. "We recognize China, lose Iran, run a great risk of a national economic catastrophe, and all you worry about is the pigmentation of my girlfriend's skin."

"The color of her skin is history," Mrs. Inudo said.

Her son pulled on his boots.

"Mom and Dad . . ." he said. Years as an orator had taught him dramatic pause. He read the anguish in their faces. "I hate to do this but I'm twenty-three now." The hope of the next generation moved into Caucasian Jane's student apartment.

Pressed for cash and feeling independent, Inudo hired on as a security guard for the Taiwanese trade office in San Jose. The presence of such a large Oriental made the trade officials feel less betrayed. He played gin rummy with them. With the Taiwanese, Inudo could generalize about Carthage, Atlantis, ancient Tyre and Babylon. They identified and felt the pangs of the ancient suffering.

"All will be lost for us too," the Taiwanese said. Their fatalism made them erratic card players and Inudo won more than his salary.

"The Eastern nations should form an OPEC of the electronics industry," he urged. "Governments are only figureheads. Real power has already shifted to transnational economic blocks. Taiwan, Korea, and Hong Kong can put the squeeze on textiles too. Fight back," he urged. "Don't be like my father who is not angry about being in an American prison camp when he was a teenager."

The Taiwanese liked his spunk. They hated Jimmy Carter more than Inudo hated the memory of Franklin Roosevelt. Beside Inudo as he ginned on the Taiwanese legates, Jane felt as if she were in the presence of the significant. She bought him a long cashmere scarf that tickled her ears when she sat behind him on the Suzuki.

H. L. Lee, the San Jose liaison, introduced Inudo to Huey "Bo" Huang, Taiwan's main man in world trade. Huang, a beaten man, stopped in San Jose on his way home after failing to even get an interview with the assistant secretary of Commerce. Huang, a wise man even in defeat, marveled at the surprising size of Slim Inudo. "A regular Wilt Chamberlain," he said.

"Don't patronize me," Slim Inudo said. "The stakes are high for your small island republic. There is no time for idle talk."

Bo Huang knew a good man when he saw one. Huang's father was related on both sides of his family to General Chiang Kai-shek. Genetics, thus, made Huang a diplomat; by inclination he preferred American sports, light reading, and the company of small-boned women.

Slim Inudo found the American abandonment of Taiwan the first great issue of his adult political life. He was too young for Vietnam, but betrayal by the West was his favorite theme.

"Woe to those who trusted in Rome," he told Huang, "and woe to the small island republic that is less than self-sufficient." He mentioned Mytilene in the Aegean Sea at the time of the Peloponnesian Wars.

"Listen," Bo Huang said over a half cup of oolong tea, "I'm on my way back to Taipei after a rough 48 hours in D.C. Give me a break." Bo took off his shoes and watched the office gin game.

Slim Inudo in his tan Burns security uniform looked like a boy scout troopmaster when on the office blackboard he outlined the major political issues of the day. Bo Huang sucked on his pipe. "A thinker like you is always useful in government," he said. "Unfortunately we Taiwanese are now cutting back on employment. No longer will we maintain full consulates throughout the world." He looked sadly at H. L. Lee and the San Jose boys. He shook his head. The gloom made Jane shiver. Slim Inudo ginned and the San Jose boys pulled out their dollars.

"It sounds abstract to most Americans," Lee said. "They can't tell one Chinaman from another. And Vietnam confused them so much they curtailed the domestic production of globes. When Americans look East they want to see what Marco Polo saw."

"Marco Polo," Inudo said, "was a popularizer, a trivializer. He was like the astronauts who go to the moon to play golf."

Huey "Bo" Huang smiled in amazement. "You should be at the U.N."

"That's what my mother says."

Jane stroked Inudo's long dark hair and peeked over his shoulder at the gin rummy hand.

"Your mother," Huang said, "knows personnel."

Inudo smiled and dropped his cards. "Listen fellas," he pleaded, "don't give up. Taiwan is already off the front pages but it will be an issue for years. Lots of Americans are with you. I am, and I'm as far from Ronald Reagan as you can get. It has nothing to do with power politics. It's a matter of small island republics."

Huang shook his head sadly. "You're a good boy, Slim, but we didn't become the free world's largest textile mill by forgetting realism. No, we won't go the way of Jonestown or Masada nor will the hunchbacked pinkos ever drink our blood. We'll just curl up and die of loneliness." Small tears rolled quickly down Mr. Huang's round cheeks. Jane reached in her purse for Kleenex. The San Jose trade mission boys scuffed their shoes and looked away from one another.

Slim Inudo said, "I'm sick of this saving-face business. You guys may be Orientals; I'm an American." He went to the phone and called Washington.

Slim Inudo's name was well known among the Washington staff of Senator B. S. Hirahimo. Some still bristled over Slim's abrupt refusal to become a page after high school. All of them knew his recent forays into Caucasian girls and the generation gap. Mrs. Inudo wrote monthly letters to the senator. The senator himself had given her the idea. When she received his monthly "Report from Washington" she decided that if the senator had the time, so did she. "The Inudo Report" reached his desk on the first of each month. His staffers jokingly put it on the top of his pile of work whenever it arrived. The name "Inudo" became in the Hirahimo office a synonym for small-town mentality. They called Jimmy Carter an Inudo. Kings and princes, governors and various federal agency directors were called either first-class or second-class Inudos. Someone from the staff thanked Mrs. Inudo each month for her report.

When Slim telephoned from the Taiwanese Trade Office, the secretary merely announced an Inudo calling. They all thought it was an Inudo from Consumer Affairs or Environmental Protection or Defense. An Inudo with the Taiwanese, a genuine Inudo, was a major diplomatic event. They paged Hirahimo from the Senate floor where he was reading last month's *Intellectual Digest*.

The senator was not as fond of the Inudo joke as his staffers were. He treated the call from Slim as a serious complaint from a constituent. He said that he too was disturbed by the Taiwanese about-face.

"When a man like Huey Huang can't even get a ten-minute appointment with the assistant secretary of Commerce, someone's looking up the wrong hole," Slim said. He was an Inudo who never minced his words.

"I'll see what I can do," the senator promised.

"I'll wait for your call," Slim said. "I'll be at this number until five."

Huey "Bo" Huang, dabbing at his cheeks with Jane's Kleenex, said, "With a few dozen like you we wouldn't need recognition from the rest of America."

•

Emily Inudo never knew how instrumental her monthly reports were in her son's sudden reawakening to civic duty. "One day he's moving in with a plain Jane," she said to the senior Inudo, "the next he's going to Washington with the Taiwan ambassador. Genius can't stay hidden for too long." The elder Inudos stored his Suzuki in the garage and promised to keep the chrome parts free of rust.

Jane bought her own half-fare ticket and accompanied him. "It's not just romance," she told the skeptical Inudos. "I'm a journalist and this may be a major story."

Emily Inudo could overlook the girlfriend. Her son was finally on his way to Washington. "When he comes back," she told her husband, "he'll have a title. I know it."

Senator Hirahimo called Commerce and made an appointment for Huey Huang of the Republic of China. "It's just kind of an embarrassment," Commerce told the Senator, "to have these Taiwan people hanging around. I mean the ax fell. You'd think they'd turn their embassy into a townhouse or something and stop dry cleaning their flags."

The senator stood firm. By four o'clock he called Slim Inudo and gave him a date and appointment time. On the spot Huey "Bo" Huang hired Slim as a Washington lobbyist for the Republic of China.

Slim Inudo turned in his Burns security outfit for a three-piece

Hong Kong suit. The tailor whistled through his teeth when he measured Inudo's inseam. "That's one Texas-size Jap," he said.

"An American," Slim Inudo corrected, "a 100% American of Oriental lineage."

Huey Huang insisted on ordering three suits for Slim. "Expense account," he said. "Washington is a dress-up city." Jane bought a shirtwaist, two pairs of low-heeled shoes, and a strapless gown. Mr. Huang put it on the tab. "You're judged by your company too." He threw in a new hairdo from Saks Fifth Avenue. "When you're representing a government, personal expenses don't mean anything," he said. "You have to think in larger terms."

An Air Taipei charter refueling in Oakland carried them first class to Washington. For Jane and Slim it was their first trip to the nation's capital. The charter was taken up by Filipinos and by Americans returning from Guam. The Taiwanese were already staying home in great numbers. Stunned and unsure of what to do next, they hoarded canned goods and awaited word on the future of their small island republic.

"We're desperate," Mr. Huang told Inudo. Jane took notes. "We're desperate and the U.S., our friend and ally, is turning her back on thirty years of friendship."

"We'll see about that," Slim Inudo said. Secure in the company of his new employee, Huey Huang relaxed for the first time since the change in the mainland wall posters.

•

Official Washington hardly noticed the new lobbyist. One more cup of bottomless coffee at the Mayflower Hotel, another pair of ninety-dollar shoes, a few appointments with underlings, extra sales of mimeo paper . . . it happened every day.

Jane and Huey "Bo" Huang knew this was different. "A single man has always been able to affect the course of events," Huang said. "Look at Simón Bolívar, Fidel Castro, Charles de Gaulle, Sun Yat-sen . . ." At Commerce where Huang wanted to talk textiles, he was told to keep a low profile and not press the Carter administration. "I know you fellas can't see things from our point of view," the assistant secretary told Huang, "but we've got a peck of trouble on our hands. Taiwan hasn't been a serious issue since

Eisenhower. It's time for everyone to look toward the twenty-first century."

Huang cabled his government in code, "H Bomb Only Hope."

"I could stay here," he confessed to Slim and Jane at dinner. "I could do very well for myself. Lots of governments would hire me as a trade consultant and IBM has made me a most attractive offer. My salary now is peanuts by comparison."

"You cannot put a price on patriotism," Slim said. "That tiny island republic needs you. The venture capitalists of the West have a host of MBA programs."

"Don't I know it," Huang said, fighting bitterness. "Haven't I lectured at Harvard, Pennsylvania, Cornell, Stanford, and UCLA breaking up a busy schedule time and again to give tips on international business free of charge."

"You should know," Inudo said, "that the European always has and always will continue to think of us as an oddity. My own projection for the next 200 years is for renewed and bitter Moslem-Christian wars. The Orient will become the world's only sanctuary with Russia and India joining the religious wars."

Jane took it all down. Columnists at nearby tables chewed lightly and ordered their waiters to stand still until Slim finished his statement. Scattered applause rang through the Sans Souci.

"But in the meantime," Huang said, "in the short run, in the next five or ten years what can we do?"

"Arm to the teeth," Inudo said. "Hire mercenaries and sign mutual defense pacts with every unaligned nation."

"Come now," said an unnamed high state department official from a secluded table at the rear. "That will only lead to total ostracism. We are still your friends. Only geopolitical events have brought us to this temporary misunderstanding about national identity and territorial aspiration."

There was much applause. "Let's get out of here," Inudo said. "I heard that in D.C. you had to watch your tongue, but I didn't expect this."

"It was worse during Watergate," Huang said. "Then everyone was routinely taping small talk. You could never flag a waiter. They were always running out to buy AA batteries for someone important. A Taiwanese engineer solved the problem with an inexpensive and portable voice-actuated device. Nobody in Washington even asked his name."

"The faceless," Inudo said, "the fodder of history." He arose and signed for his dinner. "If they look to the twenty-first century, so can we."

•

The existence of small republics coincided with the attention to size that was the graph of Slim Inudo's life. He was twelve to fifteen inches taller than any of his relatives. To Inudo love meant, early on, bending and restraint of power. He felt sometimes like a bird or animal magically able to understand human speech. In his extra long trousers and size 15 shoes he went with his father to shop in the boy's department. He was big, very big, but he felt small and he understood smallness. In crowds he suffocated even when his head bobbed above everyone else's. To his family he was a freak of nature but they felt blessed by his awesomeness, aware of the special responsibility of such an offspring. Emily Inudo likened her big boy to Samson and worried about his fate among the Philistines. When his father took two-year-old Slim for his first haircut Emily cried all day. She told her husband her ideas about Samson for, already at two, his height soared off the growth charts.

"Well, then it's better for me to take him for a haircut than his girlfriends," the senior Inudo joked, but as the boy continued to grow past the size of all their known ancestors he too began to suspect a special destiny for young Slim.

They never had to caution the boy about gentleness to his peers. On the playground he deferred to everyone. Even in high school as a star basketball forward he made his reputation on defense and gladly let others take the shots. Emily Inudo saw no hint of a Delilah in Jane Williams. There was no exoticism of dress or manner, no femaleness lying in wait with a scissors; just a very pretty brown-haired girl long from knee to thigh and aware of her blue-green eyes.

Although he had moved from their household in the spirit of youthful rebelliousness, their Slim wrote long letters from Washington explaining his preoccupation with Taiwan.

"The world," he wrote, "is in its penultimate stages of a transference from the last gasps of capitalism. Marxism too is fading like the 1920s. The future of political and social development really lies with the small republics. It was Athens, not Persia or even

Rome, that gave us our ideologies and Marxism has its best chance
in a place like Cuba. If only the big powers would let the small
republics develop independently the world might know real progress."

"Does he belong in Congress," Emily Inudo asked her husband,
"or doesn't he?" She sent copies of certain of his letters to Senator
Hirahimo.

•

Jane, too energetic for simple housekeeping, found a part-time job
with the Associated Press. She suspected that the CIA, aware of
Inudo's work and anxious to eavesdrop, somehow got her the job.
"It was so easy," she said, "no transcript, no portfolio, an interview
full of smiles and $9 an hour, set your own schedule. It's not like
the real world is supposed to be."

Mr. Huang did not take her suspicions seriously. "The CIA is
treacherous," he admitted, "but not as powerful as a beautiful
woman. Beauty always sets its own hours."

Jane blushed. "Not at SJ State it didn't." Her work put her in
instant touch with world events. Anything remotely connected to
Taiwan she clipped and stuck in her purse. But the news ran
entirely to the mainland. A few senators from rural areas wrote
letters of condolence to the Taiwan embassy but no longer could
Huey "Bo" Huang talk about the Republic of China without con-
fusing people.

Delegations from the Chinese mainland to the U.S. became routine. When Coca-Cola signed a long-term agreement with Peking,
Taiwan's nervous citizens, not trusting in the Hong Kong black
market, began to hoard Coke. Their government and the Coca-
Cola company tried to reassure them but siege mentality was
everywhere. In two weeks you couldn't find a Coke on the island.
Jane put a story on the AP wire about the Coke shortages but no
paper ran it. Instead the media covered the endless jaunts of Peking officials to prison rodeos, barbecues, and midnight dinners in
Hollywood.

"Siege mentality is not exciting news," Slim Inudo said. "You see
that it's glamour alone that brings attention."

"I would have never believed it," Jane said. "In the classroom we
are so isolated that it hurts."

Inudo and Jane huddled beside the fireplace of their Georgetown apartment planning the future of small island republics. Huang had established an office for Inudo at the embassy but Slim preferred to work at home. He registered as a representative of a foreign government, reported his salary, and claimed only himself as a deduction. In "The Inudo Report" Emily called her son a "goodwill ambassador" but in his heart malign calculation dwelled. He read history for many hours each day.

"I thought," Mr. Huang said finally, "after your exuberant success in obtaining an interview with the Commerce Department that you might work at a less leisurely pace." Bo Huang, a desperate man, did not want to offend Inudo but his small island republic showed daily signs of export slippage.

"There is no immediate hurry," Slim said after reading intelligence estimates from the Defense Department. "Your population is not in danger and there is no critical shortage of raw material. The people of the island are unified. They will triumph. I am studying options."

"We have experts and our own State Department," Huang said. "Don't try to shoulder the burden completely, just do a little public relations."

Inudo closed the covers of *Capitalism and Material Life: 1400–1800* and put a long arm around his employer. "Bo," he said, "let's get it straight. You know I'm thinking of much more than a contract or two. If I'd wanted to hawk wares I could have gone to law school or become a professional Japanese-American. I want to develop a policy for small island republics. It's not just Taiwan. There are the tourist jewels of the Caribbean, there is Madagascar, the Azores, even Israel, a tiny island republic in a sea of Arabs. Everywhere the big eat the small. It may be pure physics, the whole universe as hungry as gravity. I want small island republics to maintain their identity. I want no more Carthages, no more teeth sown in the ground of a destroyed landscape, no more Mytilenes abandoned by her trading partners, no more Pearl Harbors on quiet Sunday mornings."

Bo Huang shook his head. "I see what you're saying," he said, "the vista is too grand for my humble capacities. Essentially, I'm a salesman. Statesmanship blinds me." He buried his face in Inudo's sleeve.

"Salesmen are not superfluous," Inudo said calming his employer. "Whatever else they do small island republics will always need salesmen. The landlocked nation can be smug, brutal, and self-sufficient. The big can be indifferent. But small island republics create civilization."

•

Jane stayed patient as her tall Japanese lover buried himself in policy. She worked, cooked four-egg omelettes, made sure the FM classical station didn't fade too badly, and gave Bo Huang reports on Slim's long study and seclusion.

"He's up to something," she told Bo, "he's working day and night but it's nothing that he'll talk about. He trusts me but I think his ideas are still unformed. He'll tell you as soon as he's got something."

Bo Huang looked at Jane's gleaming complexion. She wore loneliness like an earring. "It must be hard for you," he said.

Jane tried a half smile, "I don't complain." Bo Huang appreciated her well-formed ankles and the slope of her instep as a pennyloafer dangled at the top of her foot.

"It's odd how we are thrown together," he said, "the way big destinies gobble up small ones." He removed Jane's loafer and put the ball of her foot on his knee. Her toes contracted and dug their pattern into his gray silk suit. "I was raised by important people to think of myself as an important person," Huang said. "It's hard to accept the insignificance of one's homeland. Personal relations may be all that we're left with."

When Bo pulled at her anklet Jane crumbled into his lap. "If he had paid me the slightest attention . . . " she moaned.

"I know, I know," the trade ambassador said, "living in chaotic times has made us all animals."

"If small island republics can't survive," Jane gasped, "is there any hope for personal morality?"

•

Slim Inudo saw the flowers and the notes, and he read the look in both their eyes. He said nothing nor did he vary his intense study of documentary and social history. "Personal fidelity means nothing to him," Bo Huang said. "He is a giant, truly a giant, not in body alone."

Jane wondered what her parents would think, first a Japanese-American then a Chinese trade envoy. "I guess the East is my destiny," she wrote. Her family was very impressed by the AP job. Her young brother liked the autographed pictures she sent him of all the members of the Senate. "His walls are lined with politicians," her mother wrote. "His friends come over and quiz each other about who's the senator from where. It's a wonderful way to study civics."

Inudo regularly sent requests to the Library of Congress. Since he asked on behalf of a foreign trade consulate he received same day messenger delivery of whatever he wanted. The Georgetown apartment looked like a library storage room. U.N. reports, geography textbooks, stories of fabled Atlantis, books everywhere Jane stepped. Only the kitchen remained neat. When Jane was certain he had finished with a stack of materials she took them back to the library herself. But no matter how much she returned, his requests were ever greater. Inudo stopped taking meals with her. He ate in his study at the bay window overlooking P Street.

"I don't know," Bo Huang said to Jane, "but whatever happens we have each other. Maybe that's all destiny ever intended. Maybe Taiwan existed only for you and me to share these moments."

Jane loved his boyish romanticism. On his desk were photos of a wife and three children in front of a white stone mansion in Taipei. "Yes," he said, "nobody lives without obstacles but I believe in the power of human affection."

Inudo began to make phone calls to California. He also sent telegrams to all parts of the world. After months of solitude he came out of his study and said he needed a secretary and a very secure telephone line. Huey "Bo" Huang had already given up on Inudo and happily settled for Jane. The sudden burst of activity made him nervous. He was enjoying the status quo. Inudo withered him with a glance. The secretary, a discreet Chinese male, moved into the spare bedroom.

Normalization with China progressed so smoothly that Taiwan became as obscure as the Spanish-American War. Only the CIA still seemed interested. Sometimes Jane knew she was being followed as she walked down Pennsylvania Avenue. She did not feel threatened. On windy nights she covered her typewriter and felt extra good knowing the government was watching her as she walked through unsafe neighborhoods to her apartment where three Oriental men awaited her. The secretary spent all his time typing, Bo cooked, and Inudo talked on the phone and read. Jane felt as if she were living a fairytale with Charlie Chan and his sons.

"All this intrigue," she thought, "all this mystery." She could hardly believe that only a few months ago she was writing term papers and going out with boys. Her work was exciting, her men more exciting still. At her doorstep she threw a kiss to the invisible CIA and the deities that had led her to the nation's capital in times like these.

Inudo, now and then, left the apartment. He never told Jane where he went and on two occasions he was gone overnight. Bo, who paid the bills, said there were trips to California. If not for Jane the trade ambassador would long ago have fired his large Japanese-American lobbyist. After Inudo's second trip to California and six months without any visible work, Huang in embarrassment told his superior, Ambassador V. V. Fong, that he was going to fire the only remaining trade lobbyist for lack of lobbying.

Fong shook his finger and wagged his head. "No, no, no," he said, "no, no, no." Huey realized that the matter was over his head and never mentioned it again. If whatever Inudo was doing met with the ambassador's approval Huang need not feel responsible. Textile sales firmed up, and recognized or not, the Republic of China went ahead with her national life.

●

When the news broke in the *Washington Post* Jane sobbed and pounded the pillow. "He could have given me the story," she cried. "He could have told me last night and handed me a Pulitzer Prize. This is how he got even."

Huey "Bo" Huang called Taiwan for confirmation. He shook his head in disbelief. "It's true," he said. "Of course all of the contracts are subject to a vote of the people but in our country that will be automatic."

In California the Disney executives were very subdued. They spoke about their responsibilities to the population and the need to go slowly. The best legal minds had approved the principle. "A small island republic is as individual as a corporation," Inudo said. "When I realized that, the rest was simple matchmaking. The Disneys get a highly trained work force and a prime site adjacent to the world's largest populated area. Taiwan, a no-man's land, becomes a Disneyland. What bananas are to so-called banana republics, electronics is to Disneyland. It was a match made in Heaven."

The surprised administration legally had no power to interfere with the long-term lease of an island to a corporation. "Of course,"

Inudo said, "there is no absolute security, the Communists might still attack, but historically communism is uncomfortable with tourism, uneasy with ease. And who could attack an unarmed magical kingdom," he said. "This small island republic by its merger with a corporate identity might be truly leading the way to the twenty-first century."

After the noon news conference Inudo granted Jane a private three-hour interview. It was his going away present. "I didn't keep it from you on purpose," he said. "It was not my choice to let the *Post* break the story."

"I understand," she said. "This interview and all the background stories will get me by-lines for a month." He packed for home and kissed tenderly the now experienced journalist.

Emily Inudo, seeing her son's picture on the front page, raised her joyful eyes to the heavens. "Samson destroyed," she mumbled, "Slim creates. A small island republic is just a start. Someday he'll be a senator."

ANN BEATTIE

Winter: 1978

(FROM CAROLINA QUARTERLY)

THE CANVASES were packed individually, in shipping cartons. Benton put them in the car and slammed the trunk shut.

"They'll be all right?" the man asked.

"They survived the baggage compartment of the 747, they'll do okay in the trunk," Benton said.

"I love his work," the man said to Nick.

"He's great," Nick said, and felt like an idiot.

Benton and Olivia had just arrived in L.A. Nick had gone to the airport to meet them. Olivia said she wasn't feeling well and insisted on getting a cab to the hotel, even though Nick offered to drive her and meet Benton at Allen Tompkins' house later.

The man who had also come to the airport to meet Benton was Tompkins' driver. Nick could never remember the man's name. Benton was in L.A. to show his paintings to Tompkins. Tompkins would buy everything he had brought. Benton was wary of Tompkins, and of his driver, so he had asked Nick to meet him at the airport and to go with him.

"How was your flight?" Nick said to Benton. All three of them were in the front seat of the Cadillac.

"It was okay. We were half an hour late taking off, but I guess they made up the time in the air. The plane was only a few minutes late, wasn't it?"

"Allen and I are flying to Spain for Christmas," the driver said.

On the tape deck, Orson Welles was broadcasting *The War of the Worlds*. Cars seldom passed them; the man drove sixty-five, with the car on cruise control, nervously brushing hair out of his eyes. The last time Nick rode in this car, a Jack Benny show, complete with canned laughter, had been playing on the tape deck.

"An Arab bought the house next door, and he's having a new pool put in. It's in the shape of different flowers: one part of it's tulip-shaped, and the other part is a rose. I asked, and the pool man told me it was supposed to be a rose." The driver kneaded his left shoulder with his right hand. He was wearing a leather strap around his wrist with squares of hammered silver through the middle.

"Have you been to Marbella?" the driver said. "Beverly Hills is the pits. Only *he* would want to live in Beverly Hills."

They were on Allen Tompkins' street. "Hold it," the driver said to Benton and Nick, taking the car off cruise control but slowing only slightly as he pulled into the steep driveway. He hopped out and opened the door on their side of the car.

Benton hesitated a moment before reaching into the trunk. Glued to the underside of the trunk was a picture of Raquel Welch in a sequined gown. With her white teeth and tightly clothed, sequined body she looked like a mermaid in a nightmare.

Benton was in California because Allen Tompkins paid him triple what he could get for his paintings in New York. Benton had met Tompkins years ago, when he had been framing one of his paintings, staying on after his shift at the frame shop in New Haven where he worked was over. Tompkins had asked Benton how much the picture he was working on would cost when it was framed. "It's my painting, not for sale," Benton had told him. Very politely, Tompkins had asked if he had others. That night, Benton called Nick, drunk, raving that a man he had just met had given him a thousand dollars *cash.* He had gone out with Benton the next night, Benton laughing and running from store to store, to prove to himself that the money really bought things. Benton had bought a brown tweed coat and a pipe. That joke had only turned sour when Benton's wife, Elizabeth, commended him for selecting such nice things.

Now, seven years later, Benton was wearing jeans and a black velvet jacket, and they were sitting in Tompkins' library. It was cluttered with antique Spanish furniture, the curtains closed, the room illuminated by lamps with bases in the shape of upright fish that supported huge plexiglass conch-shell globes in their mouths. The lamps cast a lavender-pink light. Three Turkish prayer rugs were lined up across the center of the room — the only floor covering on the white-painted floorboards.

"Krypto and Baby Kal-El," Tompkins said, coming toward them

with both hands outstretched. Benton smiled and shook both of Tompkins' hands. Then Nick shook his hand too, certain that any feeling of warmth came from Tompkins' just having shaken hands with Benton.

"I'm so excited," Tompkins said. He went to the long window behind where Benton and Nick sat on the sofa and pulled the string that drew the drapes apart. "Dusk falls on Gotham City," Tompkins said. He sat in the heavily carved chair beside the sofa. "All for me?" he said, raising his eyebrows at the crates. "If you like them," Benton said. The driver came into the library with a bottle of ouzo and a pitcher of orange juice on a tray. He put it on the small table midway between Benton and Tompkins.

"Sit down. Sit down and have a look," Tompkins said excitedly. The man sat on the floor by the crates, leaning against the sofa. Benton took a Swiss Army knife out of his pocket and began undoing the first one.

"I'm using my special x-ray vision," Tompkins said, "and I love it already."

Tompkins got up and crouched by the open crate, fingers on the top of the frame, obviously enjoying every second of the suspense, before he pulled the picture out.

"Money and taste," the driver said to Nick.

"You could not remember the simplest song lyric," Tompkins said to his driver, slowly drawing out the painting. "Money and *time*," he sighed, pulling the canvas out of the crate. "Money and time," he said again, but this time it was half-hearted; he was interested in nothing but the picture he held in front of him. Benton was always amazed by that expression on Tompkins' face. It made Benton as happy as he had been years before when he and Elizabeth were still married, and it had been his morning routine to go into Jason's bedroom, gently shake him awake, and see his son's soft blue eyes slowly focus on his own.

•

It was three days after Benton had sold all his paintings to Tompkins, and Nick had gone to the hotel where Olivia and Benton were staying to try to persuade them to go to lunch.

The light came into the hotel room in a strange way. The curtains were hung from brass rings, and between the rings, because the curtains did not quite come to the top of the window, light leaked in. Benton and Olivia kept the curtains closed all day — what they saw of the daylight was a pale band across the paint.

Olivia was lounging on the bed in Benton's boxer shorts and a T-shirt imprinted with a picture of the hotel, and when Nick laughed at her she pointed to his own clothing: white cowboy boots with gold-painted eagles on the toes, white jeans, a T-shirt with what looked like a TV test pattern on it. Nick had almost forgotten that he had brought Olivia a present. He took his hand out of his pocket and brought out a toy pistol in the shape of a bulldog. He pulled the trigger and the dog's mouth opened and the bulldog squeaked.

"Don't thank me," Nick said, putting it on the bedside table with the other clutter. "A blinking red light means that you have a message," he said. He picked up the phone and dialed the hotel operator. "Nothing to it," Nick said, patting Olivia's leg. "Red light blinks, you just pick up the phone and get your message. If Uncle Nickie can do it, anybody can."

He tickled Olivia's lips with an uneaten croissant from the bedside table. He was holding it so she could bite the end. She did. Nick dipped it in the butter, which had become very soft, and held it to her mouth again. She puffed on her joint and ignored him. He took a bite himself and put it back on the plate. He went to the window and pulled back the drapes, looking at the steep hill that rose in back of the hotel.

"I wish I lived in a hotel," he said. "Nice soft sheets, bathroom scrubbed every day, pick up the phone and get a croissant."

"You can get all those things at home," Benton said, wrapping a towel around him as he came out of the bathroom. The towel was too small. He gave up after several tugs and threw it over the chair.

"The sheets I slept on last night illustrated the hunt of the Unicorn. Poor bastard is not only fenced in, but I settled my ass on him. Manuela does nothing in the bathroom but run water in the tub and smoke Tiparillos. Maybe on the way home I'll stop and pick up some croissants." Nick closed the window. "Christmas decorations are already going up," he said. He took a bottle of pills out of pocket and put them on the table. The label said: "Francis Blanco: 2 daily, as directed."

"Any point in asking who Francis Blanco is?" Benton said.

"You're hovering like a mother over her chicks," Nick said.

"Some day that bottle will grow wings and fly away, and then you'll wonder why you cared so much." Nick clasped his hands behind him. "Francis Blanco just overhauled my carburetor," he said. "You don't have to look far for anything."

•

In spite of the joke about being Uncle Nickie, Nick was Benton's age and four years younger than Olivia. Nick was twenty-nine, from a rich New England family, and he had come to California four years before and made a lot of money in the record industry. His introduction to the record industry had come from a former philosophy professor's daughter's supplier. In exchange for the unlisted numbers of two Sag Harbor dope dealers, Dex Whitmore had marched Nick into the office of a man in L.A. who hired him on the spot. Nick sent a post card of the moon rising over the freeways to the professor, thanking him for the introduction to his daughter, who had, in turn, introduced him to her yoga teacher, who was responsible for his gainful employment. Dex Whitmore would have liked the continuation of that little joke; back East, he had gone to the professor's house once a week to lead the professor's daughter in "yoga exercises." That is, they had gone to the attic and smoked dope and turned somersaults. Dex had been dead for nearly a year now, killed in a freak accident that had nothing to do with the fact that he sold drugs. He had been waiting at a dry cleaner's to drop off a jacket when a man butted in front of him. Dex objected. The man took out a pistol and put a bullet in his side, shooting through a bottle of champagne Dex had clasped under his arm. Later Dex's ex-wife filed a suit for more money from his estate, claiming that he had been carrying the bottle of champagne because he was on his way to reconcile with her.

Nick hadn't succeeded in getting Benton and Olivia to leave the hotel. He was hungry, so he parked his car and went into a bakery. The cupcakes looked better than the croissants, so he bought two of them and ate them sitting at the counter. It embarrassed him that Benton and Olivia couldn't stay at his house, but the year before, when they were in L.A., his dog had tried to bite Olivia. Ilena, the woman he lived with, also disliked Olivia, and he half thought that somehow she had communicated to the dog that he should lunge and growl.

He peeled the paper off of the second cupcake. One of the

cupcakes had a little squirt of orange and red icing on top, piped out to look like maize. The other one had a crooked glob of pale brown, an attempt at a drumstick.

Nick was a friend of long standing, and used to most of Benton's eccentricities — including the fact that his idea of travel was to go somewhere and never leave the hotel. He and Benton had grown up in the same neighborhood. Benton had once supplied Nick with a fake I.D. for Christmas; Nick had turned Benton on to getting high with nutmeg. Each had talked Dorothy Birdley ("most studious") into sleeping with the other. Benton presented Nick as brilliant and sensitive; Nick told her, sitting underneath an early-flowering tree on the New Haven green, that Benton's parents beat him. In retrospect, she had probably slept with them because she was grateful anyone was interested in her: she had bottle-thick glasses and a long pointed nose, and she was very self-conscious about her appearance and defensive about being the smartest person in the high school.

It had been a real surprise for Nick when Benton began to think differently from him — when, home from college at Christmas, Benton had called to ask him if he wanted to go to the funeral parlor to pay his respects to Dorothy Birdley's father. He had never thought about facing Dorothy Birdley again, and Benton had made him feel ashamed for being reluctant. He drove and stayed in the car. Benton went in alone. Then they went to a bar in New Haven and talked about college. Benton liked it, and was going to transfer to the Fine Arts department; Nick hated the endless reading, didn't know what he wanted to study, and would never have had Benton's nerve to buck his father and change from studying business anyway. In other ways, though, Benton had become almost more prudent: "You go ahead," Benton said when the waitress came to see if they wanted another round. "I'll just have coffee." So Nick had sat there and gotten sloshed, and Benton had stayed sober enough to get them home. Then, when they graduated, Benton had surprised him again. He had gotten engaged to Elizabeth. In his letters to him that year, Benton had expressed amusement at how uptight Elizabeth was, and Nick had been under the impression that Benton was loosening up, that Elizabeth was just a pretty girl Benton saw from time to time. When Benton married her, things started to turn around. Nick, that year, stumbled into a high-paying job in New York; his rela-

tionship with his father was better, after they had a falling out and
his father called to apologize. Benton's father, on the other hand,
left home; the job Benton thought he'd landed with a gallery fell
through, and he went to work as a clerk in a framing store. In
December, six months after he married Elizabeth, she was pregnant. Then it was Nick who did the driving and Benton who
drank. Coming out of a bar together, the night Benton told Nick
that Elizabeth was pregnant, Benton had been so argumentative
that Nick was afraid he had been trying to start a fight with
him.

"I end up on the bottom, and you end up on the top, after your
father tried to talk your mother into shipping you out to his
brother's in Montana in high school, you drove him so crazy. Now
he's advising you about what stock to buy."

"What are you talking about?" Nick had said.

"I told you that. Your mother told my mother."

"You never told me," Nick said.

"I did." Benton, said rolling down the window and pitching his
cigarette.

"It must have been Idaho," Nick said. "My uncle lives in Idaho."

They rode in silence. "I'm not so lucky," Nick said, suddenly
depressed. "I might have Ilena's car, but she's in Honolulu tonight."

"What's she doing there?"

"She's with a tea merchant."

"What's she doing with a tea merchant?"

"Wearing orchids and going to pig barbecues. How do I know?"

"Honolulu," Benton said. "I don't have the money to get to
Atlantic City."

"What's there?"

"I don't have the money to eat caramel corn and see a horse
jump off a pier."

"Have you talked to her about an abortion?" Nick said.

"Sure. Like trying to convince her the moon's a yo-yo."

He rolled down his window again. Wind rushed into the car and
blew the ashes around. Nick saw the moon, burning white, out the
side window of the car.

"I don't have the money for a kid," Benton said. "I don't have
the money for popcorn."

To illustrate his point, he took his wallet out of his back pocket

and dropped it out the window. "Son of a bitch, I don't believe it,"
Nick said. They were riding on the inside lane, fast, and there was
plenty of traffic behind them. What seemed to be a quarter of a
mile beyond where Benton had thrown his wallet, Nick bumped
off the highway, emergency lights flashing. The car was nosed
down so steeply on the hill rolling beneath the emergency lane
(which he had overshot) that the door flew open when he cracked
it to get out. Nick climbed out of the car, cursing Benton. He got
a flashlight out of the trunk and started to run back, remembering
having seen some sort of sign on the opposite side of the road just
where Benton had thrown his wallet. It was bitter cold, and he was
running with a flashlight, praying a cop wouldn't come along. Mi-
raculously, he found the wallet in the road and darted for it when
traffic stopped. He ran down the center median, back to the car,
wallet in his pocket, beam from the flashlight bobbing up and
down. "God damn it," he panted, pulling the car door open.

The light came on. For a few seconds no cars passed. Everything
on their side of the highway was still. Nick's heart felt like it was
beating in his back. Benton had fallen up against the door and was
slumped there, breathing through his mouth. Nick pulled the wallet out of his pocket and put it on the seat. As he dropped it, it
flopped open. Nick was looking at a picture of Elizabeth, smiling
her madonna smile.

•

He drove back to the hotel to get Olivia and Benton for dinner.
The lobby looked like a church. There were no lights on, except
for dim spotlights over the pictures. Nobody was in the lobby. He
went over to the piano and played a song. A man came down the
steps into the room, applauding quietly when he finished.

"Quite nice," the man said. "Are you a musician?"

"No," Nick said.

"You staying here, then?"

"Some friends are."

"Strange place. What floor's your friend on?"

"Fourth," Nick said.

"Not him, then," the man said. "I'm on the third, and some man
cries all night."

He sat down and opened the newspaper. There was not enough
light in the lobby to read by. Nick played "The Sweetheart Tree,"
forgot how it went halfway through, got up, and went into the

phone booth. It was narrow and high, and when he closed the wood door he felt like he was in a confessional.

"Father I have sinned," he whispered. "I have supplied already strung-out friends with Seconal, and I have been unfriendly to an Englishman who was probably only lonesome."

He dialed his house. Ilena picked it up.

"Reconsider," he said. "Come to dinner. We're going to Mr. Chow's. You love Chow's."

"I've got nothing to say to her," Ilena said.

"Come on," he said. "Go with us."

"She's always stoned."

"Go with us," he said.

Ilena sighed. "How was work?"

"Work was great. Exciting. Rewarding. All that I always hope work will be. The road manager for Barometric Pressure called to yell about there not being any chicken tacos in the band's dressing room. Wanted to know whether I did or did not send a telegram to New York."

"Well," she said. "Now I've asked about work. Only fair that you ask me about the doctor."

"I forgot," he said. "How did it go?"

"The bastard cauterized my cervix without telling me he was going to do it."

"God. That must have hurt."

"I see why people go around stoned. I just don't want to eat dinner with them."

"Okay, Ilena. Did you walk Fathom?"

"Manuela just had him out. I threw the frisbee for him half the afternoon."

"That's nice of you."

"I can hardly stand up straight."

"I'm sorry."

"I'll see you later," Ilena said.

He went out of the phone booth and walked up the stairs. Pretty women never liked other pretty women. He rang the buzzer outside Benton and Olivia's room.

Benton opened the door in such a panic that Nick smiled, thinking he was clowning because Nick had told him earlier that he was too lethargic. It only took a few seconds to figure out it wasn't a joke. Benton had on a white shirt hanging outside his jeans and a tie hanging over his shoulder. Olivia had on a dress and was sitting, still as a mummy, hands in her lap, in a chair with its back to the desk.

"You know that call? The phone call from Ena? You know what the message was? My brother's dead. You know what the hotel told Ena days ago? That I'd checked out. She called back, and today they told her I was here. Wesley is dead."

"Oh, Christ," Nick said.

"He and a friend were on Lake Champlain. They drowned. In November, they were out in a boat on Lake Champlain. Today was the funeral. Why the hell did they tell her I'd checked out? It doesn't matter anymore why they told her that." Benton turned to Olivia. "Get up," he said. "Pack."

"There's no point in my going," she said, her voice almost a whisper. "I'll fly to New York with you and go to the apartment."

"Elizabeth would hate not to see you," Benton said. "She likes to see you and clutch Jason from the hawk."

"Elizabeth is at your mother's?" Nick said.

"Elizabeth misses no opportunity to ingratiate herself with my family. They're not at my mother's. They're at his house, in Weston, for some reason."

"I thought he lived on Park Avenue."

"He moved to Connecticut." Benton slammed his suitcase shut. "For God's sake, I've made plane reservations. Will you pack your suitcase?"

"I'll drive you to the airport," Nick said.

"God damn it," Benton said, "I don't mean to be ungracious, but I realize that, Nick." Benton was packing Olivia's suitcase. He looked at the bedside table and sighed and held the suitcase underneath it and swept everything in. He put a sign about the continental breakfast the hotel served back on the table.

"I really love you," Olivia said, "and when something awful happens, you treat me like shit."

Olivia got up and Nick put his arm around her shoulder and steered her toward the door. Benton came behind them, carrying both suitcases.

"You were lucky you could get a plane this close to Thanksgiving," Nick said.

"I guess I was. Forgot it was Thanksgiving."

"Maybe people don't go home for Thanksgiving anymore," Nick said.

Nick was remembering what Thanksgiving used to be like, and

the good feeling he got as a child when the holidays came and it snowed. One Christmas his parents had given him an archery set, and he had talked his father into setting it up outside in the snow. His father had been drunk and had taken a fruitcake from the kitchen counter and put the round, flat cake on top of his head like a hat, and stood to the side of the target, tipping his fruitcake hat, yelling to Nick to shoot it off his head while his mother rapped on the window, gesturing them inside.

"I hope you enjoyed your stay," the woman behind the desk said to Benton.

"Fine," Benton said.

"How you doing?" Dennis Hopper said.

"Fine," the woman behind the desk said. She reached around Benton and handed Dennis Hopper his mail.

The security guard was sitting on a chair drinking a Coke. He was staring at them. Nick hoped that by the time he got them to the airport that Olivia would have stopped crying.

"Want to come East and liven up the wake?" Benton said to Nick.

"They don't want to see me," Olivia said. "Why can't I go back to the apartment?"

"You're who I live with. My brother just died. We're going to be with my family."

"I wish I could go," Nick said. "I wish I could act like everybody else in my office — phone in and say I'm having an anxiety attack."

"Come with us," Olivia said, squeezing his hand. "Please."

"I can't just get on a plane," he said.

"If there's a seat," she said.

"I don't know," Nick said. "Are you serious?"

"I'm serious," Benton said. "Olivia's probably as serious as she gets on Valium."

"That was nasty," she said. "I'm not stoned."

"I don't know," Nick said. Olivia looked at him. "About the plane, I mean," he said.

"She misunderstands things when she's stoned," Benton said.

They got into Nick's car and he pulled out onto the narrow, curving road behind the hotel. "I'll call Ilena," Nick said. "Are we going to miss the plane if I go back into the hotel?"

"We've got time," Benton said. "Go on."

He left the car running and went back into the hotel. The security guard was making funny whiney noises and shuffling across the floor, and the girl behind the desk was laughing. She saw him looking at them and called out: "It's an imitation of one of the rabbits in *Watership Down*."

The security guard, amused at his own routine, crossed his eyes and wiggled his nose.

•

The house in Weston was huge. It was a ten-room house on four acres, the back lawn bordered by massive fir trees, and in front of them thick vines growing large, oblong pumpkins. Around the yard were sunflowers, frost struck, bent almost in half. Nick squatted to stare at one of their black faces.

He had seen the sunflowers curving in the moonlight when they arrived the night before and Benton's mother, Ena, lit the yard with floodlights; the flowers were just outside that aura of light, and he had squinted before he was able to make out what they were. It was morning now, and he was examining one. He ran his fingers across its rough face.

The reality of Wesley's death hadn't really hit him until he got to the house, walked across the lawn, and went inside. Then, although he hadn't seen Wesley for years, and had never been to the house, Nick felt that Ena didn't belong there, and that Wesley was very far away.

Ena had been waiting up for them, and the house had been burning with light — hard to see from the highway, she had told Benton on the phone — but inside there was a horrible pall over everything, in spite of the brightness. He had not been able to get to sleep, and when he had slept, he had dreamed about the gigantic, bent sunflowers. Wesley was dead.

The movie they had shown on the plane, which they stared at but did not listen to, had a scene in it of a car chase through San Francisco, with Orientals smiling in the back seat of a speeding car and waving little American flags. It did not seem possible that such a thing could be happening if Wesley was really dead.

Ena was at the house because she thought that assembling there was a tribute to Wesley — no matter that in the six months he'd lived there he never invited the family to his house, and that the things they saw there now made Wesley more of an enigma. And they had already begun to take his things. They obviously felt guilty or embarrassed about it, because when the three of them came in the night before, people began to confess: Elizabeth had taken Wesley's rapidograph, for Jason; for herself she had taken a dome-shaped paperweight, a souvenir of Texas with a longhorn cow facing down a cowboy with a lasso underwater, in a tableau that would fill with snow when the dome was shaken; Uncle Cal had taken a picture of Ena as a schoolgirl, in a heart-shaped frame. Ena had taken a keyring with three keys on it from Wesley's night table. She did not know what locks the keys fit, because she had tried them on everything in the house with no luck, but they were small antique keys and she wanted to get a chain for them and wear them as a necklace. Wesley was dead, drowned in Lake Champlain, two life vests floating near where the boat capsized, no explanation.

Benton came out of the house. It was a cold morning, and it was early; Nick did not feel too cold because he had found a jacket on a hook by the back door — Wesley's, no doubt — and put it on. Benton, in the black velvet jacket, hugged his arms in front of him.

"I just realized that I dragged you here from California," Benton said. "What are you doing out here?"

"I couldn't sleep. I came out to look around."

"What did you find?"

"Pumpkins still growing in his garden."

At the back of the lawn, past a tangle of leafless berry bushes, was a fallen-down chicken coop. The roof barely cleared their heads. There was a cement floor, and most of the walls were still standing, but they were caving in, or missing boards.

"Long time since this was in operation," Benton said.

"Imagine Wesley out in the country," Nick said.

Most of the back wall was missing from the coop. When they came to the end, Nick jumped down, about five feet, to the ground, and Benton jumped behind him. The woods were covered with damp leaves, thickly layered.

"Although the shape that coop was in, I guess he was hardly the gentleman farmer," Benton said. "What do you think about the way Ena's acting?"

"Ena's edgy."

"She is," Benton said. He pushed a branch out of his face; it was so brittle that it snapped. He used the piece of broken branch to poke at other branches. "I went into Jason's bedroom and thought about kidnapping him. I didn't even have the heart to wake him up to say hello."

"What time was it when you came out?"

"Seven. Seven-thirty."

They saw a white house to their left, just outside the woods, and turned back for the house. Wind chimes were clinking from a tree beside the chicken coop — long green tubes hitting together.

Nick hadn't seen the chimes when he walked back to the chicken coop earlier. They reminded him of the strange graveyard he and Wesley and Benton had gone through when they were in college and Wesley was a senior in high school, on a trip they took to see a friend who had moved to Charlemont, Massachusetts. It was Christmastime, after a snow, and Benton and Nick had been wearing high rubber boots. Wesley, as usual, had on his sneakers. They had sighted the snowy graveyard, and it had been somebody's idea to walk through it. Wesley had been the first one out of the car, and he had also been the first to sight the broomstick slanted into the ground like a flagpole, with wind chimes hanging from the top of it. It was next to one of the tombstones. There was a deep path leading to it — someone had put it there earlier in the day. It looked crazy — a touch from Mardi Gras, nothing you would expect to see standing in a graveyard. The ground was frozen beneath the snow — the person had dug hard to put the broomstick in, and the chimes tinkled and clanked together in the wind. Wesley had photographed that, and also a tombstone with a larger-than-life dog stretched on top — a Borzoi, perhaps, or some odd cross — and the dog appeared to be looking toward a tree that cast a shadow. There was snow mounded on the dog's head and back, and the tree branches it looked toward were weighted with snow.

"You know that picture Wesley took in the graveyard?" Nick said.

"The dog? The one you told him would make a fine Christmas card?"

Nick nodded yes. "You know what fascinates me about photographs? Did you ever notice the captions? Photographer gets a shot of a dwarf running out of a burning hotel and it's labeled 'New York: 1968.' Or there's a picture of two hump-backed girls on the back of a pony, and it says 'Central Park: 1966.' "

"I remember those, too," Benton said. "I wonder why he never showed them? Nobody else in this family is modest. Even Elizabeth tacks her drawings up alongside Jason's." Benton kicked some moss off of his shoe. "It irritated the hell out of him that I'd put my camera on a tripod and wait for the right shot. Remember how he used to carry on about how phony that was?" Benton had stopped to look at some mint, sticking out between the rubble. "He idolized you," Benton said.

"He's dead and I work at Boulevard Records and handle complaints about chicken that doesn't show up," Nick said. "He didn't idolize me."

They were coming closer to the house, and the tinkling of the chimes was faint. They were walking by the pumpkin vines that wove across the ground in front of the tall black-green trees.

Nick was thinking of another one of Wesley's photographs — one he had taken when he and Benton were still in college. The three of them had been in a booth in a restaurant in New Haven, on a Sunday, and Wesley had said, "Don't move." They were waiting for their order, and Nick's hands were resting on *The New York Times*. The picture was pale grey and Nick had been absolutely astonished to see what Wesley had made his hands look like. One hand seemed to be clasping the other as though it was a strange hand. Both hands had been eerily beautiful, the newspaper out of focus beneath them — hands, suspended, with one cradling, or sheltering, the other. When Wesley showed him the photograph he had been so surprised that he couldn't speak. Finally, having had time to think, he said something close to what he meant, but not exactly what he wanted to ask. "How did you get that softness?" he had asked Wesley, and Wesley had hesitated. Then he had said: "I developed it in Acufine."

They went quietly into the house and stood by the heat grate in the kitchen. Nick took down a pan hanging from a nail in the beam over the stove and filled it with water for coffee. Then he sat on the kitchen table. The only real detail they knew of Wesley's death was that the life vests had been floating near the boat. Ena had told them about it the night before. The life vests had stopped in time for Nick. She did not say anything about the color, but Nick knew as she talked that they were bright orange, and the water was grey and deep. One floated beside the boat, one farther off. He had tried to catch his breath when the image formed. He was as shocked as if he had been there when they recovered the body.

Benton was finding cups, putting the filter in the coffee pot. Benton turned off the burner. The bubbles grew smaller. Steam rose from the pan.

"We're both thinking the same thing, aren't we?" Benton said. "Capsized boat, life vests floating free, middle of winter."

" 'Lake Champlain: 1978,' " Nick said.

•

Ena was knitting. The afghan covered her lap and legs and spilled onto the floor, a wide flame pattern of brown and tan and green.

"You look like a cowboy, Nickie," she said. "Why do young men want to look like cowboys now?"

"Leave him alone," Elizabeth said.

"I didn't mean to criticize. I just wanted to know."

"What am I supposed to dress like?" Nick said.

"My husband wore three-piece suits, and ties even on Saturday, and after thirty-five years of marriage he left me to marry his mistress, by whom he had a five-year-old son."

"Forget it," Uncle Cal said. He was leaning against the fireplace, tapping his empty pipe against the wood, looking at Ena through yellow-tinted aviator glasses. "Spilled milk," he said. "My brother's a fool, and pretty soon he's going to be an old fool. Then see how she likes him when he dribbles his martini."

"You never got along with him before he left me," Ena said. "You can't feign objectivity."

"Don't talk about it in front of Jason," Elizabeth said.

Jason and Benton had just come inside. Benton had been holding a flashlight while Jason picked the mint Benton and Nick had discovered earlier.

"Pick off the leaves that the frost got, and then we'll tie the stalks with rubber bands and hang them upside down to dry," Benton said.

It had gotten colder outside. The cold had come in with them and spread like a cloud to the living room where it stayed for a minute until the heat began to absorb it.

"Why do they have to be upside down?"

"So the leaves can't speak and criticize us for picking them."

"You don't hear all that stuff about plants having feelings anymore," Uncle Cal said. "That was a big item, wasn't it? Tomato plants curling their leaves when the guy who'd burned them the day before stuck a book of matches in their face the next day." He lit his pipe.

Squeals from the kitchen as Benton held Jason upside down. "Can you talk upside down?" Benton said. "Talk to Daddy."

Jason was yelling and laughing.

"Put him right side up," Elizabeth said, going and standing in the doorway that separated the kitchen from the living room.

Benton stood Jason back on his feet.

"Aw, Lizzie," Benton said.

"Who's Lizzie?" Jason said.

"She is. Lizzie is a nickname for Elizabeth."

"No one has ever called me Lizzie in my life," Elizabeth said.

Uncle Cal was putting logs in the fireplace. Above the mantle was a poster of the Lone Ranger and Tonto on horseback. Cloudy sky. Mountains behind them. The Lone Ranger was positioned directly in front of a tall cactus, so that it appeared the cactus was rising out of his hat.

"Lizzie is also the nickname for a lizard," Benton said.

"It's nice you're so clever," Elizabeth said to Benton.

"Lizzie loves me," Benton said. He put his thumb to his lip and flipped it forward, blowing her a kiss.

"Beautiful, beautiful," Uncle Cal said. He was admiring the fire, with strong yellow flames crackling out of the logs. Ena had explained to them that there was only wood for one fire, and she had decided to save it until the family could be together. It seemed impossible for everyone to be in the same room at the same time, though, so finally she had told Cal to lay the fire. Benton and Jason were in the kitchen; Olivia was upstairs taking a bath. She was humming loudly.

"I'm going to stay here a while," Ena said. "No one should feel that they have to stay with me."

"I'm staying," Uncle Cal said.

"I've already called Hanley Paulson, and he's delivering more firewood tonight. I can always count on Hanley. I think Wesley would have liked him, and the other people around here. Wesley didn't move here just to take care of me."

"Is there something wrong with you?" Uncle Cal said.

"No. Nothing is wrong with me. He wanted to be closer to me because sometimes I get lonesome."

"Don't tell me you ran down some sob story that made Wesley feel guilty for living in the city," Benton said, coming to the doorway.

"Some people," Ena said, staring at him with eyes hot from the fire, "think about the needs of others without having to be told."

"Christ," Benton said in disgust. "Is that what you did to Wesley?"

"I love it," Uncle Cal said. "I wish I'd never blocked up my fireplace."

"Take down the paneling," Elizabeth said.

"And I wish I'd never painted my living room green," Uncle Cal said.

Nick was playing solitaire. Elizabeth was sitting and looking bored, shifting her eyes from the fireplace to the empty doorway to the kitchen. When things were silent in there too long, she got up to investigate. Benton was holding Jason on his shoulders, and Jason was fastening the bunches of mint to the wooden ceiling beams with tacks.

"Come to kiss us?" Benton said to Elizabeth. "Legend has it that when you stand under mistletoe — or mint — you have to be kissed."

She looked at Jason, grinning as he sat high above them, one bunch of mint left in his hand. She went over to Jason and kissed his hand.

"Kiss Daddy," he said.

Benton was standing with his eyes closed, lips puckered in exaggeration, bending forward.

Elizabeth walked out of the room.

"Kiss him," Jason hollered, and kicked his feet, in damp brown socks, against Benton's chest.

"Kiss him," Jason called again.

Elizabeth sighed and went upstairs, leaving Benton to deal with the situation he'd created. Nick put an ace on top of a deuce and had no more cards to play. He went to the kitchen and poured a shotglass full of bourbon.

"Would anyone else like a drink?" Nick said, coming back into the living room.

"I swore off," Uncle Cal said, tapping his chest.

"Give me whatever you're drinking," Ena said to Nick.

Everyone was ignoring Jason, crying in the kitchen, and Benton, whispering to him.

Nick went into the kitchen to get Ena a drink, and Jason broke away from Benton and tried to kick Nick. When Nick drew away in time, Jason made fists and stood there, crying.

"I'm your friend," Nick said. He put half a shot of bourbon in a glass and filled it with water. He dropped in an ice cube.

"I go to bed at ten," Uncle Cal said.

"Why *can't* I?" Jason screamed in the kitchen.

"Because she's a naked lady. Decency forbids," Benton said. "It will take me one minute to tell her she's been in there long enough."

Olivia was singing very loudly.

"I want to come with you," Jason said.

Benton walked out of the kitchen and went to get Olivia out of her bath. She was doing her Judy Collins imitation, loudly, which she only did when she was stoned. Obviously, she had taken a joint into the bathroom.

Uncle Cal followed Benton up the stairs. It was nine-thirty.

"Early to bed, clears up the head," Uncle Cal said. He was sleeping in Ena's room, on a Futon mattress he had brought with him that he tried to get everyone to try out. Jason liked it best. He used it as a trampoline.

"I don't think Hanley is coming tonight," Ena said. She had gotten herself another drink. The fire was ash. She got out of the chair and turned up the thermostat, and instead of coming back to the living room, she began to climb the stairs, calling to Uncle Cal that he should do yoga exercises in the morning instead of at night, because if his back went out, she wouldn't know who to call in the middle of the night.

·

The next evening Nick talked to Ilena. Manuela picked up the phone and started telling him about his messages. He cut her off. Then she told him about what had been delivered that day — as she described it, it was a milk-chocolate top of a woman's body. She and Ilena had stood it up on the kitchen table, and the table was far enough away from the window that the sun wouldn't melt it. Manuela told him not to worry. She read him the message on the card that was enclosed. It was from Mr. Bornstein, a man he vaguely remembered from some party in Beverly Hills. Mr. Bornstein was with Fat Productions. He had another company called Fat Chance.

Ilena got on the phone. "Hi, Nick," she said.

"It's winter here," he said. "You should see it."

"I wasn't invited," she said.

"You hate Olivia," he said. "Anyway — it's not the time to bring somebody new into the house when Wesley just died."

"I wouldn't have come," Ilena said. "I just felt like sulking."

"So what's up?" he said. "You there sulking?"

"My cervix hurts. And somebody stole our hose. Unless you did something with the hose."

"The garden hose? What would I do with it?"

"That's what I thought. So somebody must have stolen it."

"What would they want with it?" he said.

"Strangle a Puerto Rican, maybe."

"How's the dog?" he said.

"He missed you and wouldn't eat, so Manuela poached a chicken for him. The chicken made him forget his grief."

"Good," he said.

"When are you coming back?"

"Pretty soon. Tomorrow or the next day, I guess. I was hoping it would snow."

"That creepy man keeps calling. The one Benton sells his stuff to. He's having a costume party, and he called yesterday to say that somebody was still needed to dress as Commissioner Gordon. Then he called this morning to say that somebody named Turaj was going as Gordon, but he still needed to find somebody to be the mother of Kal-El. Tell me there's not going to be a lot of coke at that party."

"Yeah," Nick said. "I guess that's where the snow is."

"He's so creepy. He gives me the creepy-crawls. I hope he doesn't call here anymore."

"Just tell him that I can't do it."

"That chocolate body in the other room gives me the creeps too."

"Other than that," he said, "is everything all right there?"

"Manuela wanted a raise, so I gave her one."

"Does that mean she's going to clean the bathroom?"

"I told her you didn't like her smoking cigars. She said she wouldn't anymore."

"Great. Sounds like everything will be perfect when I get back."

"What would you know about perfection? I'm perfect, and you don't appreciate me. I don't even have an eroded cervix anymore."

"I hope you feel better soon, Ilena."

"Thanks," she said. "See you when I see you. I might go to Ojai with Perry Dwyer and his sister this weekend."

"Have a good time in Ojai," he said.

They said goodbye and he hung up the kitchen phone. Elizabeth was leaning against the stove, staring at him. He waited for her to say something, but she didn't. She went to the window and looked at Jason and Benton, playing tag in the circle of light in the back-yard.

"He must be doing well," she said. "He's been paying child support."

"He's got quite a reputation on the West Coast."

"Do you know the man he sells the paintings to?"

"I saw him again when Benton was in L.A."

"Is he crazy, or does Benton exaggerate?"

"Crazy," Nick said.

Nick stood beside her and watched Benton chugging along, pretending to be running as fast as he could to catch Jason, then moving in comic slow motion.

"That's like the picture," Elizabeth said.

"What is?"

"That."

She was pointing to his hands, folded on the window sill. He felt a tingling in his fingers, as if his hands were about to move.

"Benton told me that picture always embarrassed you," she said. "You know — everybody in this family is embarrassed by beautiful things. That's why Benton never shows Ena or Cal his paintings. Even Benton's given in to it: he made fun of me for putting one of my watercolors up on the bulletin board alongside Jason's. You've probably hung around all these people so long that you've fallen into the pattern."

"I'm not embarrassed by it. It was just a picture he took one day when I was sitting in some diner."

"You look like a holy person when you clasp your hands."

She looked out the window again.

"What did you want to say to me when I was on the phone, Elizabeth?"

"Nothing," she said. "I was being envious. I was thinking how nice it is that he has a friend who'll fly from one coast to the other to pal around with him." She coughed. "And I've always been a little jealous of you — that people study you, photograph you — and they don't pay attention to me." She put her nose against the window. "Saying that Lizzie was a nickname for a lizard," she said.

•

Benton did not go to Westport with them because Jason acted up. Jason said that Benton had promised that the two of them could play tag. He was about to cry, and Benton had been trying since the day before to get back into Jason's good graces.

After Nick had opened the door on the driver's side of Elizabeth's car, he realized that he had made a silly, macho move. She was sober, and he had been drunk since before he called Ilena. He should have let her drive the car.

Elizabeth was shivering, her scarf over her mouth, staring straight ahead. He couldn't think of anything to say. It had been her idea to get out of the house and go get a drink, and he was surprised that he had agreed. Finally she said something. "Turn right," she said.

He turned, and was on a narrow road he wished she was navigating. "Hard to believe we're an hour outside New York," she said. "It's nice, when it isn't pitch black. This road reminds me of a road that winds in back of my grandmother's house in Pennsylvania."

She reached over and pushed down a lever. The heat came on.

"What kills me is that she knows Hanley Paulson charges outrageous prices for firewood, and she still won't consider having anyone else deliver it because Hanley is an old-timer, and she's so charmed by people who hang on."

She adjusted the heater to low. This time Nick remembered to look at the road, and not at what she was doing. He was trying to remember if he had just been told that his dog was, or was not, eating. A small animal ran in front of the car and made it to the other side. "Again," she said, and pointed for him to turn right.

They went to a bar with a lot of cars parked outside. A man was inside, sitting on a stool, collecting money. "Zenith String Band," he said, although neither of them had asked.

They sat side by side behind a small round table. One of the people on stage had broken a string, and another member of the band had stopped playing to pretend to beat him over the head with his fiddle. They ordered bourbon. A curly-haired girl handed another guitar up onto the stage, and everyone was playing together again.

"I hated it that he turned everybody against me," she said. "He was so angry that I wouldn't have an abortion, and look at the way he loves Jason. You'd think he'd be glad I didn't listen to him, but he's still making jokes, and I'm still the villain."

She was speaking quite loudly. The people at the next table were looking at them and pretending not to. He knew he should do something to pass it off, so he gave them a little smile, but he was drunk and the smile spread too far over his face; what he was giving them was an evil smirk.

"What a family. Cal with his mansion on Long Island, never liking what the decorator does, having some God damn vegetarian decorator who paints the walls the color of carrots and turnips. He gives better Christmas presents to his decorator than he does to Jason. Poor Cal, out in East Hampton, and poor Ena, who's staying in Wesley's house when he's dead because he wouldn't have her there when he was alive. The only person in the family worth anything was Wesley."

They sat in silence, drinking, until the set was over. It was slowly starting to sink in that he was not in California — that lantana would not be growing outside when they went out, that it would be dark and cold. He usually said that he loved California, but when he was back East he felt much better. He began to wish for snow again. When the musicians climbed down from the stage he asked for the check. He left money on the table, wondering if he was crazy to suspect that the people at the next table were going to take the money. Since no one ran out of the bar after them in all the time it took to start Elizabeth's car in the cold, he decided that it was paranoia.

He thought that he remembered the way back and was glad that he did. Elizabeth's eyes were closed. He put on the heater. Elizabeth put it off.

"It's cold," he said.

"Better ways to keep warm."

He was looking at the speedometer, to make sure he was driving fast enough. It felt like he was floating. He accelerated a little, watched the needle climb. Drunken driving.

"Pull over," Elizabeth said, hand over her mouth, other hand on his wrist. He did, quickly, expecting her to be sick.

Wind blew in the car as she jumped out and ran through the leaves unsteadily, over to a stone wall. He looked away as she bent over.

She came back to the car carrying a cat.

"I got myself something nice," she said, shivering.

"It's somebody's cat," he said.

"He might be your friend, but he's a real bastard. Telling Jason that lizards are called Lizzie."

"Get even with Benton," he said. "Don't get even with me."

She looked at him, and he knew exactly where Jason got his perturbed expression, the looked that crossed his face when his mother told him that Uncle Cal's mattress was not a toy.

"That's what they're all doing," she said. "They're all at Wesley's house getting even. Olivia singing in the tub to pretend that everything's cool, Cal being nice to Ena because his last EKG readout scared him and he wants to be sure she'll nurse him. Benton playing Daddy. That one really kills me."

The cat hopped into the back seat. He looked at it. Its eyes were glowing.

"What I like about animals is that they're not pretentious," she said.

"You've taken somebody's cat," he said.

She was pathetic and ridiculous, but neither of those things explained why the affection he felt for her was winning out over annoyance. He couldn't remember if she had propositioned him, or if he had just imagined it. He put his head against the window. It seemed like a situation he would have found himself in in college. It was a routine from years ago. He took her hand.

"This is silly," he said.

•

He did not know her license plate number, so he put down *?—#! on the registration form. Then, realizing what he had done, he blacked that out and wrote in a series of imaginary numbers.

The motel was on route 58, just off the Merritt Parkway. He was careful to notice where he was, because he thought that when he went out to the parking lot, she might simply have driven away. He gave the woman his credit card, got it back, slipped the room key across the counter until it fell off the edge into his hand instead of trying to pick it up with his fingers, and went out to the parking lot. She was in the car, holding the cat. He knocked on her window. She got out of the car. The cat, in her arms, looked all around.

"I know where there's an all-night diner," she said drunkenly.

"You seem to know your way around very well."

"I used to come see Wesley," she said.

She said it matter-of-factly, climbing the stairs in back of him, and at first he didn't get it. "And I know for a fact that he didn't intend to use all the servicemen Ena used, and that when he had wood delivered it wasn't going to be the famous Hanley Paulson who brought it," she said, as he put the key in the lock and opened the door. "He might have left New York to nursemaid Ena, but he was only going so far. He was a nice person, and people took advantage of him."

He held her. He put his arms around her back and hugged her. This was Benton's ex-wife, Wesley's lover, standing in front of him in a black sweater and black silk underpants, and instead of its seeming odd to him, it only made him feel left out that he was the only one who had no connection with her.

"Who was that man who drowned with him?" she said, as if Nick would know. "Nobody he cared about, because I never heard of him. I didn't even know he was Wesley's friend."

The cat was watching them. It was sitting in a green plastic chair, and when he looked at the cat the cat began to lick its paw. Elizabeth drew away from him to see why he had stopped stroking her back.

"Would you like to forget about it and go to the diner?" she said.

"I was thinking about the cat," he said. "We ought to return the cat."

"If you want to return the cat, you go return the cat."

"We can do it later," he said.

Later, he got hopelessly lost looking for the road where they had gotten the cat. He thought that he had found just the place, but when he got out of the car he saw that there was no stone wall. He carried the cat back to the car and consulted Elizabeth. She had no idea where they were. Finally he had to backtrack all the way to the bar and find the road from there that they had been on earlier. He got out of the car, carrying the cat. He dropped it on the stone wall. It didn't move.

"It wants to go with us," Elizabeth called out the window.

"How do you know?" he said. He felt foolish for asking, for assuming that she might know.

"Bring it back," she said.

The cat sat and stared. He picked it up again and walked back to the car with it. It jumped out of his arms, into the back seat.

"What he says to Jason is very clever," Elizabeth said, as he started the car. "I'd be amused, if Jason weren't my son."

When he found out that she and Wesley had been lovers, it had been clear to him that she was sleeping with him to exorcise Wesley's ghost, or to get even with him for dying; now he wondered if she had told him to go to the motel to get even with Benton, too.

"If you want Benton to know about what happened tonight, you're going to have to tell him yourself. I'm not telling him," he said.

Her face was not at all the face in the picture of Benton's wallet from years ago. Her eyes were shut as if she were asleep, but her face was not composed.

"I didn't mean to insult you," he said. "I'm sorry."

"I'm used to it," she said. She rummaged in her purse and pulled her brush out and began brushing her hair. "If the family had known about Wesley and me, they'd write that off as retaliation, too. They love easy answers."

They were on the road that led to the house, passing houses that stood close to the road. There was nothing in California that corresponded to the lights burning in big old New England houses at night. It made him want to live in this part of the world again, to be able to drive and see miles of dark fields. The apple orchards, the low rock walls, the graveyards. A lot of people went through them, and it did not mean that they were preoccupied with death. The car filled with light when a car with its high beams on came toward them. For a few seconds he saw his hands on either side of the wheel and thought, sadly, that what Wesley had seen about them had never come true.

"At the risk of being misunderstood as looking for sympathy, there's one other thing I want to tell you about Benton," Elizabeth said. "He used to put his camera on his tripod and take pictures of Jason when he was an infant — roll after roll. He'd stand by his crib and take pictures of Jason when he was sleeping. I remember asking him why he was taking so many pictures when Jason's expression wasn't changing, and you know what he said? He said that he was photographing light."

•

Déjà vu: Ena with the afghan, Uncle Cal circling figures on the stock page, knocking his empty pipe against the old wooden chest in front of the sofa with the regular motion of a metronome,

Elizabeth reading a book, her feet tucked primly beneath her, coffee steaming on the table by her chair.

"Went out and got drunk," Uncle Cal said in greeting. "I couldn't." He tapped his shirt pocket. It made a crinkling noise. Pipe cleaners stuck out of the pocket, next to the pack of cigarettes.

Elizabeth was reading *A Tale of Two Cities*. She continued to read as if he hadn't come into the room. The cat was curled by the side of the chair.

"Hanley Paulson isn't coming," Elizabeth said.

"We can go to lunch and leave him a note and the check," Uncle Cal said.

"That would be just fine," Ena said. "He's not a common delivery person — he's a friend of long standing."

"Maybe someone told him Wesley was dead, and he isn't coming."

"I called him," Ena said. "Not Wesley."

"Wesley wouldn't have paid seventy-five dollars for half a cord of wood." Elizabeth said.

"Everyone is perfectly free to go out," Ena said.

Nick went into the kitchen. He saw Benton and Jason and Olivia, all red-cheeked, with puffs of air coming out of their mouths. They were playing some sort of game in which they came very close to Olivia and ducked at the last second, so she couldn't reach out and touch them. The sky was grey-white, and it looked like snow. Olivia was loosening the scarf around her neck and lighting one of her hand-rolled narrow cigarettes. Either that, or she had stopped caring and was smoking a joint. He watched her puff. A regular cigarette. Olivia's jeans were rolled to the knee, and the bright red socks she wore reminded him of the large red stocking his uncle had hung by the mantle for him when he was young. "Let's see Santa fill that," his uncle had laughed, as the toe of the stocking grazed the hearth. In the morning, his usual stocking was in the toe of the large stocking, and his father was glaring at his uncle. His father did not even like his brother — how could he have wanted to send him to live with him?

Uncle Cal came into the kitchen and took cheese out of the refrigerator.

"I'm going to grill some French bread with cheese on top," he said. "Will anyone share my lunch?"

"Give me whatever you're having," Ena said.

"No thank you," Elizabeth said.

"Not good for me, but I love it," Uncle Cal said to Nick. "You?"

"Sure," Nick said.

"You watch it so it doesn't get too brown," Uncle Cal said, smoothing Brie over the two halves of bread. "I'm going out for a second to clear my lungs."

Nick looked out the window. Uncle Cal was bending forward, cupping his hands, lighting a cigarette. He had only taken one puff when a car pulled into the driveway.

"Is that Hanley's truck?" Ena called.

"It's just a car," Nick said.

"I hope it isn't someone coming to express sympathy unannounced," Ena said. She was still wearing her pajamas, and a quilted Chinese coat.

Nick watched as a boy got out of the car and Benton went to talk to him. Benton and the boy talked for a while, and then Benton left him standing there, Jason circling his car with one arm down, one arm high, buzzing like a plane. Benton pushed open the kitchen door.

"Where do you want the wood stacked?" he called.

"Is that Hanley Paulson?" Ena asked, getting up.

"It's his son. He wants to know where to put the wood."

"Oh dear," Ena said, pulling off her jacket and going to the closet for her winter coat. "Outside the kitchen door where it will be sheltered, don't you think?"

Benton closed the kitchen door.

"Where's Hanley?" Ena said, hurrying past Nick. Still in her slippers, she went onto the lawn. "Are you Hanley's son?" Nick heard her say. "Please come in."

The boy walked into the kitchen behind Ena. He had a square face, made squarer by dirty blond bangs, cut straight across. He stood in the kitchen, hands plunged in his pockets, looking at Ena.

"Where would you like the wood, ma'am?" he said.

"Oh," she said, "well Hanley always stacks it at my house under the overhang by the kitchen door. We can do the same thing here, don't you think?"

"It's ten dollars extra for stacking," the boy said.

When the boy left the kitchen, Ena went out behind him. Nick watched her standing outside the door as the boy went to his car and backed it over the lawn. He opened the back hatch and began to load the wood out.

"This is very dry wood?" Ena said.

"This is what he gave me to deliver," the boy said.

Jason put his arms up for a ride, and Benton plopped him on his shoulders. Jason's dirty shoes had made streaks down the front of Benton's jacket. Uncle Cal put his arm through Olivia's, and the two of them began to walk toward the back of the property. Nick watched Ena as she looked first toward Uncle Cal and Olivia, then to Benton and Jason, charging a squirrel, Benton hunching forward like a bull.

"Everyone has forgotten about lunch," Ena said, coming back into the kitchen. She broke off a piece of the cooked bread and took a bite. She put it on the counter and poured herself a drink, then went back into the living room with the piece of bread and the glass of bourbon and sat in her chair, across from Elizabeth.

"Hanley Paulson would have come in for coffee," Ena said. "I don't know that I would have wanted that young man in for coffee."

He tore off a piece of bread and went into the living room. Ena was knitting. Elizabeth was reading. He thought that he might as well get the plane that night for California. He stood up to answer the phone, hoping it was Ilena, but Elizabeth got up more quickly than he, and she went into the dining room and picked it up. She spoke quietly, and he could only catch a few words of what she said. Since Ena could hear no better than he could, he did not think she was crying because the phone calls expressing sympathy about Wesley's death made her remember. He felt certain that she was weeping because of the way things had worked out with Hanley Paulson's son. It was the first time he had ever seen Ena cry. She kept her head bent and sniffed a little. Elizabeth was on the phone a long while, and after a few deep sniffs Ena finally raised her head.

"How do your parents like Scottsdale, Nickie?" she said.

"They like it," he said. "They always wanted to get away from these cold winters."

"The winter is bad," Ena said, "but the people have great character. At least they used to have great character." She began to knit again. "I can't imagine why Cal would leave that fabulous house in Essex for that monstrosity in East Hampton. You always liked it here, didn't you, Nickie?"

"I was hoping it would snow," he said. "But I guess with just my cowboy suit, I'm not really prepared for it."

Uncle Cal came into the living room and asked Ena if he should tip Hanley Paulson's son. Ena told him that she didn't see why, but Nick could tell from Uncle Cal's expression that he intended to do it anyway.

"He wants to know if it's all right to take a few of the pumpkins," Uncle Cal said. Before Ena answered, he said: "Of course I told him to help himself."

"We're going to play baseball," Jason shouted, running into the living room. "And I'm first at bat, and you're first base, and Nick can pitch."

Olivia came in and sat down, still in her coat, shivering.

"You don't mind, do you?" Uncle Cal said to Ena. "He's just taking a few pumpkins we don't have any use for."

"Come on," Jason said, tugging Nick's arm. "Please."

"Leave him alone if he doesn't want to do what you want him to do, Jason," Elizabeth said. She had just come back into the room.

"Who was that on the phone?" Ena said. She took a drink of bourbon. Nick noticed that she had put a sprig of mint in the glass.

"That person named Richard. He read something from a book called *An Exaltation of Larks.*" Elizabeth shook her head. "He's the one you call The Poet, isn't he, Cal? Wasn't the man who called two days ago and read that long poem by Donne named Richard?"

"It's not a practice I've ever heard of," Ena said. "I think it was the same man."

"Come on," Jason whined to Elizabeth. "Aren't you going to come out and play baseball?"

"I wasn't invited."

"You're so touchy," he said. "You're invited. Come on."

Nick and Elizabeth got their coats and walked out the back door into the cold. Benton had found a chewed-up baseball bat in the back of the garage, and a yellow tennis ball. As they got into position to play, Hanley Paulson's son passed through the game area, carrying an armful of pumpkins. The back hatch of his car was open, and there were already about a dozen pumpkins inside. He closed the hatch and started the car and bumped down the driveway, raising his fist and shaking it from side to side when Uncle Cal waved goodbye.

Looking at his watch, Nick wondered if it could be possible that the boy had stacked all the wood and gathered the pumpkins in only half an hour. It was amazing what could be accomplished in half an hour.

•

The night before Nick left for L.A., there was a big dinner. Ena cooked it, saying that it was to make up for the Thanksgiving dinner she hadn't felt like fixing. Everyone said that this dinner was very good and that on Thanksgiving no one had been hungry.

"I would have made a pumpkin pie, but the pumpkins disappeared," Ena said, looking across the table at Uncle Cal.

"What do you mean?" he said. "The kid took two or three pumpkins. There must be a dozen left out there."

"He took all the pumpkins," Ena said.

"You're being ridiculous," Uncle Cal said. "Where's the flashlight? I'll go out and get you a pumpkin."

Uncle Cal and Ena were both drunk. She had not wanted to make a pie, and he did not want to go outside in the cold to shine a flashlight into the pumpkin patch.

"I was mistaken," Ena said finally. "I thought you had given him all the pumpkins."

"He got them himself," Uncle Cal said. "I didn't give him anything. I let him round them up." He cut into his roast beef. "He was just a kid," he said.

"Olivia hasn't touched her roast beef," Ena said.

"You talk about me as though I'm not here," Olivia said.

"What does she mean?" Ena said.

"I mean that you don't address me directly. You talk *about* me, as though I'm not here."

"I realize that you are here," Ena said.

"It's great roast beef," Ena said. "I want everybody to enjoy it."

"I'm enjoying it," Uncle Cal said. "If Morris could see me now, he'd die," Uncle Cal said. "Morris is my decorator. Doesn't eat meat. Talks about it all the time, though, so that you'd think there were plates of meat all over *reminding* him about how much *meat* there was in the world."

"Your decorator," Olivia said.

"Yes?" Uncle Cal said.

"Don't be pissy," Benton said.

"I don't think anybody even remembers why we're here. It seems to me that this is just another family gathering where everybody lolls around by the fireplace and drinks." Olivia took a sip of her wine. Nick winced, because he had seen her taking Valium in the kitchen before dinner.

"That's uncivilized," Ena said.

"*This* is uncivilized," Olivia said.

Nick had expected one of them — probably Olivia — to begin crying. But it was Jason who began to cry, and who ran from the table.

Elizabeth had left the table to go after Jason, and Benton had followed her upstairs without saying anything else to Olivia.

"You said what you thought," Uncle Cal said to Olivia. "Nothing wrong with that."

Olivia got up and stalked away from the table.

"She did what she felt like doing," Uncle Cal said to Ena. "Nothing wrong with that."

"Oh, nothing's wrong with anything, is it?" Ena said to Cal.

"My heart," he said. "You should see that last EKG. Looked like an ant's eye view of the Himalayas, where there should have been a pretty straight line. Of course you have a straight line, straight as a piece of string, you're dead. It should have been bumpy, I mean — but not like it was."

"Then what are you doing yoga for?" Ena said. "You'll kill yourself twisting into all those stupid positions."

"Probably going to be dead anyway," Uncle Cal said, tapping his pocket.

"Stop being morose," Ena said.

"Might stop being anything," Cal said.

"Stop worrying about your *health*," Ena said. "It's what's in the cards. Wesley was a young man, and he drowned."

"That was an accident," Uncle Cal said. "An accident."

"It wasn't any accident," Olivia hollered from the living room.

"It *was*," Elizabeth said. She had come downstairs again, and she looked like she was about to murder somebody.

"Elizabeth — " Nick said.

Elizabeth sat down and smoothed her skirt and smiled to show that she was all right, calm and all right. Then she began to cry.

Nick got up and put his arm around her, sitting on his heels and crouching by her chair. He said her name again, but it didn't do any good. It hadn't done any good the night before, either, in the motel room.

·

Upstairs, Jason was pretending to be a baby. Benton had gotten him into his pajamas and had taken the sheet from the bed and was holding Jason, sheet thrown around him like a huge poncho, facing the window. Jason was afraid, and he was trying to pretend that it was animals he was afraid of. He wanted to know if there were bears in the woods. "Not around here," Benton said. Fox, then? Maybe — "but they don't attack people. Maybe none around here, anyway." Jason wanted to know where all the animals came from.

"You know where they came from. You know about evolution."

"I don't know," Jason said. "Tell me."

"Tell you the whole history of evolution? You think I went to school yesterday?"

"Tell me something," Jason said.

Benton told him this fact of evolution: that one day dinosaurs shook off their scales and sucked in their breath until they became much smaller. This caused the dinosaurs' brains to pop through their skulls. The brains were called antlers, and the dinosaurs deer. That was why deer had such sad eyes, Benton told Jason — because they were once something else.

ROBERT COOVER

A Working Day

(FROM THE IOWA REVIEW)

SHE ENTERS, deliberately, gravely, without affectation, circumspect in her motions (as she's been taught), not stamping too loud, nor dragging her legs after her, but advancing sedately, discreetly, glancing briefly at the empty rumpled bed, the cast-off night-clothes. She hesitates. No. Again. She enters. Deliberately and gravely, without affectation, not stamping too loud, nor dragging her legs after her, not marching as if leading a dance, nor keeping time with her head and hands, nor staring or turning her head either one way or the other, but advancing sedately and discreetly through the door, across the polished floor, past the empty rumpled bed and cast-off nightclothes (not glancing, that's better), to the tall curtains along the far wall. As she's been taught. Now, with a humble yet authoritative gesture, she draws the curtains open: Ah! the morning sunlight comes flooding in over the gleaming tiles as though (she thinks) flung from a bucket. She opens wide the glass doors behind the curtains (there is such a song of birds all about!) and gazes for a moment into the garden, quite prepared to let the sweet breath of morning blow in and excite her to the most generous and efficient accomplishments, but her mind is still locked on that image, at first pleasing, now troubling, of the light as it spilled into the room: as from a bucket . . . She sighs. She enters. With a bucket. She sets the bucket down, deliberately, gravely, and walks (circumspectly) across the room, over the polished tiles, past the empty rumpled bed (she doesn't glance at it), to draw open the tall curtains at the far wall. Buckets of light come flooding in (she is not thinking about this now) and the room, as she opens wide the glass doors, is sweetened by the fresh morning air blowing in from the garden. The sun is fully risen and the pink clouds of dawn are all gone out of the sky (the time lost: this is what she is thinking about), but the dew is still on every plant in the garden, and everything looks clean and bright. As will his room when she is done with it.

●

He awakes from a dream (something about utility, or futility, and a teacher he once had who, when he whipped his students, called it his "civil service"), still wrapped in darkness and hugged close to the sweet breast of the night, but with the new day already hard upon him, just beyond the curtains (he knows, even without looking), waiting for him out there like a brother: to love him or to kill him. He pushes the bedcovers back and sits up groggily to meet its challenge (or promise), pushes his feet into slippers, rubs his face, stretches, wonders what new blunders the maid (where is she?) will commit today. Well. I should at least give her a chance, he admonishes himself with a gaping yawn.

●

Oh, she knows her business well: to scrub and wax the floors, polish the furniture, make the master's bed soft and easy, lay up his nightclothes, wash, starch, and mend the bedlinens as necessary, air the blankets and clean the bathroom, making certain of ample supplies of fresh towels and washclothes, soap, toilet paper, razor blades and toothpaste — in short, to see that nothing be wanting which he desires or requires to be done, being always diligent in endeavoring to please him, silent when he is angry except to beg his pardon, and ever faithful, honest, submissive, and of good disposition. The trivial round, the common task, she knows as she sets about her morning's duties, will furnish all she needs to ask, room to deny herself, a road (speaking loosely) to bring her daily nearer God. But on that road, on the floor of the bathroom, she finds a damp towel and some pajama bottoms, all puddled together like a cast-off mop-head. Mop-head? She turns and gazes in dismay at the empty bucket by the outer door. Why, she wants to know, tears springing to the corners of her eyes, can't it be easier than this? And so she enters, sets her bucket down with firm deliberation, leans her mop gravely against the wall. Also a broom, brushes, some old rags, counting things off on her fingers as she deposits them. The curtains have been drawn open and the room is already (as though impatiently) awash with morning sunlight. She crosses the room, past the (no glances) empty rumpled bed, and opens wide the glass doors leading out into the garden, letting in the sweet breath of morning, which she hardly notices. She has resolved this morning — as every morning — to be cheerful and good-natured, such that if any accident should happen to test that resolution, she should not suffer it to put her out of temper with everything besides, but such resolutions are more easily sworn than obeyed. Things are already in such a state! Yet: virtue is made for difficulties, she reminds herself, and grows stronger and brighter for such trials, *"Oh, teach me, my God and King, in all things thee to see, and what I do in any thing, to do it as for thee!"* she sings out to the garden and to the room, feeling her heart lift like a sponge in a bucket. *"A servant with this clause makes drudgery divine: who sweeps a room, as for thy laws, makes that and th'action fine!"* And yes, she can still recover the lost time. She has everything now, the mop and bucket, broom, rags, and brushes, her apron pockets are full of polishes, dustcloths, and cleaning powders, the cupboards are well stocked with fresh linens, all she really needs now is to keep — but ah! is there, she wonders anxiously, spinning abruptly on her heels as she hears the master relieving himself noisily in the bathroom, any *water* in the bucket — ?!

•

He awakes, squints at his watch in the darkness, grunts (she's late, but just as well, time for a shower), and with only a moment's hesitation, tosses the blankets back, tearing himself free: I'm so old, he thinks, and still every morning is a bloody new birth. Somehow it should be easier than this. He sits up painfully (that divine government!), rubs his face, pushes his feet into slippers, stands, stretches, then strides to the windows at the far wall and throws open the tall curtains, letting the sun in. The room seems almost to explode with the blast of light: he resists, then surrenders to, finally welcomes its amicable violence. He opens wide the glass doors that lead out into the garden and stands there in the sunshine, sucking in deeply the fresh morning air and trying to recall the dream he's just had. Something about a teacher who had once lectured him on humility. Severely. Only now, in the dream, he was himself the teacher and the student was a woman he knew, or thought he knew, and in his lecture "humility" kept getting mixed up somehow with "humor," such that, in effect, he was trying, in

all severity, to teach her how to laugh. He's standing there in the
sunlight in his slippers and pajama bottoms, remembering the curious strained expression on the woman's face as she tried — desperately, it seemed — to laugh, and wondering why this provoked
(in the dream) such a fury in him, when the maid comes in. She
gazes impassively a moment (yet humbly, circumspectly) at the
gaping fly of his pajamas, then turns away, sets her bucket down
against the wall. Her apron strings are loose, there's a hole in one
of her black stockings, and she's forgotten her mop again. I'd be a
happier man, he acknowledges to himself with a wry sigh, if I
could somehow fail to notice these things. "I'll start in the bathroom," she says discreetly. "Sir," he reminds her. "Sir," she says.

•

And she enters. Deliberately and gravely, as though once and for
all, without affectation, somewhat encumbered by the vital paraphernalia of her office, yet radiant with that clear-browed self-
assurance achieved only by long and generous devotion to duty.
She plants her bucket and brushes beside the door, leans the mop
and broom against the wall, then crosses the room to fling open
(humbly, authoritatively) the curtains and the garden doors: the
fragrant air and sunlight come flooding in, a flood she now feels
able to appreciate. The sun is already high in the sky, but the
garden is still bejeweled with morning dew and (she remembers to
notice) there is such a song of birds all about! What inspiration!
She enjoys this part of her work: flushing out the stale darkness of
the dead night with such grand (yet circumspect) gestures — it's
almost an act of magic! Of course, she takes pleasure in *all* her
appointed tasks (she reminds herself), whether it be scrubbing
floors or polishing furniture or even scouring out the tub or toilet,
for she knows that only in giving herself (as he has told her) can
she find herself: true service (he doesn't have to tell her!) is perfect
freedom. And so, excited by the song of the birds, the sweet breath
of morning, and her own natural eagerness to please, she turns
with a glad heart to her favorite task of all: the making of the bed.
Indeed, all the rest of her work is embraced by it, for the opening
up and airing of the bed is the first of her tasks, the making of it
her last. Today, however, when she tosses the covers back, she
finds, coiled like a dark snake near the foot, a bloodstained leather
belt. She starts back. The sheets, too, are flecked with blood. Shadows seem to creep across the room and the birds fall silent. Per-

haps, she thinks, her heart sinking, I'd better go out and come in again . . .

•

At least, he cautions himself while taking a shower, give her a chance. Her forgetfulness, her clumsiness, her endless comings and goings and stupid mistakes are a trial of course, and he feels sometimes like he's been living with them forever, but she means well and, with patience, instruction, discipline, she can still learn. Indeed, to the extent that she fails, it could be said, *he* has failed. He knows he must be firm, yet understanding, severe if need be, but caring and protective. He vows to treat her today with the civility and kindness due to an inferior, and not to lose his temper, even should she resist. Our passions (he reminds himself) are our infirmities. A sort of fever of the mind, which ever leaves us weaker than it found us. But when he turns off the taps and reaches for the towel, he finds it damp. Again! He can feel the rage rising in him, turning to ash with its uncontrollable heat his gentler intentions. Has she forgotten to change them yet again, he wonders furiously, standing there in a puddle with the cold wet towels clutched in his fists — or has she not even come yet?

•

She enters once and for all encumbered with her paraphernalia which she deposits by the wall near the door, thinking: it should be easier than this. Indeed, why bother at all when it always seems to turn out the same? Yet she cannot do otherwise. She is driven by a sense of duty and a profound appetite for hope never quite stifled by even the harshest punishments: this time, today, perhaps it will be perfect . . . So, deliberately and gravely, not staring or turning her head either one way or the other, she crosses the room to the far wall and with a determined flourish draws open the tall curtains, flooding the room with buckets of sunlight, but her mind is clouded with an old obscurity: When, she wants to know as she opens wide the glad doors to let the sweet breath of morning in (there are birds, too, such a song, she doesn't hear it), did all this really begin? When she entered? Before that? Long ago? Not yet? Or just now as, bracing herself as though for some awful trial, she turns upon the bed and flings the covers back, her morning's tasks begun. "Oh!" she cries. "I beg your pardon, sir!" He stares groggily down at the erection poking up out of the fly of his pajama pants, like (she thinks) some kind of luxuriant but dangerous dew-bejeweled blossom: a monster in the garden. "I was having a dream," he announces sleepily, yet gravely. "Something about tumidity. But it kept getting mixed up somehow with — " But she is no longer listening. Watching his knobby plant waggle puckishly in the morning breeze, then dip slowly, wilting toward the shadows like a closing morning glory, a solution of sorts has occurred to her to that riddle of genesis that has been troubling her mind: to wit, that a condition *has* no beginning. Only *change* can begin or end.

•

She enters, dressed crisply in her black uniform with its starched white apron and lace cap, leans her mop against the wall like a standard, and strides across the gleaming tile floor to fling open the garden doors as though (he thinks) calling forth the morning. What's left of it. Watching her from behind the bathroom door, he is moved by her transparent earnestness, her uncomplicated enthusiasm, her easy self-assurance. What more, really, does he want of her? Never mind that she's forgotten her broom again, or that her shoe's unbuckled and her cap on crooked, or that in her exuberance she nearly broke the glass doors (and sooner or later will), what is wonderful is the quickening of her spirits as she enters, the light that seems to dawn on her face as she opens the room, the way she makes a maid's oppressive routine seem like a sudden invention of love. See now how she tosses back the blankets and strips off the sheets as though, in childish excitement, unwrapping a gift! How in fluffing up the pillows she seems almost to bring them to life! She calls it: "doing the will of God from the heart!" *"Teach me, my God and King, in all things thee to see,"* she sings, *"and what I do in any thing, to do it as for thee!"* Ah well, he envies her: would that he had it so easy! All life is a service, he knows that. To live in the full sense of the word is not to exist or subsist merely, but to make oneself over, to *give* oneself: to some high purpose, to others, to some social end, to life itself beyond the shell of ego. But he, lacking superiors, must devote himself to abstractions, never knowing when he has succeeded, when he has failed, or even if he has the abstractions right, whereas she, needing no others, has him. He would like to explain this to her, to ease the pain of her routine, of her chastisement — what he calls his disciplinary interventions — but he knows that it is he, not she, who is forever in need of such explanations. Her mop fairly flies over the tiles (today she has remembered the mop), making them gleam like mirrors, her face radiant with their reflected light. He checks himself in the bathroom mirror, flicks lint off one shoulder, smoothes the ends of his moustache. If only she could somehow understand how difficult it is for me, he thinks as he steps out to receive her greeting: "Good morning, sir." "Good morning," he replies crisply, glancing around the room. He means to give her some encouragement, to reward her zeal with praise or gratitude or at least a smile to match her own, but instead he finds himself flinging his dirty towels at her feet and snapping: "These towels are damp! See to it that they are replaced!" "Yes, sir!" "Moreover, your apron strings are dangling untidily and there are flyspecks on the mirror!" "Sir." "And another thing!" He strides over to the bed and tears it apart. "Isn't it about time these sheets were changed? Or am I supposed to wear them through before they are taken to be washed?" "But, sir, I just put new — !" "What? *WHAT* — ?" he storms. "Answering back to a reproof? Have you forgotten all I've taught you?" "I — I'm sorry, sir!" "Never answer back if your master takes occasion to reprove you, except — ?" "Except it be to acknowledge my fault, sir, and that I am sorry for having committed it, promising to amend for the time to come, and to . . . to . . ." "Am I being unfair?" he insists, unbuckling his belt. "No, sir," she says, her eyes downcast, shoulders trembling, her arms pressed tight to her sides.

•

He is strict but not unkindly. He pays her well, is grateful for her services, treats her respectfully, she doesn't dislike him or even fear him. Nor does she have to work very hard; he is essentially a tidy man, picks up after himself, comes and goes without disturbing things much. A bit of dusting and polishing now and then, fold his pajamas, change the towels, clean the bathroom, scrub the floor, make his bed; really there's nothing to complain about. Yet, vaguely, even as she opens up the garden doors, letting the late morning sunshine and freshness in, she feels unhappy. Not because of what she must do — no, she truly serves with gladness. When she straightens a room, polishes a floor, bleaches a sheet or scrubs a tub, always doing the very best she can, she becomes, she knows, a part of what is good in the world, creating a kind of beauty, revealing a kind of truth. About herself, about life, the things she touches. It's just that, somehow, something is missing. Some response, some enrichment, some direction . . . it's, well, it's too repetitive. Something like that. That's part of the problem anyway. The other part is what she keeps finding in his bed. Things that oughtn't to be there, like old razor blades, broken bottles, banana skins, bloody pessaries, crumbs and ants, leather thongs, mirrors, empty books, old toys, dark stains. Once, even, a frog jumped out at her. No matter how much sunlight and fresh air she lets in, there's always this dark little pocket of lingering night which she has to uncover. It can ruin everything, all her careful preparations. This morning, however, all she finds is a pair of flannelette drawers. Ah: she recognizes them. She glances about guiltily, pulls them on hastily. Lucky the master's in the bathroom, she thinks, patting down her skirt and apron, or there'd be the devil to pay.

·

Something about scouring, or scourging, he can't remember, and a teacher he once had who called his lectures "lechers." The maid is standing over him, staring down in some astonishment at his erection. "Oh! I beg your pardon, sir!" "I was having a dream . . ." he explains, trying to bring it back. "Something about a woman . . ." But by then he is alone again. He hears her in the bathroom, running water, singing, whipping the wet towels off the racks and tossing them out the door. Ah well, it's easy for her, she can come and go. He sits up, squinting in the bright light, watching his erection dip back inside his pajamas like a sleeper pulling the blankets over his head (oh yes! to return there!), then dutifully shoves his feet into slippers, stretches, staggers to the open garden doors. The air is fragrant and there's a morning racket of birds and insects, vaguely threatening. Sometimes, as now, scratching himself idly and dragging himself still from the stupor of sleep, he wonders about his calling, how it came to be his, and when it all began: on his coming here? on *her* coming here? before that, in some ancient time beyond recall? And has he chosen it? or has he, like that woman in his dream, showing him something that for some reason enraged him, been "born with it, sir, for your very utility"?

·

She strives, understanding the futility of it, for perfection. To arrive properly equipped, to cross the room deliberately, circumspectly, without affectation (as he has taught her), to fling open the garden doors and let the sweet breath of morning flow in and chase the night away, to strip and air the bed and, after all her

common tasks, her trivial round, to remake it smooth and tight, all
the sheets and blankets tucked in neatly at the sides and bottom,
the upper sheet and blankets turned down at the head just so far
that their fold covers only half the pillows, all topped with the
spread, laid to hang evenly at all sides. And today — perhaps at
last! She straightens up, wipes her brow, looks around: yes! he'll
be so surprised! Everything perfect! Her heart is pounding as the
master, dressed for the day, steps out of the bathroom, marches
directly over to the bed, hauls back the covers, picks up a pillow,
and hits her in the face with it. Now what did he do that for? "And
another thing!" he says.

•

He awakes, feeling sorry for himself (he's not sure why, something
he's been dreaming perhaps, or merely the need to wake just by
itself: come, day, do your damage!), tears himself painfully from
the bed's embrace, sits up, pushes his feet into slippers. He grunts,
squinting in the dimness at his watch: she's late. Just as well. He
can shower before she gets here. He staggers into the bathroom
and drops his pajamas, struggling to recall his dream. Something
about a woman in the civil service, which in her ignorance or
cupidity, she insisted on calling the "sybil service." He is relieving
himself noisily when the maid comes in. "Oh! I beg your pardon,
sir!" "Good morning," he replies crisply, and pulls his pajamas up,
but she is gone. He can hear her outside the door, walking quickly
back and forth, flinging open the curtains and garden doors, singing to herself as though lifted by the tasks before her. Sometimes
he envies her, having him. Her footsteps carry her to the bed and
he hears the rush and flutter of sheets and blankets being thrown
back. Hears her scream.

•

He's not unkind, demands no more than is his right, pays her well,
and teaches her things like, "All life is a service, a consecration to
some high end," and, "If domestic service is to be tolerable, there
must be an attitude of habitual deference on the one side and one
of sympathetic protection on the other." "Every state and condition of life has its particular duties," he has taught her. "The duty
of a servant is to be obedient, diligent, sober, just, honest, frugal,
orderly in her behavior, submissive and respectful toward her
master. She must be contented in her station, because it is necessary that some should be above others in this world, and it was the

will of the Almighty to place you in a state of servitude." Her soul, in short, is his invention, and she is grateful to him for it. *"Whatever thy hand findeth to do,"* he has admonished her, *"do it with all thy might!"* Nevertheless, looking over her shoulder at her striped sit-me-down in the wardrobe mirror, she wishes he might be a little less literal in applying his own maxims: *he's drawn blood!*

•

He awakes, mumbling something about a dream, a teacher he once had, some woman, infirmities. "A sort of fever of the mind," he explains, his throat phlegmy with sleep. "Yes, sir," she says, and flings open the curtains and the garden doors, letting light and air into the stale bedroom. She takes pleasure in all her appointed tasks, but enjoys this one most of all, more so when the master is already out of bed, for he seems to resent her waking him like this. Just as he resents her arriving late, after he's risen. Either way, sooner or later, she'll have to pay for it. "It's a beautiful day," she remarks hopefully. He sits up with an ambiguous grunt, rubs his eyes, yawns, shudders. "You may speak when spoken to," he grumbles, tucking his closing morning glory back inside his pajamas (behind her, bees are humming in the garden and there's a crackly pulsing of insects, but the birds have fallen silent: she had thought today might be perfect, but already it is slipping away from her), "unless it be to deliver a message or ask a necessary question." "Yes, sir." He shoves his feet into slippers and staggers off to the bathroom, leaving her to face (she expects the worst) — shadows have invaded the room — the rumpled bed alone.

•

It's not just the damp towels. It's also the streaked floor, the careless banging of the garden doors, her bedraggled uniform, the wrinkled sheets, the confusion of her mind. He lectures her patiently on the proper way to make a bed, the airing of the blankets, turning of the mattress, changing of the sheets, the importance of a smooth surface. "Like a blank sheet of crisp new paper," he tells her. He shows her how to make the correct diagonal creases at the corners, how to fold the top edge of the upper sheet back over the blankets, how to carry the spread under and then over the pillows. Oh, not for his benefit and advantage — he could sleep anywhere or for that matter (in extremity) could make his own bed — but for hers. How else would she ever be able to realize what is best for herself? "A little arrangement and thought will give you method and habit," he explains (it is his "two fairies" lecture), but though she seems willing enough, is polite and deferential, even eager to please, she can never seem to get it just right. Is it a weakness on her part, he wonders as he watches her place the pillows on the bed upside down, then tug so hard on the bottom blanket that it comes out at the foot, or some perversity? Is she testing him? She refits the bottom blanket, tucks it in again, but he knows the sheet beneath is now wrinkled. He sighs, removes his belt. Perfection is elusive, but what else is there worth striving for? "Am I being unfair?" he insists.

•

He's standing there in the sunlight in his slippers and pajama bottoms, cracking his palm with a leather strap, when she enters (once and for all) with all her paraphernalia. She plants the bucket and brushes beside the door, leans the mop and broom against the wall, stacks the fresh linens and towels on a chair. She is late — the curtains and doors are open, her circumspect crossing of the room no longer required — but she remains hopeful. Running his maxims over in her head, she checks off her rags and brushes, her polishes, cleaning powders, razor blades, toilet paper, dustpans — oh no . . . ! Her heart sinks like soap in a bucket. The soap she has forgotten to bring. She sighs, then deliberately and gravely, without affectation, not stamping too loud, nor dragging her legs after her, not marching as if leading a dance, nor keeping time with her head and hands, nor staring or turning her head either one way or the other, she advances sedately and discreetly across the gleaming tiles to the bed, and tucking up her dress and apron, pulling down her flannelette drawers, bends over the foot of it, exposing her soul's ingress to the sweet breath of morning, blowing in from the garden. "I wonder if you can appreciate," he says, picking a bit of lint off his target before applying his corrective measures to it, "how difficult this is for me?"

•

He awakes, vaguely frightened by something he's dreamt (it was about order or odor and a changed condition — but how did it begin . . . ?), wound up in damp sheets and unable at first even to move, defenseless against the day already hard upon him. Its glare blinds him, but he can hear the maid moving about the room, sweeping the floor, changing the towels, running water, pushing furniture around. "Good morning, sir," she says. "Come here a moment," he replies gruffly, then clears his throat. "Sir?" "Look under the bed. Tell me what you see." He expects the worst: blood, a decapitated head, a bottomless hole . . . "I'm — I'm sorry, sir," she says, tucking up her skirt and apron, lowering her drawers, "I thought I *had* swept it . . ."

•

No matter how much fresh air and sunlight she lets in, there is always this little pocket of lingering night which she has to un-cover. Once she found a dried bull's pizzle in there, another time a dead mouse in a trap. Even the nice things she finds in the bed are somehow horrible; the toys broken, the food moldy, the cloth-ing torn and bloody. She knows she must always be circumspect and self-effacing, never letting her countenance betray the least dislike toward any task, however trivial or distasteful, and she re-solves every morning to be cheerful and good-natured, letting nothing she finds there put her out of temper with everything besides, but sometimes she just cannot help herself. "Oh, teach me, my God and King, in all things thee to see, and what I do in any thing, to do it as for thee," she tells herself, seeking courage, and flings back the sheets and blankets. She screams. But it's only money, a little pile of gold coins, agleam with promise. Or chal-lenge: is he testing her?

•

Ah well, he envies her, even as that seat chosen by Mother Nature for such interventions quivers and reddens under the whistling strokes of the birch rod in his hand. "Again!" "Be . . . be diligent in endeavoring to please your master — be faithful and . . . and . . ." Swish — *SNAP!* "Oh, sir!" "Honest!" "Yes, sir!" She, after all, is free to come and go, her correction finitely inscribed by time and the manuals, but he . . . He sighs unhappily. How did it all begin, he wonders. Was it destiny, choice, generosity? If she would only get it right for once, he reasons, bringing his stout engine of duty down with a sharp report on her brightly striped but seem-ingly unimpressionable hinder parts, he might at least have time for a stroll in the garden. Does she — *CRACK!* — think he enjoys this? "Well?" "Be . . . be faithful, honest, and submissive to him, sir, and — " Whish — *SLASH!* "And — *gasp!* — do not incline to be slothful! Or — " *THWOCK!* "Ow! Please, sir!" Hiss — *WHAP!* She groans, quivers, starts. The two raised hemispheres upon which the blows from the birch rod have fallen begin (predictably) to make involuntary motions both vertically and horizontally, the constrictor muscle being hard at work, the thighs also participating in the general vibrations, all in all a dismal spectacle. And for nothing? So it would seem . . . "Or?" "Or lie long in bed, but rise . . . rise early in a morning!" The weals crisscross each other on her flushed posteriors like branches against the pink clouds of dawn, which for some reason saddens him. "Am I being unfair?" "No — no, s — " Whisp — *CRACK!* She shows no tears, but her face pressed against the bedding is flushed, her lips trembling, and she breathes heavily as though she's been running, confirming the quality of the rod which is his own construction. "Sir," he reminds her, turning away. "Sir," she replies faintly. "Thank you, sir."

•

She enters, once and for all, radiant and clear browed (a long devotion to duty), with all her paraphernalia, her mop and bucket, brooms, rags, soaps, polishes, sets them all down, counting them off on her fingers, then crosses the room deliberately and circumspectly, not glancing at the rumpled bed, and flings open the curtains and the garden doors to call forth the morning, what's left of it. There is such a song of insects all about (the preying birds are silent) — what inspiration! "Lord, keep me in my place!" The master is in the shower: she hears the water. "Let me be diligent in performing whatever my master commands me," she prays, "neat and clean in my habit, modest in my carriage, silent when he is angry, willing to please, quick and neat-handed about what I do, and always of an humble and good disposition!" Then, excited to the most generous and efficient accomplishments, she turns with a palpitating heart (she is thinking about perfect service and freedom and the unpleasant things she has found) to the opening up and airing of the bed. She braces herself, expecting the worst, but finds only a wilted flower from the garden: ah! today then! she thinks hopefully — perhaps at last! But then she hears the master turn the taps off, step out of the shower. Oh no . . . ! She lowers her drawers to her knees, lifts her dress, and bends over the unmade bed. *"These towels are damp!"* he blusters, storming out of the bathroom, wielding the fearsome rod, that stout engine of duty, still wet from the shower.

•

Sometimes he uses a rod, sometimes his hand, his belt, sometimes a whip, a cane, a cat-o'-nine-tails, a bull's pizzle, a hickory switch, a

martinet, ruler, slipper, a leather strap, a hairbrush. There are
manuals for this. Different preparations and positions to be assumed, the number and severity of the strokes generally prescribed to fit the offense, he has explained it all to her, though it is
not what is important to her. She knows he is just, could not be
otherwise if he tried, even if the relative seriousness of the various
infractions seems somewhat obscure to her at times. No, what matters to her is the idea behind the regulations that her daily tasks,
however trivial, are perfectible Not absolutely perhaps, but at least
in terms of the manuals. This idea, which is almost tangible —
made manifest, as it were, in the weals on her behind — is what
the punishment is for, she assumes. She does not enjoy it certainly,
nor (she believes — and it wouldn't matter if he did) does he.
Rather, it is a road (speaking loosely), the rod, to bring her daily
nearer God — and what's more, it seems that she's succeeding at
last! Today everything has been perfect: her entry, all her vital
paraphernalia, her circumspect crossing of the room and opening
of the garden doors, her scrubbing and waxing and dusting and
polishing, her opening up and airing and making of the master's
bed — everything! True service, she knows (he has taught her!), is
perfect freedom, and today she feels it: almost like a breeze — the
sweet breath of success — lifting her! But then the master emerges
from the bathroom, his hair wild, fumbles through the clothes
hanging in the wardrobe, pokes through the dresser drawers,
whips back the covers of her perfectly made bed. "What's this
doing here — ?!" he demands, holding up his comb. "I — I'm
sorry, sir! It wasn't there when I — " "What? *What* — ?!" He seizes
her by the elbow, drags her to the foot of the bed, forces her to
bend over it. "I have been very indulgent to you up to now, but
now I am going to punish you severely, to cure you of your inso-
lent clumsiness once and for all! So pull up your skirt — come!
pull it up! you know well enough that the least show of resistance
means ten extra cuts of the — *what's this* — ?!" She peers round
her shoulder at her elevated sit-me-down, so sad and pale above
her stockings. "I — I don't understand, sir! I had them on when I
came in — !"

•

Perhaps he's been pushing her too hard, he muses, soaping himself in the shower and trying to recall the dream he was having
when she woke him up (something about ledgers and manual po-

robe door. In the mirror, she sees the bed. The spread and blankets have been thrown back, the sheets pulled out. In the bathroom doorway, the master taps his palm with the stretched-out bull's pizzle, testing its firmness and elasticity, which she knows to be terrifying in its perfection. She remakes the bed tight and smooth, not knowing what else to do, vaguely aware as she finishes of an unpleasant odor. Under the bed? Also her apron is missing and she seems to have a sheet left over. Shadows creep across the room, silent now but for the rhythmic tapping of the pizzle in the master's hand and the pounding of her own palpitating heart.

·

Sometimes he stretches her across his lap. Sometimes she must bend over a chair or on the bed, or lie flat out on it, or be horsed over the pillows, the dresser or a stool, there are manuals for this. Likewise her drawers: whether they are to be drawn tight over her buttocks like a second skin or lowered, and if lowered, by which of them, how far, and so on. Her responses are assumed in the texts (the writhing, sobbing, convulsive quivering, blushing, moaning, etc.), but not specified, except insofar as they determine his own further reactions — to resistance, for example, or premature acquiescence, fainting, improper language, an unclean bottom, and the like. Thus, once again, her relative freedom: her striped buttocks tremble and dance spontaneously under the whip which his hand must bring whistling down on them according to canon — ah well, it's not so much that he envies her (her small freedoms cost her something, he knows that), but that he is saddened by her inability to understand how difficult it is for him, and without that understanding it's as though something is always missing, no matter how faithfully he adheres to the regulations. "And — ?" "And be neat and clean in your — " whisp — *CRACK!* " — *OW!* habit! Oh! and wash yourself all over once a day to avoid bad smells and — " hiss — *SNAP!* " — and — *gasp!* — wear strong decent underclothing!" The whip sings a final time, smacks its broad target with a loud report, and little drops of blood appear like punctuation, gratitude, morning dew. "That will do, then. See that you don't forget to wear them again!" "Yes, sir." She lowers her black alpaca skirt gingerly over the glowing crimson flesh as though hooding a lamp, wincing at each touch. "Thank you, sir."

·

For a long time she struggled to perform her tasks in such a way as to avoid the thrashings. But now, with time, she has come to understand that the tasks, truly common, are the only peripheral details in some larger scheme of things which includes her punishment — indeed, perhaps depends upon it. Of course she still performs her duties *as though* they were perfectible and her punishment could be avoided, ever diligent in endeavoring to please him who guides her, but though each day the pain surprises her afresh, the singing of the descending instrument does not. That God has ordained bodily punishment (and Mother Nature designed the proper place of martyrdom) is beyond doubt — every animal is governed by it, understands and fears it, and the fear of it keeps every creature in its own sphere, forever preventing (as he has taught her) that natural confusion and disorder that would instantly arise without it. Every state and condition of life has its particular duties, and each is subject to the divine government of pain, nothing could be more obvious, and looked on this way, his chastisements are not merely necessary, they might even be beautiful. Or so she consoles herself, trying to take heart, calm her rising panic, as she crosses the room under his stern implacable gaze, lowers her drawers as far as her knees, tucks her skirt up, and bends over the back of a chair, hands on the seat, thighs taut and pressed closely together, what is now her highest part tensing involuntarily as though to reduce the area of pain, if not the severity. "It's . . . it's a beautiful day, sir," she says hopefully. "What? *WHAT — ?!*"

•

Relieving himself noisily in the bathroom, the maid's daily recitals in the next room (such a blast of light out there — even in here he keeps his eyes half closed) thus drowned out, he wonders if there's any point in going on. She is late, has left half her paraphernalia behind, is improperly dressed, and he knows, even without looking, that the towels are damp. Maybe it's some kind of failure of communication. A mutual failure. Is that possible? A loss of syntax between stroke and weal? No, no, even if possible, it is unthinkable. He turns on the shower taps and lets fall his pajama pants, just as the maid comes in with a dead fetus and drops it down the toilet, flushes it. "I found it in your bed, sir," she explains gratuitously (is she testing him?), snatching up the damp towels, but failing to replace them with fresh ones. At least she's remembered her drawers today: she's wearing them around her ankles. He sighs, as she shuffles out. Maybe he should simply forget it, go for a stroll in the garden or something, crawl back into bed (a dream, he recalls now: something about lectures or ledgers — an inventory perhaps — and a bottomless hole, glass breaking, a woman doing what she called "the hard part" . . . or did she say "heart part"?), but of course he cannot, even if he truly wished to. He is not a free man, his life is consecrated, for though he is *her* master, her failures are inescapably *his*. He turns off the shower taps, pulls up his pajama pants, takes down the six-thonged martinet. "I have been very indulgent to you up to now," he announces, stepping out of the bathroom, "but now I am going to punish you severely, so pull up your skirt, come! pull it up!" But, alas, it is already up. She is bent over the foot of the bed, her pale hinder parts already exposed for his ministrations, an act of insolence not precisely covered by his manuals. Well, he reasons wryly, making the martinet sing whole chords, if improvisation is denied him, interpretation is not. "Ow, sir! Please! *You'll draw blood, sir!*"

•

"Neat and clean in habit, modest — " WHACK! " — in . . . in carriage, silent when — " Whisp — SNAP! "OW!!" "Be careful! If you move, the earlier blow won't count!" "I — I'm sorry, sir!" Her soul, she knows, is his invention and she is grateful to him for it, but exposed like this to the whining slashes of the cane and the sweet breath of mid-afternoon which should cool his righteous ardor but doesn't (once a bee flew in and stung him on the hand: what did it mean? nothing: she got it on her sit-me-down once, too, and he took the swelling for a target), her thighs shackled by flannelette drawers and blood rushing to her head, she can never remember (for all the times he has explained it to her) why it is that Mother Nature has chosen that particular part of her for such solemnities: it seems more like a place for letting things out than putting things in. "Well? Silent when — ?" "Silent when he is angry, willing to please, quick and — " swish — CRACK! " — and of good disposition!" "Sir," he reminds her: THWOCK! "SIR!" she cries. "Very well, but you must learn to take more pleasure in your appointed tasks, however trivial or unpleasant, and when you are ordered to do anything, do not grumble or let your countenance betray any dislike thereunto, but do it cheerfully and readily!" "Yes, sir! Thank you, sir!" She is all hot behind, and peering over her shoulder at herself in the wardrobe mirror after the master has gone to shower, she can see through her tears that it's like on fire, flaming

crimson it is, with large blistery welts rising and throbbing like
things alive: he's drawn blood! She dabs at it with her drawers,
recalling a dream he once related to her about a teacher he'd had
who called his chastisements "scripture lessons," and she understands now what he's always meant by demanding "a clean sheet
of paper." Well, certainly it has always been clean, neat and clean
as he's taught her, that's one thing she's never got wrong, always
washing it well every day in three hot lathers, letting the last lather
be made thin of the soap, then not rinsing it or toweling it, but
drying it over brimstone, keeping it as much from the air as possible, for that, she knows, will spoil it if it comes to it. She finishes
drying it by slapping it together in her hands, then holding it
before a good fire until it be thoroughly hot, then clapping it and
rubbing it between her hands from the fire, occasionally adding to
its fairness by giving it a final wash in a liquor made of rosemary
flower boiled in white wine. Now, she reasons, lifting her drawers
up gingerly over the hot tender flesh, which is still twitching con-
vulsively, if she could just apply those same two fairies, method
and habit, to the rest of her appointed tasks, she might yet find
in them that pleasure he insists she take, according to the manuals. Well, anyway, the worst is past. Or so she consoles herself as, smoothing down her black skirt and white lace apron, she
turns to the bed. *"Oh, teach me, my God and King, in all things
thee to . . ."* What — ? There's something under there! *And it's
moving . . . !*

•

"Thank you sir." "I know that perfection is elusive," he explains,
putting away his stout engine of duty, while she staggers over, her
knees bound by her drawers, to examine her backside in the wardrobe mirror (it is well cut, he knows, and so aglow one might cook
little birds over it or roast chestnuts, as the manuals suggest), "but
what else is there worth striving for?" "Yes, sir." She shows no
tears, but her face is flushed, her lips are trembling, and she
breathes as though she has just been running. He goes to gaze out
into the garden, vaguely dissatisfied. The room is clean, the bed
stripped and made, the maid whipped, why isn't that enough? Is
there something missing in the manuals? No, more likely, he has
failed somehow to read them rightly. Yet again. Outside in the
sleepy afternoon heat of the garden, the bees are humming, insects chattering, gentler sounds to be sure than the hiss of a birch
rod, the sharp report as it smacks firm resonant flesh, yet strangely

alien to him, sounds of natural confusion and disorder from a
world without precept or invention. He sighs. Though he was
thinking "invention," what he has heard in his inner ear was "intention," and now he's not sure which it was he truly meant. Perhaps he should back off a bit — or even let her off altogether for
a few days. A kind of holiday from the divine government of pain.
Certainly he does not enjoy it nor (presumably) does she. If he
could ever believe in her as she believes in him, he might even
change places with her for awhile, just to ease his own burden and
let her understand how difficult it is for him. A preposterous idea
of course, pernicious in fact, an unthinkable betrayal . . . yet sometimes, late in the day, something almost like a kind of fever of the
mind (speaking loosely) steals over — enough! *enough!* no shrinking! "And another thing!" he shouts, turning on the bed (she is at
the door, gathering up her paraphernalia) and throwing back the
covers: at the foot on the clean crisp sheets there is a little pile of
wriggling worms, still coated with dirt from the garden. "WHAT
DOES THIS MEAN — ?!" he screams. "I — I'm sorry, sir! I'll
clean it up right away, sir!" Is she testing him? taunting him? It's
almost an act of madness! "Am I being unfair?" "But, sir, you've
already — !" "What? *WHAT* — ?! Is there to be no *end* to
this — ?!"

•

He holds her over his left knee, her legs locked between his, wrist
clamped in the small of her back, her skirt up and her drawers
down, and slaps her with his bare hand, first one buttock, reddening it smartly in contrast to the dazzling alabaster (remembering
the manuals) of the other, then attacking its companion with equal
alacrity. "Ow! Please, sir!" "Come, come, you know that the least
show of resistance means ten extra cuts of the rod!" he admonishes
her, doubling her over a chair. "When you are ordered to do
anything, do not grumble or let your countenance betray any dislike thereunto, but do it cheerfully and generously!" "Yes, sir,
but — " "What? *WHAT* — ?!" Whish — *CRACK!* "OW!" *SLASH!*
Her crimson bottom, hugged close to the pillows, bobs and dances
under the whistling cane. "When anyone finds fault with you, do
not answer rudely!" Whirr — *SMACK!* "NO, SIR!" Each stroke,
surprising her afresh, makes her jerk with pain and wrings a little
cry from her (as anticipated by the manuals when the bull's tizzle
is employed), which she attempts to stifle by burying her face in
the horsehair cushion. "Be respectful — ?" "Be respectful and obe-

dient, sir, to those — " swish — *THWOCK!* " — placed — OW! —
placed OVER you — AARGH!" Whizz — *SWACK!* "With fear and
trembling — " *SMASH!* " — and in singleness of your heart!" he
reminds her gravely as she groans, starts, quivers under his patient
instruction. "Ouch! Yes, sir!" The leather strap whistles down to
land with a loud crack across the center of her glowing buttocks,
seeming almost to explode, and making what lilies there are left
into roses. *SMACK!* Ker-*WHACK!* He's working well now. "Am I
being unfair?" "N-no, sir!" *WHAP! SLAP!* Horsed over the dresser
her limbs launch out helplessly with each blow. *"Kneel down!"* She
falls humbly to her hands and knees, her head bowed between his
slippered feet, that broad part destined by Mother Nature for such
devotions elevated but pointed away from toward the wardrobe
mirror (as though trying, flushed and puffed up, to cry out to
itself), giving him full and immediate access to that large division
referred to in the texts as the Paphian grove. "And resolve every
morning — ?" "Resolve — *gasp!* — resolve every morning to be
cheerful and — " He raises the whip, snaps it three times around
his head, and brings it down with a crash on her hinder parts,
driving her head forward between his legs. "And — *YOW!* — and
good-natured that . . . that day, and if any . . . if any accident —
groan! — should happen to — " swish — *WHACK!* " — to break
that resolution, suffer it . . . suffer it not — " *SLASH!* "Oh, sir!"
SWOCK! He's pushing himself, too hard perhaps, but he can't —
"Please, sir! *PLEASE!*" She is clinging to his knee, sobbing into his
pajama pants, the two raised hemispheres upon which the strokes
have fallen making involuntary motions both vertically and horizontally as though sending a message of distress, all the skin wrinkling like the surface of a lake rippled by the wind. "What are you
doing?! *WHAT DOES THIS MEAN* — ?!" He spanks her with a
hairbrush, lashes her with a cat-o'-nine-tails, flagellates her with
nettles, not shrinking from the hard service to be done, this divine
drudgery, clear-browed in his devotion to duty. Perhaps today . . . ! "SIR!" He pauses, breathing heavily. His arm hurts.
There is a curious strained expression on her face, flushed like her
behind and wet with tears. "Sir, if you . . . if you don't stop — "
"What? *WHAT* — ?!" "You — you won't know what to do *next!*"
"Ah." He has just been smacking her with a wet towel, and the
damp rush and pop, still echoing in his inner ear, reminds him
dimly of a dream, perhaps the one she interrupted when she ar-

rived. In it there was something about humidity, but it kept getting
mixed up somehow with hymnody, such that every time she
opened her mouth (there was a woman in the dream) damp chords
flowed out and stained his ledgers, bleached white as clean sheets.
"I'm so old," he says, letting his arm drop, "and still each day . . ."
"Sir?" "Nothing. A dream . . ." Where was he? It doesn't matter.
"Why don't you go for a stroll in the garden, sir? It's a beautiful
day." Such impudence: he ignores it. "It's all right," he says, drap-
ing the blood-flecked towel over his shoulder, scratching himself
idly. He yawns. "The worst is past."

•

Has he devoted himself to a higher end, he wonders, standing
there in the afternoon sunlight in his slippers and pajama bottoms,
flexing a cane, testing it, snapping it against his palm, or has he
been taken captive by it? Is choice itself an illusion? Or an act of
magic? And *is* the worst over, or has it not yet begun? He shudders,
yawns, stretches. And the manuals . . . He is afraid even to ask,
takes a few practice strokes with the cane against a horsehair cushion instead. When the riddles and paradoxes of his calling over-
take him, wrapping him in momentary darkness, he takes refuge
in the purity of technique. The proper stretching of a bull's pizzle,
for example, this can occupy him for hours. Or the fabrication of
whipping chairs, the index of duties and offenses, the synonymy
associated with corporal discipline and with that broad part destined by Mother Nature for such services. And a cane is not simply
any cane, but preferably one made like this one of brown Malacca
— the stem of an East Indian rattan palm — about two and a half
feet long (give or take an inch and a half) and a quarter of an inch
thick. Whing-*SNAP!* listen to it! Or take the birch rod, not a mere
random handful of birchen twigs, as often supposed, but an instrument of precise and elaborate construction. First, the twigs
must be meticulously selected for strength and elasticity, each
about two feet long, full of snap and taken from a young tree, the
tips sharp as needles. Then carefully combining the thick with the
thin and slender, they must be bound together for half their
length, tightly enough that they might enjoy long service, yet not
too tightly or else the rod will be like a stick and the twigs have no
play. The rod must fit conveniently to the hand, have reach and
swing so as to sing in the air, the larger part of all punishments
being the anticipation, not the pain of course, and immediately

raise welts and blisters, surprising the chastised flesh afresh with each stroke. To be sure, it is easier to construct a birch rod than to employ it correctly — that's always the hard part, he doesn't enjoy it, nor does she surely, but the art of the rod is incomplete without its perfect application. And though elusive, what else is there worth striving for? Indeed, he knows he has been too indulgent to her up till now, treating her with the civility and kindness due to an inferior, but forgetting the forging of her soul by way of those "vivid lessons," as a teacher he once had used to put it, "in holy scripture, hotly writ." So when she arrives, staggering in late with all her paraphernalia, her bucket empty and her bib hanging down, he orders her straight to the foot of the bed. "But, sir, I haven't even — " "Come, come, no dallying! The least show of resistance will double the punishment! Up with your skirt, up, up! for I intend to — WHAT? IS THERE TO BE NO END TO THIS — ?!" "I — I'm sorry! I was wearing them when I came — I must have left them somewhere . . .!" Maybe it's some kind of communication problem, he thinks, staring gloomily at her soul's ingress which confronts him like blank paper, laundered tiffany, a perversely empty ledger. The warm afternoon sun blows in through the garden doors, sapping his brave resolve. He feels himself drifting, yawning, must literally shake himself to bring the manuals back to mind, his duties, his devotion . . . "Sir," she reminds him. "Sir," he sighs.

•

It never ends. Making the bed, she scatters dust and feathers afresh or tips over the mop bucket. Cleaning up the floor, she somehow disturbs the bed. Or something does. It's almost as if it were alive. Blankets wrinkle, sheets peek perversely out from under the spread, pillows seem to sag or puff up all by themselves if she turns her back, and if she doesn't, then flyspecks break out on the mirror behind her like pimples, towels start to drip, stains appear on her apron. If she hasn't forgotten it. She sighs, turns once more on the perfidious bed. Though always of an humble and good disposition (as she's been taught), diligent in endeavoring to please him, and grateful for the opportunity to do the will of God from the heart by serving him (true service, perfect freedom, she knows all about that), sometimes, late in the day like this (shadows are creeping across the room and in the garden the birds are beginning to sing again), she finds herself wishing she could make the bed once and for all: glue down the sheets, sew on the pillows, stiffen the blankets as hard as boards and nail them into place. But then what? She cannot imagine. Something frightening. No, no, better this trivial round, these common tasks, and a few welts on her humble sit-me-down, she reasons, tucking the top sheet and blankets in neatly at the sides and bottom, turning them down at the head just so far that their fold covers half the pillows, than be overtaken by confusion and disorder. *"Teach me, my God and King,"* she sings out hopefully, floating the spread out over the bed, allowing it to fall evenly on all sides, *"in all things thee to — "* But then, as the master steps out of the bathroom behind her, she sees the blatant handprints on the wardrobe mirror, the streamers of her lace cap peeking out from under the dresser, standing askew. "I'm sorry, sir," she says, bending over the foot of the bed, presenting to him that broad part destined by Mother Nature for the arduous invention of souls. But he ignores it. Instead he tears open the freshly made bed, crawls into it fully dressed, kicking her in the face through the blankets with his shoes, pulls the sheets over his head, and commences to snore. Perhaps, she thinks her heart sinking, I'd better go out and come in again . . .

•

Perhaps I should go for a stroll in the garden, he muses, dutifully reddening one resonant cheek with a firm volley of slaps, then the other, according to the manuals. I'm so old, and still . . . He sighs ruefully, recalling a dream he was having when the maid arrived (when was that?), something about a woman, bloody morning glories (or perhaps in the dream they were "mourning" glories: there was also something about a Paphian grave), and a bee that flew in and stung him on his tumor, which kept getting mixed up somehow with his humor, such that, swollen, with pain, he was laughing like a dead man . . . "Sir?" "What? *WHAT* — ?!" he cries, starting up, "Ah." His hand is resting idly on her flushed behind as though he meant to leave it there. "I . . . I was just testing the heat," he explains gruffly, taking up the birch rod, testing it for strength and elasticity to wake his fingers up. "When I'm finished, you'll be able to cook little birds over it or roast chestnuts!" He raises the rod, swings it three times round his head, and brings it down with a whirr and a slash, reciting to himself from the manuals to keep his mind, clouded with old obscurities, on the task before him: "Sometimes the operation is begun a little above the garter — "

whish-*SNAP!* " — and ascending the pearly inverted cones — "
hiss-*WHACK!* " — is carried by degrees to the dimpled promon-
tories — " *THWOCK!* " — which are vulgarly called the buttocks!"
SMASH! "Ow, sir! PLEASE!" She twists about on his knee, biting
her lip, her highest part flexing and quivering with each blow, her
knees scissoring frantically between his legs. "Oh, teach me," she
cries out, trying to stifle the sobs, "my God and — " whizz —
CRACK! " — King, thee — *gasp!* — to — " *WHAP!* " — SEE!"
Sometimes, especially late in the day like this, watching the weals
emerge from the blank page of her soul's ingress like secret writing, he finds himself searching it for something, he doesn't know
what exactly, a message of sorts, the revelation of a mystery in the
spreading flush, in the pout and quiver of her cheeks, the re-
pressed stutter of the little explosions of wind, the — whush-
SMACK! — dew-bejeweled hieroglyphs of crosshatched stripes.
But no, the futility of his labors, that's all there is to read there.
Birdsong, no longer threatening, floats in on the warm afternoon
breeze while he works. There *was* a bee once, he remembers, that
part of his dream was true. Only it stung him on his hand, as
though to remind him of the painful burden of his office. For a
long time after that he kept the garden doors closed altogether,
until he realized one day, spanking the maid for failing to air the
bedding properly, that he was in some wise interfering with the
manuals. And what has she done wrong today? He wonders, tracing the bloody welts with his fingertips. He has forgotten. It
doesn't matter. He can lecture her on those two fairies, confusion
and disorder. Method and habit, rather . . . "Sir . . . ?" "Yes, yes,
in a minute . . ." He leans against the bedpost. To live in the full
sense of the word, he reminds himself, is not to exist or subsist
merely, but to . . . to . . . He yawns. He doesn't remember.

•

While examining the dismal spectacle of her throbbing sit-me-
down in the wardrobe mirror (at least the worst is past, she consoles herself, only half believing it), a solution of sorts to that
problem of genesis that's been troubling her occurs to her: to wit,
that change (she is thinking about change now, and conditions) is
eternal, has no beginning — only conditions can begin or end.
Who knows, perhaps he has even taught her that. He has taught
her so many things, she can't be sure of anymore. Everything from
habitual deference and the washing of tiffany to pillow fluffing,

true service and perfect freedom, the two fairies that make the work (speaking loosely) disappear, proper carriage, sheet folding, and the divine government of pain. Sometimes, late in the day, or on being awakened, he even tells her about his dreams, which seem to be mostly about lechers and ordure and tumors and bottomless holes (once he said "souls"). In a way it's the worst part of her job (that and the things she finds in the bed; today it was broken glass). Once he told her of a dream about a bird with blood in its beak. She asked him, in all deference, if he was afraid of the garden, whereupon he ripped her drawers down, horsed her over a stool, and flogged her so mercilessly she couldn't stand up after, much less sit down. Now she merely says, "Yes, sir," but that doesn't always temper the vigor of his disciplinary interventions, as he likes to call them. Such a one for words and all that! Tracing the radiant weals on that broad part of her so destined with her fingertips, she wishes that just once she might hear something more like, "Well done, thou good and faithful servant, depart in peace!" But then what? When she returned, could it ever be the same? Would he even want her back? No, no, she thinks with a faint shudder, lifting her flannelette drawers up gingerly over her soul's well-ruptured ingress (she hopes more has got in than is leaking out), the sweet breath of late afternoon blowing in to remind her of the time lost, the work yet to be done: no, far better her appointed tasks, her trivial round and daily act of contrition, no matter how pitiless the master's interpretation, than consequences so utterly unimaginable. So, inspirited by her unquenchable appetite for hope and clear-browed devotion to duty, and running his maxims over in her head, she sets about doing the will of God from the heart, scouring the toilet, scrubbing the tiled floor, polishing the furniture and mirrors, checking supplies, changing the towels. All that remains finally is the making of the bed. But how can she do that, she worries, standing there in the afternoon sunlight with stacks of crisp clean sheets in her arms like empty ledgers, her virtuous resolve sapped by a gathering sense of dread as penetrating and aseptic as ammonia, if the master won't get out of it?

•

She enters, encumbered with her paraphernalia, which she deposits by the wall near the door, crosses the room (circumspectly, precipitately, etc.), and flings open the garden doors, smashing the glass, as though once and for all. "Teach me, my God and King," she remarks ruefully (such a sweet breath of amicable violence all about!), "in all things thee to — oh! I beg your pardon, sir!" "A . . . a dream," he stammers, squinting in the glare. He is bound tightly in the damp sheets, can barely move. "Something about blood and a . . . a . . ." I'm so old, and still each day — "Sir . . . ?" He clears his throat. "Would you look under the bed, please, and tell me what you see?" "I — I'm sorry, sir," she replies kneeling down to look, a curious strained expression on her face. With a scream, she disappears. He awakes, his heart pounding. The maid is staring down at his erection as though frightened of his right-eous ardor: "Oh, I beg your pardon, sir!" "It's nothing . . . a dream," he explains, rising like the pink clouds of dawn. "Some-thing about . . ." But he can no longer remember, his mind is a blank sheet. Anyway, she is no longer listening. He can hear her moving busily about the room, dusting furniture, sweeping the floor, changing the towels, taking a shower. He's standing there abandoned to the afternoon sunlight in his slippers and pajama bottoms, which seem to have imbibed an unhealthy kind of damp-ness, when a bird comes in and perches on his erection, what's left of it. "Ah — !" "Oh, I beg your pardon, sir!" "It's — it's nothing," he replies hoarsely, blinking up at her, gripped still by claws as fine as waxed threads. "A dream . . ." But she has left him, gone off singing to her God and King. He tries to pull the blanket back over his head (the bird, its beak opening and closing involuntarily like whipped thighs, was brown as a chestnut, he recalls, and still smoldering), but she returns and snatches it away, the sheets too. Sometimes she can be too efficient. Maybe he has been pushing her too hard, expecting too much too soon. He sits up, feeling rudely exposed (his erection dips back into his pajamas like a frog diving for cover — indeed, it has a greenish cast to it in the half-light of the curtained room: what? isn't she here yet?), and lowers his feet over the side shuffling dutifully for his slippers. But he can't find them. He can't even find the floor! He jerks back, his skin wrinkling in involuntary panic, but feels the bottom sheet slide out from under him — "What? *WHAT* — *?!*" "Oh, I beg your pardon, sir!" "Ah . . . it's nothing," he gasps, struggling to awaken, his heart pounding still (it should be easier than this!), as, scream-ing, she tucks up her skirt. "A dream . . ."

•

She enters, as though once and for all, circumspectly deposits her
vital paraphernalia beside the door, then crosses the room to fling
open (humbly yet authoritatively) the curtains and the garden
doors: there is such a song of birds all about! Excited by that, and
by the sweet breath of late afternoon, her own eagerness to serve,
and faith in the perfectibility of her tasks, she turns with a glad
heart and tosses back the bedcovers: "Oh! I beg your pardon, sir!"
"A . . . a dream," he mutters gruffly, his erection slipping back
inside his pajamas like an abandoned moral. "Something about
glory and a pizzle — or puzzle — and a fundamental position in
the civil service . . ." But she is no longer listening, busy now at her
common round, dusting furniture and sweeping the floor: so
much to do! When (not very willingly, she observes) he leaves the
bed at last, she strips the sheets and blankets off, shaking the dead
bees into the garden, fluffs and airs the pillows, turns the mattress.
She hears the master relieving himself noisily in the bathroom:
yes, there's water in the bucket, soap too, a sponge, she's remembered everything! Today then, perhaps at last . . . ! Quickly she
polishes the mirror, mops the floor, snaps open the fresh sheets
and makes the bed. Before she has the spread down, however, he
comes out of the bathroom, staggers across the room muttering
something about a "bloody new birth," and crawls back into it.
"But, sir — !" "What, what?" he yawns, and rolls over on his side,
pulling the blanket over his head. She snatches it away. He sits up,
blinking, a curious strained expression on his face. "I — I'm sorry,
sir," she says, and pushing her drawers down to her knees, tucking
her skirt up and bending over, she presents to him that broad part
preferred by him and Mother Nature for the invention of souls.
He retrieves the blanket and disappears under it, all but his feet,
which stick out at the bottom, still slippered. She stuffs her drawers
hastily behind her apron bib, knocks over the mop bucket, smears
the mirror, throws the fresh towels in the toilet, and jerks the
blanket away again. "I — I'm sorry, sir," she insists, bending over
and lifting her skirt: "I'm sure I had them on when I came in . . ."
What? Is he snoring? She peers at him past what is now her highest
part, that part invaded suddenly by a dread as chilling as his chastisements are, when true to his manuals, enflaming, and realizes
with a faint shudder (she cannot hold back the little explosions of
wind) that change and condition are coeval and everlasting: a truth
as hollow as the absence of birdsong (but they are singing!) . . .

•

So she stands there in the open doorway, the glass doors having long since been flung open (when was that? she cannot remember), her thighs taut and pressed closely together, her face buried in his cast-off pajamas. She can feel against her cheeks, her lips the soft consoling warmth of them, so recently relinquished, can smell in them the terror — no, the painful sadness, the divine drudgery (sweet, like crushed flowers, dead birds) — of his dreams, Mother Nature having provided, she knows all too well, the proper place for what God has ordained. But there is another odor in them too, musty, faintly sour, like that of truth or freedom, the fear of which governs every animal, thereby preventing natural confusion and disorder. Or so he has taught her. Now, her face buried in this pungent warmth and her heart sinking, the comforting whirr and smack of his rod no more than a distant echo, disappearing now into the desolate throb of late-afternoon birdsong, she wonders about the manuals, his service to them and hers to him, or to that beyond him which he has not quite named. Whence such an appetite? — she shudders, groans, chewing helplessly on the pajamas — So little relief?

•

Distantly blows are falling, something about freedom and government, but he is strolling in the garden with a teacher he once had, discussing the condition of humanity, which keeps getting mixed up somehow with homonymity, such that each time his teacher issues a new lament it comes out like slapped laughter. He is about to remark on the generous swish and snap of a morning glory that has sprung up in their path as though inspired ("Paradox, too, has its techniques," his teacher is saying, "and so on . . ."), when it turns out to be a woman he once knew on the civil surface. "What? WHAT — ?!" But she only wants him to change his position, or perhaps his condition ("You see!" remarks his teacher sagely, unbuckling his belt, "it's like a kind of callipygomancy, speaking loosely — am I being unfair?"), he's not sure, but anyway it doesn't matter, for what she really wants is to get him out of the sheets he's wrapped in, turn him over (he seems to have imbibed an unhealthy kind of dampness), and give him a lecture (she says "elixir") on method and fairies, two dew-bejeweled habits you can roast chestnuts over. What more, really, does he want of her? (Perhaps his teacher asks him this, buzzing in and out of his ear

like the sweet breath of solemnity: whirr-*SMACK!*) His arm is rising and falling through great elastic spaces as though striving for
something fundamental like a forgotten dream or lost drawers. "I
— I'm sorry, sir!" Is she testing him, perched there on his stout
engine of duty like a cooked bird with the lingering bucket of
night in her beak (see how it opens, closes, opens), or is it only a
dimpled fever of the mind? He doesn't know, is almost afraid to
ask. "Something about a higher end," he explains hoarsely, taking
rueful refuge, "or hired end perhaps, and boiled flowers, hard
parts — and another thing, what's left of it . . ." She screams. The
garden groans, quivers, starts, its groves radiant and throbbing.
His teacher, no longer threatening, has withdrawn discreetly to a
far corner with diagonal creases, where he is turning what lilacs
remain into roses with his rumpled bull's pizzle: it's almost an act
of magic! Still his arm rises and falls, rises and falls, that broad
part of Mother Nature destined for such inventions dancing and
bobbing soft and easy under the indulgent sun: "It's a beautiful
day!" "What? *WHAT* — ?! Answering back to a reproof?" he in-
quires gratefully, taunting her with that civility and kindness due
to an inferior, as — hiss — *WHAP!* — flicking lint off one shoulder and smoothing the ends of his moustache with involuntary
vertical and horizontal motions, he floats helplessly backwards
("Thank you, sir!"), twitching amicably yet authoritatively like a
damp towel, down a bottomless hole, relieving himself noisily:
"Perhaps today then . . . at last!"

VINCENT G. DETHIER

The Moth and the Primrose

(FROM THE MASSACHUSETTS REVIEW)

PROUT'S HEAD lay its mile-long granitic masses supine in the cold waters of the Bay, like some geologic monster that had come to drink and was congealed forever by the kiss of the Labrador Current. Until man scarified the Head with a ragged twisting road there was nothing but an even, green pelt on the entire peninsula. And there was, to the casual eye, nothing to hint at the mystery of this primeval land, of the inexorable forces that worked upon it, and the portentous roles that even the least of things played in shaping its destiny.

The road had no name; it was simply the road to Prout's Head, a twisting trickle of dust that felt its exploratory way to the sea in emulation of the two brooks it crossed, a poor dry thing that was a mere skeleton of a water course. Yet surely as a water course it eventually found its way to the sea and having arrived was denied all the fulfillment of a stream. At the end of the peninsula it shriveled and died.

It had no history as man records history and no importance as man reckons importance. At the seaward end it came to the house of Old Prout, the clam digger; at the landward end it lost itself in the village.

The clam digger did great good simply because he did no harm. He was one of those least of all creatures, of importance only to God. One might have thought his a selfish life in the sense that he lived, to all appearances, entirely for himself. Yet simply in living his life he affected the lives of all others. He had given his name to the Head, or rather the Head had become identified with him until the name stuck. He had built the road, or rather, by use he had created the road. Although he did not know it, with the road he had made possible a whole cosmos. He had made possible the primroses. Without the road there would have been none because they grew nowhere else. Without the primroses there would have been no moths because they too could exist nowhere else.

In the final reckoning Prout gave life to the primroses. This plant could not live in the dark recesses of the forest. In the sunny fields the impatient grasses would not wait for its slow growth. But along the edge of the road where the impoverished soil lent scant encouragement, the primroses survived to create beauty from dust and barrenness.

During spring the carrotlike roots of the overwintering plants fed the tentative new growth. The interminable rain, so defeating to the village, so erosive to the road, put into solution the mineral wealth of the soil. By the time the sun had at long last asserted itself, the plants of last year had grown a full twelve inches. In a hint of the autumn colors which still lay ahead of them they disclosed a pink suffusion along the lengths of their stems even to the midvein of the new leaves. At the apex of each plant minute villi, buds yet unformed, lay packed so tightly together that the young cushion of the plant looked like a miniature hooked rug with a roseate center. The insistent hints of pink, the stems, the leaf veins, the center buds, were as the pinkness of a young child and gave an illusion that the same red blood coursed through the channels and gateways of the plant's inner structure. But it was only an illusion for the primrose was a cold and bloodless creature even though it reached for the sun as no animal would. It was a creature torn, stretched between the sun and the soil, the two poles of its existence.

It grew in clusters preordained by the casting of last year's seeds. Every place where the edge of the road lay in sun the plants grew in profusion. And the sunniest stretches of the road were those where aged trees of the encroaching, lowering forest had finally crashed, tearing a ragged hole in the foliage canopy, wiping out in an instant years of growth and balance and causing the whole floral succession to commence anew.

For the road such an event was not catastrophic but incentive. As the sunlight poured in the roadside, plants burst forth as though from nowhere testifying to the immense opportunistic fertility of the land. How many countless seeds, spores, and dormant things inhabited the land and awaited only the moment of chance!

As the road gradually abandoned the outside boundaries of its curves, the forest advanced with shade and moisture to drive out the primroses. So the whole road stole new space on its inside boundaries, and the primroses colonized the new gains. By blueberry time they had reached full bud. Around them clustered hundreds of minute seedlings. Already next year's life with its overlapping continuity had begun and with it the essence of eternity and immutability. This is the sadness of extinction. The last of a species is the denial of immortality.

On July evenings when Prout turned his back on the deepening dusk, like his neighbors, to fortify himself against the night, the primroses unclasped their petals and presented themselves to the night.

The July nights were the lovely nights, the nights of promise. There have been millions of them, no two ever alike. Like time, of which they are a passing fragment, no one can ever be repeated. Each is unique. There are the cold nights when the dew lies heavy on the foliage as soon as the sun withdraws its warmth. There are the dark nights, pitch black, when blackness seems less the absence of light than something of substance. There are the windy nights when few animals venture abroad. There are the silent nights when for no reason known to man the voices of nature are stilled.

There is the night of the full moon. On such a night the sun has hardly abandoned the world before the burnished moon rises dripping out of the bay and drops its shining ladder across the water to shore, a ladder composed of a fantasy of millions of golden fishes transported from an oriental fairy tale. The flight of the sun has left the western sky a cold ashen white. The moon climbs higher and higher into shoals of low smoky clouds which turn down the wick of its light on the waters, ever shorter, till extinguished.

Choruses of birds pour forth their loveliest songs as though they were not to live to sing again. As the light fades the wood warblers are the first to hush. A purple finch clings to the topmost spire of a towering spruce to catch the last ray of light and sings as though the spell of his song would stay the passing of day. In the already darkened thickets along the edge of the road a white-throated sparrow repeats again and again his pensive phrase, forever unable to compose any more of his symphony. From a gable of Prout's house a song sparrow chants vespers and departs. At the edge of the woods the querulous robins shout back at one another and the ovenbird scolds "teacher! teacher! teacher!" Until finally there is only the hermit thrush calling plaintively from the deep woods. And when his hauntingly lovely silver bell is hushed the land becomes still. From far out on the bay drifts in the banshee wail of a gull and still more faintly the shrill bickering of a pair of terns. Then even the sea is quiet.

The crickets and katydids, young, wingless neophytes, have not yet tuned their fiddles. Mute fireflies flash their cold lanterns in the fields around Prout's house and along the road. Occasionally at the top of a tall poplar a single restless leaf shivers to a stray breath of wind. A plump snowshoe hare ventures out to nibble at the plantain along the road's edge, hind legs tucked like a wound spring, prepared for instant flight. So still lies the night that the fretful barking of one of the dreaming village dogs carries his dream across the bay.

At this time of year the creatures of night are creatures of silence. When man and others among the strong retreat and guard themselves against the night, the soft-bodied creatures, the delicate and vulnerable expose themselves with implicit trust. The stealthy also are abroad, among them the mosquitoes of the north country, voracious seekers of blood whose implacability science has acknowledged with the given names *vexans, irritans, excrucians.*

On occasion someone would make a misstep in the woods; a leaf would rustle, a twig would snap. Sometimes a bird at roost would cry out in a brief instant of agony between sleep and death as a weasel plucked it from a limb. The objectivity of nature denies it even the small mercy of not waking.

For all of that, these were the nights of promise. Though the village was barren and beds creaked only to the tortured turnings of bodies too tired to sleep, the night throbbed with fertility. The warmth and dampness alone seemed almost sufficient for creation, for these are the prime ingredients of life. The old and the wizened are devoid of them; like the others Old Prout enshrouded himself in blankets ever seeking outside himself for warmth. And even then no perspiration came to his brow.

But in fact the warmth and moisture of the night were not sufficient, and for many fulfillment lay in the whims of others. The captive creatures like the primrose could only wait. Their lot had been cast with the seed. They were as alive as the nighthawk who wheeled in the darkness above, as the wood frog who called sepulchrally from the damp woods, as the beetle who gnawed their leaves — as alive as Old Prout himself. They were made of the same stuff. They were born, they grew, and they died. But they were voiceless, and they lived out their lives without pain, and they were captives in the soil. So they could not seek fulfillment.

For many blossoms fulfillment never came. A few anticipated the season, a few came too late. These waited a few nights, alone and unattended, then faded and were gone. But as each faded, another replaced it, and each for its brief span filled the night with a heady and intoxicating perfume. Had Old Prout walked the road at night he would have walked in enchantment. Blurred though the eye may be and stultified the fantasy, the world of scent strikes at a more primitive fiber in man and can stir him when all else is denied entry into his consciousness. Even in man, the creature of vision, olfaction is the provocative remnant of a once powerful faculty by which his remote animal ancestors could discriminate friend from foe, the edible from the inedible. It is the lure of procreative love which brings the buck and the doe together and the moth to his partner.

The scent of the primrose is a feminine thing. It misses no places; it goes everywhere. It touches lightly on the grasses and sedges. It passes where the moth clings, its great sensitive antennae spread in the night. For the primrose fulfillment is at hand.

All the winter the moth had lain, a brown sarcophagus in the soil, prey to a surfeit of moisture and a surfeit of dryness, vulnerable to the malignant fungi of the soil and the predators in the world above who would scent out its presence. A strange creature this pupa, yet neither caterpillar nor moth, neither past nor future. When did the individual that was the caterpillar, a superbly organized creature living in delicate balance with the primrose, become the individual that was the moth? When does the child become the man? Even so, when does the man become the spirit?

Tonight the moth in essence began its life. It had no memories; it had no age. And by some subtle ordering of nature it and its kin attained the apogee of their development at the same time as the primrose. The two shared nothing in common and they had everything in common. One a creature of the soil, the other a creature of the air, until this night they had no material bond. The primrose grew through the long spring in cadence with the heat and cold, the wetness and dryness. All through the long nights and short days of spring it grew until the days stretched ever longer and the nights shorter. Then it bloomed, while the moth in its earthen crypt saw neither night nor day and lay surrounded by a subterranean cold. All the while the preordained working of its juices organized its tissues, machined its wings, shingled them with bright scales until at a moment as awful as resurrection it shrugged off its shroud and climbed from the soil. Neither the movement of galaxies in deepest space nor space itself were any grander or more remote from understanding than the rebirth of this insignificant creature.

As it spread the net of its antennae to seine the night breeze, it caught the perfume of the primroses. The scent became enmeshed in its plumes, became in truth a part of the moth, and stirred strange energies in its frail body. Slave to the wanton call, the moth spread its wings for the first time and bore off into the wind, winding up the tangled skein of the perfume.

This first night was for gourmandizing. Inactive though the winter had been, it had consisted of the lean days of tissue reorganization. Much energy was required to transform a caterpillar into a moth. The moth, like bigger and smaller creatures, began life hungry. When the introduction of life might have been a grand event it comes to all as a time of danger, discomfort, and above all of hunger.

The primroses' butter yellow petals wasted their color in the darkness. On this night the moth could neither see the road nor the flowers along the road's edge, but the scent drew her unerringly to the nearest blossom. There she settled with much trembling of wings in an excitement of denial and anticipation. Without ever having done it before, unlearned in the ways of life, she uncoiled the watch-spring of her tongue and insinuated the tip deeply into the honey stores of the flower whence she pumped up microscopic draughts of sweetness.

The night lay warm on the land, its breezes at best a caress, gentle enough to waft the scent, far too delicate even to tremble the flowers. The moth flew from blossom to blossom, traversing the twisting mile of the road, passing others of her kind navigating the scented airways. Some as they sailed away from the safety of the foliage were plucked skillfully in flight by the patrolling bats. Others hearing the shrill echo-locating cry of the marauder dived for the tangled shelter of the roadside plants for even at night the road was a ribbon of danger. Great though its bounty in comparison to the barren forest, the price could be high.

Even the airways were not free. Hard-working spiders strung their cables across the open spaces and set their strategic nets for the unwary. And some moths, unable to sound the snares, hurtled to destruction. Some of these were newly emerged, resplendently pink moths which had not yet found their first primrose and were snared without ever discovering what lay at the end of the trail of scent. Others were tattered derelicts whose frayed wings hardly sufficed to keep them aloft. In any case, for these, the work of the long winter of gestation had come to nought. The marvels of organization and tissue architecture meant nothing to the spider beyond sustenance. He enshrouded each victim with impartial efficiency.

But other moths survived. Inner hungers and tantalizing scents drove them up and down the ribbon of the road, never venturing into the closeness of the forest, resting only on the primroses. Their flight was deceptively leisurely as they drew slow arcs and zigzags into the darkness, but the urgency of the effort was prodigious. Their wings blurred in the speed of the beat. It seemed inconceivable that so frail a foil as those with which the moth rowed the air could long survive the wear.

Until the fatigue of tippling and the slight chill that signaled predawn put an end to activity, the moths sampled every blossom. Not without cost, however, because the penalty for the invasion of privacy was a thorough dusting with pollen. Before the night had ended an orgy of miscegenation had been wrought. The primroses had found fulfillment.

Dawn found the moth clinging immobile to the last blossom to which she had the strength to fly. She clung immensely fatigued and perhaps just a little bit tipsy. As the pale weak light of the new day, enfeebled by the ground fog, filtered through the bordering trees and came at last to rest on the primrose, the blossom ever so slowly drew its petals together and enclosed the sleeping moth in a gossamer embrace until its head and vulnerable parts were completely protected and only the canopy of its painted wings were exposed to the outside.

The bacchanal had ended. Moth and flower alike were spent. No further scent effused from the primroses as they locked out the busybody bees and bristly flowerflies. The moth and all the

other night creatures slept. The gray world of night surrendered
to the unrestful colors of day.

•

Old Prout awoke. After a frugal breakfast he headed down the
road essaying this time its entire length and then, perhaps, even
the additional distance to the village. He passed one clump of
primroses after another, but it is doubtful that he saw a single one
of them — which was a pity because this morning they presented
a breathtakingly novel sight. Many of the plants appeared to have
flaunted their heritage and produced alien blossoms of startling
pink, pink of a hue seldom seen in nature. Sometimes a plant was
a complete sport with as many as five blossoms that had not bred
true. And here and there was a rare double-blossom where two
moths had crawled into the same blossom. These two creatures of
night, the yellow primrose and the pink moth, together composed
an impression that would have delighted Monet. One might have
expected them to have been clothed in the dull trappings of darkness because during the periods of their greatest activity there was
none to see. Instead they were adorned as creatures of sunlight.
Their brilliant colors matched beautifully all the other bright colors of day. In their gaiety they found safety. So they slept in peace.
  While the moths idled the day, the creatures of light labored
and hastened to store. The bumblebees, the honeybees, and the
harvest ants worked unceasingly. Ironically this time of year so
baroque in beauty, so conducive to poetry, so gay, had to be a time
of labor. The long struggle to store for the fruitless months of
winter began now. The men of the village found little time for
fishing or hunting. The grass waved long in the fields; the barns
yawned to be filled. All day long plodding horses pulled the mow-
ing machines. Every field, however small, was harvested even to
the very edges of the fences and roads. As a result the forests
never encroached on the fields, the woody plants never secured a
foothold, plants like the primroses never invaded. The fields remained nearly pure stands of grass. Everyone worked at a feverish
pace. No time remained to admire the cloud patterns of the summer day, the swallows gyrating over the village or skimming the
placid mirror of the mill pond. No one could pause long enough
to inhale the incense of the shorn fields, to look down the bay and
wonder to what far places the sea led, or to watch the changing
colors in the village as the sun, like an indomitable checker player,

moved its shadows from east to west. Even Old Prout, who now had the time, lacked the inclination. There was no one to see beauty in the day of which the moths and the primrose were a part. So again the day spent itself, bright in toil, until in the fading light the primroses again released the moths and floated their wanton perfume on the night to lure them back again.

As the days succeeded the nights the villagers toiled on and both the moths and the primroses aged. Their appearances changed. The tight rosette at the crown of the plant kept giving off buds and elongating so that the plant continued to grow taller. Halfway down the stem the flowers had now become seed pods. The whole life of the plant was chronicled from stem to apex. It was as though a person could see simultaneously the child, the youth, the man, l'ancien. As the stem aged, becoming coarse, brittle, and fibrous, the apex was being born: youth and age in the same body.

The moth only aged, its wings becoming more perceptibly frayed from the constant airflow of flight and the pink beginning to fade as here and there a minute scale tore off in the turbulence of the little tempests that the wings excited. The appetites of youth lost their edge. For the moths, the primrose became less a banquet table, more a meeting place.

Drawn together by the elusive scent the moths took notice of one another. At close quarters their own perfumes of love evoked new behaviors in which the flowers were no longer a central part. It is true of course that pollen still came to be transferred from plant to plant, but fulfillment had also come to the moth. Now as the primroses clasped their petals with the lightening of dawn many blossoms enclosed two moths. And then as the season contin-ued its advance the females flew their independent ways. The primrose had served in turn as banquet table and place of ac-couchement. It now assumed the role of cradle as the females returned to tuck their creamy eggs one by one among the yet unformed flowers.

With the end of July more and more spent blossoms dropped from the primrose plants. In aging they tarnished until almost orange. The petals folded moth-like. Now the aging moths, fast losing their brightness, blended perfectly with the wizened flow-ers. The age of both partners had perfected the camouflage. It deceived the eye of all but the most astute predators, the spider in ambush and the hunting robber fly. The patrolling bats sought other victims. At the apices of aging plants new blossoms spread their petals to an empty night. Hardly begun, the season of promise ended.

One of the first eggs laid hatched during the early days of August. The caterpillar, which was all head, like most newborn things, hatched from the egg by the simple expedient of eating his way out. After he had emerged, the remnants of the vacated shell, iridescent ribs against a glassy background, looked exactly like a microscopic cathedral with traceries of stained-glass windows. The egg possessed greater beauty without the substance of the caterpillar within, but the shell itself had no permanency and no future while the caterpillar was the future.

Having consumed only slightly more of the egg than was necessary to effect escape, the caterpillar spent the next hour exploring the tightly closed bud upon which the egg had been placed. It explored like a blind creature, feeling, palpating, smelling, because its primitive eyes told it only light from dark and nothing of the subtleties of its world. For the moment its world consisted of that particular bud. Worlds beyond that did not exist. Even the rest of the primrose was beyond its experience. The primrose, the larger world of the road, and the village beyond were finite to Old Prout and to many of the larger and swifter animals, but for the microscopic caterpillar infinity began on the next bud.

Minute though it was, the caterpillar's softness and defenselessness invited attack from predators and parasites. The bud provided sustenance and shelter. Having found the exterior to its satisfaction it proceeded to eat its way to the inside. By nightfall nothing remained of its presence but the ruined eggshell and a neat round hole halfway down the side of the elongated bud.

The world outside continued its march as though the caterpillar did not exist, which is not to say that it counted for nothing. But its influence was a statistical one, as is that of a single grain of sand upon the beach, and its existence produced no immediate effect on the world.

The night wind freshened coming in over the Head from the sea. Within its cornucopia the caterpillar experienced at most the gentle swaying of the parent plant. The motion was probably of no more import to it than was the revolving of the earth in space to Old Prout. Around the stalks of the aging primroses hundreds of minute seedlings from last year's sowing struggled as fiercely for survival. The occasional rains that gullied the road washed some away in a torrent of pebbles. Old Prout crushed under foot others too far from the edge of the road. And the slow were trapped in the shadows of the quick and perished for want of sun.

It was difficult to imagine that this old man moving down the road was indeed the ultimate agent of all the things that the road was and represented. Surely his one passage had no effect on the life of the road except to scare off a chipmunk which sat on a roadside boulder, cause the red squirrel in an overhead spruce to scold in alarm and kick up dusk which hung in the hollows as its motes danced, golden in the sunlight. A less likely architect could not be imagined. He could no more control the events he had set in motion than he could control the existence of his own shadow. Nonetheless, the caterpillar in the bud was there because Prout was there.

The caterpillar did not toil. It had only to eat. To consume the entire contents of the bud was but the work of a few days. Now the seed would never mature, never unfold to the night, never send a lorelei scent into the wind. The substance that had been the bud was now the caterpillar. Inevitably the caterpillar had grown, though its skin had not. But the humors of its body worked in marvelous harmony on its ever-growing tissues so that a new and larger skin came into existence beneath the old. At the right moment the caterpillar exerted itself, split asunder its tight corset, and crawled forth from it and from the bud a freer and hungrier creature.

Now larger, tougher, and camouflaged in green with hazy dull lines of pink it abandoned the buds for the seed pods which the moths had made possible. It wore just the proper harmony of green and pink to match the color scheme of the primrose plant. It had gnawed a hole in a large pod, thrust its head inside, and began to consume the seeds, the ovules of the plant. As it ate the ones at the top, it had to crawl farther and farther in, finally reaching the bottom of the pod. When the pod was empty the caterpillar moved to another. For the rest of its days it would never see beyond the darkness of its own private food-bag. As it grew larger, shedding one coat after another, the horizon in its world lifted beyond a single bud, to a whole plant, and finally beyond that plant to a neighboring one.

On every primrose that the moths had visited, caterpillars now raped the pods. Some plants that had been sparing of flowers lost all of their seed to the caterpillars who then had to abandon them to set off blindly for another plant, not knowing in which direction it lay, not even knowing if there was another plant.

In a sense the relationship between moth and primrose had come full cycle. The fresh young primroses of early summer had courted the moths extravagantly for their own selfish ends, and the moths had come greedily, for their own selfish ends. Now the primroses faced sterility, and even communal extinction, as every one up and down the road was ravished by caterpillars serving their own selfish ends. But in being so prodigal of their sustenance the caterpillars had become the potential instruments of their own destruction. Many of them consumed pods so methodically and so efficiently that they eventually were forced to seek new plants. This time of search was the time of peril.

If a primrose grew apart from the others its emigrating caterpillars wandered aimlessly in an impenetrable jungle of stems with failure the inevitable outcome of their search. If the parent plant had grown in the company of others, some caterpillars had a chance of success, but emigration was the great equalizing phenomenon, for it was a time of incredible hazard. Hard, lean ants roamed the edge of the road, always hungry, driven not only by their own hunger but as urgently by hunger of the colony. The wolf spider stalked the stem jungle; the orb spider spun its snares. By night there were predacious ground beetles, wood frogs, shrews, and countless others; by day, the hunting wasps, the robber flies, parasites no less dangerous because of their insidious ways. There were the white-throated sparrow, the chipping sparrow, the goldfinches, the yellowthroat, and the other warblers. And always the ants, running, running, running.

Along the roadside the primroses no longer stood in beauty. Age and the caterpillars had robbed them of that. Pods had become mere shells riddled with holes. Stems, leaves, and leaf axils were soiled with the caterpillars' refuse. Stems had become fibrous with age. Leaves curled, twisted, tore, and contorted themselves in tortured, grotesque shapes. Where before there had been a gothic grace in their fanning and arching from the stalk, now there were only tiered gargoyles. The gentle red suffusion which earlier had given the plant a touch of animal warmth, deepened and spread becoming the floridness of decadence. The primroses were untidy, spent, and old.

But even the caterpillars lacked the efficiency which man in his pride presumes himself to have. Many pods escaped complete annihilation; some pods were overlooked completely. The success of nature is built upon inefficiency. A beautiful balance had been struck so that some pods would survive and some caterpillars would perish. The caterpillars that perished, perished for the survival of the species, and in a way, accomplished as much for the species as those which survived. And the same was true of the primroses, and there would always be moths — as long as the road existed.

Of the primroses there remained only the leaves, red-tipped as though dipped untidily into a pot of bright paint, and the steepled stalks beaded with pods, many mere shells, a small few with fertile seeds. In its Jekyll and Hyde existence the moth had made fertile the pod and in its own seed lay the destruction of that fertility. The successful caterpillars, replete with stored fat, had abandoned the precarious life on the stalks and crept away to the detritus of the road's edge to a deceptively safer place of hibernation.

•

Late that night a fine driving rain began to fall. The year had begun in weeping; it was ending in weeping. The rain wet down the desiccated cedar shingles of the house until they began to relax their crustiness and uncurl. On the gray rocks above the high-tide mark the lichens relaxed under the rain's caress. And the rain continued to work upon them till the rocks softened in delicate lichen blues and greens and siennas, golds, and earthy browns.

By morning the rain had sought out every crack and crevice, every twig, needle, and leaf, so the trees stood weeping. It worked into the ground until the roots relaxed their firm grip on the soil. The wind freshened to the south. Though the trees shook themselves almost like drenched animals, the rain came too fast. Everything lay soaking. And over all gusted the strange warm wind.

When Prout awoke the bay was boiling, white-capped. The wind played a throaty tune on the slatted window-blind of the bedroom. The hot, sticky air, for all its violent movement, seemed to clutch at his throat. The crickets of yesterday were silent. No birds were to be seen, not even the herring gulls that usually rode the storm scud.

Along the road the wind did reach all the way to the ground. The border plants lashed to and fro as though they would surely escape bondage in the clutch of the soil. The primroses thrashed as wildly. Down in the trash and soil the caterpillars heard nothing, felt nothing, and were probably the least sentient of all creatures as they lay coiled in prepupal stupor.

At noontime the wind curled under Prout's overturned dory resting above the high-tide mark and with a casual flip flung it toward the beach. This was too much for the old man, who had been watching the surf from the kitchen window. He struggled into his sou'wester and boots and hobbled to the door. It tore from his grasp as soon as he released the latch. He fought it closed behind him. As he bent his way toward the toolshed to fetch a coil of rope, he noticed that three shingles had been torn from the roof and that the side of the house in the lee of the poplar was papered with the green fragments of leaves shredded from the tree.

Now it could be heard, a biblical wind. He did not have to look up where it million-fingered through the oaks and tousled their crowns to know that this surpassed common winds. He might have wondered if the tousling of the trees was the sort of sensation that reached even to the roots, whether the tree stirred where it was bound. He might have wondered what manner of creatures were these trees that felt not. Instead his thoughts were captured by the sound of the village church bell. Faintly above the continuing roar of the wind and the pounding of the surf he heard it. It came only intermittently as the gale again and again snatched away the sound. It was obvious, however, that the bell was being rung in desperation. It could only mean fire. Somebody's chimney had probably blown down. There would be no chance of saving the house in this wind. In this country of wooden frame houses and small isolated villages fire meant the end of everything. The lucky ones got themselves out and, on rare occasions, a few of their most precious belongings. He paused to look up at his own chimney. The wind sucked at it with great, greedy gulps. Sparks flew horizontally from the lee side as twisting fire-worms. Otherwise all seemed shipshape.

By the time Prout had found the rope, reached, and again overturned the dory, the world which had been in turmoil all night hushed as though a spell had been cast upon it. In an instant the water in the bay turned thick and sluggish. Save for a lingering catspaw here and there the storm might never have been. Time stood still. No storm in his experience had ever ceased so abruptly.

The illusion of peace did not last, however. In his preoccupation Prout had not noticed that the catspaws now came from the north. The light breeze had quartered around. Then, with no warning whatsoever, the storm bore out of the north, ravished across the Head snapping the tops of ancient white pines, plucking firs and spruce like weeds from a garden, and hastening the ebb tide from the beach. In an instant it caught the dory again with the futile old man attached as tenaciously as a barnacle and flung the pair onto the granite ledges. Two planks and three ribs of the dory were stove in beyond repair. And the storm continued unabated the rest of the afternoon. By nightfall it was spent.

Along the roadside the pod-laden primroses swayed gently as though nothing at all had happened. The caterpillars in the soil slept on undisturbed. Prout's house too survived the full force of the wind. It looked as it always looked except that no smoke curled from the chimney. The stricken dory lay inextricably wedged among the rocks where the storm had cached it. On the beach not far away the wavelets of the rising tide tried in vain to cover Old Prout, but there had not been much time and in this rocky land there was little sand.

•

It was still raining, lightly, the day they buried Old Prout. A pathetically small group stood around the open grave. Each stood more or less separately because in this relationship to the old man they had little in common with one another and nothing in common with him. It is difficult to say why they were there. None could honestly say that he grieved. The penalty of living alone is that there is no one to grieve. Prout owed them nothing, and they owed him nothing. They wished the parson would get on with it. The parson had problems of his own. He had not known Prout in life; he was at a loss as to how to speak in his behalf in death. Perhaps the need to say something for the lowly was greater than that of eulogizing the mighty. But what could he possibly say about the old man? As far as he was aware, the old fellow had never done anything — for or against any man. He had been neither a good neighbor nor a bad one. What had he given the world? He had neither kith nor kin to anyone's knowledge. He left no lineage.

Whatever immortality there may be in the germ plasma, Prout's had ceased to exist.

The house would gradually be eroded by the weather without and the carefree tenants within. In full time it would be window-less, its roof cracked open to the sky, its floors collapsing. By some subtle and mysterious alchemy the emptiness of the house — not merely its physical emptiness but its emptiness of purpose — would leach the quicksilver from the weathered fabric. The silvery sheen of the shingles would dull and darken as the light went out. And nobody would care.

With the house purposeless there would be no need of a road. Trees felled by the burden of winter snows or undermined by spring freshets would lie undisturbed. The endless rains would burrow industriously in their tortured gullies in frantic search for the sea. Seed which before had been trod underfoot would sprout with impunity in the uncrowded road. Grass would begin to grow between the ruts undisturbed by the harrow-sharp hooves of the oxen. White clover would extend its inquisitive roots among the pebbles; miniature blackberry plants would bind the gravel with their runners. Other lesser-known weeds, plantains, dandelions, lambs-quarters, and even primrose seedlings, would steal back to reclaim the road from sterility. Near the brooks the scouring rushes would climb the banks to clothe the sandy spots. Every-where there would be sour-grass in abundance. From the great press and competition of the roadside, jungle plants would escape to the open frontier.

All of these diminutive plants would shelter the road from the tattoo of the rain, impede the rivulets that ate away at the soil, and on the dry days capture and retain the dew formed during the cool evenings. When they died in the fall, the gravel of the road would be just a bit richer for their having grown there, a bit more cohesive, a shade more colorful.

By the second year asters would have ventured out beyond the sheltered roadside, accompanied by the wild sarsaparilla. In the more moist sections where the canopy of greater trees protected the road from desiccating sun and winds, the plants of the woods would finally have followed the shadows and shade of the plants already growing there. There would be scattered shooting stars, the bunchberry, wild lily-of-the-valley, and club mosses. The road would be becoming wetter, softer, more pliant, more receptive. It

would come alive. From overhead the maples, birches, and coni-
fers would cast their leafy raiments in preparation for winter.
Leaves would accumulate in the ruts, in hoof-prints, in all of the
depressions where the wind was unable to rouse them.

By the third year the cinnamon ferns, the interrupted ferns,
and the bracken would have found the road amicable. From the
high crossing branches of the spruces and balsams, where the red
squirrel sat shelling cones, crumbs of seed would have fallen so
that by now miniature evergreens would take their places among
the pioneers.

While all of the colonization of the abandoned road would be
going on, the roadside plants would lean farther and farther into
the sun, no longer brushed back by the plodding oxen, broken by
the passing wagon, or throttled by the rising dust. Together the
new plants and the old would begin to cover the scar that was the
road to Prout's Head.

At first the community of primroses would expand into the new
space, ever seeking room and sunlight. Each new plant would
spread its rosette of leaves, making that circle of space unavailable
to others. Underground its roots would worm blindly through the
earth usurping space there too. The first plants to gain foothold
would impede the colonization of their congeners, but, ironically,
their presence would be sealing their own doom by rendering the
road more suitable to more aggressive plants. The road would
become less a road, more a field at first, then a glade in the forest.
The encroaching shade and the woodland plants would thin the
ranks of the primroses.

As the primroses first increased in number there would be more
pods saved from the rape of the caterpillar. But the moths would
find plants closer together. There would be less need to venture
farther afield where they would expose themselves to the hazards
of long stretches of open road. The moth population would grow.
Inevitably, however, the primroses would lose their struggle
against the forest. Their seedlings would perish, their numbers
decrease. The hungry generations of caterpillars would eat far
more than their share of seeds. The delicate balance of moth and
primrose would shift again. No longer would the moths be able to
trail the obsessive scent up and down an open road.

Pursuing their fruitless search the moths would cover greater
distances, remain longer on the wing, expose themselves longer to

the winged assassins of the night. Confined to the narrow twisting gallery in the forest they would only be able to shuttle endlessly back and forth. Most would perish. A few would come by chance to the end of the road, where the world beyond invited exploration. They would burst into the infinity of space, voyagers in a new world, pursuers of a phantom scent. And again by sheer chance a few, caught up in the vast flowing currents of the sky, would find in a distant place, another road, another primrose. And the species would go on, continuing from the hidden springs of its mysterious drive as it had for millennia, as with all life, never content to rest, but forever enlarging, expanding, duplicating.

In ten years the scar that Prout and his oxen had made in the coverlet of green lying on the granite masses of the Head would have healed completely. The dark forest would roll unbroken from the sea to the village. People in the village would say that there had once been a road to the Head, but that now it was gone.

The parson had no knowledge of any of these things. Perhaps these things were of no importance. For a flash in time, as the ages are measured, a whole world had existed, a complex interacting world, life in its manifest forms. Then it was gone as though it had never been. Somewhere else on the planet the story was repeating itself. The locale would be different, the circumstances altered, unique to the place; but the life there would all be tied to the past by the same mysterious thread that is woven in cryptic design.

And of Old Prout? Perhaps he was of no importance either. Like the moths and the primroses he existed for a time as part of the world of the road. Like them he was an extension of the past. He had occupied top place in the whole hierarchy; he was its prime agent. With his passing that complex ceased to exist. He did not exist apart from these things. If he moved in a vacuum, it was only one of his own making. If he lived in ignorance of the moth, the primrose, and all the other beings of the road, even that did not set him apart. Each of them lived in ignorance of him. So the interdependence of all balanced them in some kind of anonymous equality.

But possibly, just possibly, all of these things were important. And in some unfathomable manner Prout was perfected in the being of the moth and the primrose. Perhaps it was right that all of these things ceased in time to exist after the old man had gone.

For nothing really survives the man — a trace, perhaps, a pyramid, a web; but these must be empty symbols.

The parson knew none of these things. He knew nothing of the road, Old Prout, or the past — any more than he knew of the future. He only knew that Old Prout, the least of God's creatures, was gone. Acutely aware of his inadequacy, he asked for a minute of silent prayer. Self-consciously the five bowed their heads and waited out the time. Wraiths of mist emerged from the sea, stole around the ancient grave stones, and set the trees to weeping.

ANDRE DUBUS

The Winter Father

(FROM THE SEWANEE REVIEW)

THE JACKMANS' MARRIAGE had been adulterous and violent, but in its last days they became a couple again, as they might have if one of them were slowly dying. They wept together, looked into each other's eyes without guile, distrust, or hatred, and they planned Peter's time with the children. On his last night at home he and Norma, tenderly, without a word, made love. Next evening, when he got home from Boston, they called David and Kathi in from the snow and brought them to the kitchen.

David was eight, slender, with light brown hair neatly to his shoulders, a face that was still pretty; he seemed always hungry, and Peter liked watching him eat. Kathi was six, had long red hair and a face that Peter had fallen in love with, a face that had once been pierced by glass the shape of a long dagger blade. In early spring a year ago — he still had not taken the storm windows off the screen doors — he was bringing his lunch to the patio; he did not know Kathi was following him, and holding his plate and mug he had pushed the door open with his shoulder, stepped outside, heard the crash and her scream, and turned to see her gripping the long shard, then pulling it from her cheek. She got it out before he reached her. He picked her up and pressed his handkerchief to the wound, midway between her eye and throat, and held her as he phoned his doctor, who said he would meet them at the hospital and do the stitching himself because it was cosmetic and that beautiful face should not be touched by residents. Norma was not at home. Kathi lay on the car seat beside him, and he held his handkerchief on her cheek, and in the hospital he held her hands while she lay on the table. The doctor said it would only take about four stitches and it would be better without anesthetic, because sometimes that puffed the skin, and he wanted to fit the cut together perfectly, for the scar; he told this very gently to Kathi, and he said that as she grew the scar would move down her face and finally would be under her jaw. Then she and Peter squeezed each other's hands as the doctor stitched and she gritted her teeth and stared at pain.

She was like that when he and Norma told them. It was David who suddenly cried, begged them not to get a divorce, and then fled to his room and would not come out, would not help Peter load his car, and only emerged from the house as Peter was driving away: a small running shape in the dark, charging the car, picking up something and throwing it, missing, crying *You bum You bum You bum . . .*

Drunk that night in his apartment, whose rent he had paid and keys received yesterday morning, before last night's grave love-making with Norma, he gained through the blur of bourbon an intense focus on his children's faces as he and Norma spoke: We fight too much, we've tried to live together but can't; you'll see, you'll be better off too, you'll be with Daddy for dinner on Wednesday nights, and on Saturdays and Sundays you'll do things with him. In his kitchen he watched their faces.

Next day he went to the radio station. After the news at noon he was on; often, as the records played, he imagined his children last night, while he and Norma were talking, and after he was gone. Perhaps she took them out to dinner, let them stay up late, flanking her on the couch in front of the television. When he talked, he listened to his voice: it sounded as it did every weekday afternoon. At four he was finished. In the parking lot he felt as though, with stooped shoulders, he were limping. He started the forty-minute drive northward, for the first time in twelve years going home to empty rooms. When he reached the town where he lived, he stopped at a small store and bought two lamb chops and a package of frozen peas. *I will take one thing at a time,* he told himself. Crossing the sidewalk to his car, in that short space, he felt the limp again, the stooped shoulders. He wondered if he looked like a man who had survived an accident which had killed others.

·

That was on a Thursday. When he woke Saturday morning, his first thought was a wish: that Norma would phone and tell him they were sick — and that he should wait to see them Wednesday. He amended his wish, lay waiting for his own body to let him know it was sick, out for the weekend. In late morning he drove to their coastal town; he had moved fifteen miles inland. Already the snow-plowed streets and country roads leading to their house felt like parts of his body: intestines, lung, heart-fiber lying from his door to theirs. When they were born, he had smoked in the waiting room with the others. Now he was giving birth: stirruped, on his back, waves of pain. There would be no release, no cutting of the cord. Nor did he want it. He wanted to grow a cord.

Walking up their shoveled walk and ringing the doorbell, he felt at the same time like an inept salesman and a con man. He heard their voices, watched the door as though watching the sounds he heard, looking at the point where their faces would appear; but when the door opened he was looking at Norma's waist; then up to her face, lipsticked, her short brown hair soft from that morning's washing. For years she had not looked this way on a Saturday morning. Her eyes held him: the nest of pain was there, the shyness, the coiled anger. But there was another shimmer: she was taking a new marriage vow: *This is the way we shall love our children now; watch how well I can do it.* She smiled and said: "Come in out of the cold and have a cup of coffee."

In the living room he crouched to embrace the hesitant children. Only their faces were hesitant. In his arms they squeezed, pressed, kissed. David's hard arms absolved them both of Wednesday night. Through their hair Peter said pleasantly to Norma that he'd skip the coffee this time. Grabbing caps and unfurling coats, they left the house, holding hands as they walked to the car.

He showed them his apartment: they had never showered behind glass; they slid the doors back and forth . . . Sand washing down the drain, their flesh sunburned, a watermelon waiting in the refrigerator.

"This summer — "

They turned from the glass, looked up at him.

"When we go to the beach. We can come back here and shower."

Their faces reflected his bright promise, and they followed him to the kitchen; on the counter were two cans of kidney beans, Jalapeno peppers, seasonings. Norma kept her seasonings in small jars. Two years ago when David was six and came home bullied and afraid of next day at school, Peter asked him if the boy was bigger than he was, and David said a lot, and showed him the boy's height with one hand, his breadth with two. Peter took the glass stopper from the cinnamon jar, tied it in a handkerchief corner, and struck his palm with it, so David would know how hard it was, would believe in it. Next morning David took it with him. On the schoolground, when the bully shoved him, he swung it up from his back pocket and down on the boy's forehead. The boy cried and went away. After school David found him on the sidewalk and hit his jaw with the weapon he had sat on all day, chased him two blocks swinging at his head, and came home with delighted eyes, no damp traces of yesterday's shame and fright, and Peter's own pain and rage turned to pride, then caution, and he spoke gently, told David to carry it for a week or so more, but not to use it unless the bully attacked; told him we must control our pleasure in giving pain.

Now, reaching into the refrigerator, he felt the children behind him; then he knew it was not them he felt, for in the bathroom when he spoke to their faces he had also felt a presence to his rear, watching, listening. It was the walls, it was fatherhood, it was himself. He was not an early drinker, but he wanted an ale now; looked at the brown bottles long enough to fear and dislike his reason for wanting one; then he poured two glasses of apple cider and, for himself, cider and club soda. He sat at the table and watched David slice a Jalapeno over the beans, and said, "Don't ever touch one of those and take a leak without washing your hands first."

"Why?"

"I did it once. Think about it."

"Wow."

They talked of flavors as Kathi, with her eyes just above rim-level of the pot, her wrists in the steam, poured honey, and shook paprika, basil, parsley, Worcestershire, wine vinegar. In a bowl they mixed ground meat with a raw egg: jammed their hands into it, fingers touching; scooped and squeezed meat and onion and celery between their fingers. The kitchen smelled of bay leaf in the simmering beans, and then of broiling meat. They talked about the food as they ate, pressing thick hamburgers to fit their mouths, and only then Peter heard the white silence coming at them like afternoon snow. They cleaned the counter and table and what they had used; and they spoke briefly, quietly; they smoothly passed things; and when Peter turned off the faucet, all sound stopped, the kitchen was multiplied by silence, the apartment's walls grew longer, the floors wider, the ceilings higher. Peter walked the distance to his bedroom, looked at his watch, then quickly turned to the morning paper's television listing and called: "Hey! *The Magnificent Seven*'s coming on."

"All *right*," David said, and they hurried down the short hall, light footsteps whose sounds he could name: Kathi's, David's, Kathi's. He lay between them, bellies down, on the bed.

"Is this our third time or fourth?" Kathi said.

"I think our fourth. We saw it in a theater once."

"I could see it every week," David said.

"Except when Charles Bronson dies," Kathi said. "But I like when the little kids put flowers on his grave. And when he spanks them."

The winter sunlight beamed through the bedroom window, the afternoon moving past him and his children. Driving them home he imitated Yul Brynner, Eli Wallach, Charles Bronson; the children praised his voices, laughed, and in front of their house they kissed him and asked what they were going to do tomorrow. He said he didn't know yet; he would call in the morning, and he watched them go up the walk between snow as high as Kathi's waist. At the door they turned and waved; he tapped the horn twice, and drove away.

That night he could not sleep. He read *Macbeth*, woke propped against the pillows, the bedside lamp on, the small book at his side. He put it on the table, turned out the light, moved the pillows down, and slept. Next afternoon he took David and Kathi to a movie.

•

He did not bring them to his apartment again, unless they were on the way to another place, and their time in the apartment was purposeful and short: Saturday morning cartoons, then lunch before going to a movie or museum. Early in the week he began reading the movie section of the paper, looking for matinees. Every weekend they went to a movie, and sometimes two, in their towns and other small towns and in Boston. On the third Saturday he took them to a PG movie which was bloody and erotic enough to make him feel ashamed and irresponsible as he sat between his children in the theater. Driving home, he asked them about the movie until he believed it had not frightened them or made them curious about bodies and urges they did not yet have. After that he saw all PG movies before taking them, and he was angry at mothers who left their children at the theater and picked them up when the movie was over, and left him to listen to their children exclaiming at death, laughing at love; and often the children roamed the aisles going to the concession stand, and distracted him from this weekly entertainment which he suspected he waited for and enjoyed more than David and Kathi. He had not been an indiscriminate moviegoer since he was a child. Now what had started as a duty was pleasurable, relaxing. He knew that beneath this lay a base of cowardice, but he told himself it would pass. A time would come when he and David and Kathi could sit in his living room, talking like three friends who had known each other for eight and six years.

Most of the people he entertained on weekday afternoons were women. Between love songs he began talking to them about movie ratings. He said not to trust the ratings. He asked what they felt about violence and sex in movies, whether or not they were bad for children. He told them he didn't know; that many of the fairy tales and all the comic books of his boyhood were violent; and so were the westerns and serials on Saturday afternoons. But there was no blood. And he chided the women about letting their children go to the movies alone.

He got letters and read them in his apartment at night. Some thanked him for his advice about ratings. Many told him it was all right for him to talk: he wasn't with the kids every afternoon after school and all weekends and holidays and summer; the management of the theater was responsible for quiet and order during the movies; they were showing the movies to attract children, and they were glad to take the money. The children came home happy and did not complain about other children being noisy. Maybe he should stop going to matinees, should leave his kids there and pick them up when it was over. *It's almost what I'm doing,* he thought; and he stopped talking about movies to the afternoon women.

•

He found a sledding hill, steep and long, and at its base a large frozen pond. David and Kathi went with him to buy his sled, and with a thermos of hot chocolate they drove to the hill near his apartment. Parked cars lined the road, and children and some parents were on the hill's broad top. Red-faced children climbed back, pulling their sleds with ropes. Peter sledded first; he knew the ice on the pond was safe, but he was beginning to handle fatherhood as he did guns: always as if they were loaded, when he knew they were not. There was a satisfaction in preventing even dangers which did not exist.

The snow was hard and slick, rushed beneath him; he went over a bump, rose from the sled, nearly lost it, slammed down on it, legs outstretched, gloved hands steering around the next bump but not the next one suddenly rising toward his face, and he pressed against the sled, hugged the wood-shock to his chest, yelled with delight at children moving slowly upward, hit the edge of the pond, and sledded straight out, looking at the evergreens on its far bank. The sled stopped near the middle of the pond; he stood and waved to the top of the hill, squinting at sun and bright snow, then two silhouettes waved back, and he saw Kathi's long red hair. Holding the sled's rope he walked on ice, moving to his left as David started down and Kathi stood waiting, leaning on her sled. He told himself he was a fool: had lived winters with his children, yet this was the first sled he had bought for himself; sometimes he had gone with them because they asked him to, and he had used their sleds. But he had never found a sledding hill. He had driven past them, seen the small figures on their crests and slopes, but no more. Watching David swerve around a bump and Kathi, at the top, pushing her sled, then dropping onto it, he forgave himself; there was still time; already it had begun.

But on that first afternoon of sledding he made a mistake: within an hour his feet were painfully cold, his trousers wet, and his legs cold; David and Kathi wore snow pants. Beneath his parka he was sweating. Then he knew they felt the same, yet they would sled as long as he did, because of the point and edges of divorce that pierced and cut all their time together.

"I'm freezing," he said. "I can't move my toes."

"Me too," David said.

"Let's go down one more time," Kathi said.

Then he took them home. It was only three o'clock.

After that he took them sledding on weekend mornings. They brought clothes with them, and after sledding they went to his apartment and showered. They loved the glass doors. On the first day they argued about who would shower first, until Peter flipped a coin and David won, and Peter said Kathi would have the first shower next time and they would take turns that way. They showered long, and when Peter's turn came the water was barely warm and he was quickly in and out. Then in dry clothes they ate lunch and went to a movie.

•

Or to another place, and one night, drinking bourbon in his living room, lights off so he could watch the snow falling, the yellowed gentle swirl at the corner streetlight, the quick flakes at his window, banking on the sill, and across the street the grey-white motion lowering the sky and making the evergreens look distant, he thought of owning a huge building to save divorced fathers. Free admission. A place of swimming pool, badminton and tennis courts, movie theaters, restaurants, soda fountains, batting cages, a zoo, an art gallery, a circus, aquarium, science museum, hundreds of restrooms, two always in sight, everything in the tender charge of women trained in first aid and in Montessori, no uniforms, their only style warmth and cheer. A father could spend entire days there, weekend after weekend, so in winter there would not be all this planning and driving. He had made his cowardice urbane, mobile, and sophisticated; but perhaps at its essence cowardice knows it is apparent: he believed David and Kathi knew that their afternoons at the aquarium, the Museum of Fine Arts, the Science Museum, were houses Peter had built, where they could be together as they were before, with one difference: there was always entertainment.

Frenetic as they were, he preferred weekends to the Wednesday nights when they ate together. At first he thought it was shyness. Yet they talked easily, often about their work, theirs at school, his as a disc jockey. When he was not with the children, he spent much time thinking about what they said to each other. And he saw that in his eight years as a father he had been attentive, respectful, amusing; he had taught and disciplined. But no: not now: when they were too loud in the car or they fought, he held onto his anger, his heart buffeted with it, and spoke calmly, as though to another man's children, for he was afraid that if he scolded as he had before, the day would be spoiled, they would not have the evening at home, the sleeping in the same house, to heal them; and they might not want to go with him next day or two nights from now or two days. During their eight and six years with him, he had shown them love and made them laugh. But now he knew that he had remained a secret from them. What did they know about him? What did he know about them?

He would tell them about his loneliness, and what he had learned about himself. When he wasn't with them, he was lonely all the time, except while he was running or working, and sometimes at the station he felt it waiting for him in the parking lot, on the highway, in his apartment. He thought much about it, like an athletic man considering a sprained ligament, changing his exercises to include it. He separated his days into parts, thought about each one, and learned that not all of them were bad. When the alarm woke him in the winter dark, the new day and waiting night were the grey of the room, and they pressed down on him, fetid repetitions bent on smothering his spirit before he rose from the bed. But he got up quickly, made the bed while the sheets still held his warmth, and once in the kitchen with coffee and newspaper he moved into the first part of the day: bacon smell and solemn disc jockeys with classical music, an hour or more at the kitchen table, as near-peaceful as he dared hope for; and was grateful for too, as it went with him to the living room, to the chair at the southeast window where, pausing to watch traffic and look at the snow and winter branches of elms and maples in the park across the street, he sat in sun-warmth and entered the cadence of Shakespeare. In mid-morning he vaselined his face and genitals and, wearing layers of nylon, he ran two and a half miles down the road which at his corner was a town-road of close houses but which soon was climbing and dropping past farms and meadows; at the crest of a hill, where he could see the curve of trees on the banks of the Merrimack, he turned and ran back.

The second part began with ignition and seat belt, driving forty minutes on the highway, no buildings or billboards, low icicled cliffs and long white hills, and fields and woods in the angled winter sun, and in the silent car he received his afternoon self: heard the music he had chosen, popular music he would not listen to at home but had come to accept and barely listen to at work, heard his voice in mime and jest and remark, often merry, sometimes showing off and knowing it, but not much, no more than he had earned. That part of his day behind glass and microphone, with its comfort drawn from combining the familiar with the spontaneous, took him to four o'clock.

The next four hours, he learned, were not only the time he had
to prepare for, but also the lair of his loneliness, the source of
every quick chill of loss, each sudden whisper of dread and futility.
For if he could spend them with a woman he loved, drink and
cook and eat with her while day changed to night (though now, in
winter, night came as he drove home), he and this woman huddled
in the light and warmth of living room and kitchen, gin and meat,
then his days until four and nights after eight would demand less
from him of will, give more to him of hopeful direction. After
dinner he listened to jazz and read fiction or watched an old movie
on television until, without lust or even the need of a sleeping
woman beside him, he went to bed: a blessing, but a disturbing
one. He had assumed, as a husband and then an adulterous one,
that his need for a woman was as carnal as it was spiritual. But now
celibacy was easy; when he imagined a woman, she was drinking
with him, eating dinner. So his most intense and perhaps his only
need for a woman was then; and all the reasons for the end of his
marriage became distant, blurred, and he wondered if the only
reason he was alone now was a misogyny he had never recognized:
that he did not even want a woman except at the day's end, and
had borne all the other hours of woman-presence only to have her
comfort as the clock's hands moved through their worst angles of
the day.

Planning to tell all this to David and Kathi, knowing he would
need gin to do it, he was frightened, already shy as if they sat with
him now in the living room. A good sign: if he were afraid, then it
took courage; if it took courage, then it must be right. He drank
more bourbon than he thought he did, and went to bed excited by
intimacy and love.

He slept off everything. In the morning he woke so amused at
himself that, if he had not been alone, he would have laughed
aloud. He imagined telling his children, over egg rolls and mar-
tinis and Shirley Temples, about his loneliness and his rituals to
combat it. And *that* would be his new fatherhood, smelling of duck
sauce and hot mustard and gin. Swallowing aspirins and orange
juice, he saw clearly why he and the children were uncomfortable
together, especially at Wednesday night dinners: when he lived
with them, their talk had usually dealt with the immediate (*I don't
like playing with Cindy any more; she's too bossy. I wish it would snow; it's
no use being cold if it doesn't snow*); they spoke at dinner and breakfast and, during holidays and summer, at lunch; in the car and

stores while running errands; on the summer lawn while he prepared charcoal; and in their beds when he went to tell them good-
night. Most of the time their talk was deep only because it was
affectionate and tribal, sounds made between creatures sharing
the same blood. Now their talk was the same, but it did not feel
the same. They talked in his car and in places he took them,
and the car and each place would not let them forget they were
there because of divorce.

So their talk had felt evasive, fragile, contrived, and his drunken
answer last night had been more talk: courageous, painful, honest.
My God, he thought, as in a light snow that morning he ran out of
his hangover, into lucidity. *I was going to have a goddamn therapy
session with my own children.* Breathing the smell of new snow and
winter air, he thought of this fool Peter Jackman, swallowing his
bite of pork-fried rice, and saying: And what do you feel at school?
About the divorce, I mean. Are you ashamed around the other
kids? He thought of the useless reopening and sometimes celebrating of wounds he and Norma had done with the marriage
counselor, a pleasant and smart woman; but what could she do
when all she had to work with was wounds? After each session he
and Norma had driven home, usually mute, always in despair.
Then, running faster, he imagined a house where he lived and the
children came on Friday nights and stayed all weekend, played
with their friends during the day, came and left the house as they
needed, for food, drink, bathroom, diversion, and at night they
relaxed together as a family; saw himself reading as they painted
and drew at the kitchen table . . .

That night they ate dinner at a seafood restaurant thirty minutes
from their town. When he drove them home he stayed outside
their house for a while, the three of them sitting in front for
warmth; they talked about summer and no school and no heavy
clothes and no getting up early when it was still dark outside. He
told them it was his favorite season too because of baseball and the
sea. Next morning, when he got into his car, the inside of his
windshield was iced. He used the small plastic scraper from his
glove compartment. As he scraped the middle and right side, he
realized the grey ice curling and falling from the glass was the
frozen breath of his children.

•

At a bar in the town where his children lived, he met a woman.
This was on a Saturday night, after he had taken them home from

the Museum of Fine Arts. They had liked Monet and Cézanne, had shown him light and color they thought were pretty. He told them Cézanne's *The Turn in the Road* was his favorite, that every time he came here he stood looking at it and he wanted to be walking up that road, toward the houses. But all afternoon he had known they were restless. They had not sledded that morning. Peter had gone out drinking the night before, with his only married friend who could leave his wife at home without paying even a subtle price; and he had slept through the time for sledding, had apologized when they phoned and woke him, and on the drive to the museum had told them he and Sibley (whom they knew as a friend of their mother too) had been having fun and had lost track of time until the bar closed. So perhaps they wanted to be outdoors. Or perhaps it was the old resonance of place again, the walls and ceiling of the museum, even the paintings telling them: *You are here because your father left home.*

He went to the bar for a sandwich, and stayed. Years ago he had come here often, on the way home from work, or at night with Norma. It was a neighborhood bar then, where professional fishermen and lobstermen drank, and other men who worked with their hands, and sometimes their wives. Then someone from Boston bought it, put photographs and drawings of fishing and pleasure boats on the walls, built a kitchen which turned out quiche and crepes, hired young women to tend the bar and musicians to play folk and bluegrass. The old customers left. The new ones were couples and people trying to be a couple for at least the night, and that is why Peter stayed after eating his sandwich.

Within an hour she came in and sat at the bar, one empty chair away from him: a woman in her late twenties, dark eyes and light brown hair. Soon they were talking. He liked her because she smiled a lot. He also liked her drink: Jack Daniel's on the rocks. Her name was Mary Ann; her last name kept eluding him. She was a market researcher, and, like many people Peter knew, she seemed to dismiss her work, though she was apparently good at it; her vocation was recreation: she skied down and across, backpacked, skated, camped, ran, and swam. He began to imagine doing things with her, and he felt more insidious than if he were imagining passion: he saw her leading him and Kathi and David up a mountain trail. He told her he spent much of his life prone or sitting, except for a daily five-mile run, a habit from the Marine

Corps (she gave him the sneer, and he said: Come on, that was a
long time ago, it was peacetime, it was fun), and he ran now for
the same reasons everyone else did, or at least everyone he knew
who ran: the catharsis, which kept his body feeling good, and his
mind more or less sane. He said he had not slept in a tent since
the Marines — probably because of the Marines. He said he
wished he did as many things as she did, and he told her why.
Some time in his bed during the night, she said: "They probably
did like the paintings. At least you're not taking them to all those
movies now."

"We still go out about once a week."

"Did you know Lennie's has free matinees for children? On
Sunday afternoons?"

"No."

"I have a divorced friend; she takes her kids almost every Sunday."

"Why don't we go tomorrow?"

"With your kids?"

"If you don't mind."

"Sure. I like kids. I'd like to have one of my own, without a
husband."

As he kissed her belly he imagined her helping him pitch the
large tent he would buy, the four of them on a weekend of cold
brook and trees on a mountainside, a fire, bacon in the skillet . . .

In the morning he scrambled their eggs, then phoned Norma.
He had a general dislike of telephones: talking to his own hand
gripping plastic, pacing, looking about the room; the timing of
hanging up was tricky. Nearly all these conversations left him feeling as disconnected as the phone itself. But talking with Norma
was different: he marveled at how easy it was. The distance and
disembodiment he felt on the phone with others were good here.
He and Norma had hurt each other deeply, and their bodies had
absorbed the pain: it was the stomach that tightened, the hands
that shook, the breast that swelled, then shriveled. Now, fleshless,
they could talk by phone, even with warmth, perhaps alive from
the time when their bodies were at ease together. He thought of
having a huge house where he could live with his family, seeing
Norma only at meals, shared for the children, he and Norma talking to David and Kathi; their own talk would be on extension
phones in their separate wings: they would discuss the children

and details of running the house. This was of course the way they
had finally lived, without the separate wings, the phones. And one
of their justifications as they talked of divorce was that the children
would be harmed, growing up in a house with parents who did not
love each other, who rarely touched, and then by accident. There
had been moments near the end when, brushing against each
other in the kitchen, one of them would say: Sorry. Now, as Mary
Ann Brighi (he had waked knowing her last name) spread jam on
toast, he phoned.

"I met this woman last night."

Mary Ann smiled; Norma's voice did.

"It's about time. I was worried about your arm going."

"What about you?"

"I'm doing all right."

"Do you bring them home?"

"It's not them, and I get a sitter."

"But he comes to the house? To take you out?"

"Peter?"

"What?"

"What are we talking about?"

"I was wondering what the kids would think if Mary Ann came
along this afternoon."

"What they'll think is Mary Ann's coming along this afternoon."

"You're sure that's all?"

"Unless you fuck in front of them."

He turned his face from Mary Ann, but she had already seen his
blush; he looked at her smiling with toast crumbs on her teeth. He
wished he were married and lovemaking were simple. But after
cleaning the kitchen he felt passion again, though not much; in his
mind he was introducing the children to Mary Ann. He would
make sure he talked to them, did not leave them out while he
talked to her. He was making love while he thought this; he hoped
they would like her; again he saw them hiking up a trail through
pines, stopping for Kathi and David to rest; a sudden bounding
deer; the camp beside the stream; he thanked his member for
doing its work down there while the rest of him was in the mountains in New Hampshire.

●

As he walked with David and Kathi he held their hands; they were
looking at her face watching them from the car window.

"She's a new friend of mine," he said. "Just a friend. She wants to show us this nightclub where children can go on Sunday afternoons."

From the back seat they shook hands, peered at her, glanced at Peter, their eyes making him feel that like adults they could sense when people were lovers; he adjusted the rearview mirror, watched their faces, decided he was seeing jumbled and vulnerable curiosity: Who was she? Would she marry their father? Would they like her? Would their mother be sad? And the nightclub confused them.

"Isn't that where people go drink?" Kathi said.

"It's afternoon too," David said.

Not for Peter; the sky was grey, the time was grey, dark was coming, and all at once he felt utterly without will: all the strength he had drawn on to be with his children left him like one long spurt of arterial blood: all this time with his children was grey, with night coming; it would always be; nothing would change: like three people cursed in an old myth, they would forever be thirty-three and eight and six, in this car on slick or salted roads, going from one place to another. He disapproved of but understood those divorced fathers who fled to live in a different pain far away. Beneath his despair he saw himself and his children sledding under a lovely blue sky, heard them laughing in movies, watching in awe like love a circling blue shark in the aquarium's tank; but these images seemed beyond recapture.

He entered the highway going south, and that quick transition of hands and head and eyes as he moved into fast traffic snapped him out of himself, into the sound of Mary Ann's voice: with none of the rising and falling rhythm of nursery talk, she was telling them, as if speaking to a young man and woman she had just met, about Lennie's. How Lennie believed children should hear good music, not just the stuff on the radio. She talked about jazz. She hummed some phrases of "Somewhere over the Rainbow," then improvised. They would hear Gerry Mulligan today, she said, and as she talked about the different saxophones, Peter looked in the mirror at their listening faces.

"And Lennie has a cook from Tijuana in Mexico," Mary Ann said. "She makes the best chili around."

Walking into Lennie's with a pretty woman and his two healthy and pretty children, he did not feel like a divorced father looking for something to do; always in other places he was certain he looked that way, and often he felt guilty when talking with waitresses. He paid the cover charge for himself and Mary Ann, and she said: "All right, but I buy the first two rounds," and he led her and the children to a table near the bandstand. He placed the children between him and Mary Ann. Bourbon, Cokes, bowls of chili. The room was filling and Peter saw that at most tables there were children with parents, usually one parent, usually a father. He watched his children listening to Mulligan. His fingers tapped the table with the drummer. He looked warmly at Mary Ann's profile until she turned and smiled at him.

Often Mulligan talked to the children; explained how his saxophone worked; his voice was cheerful, joking, never serious, as he talked about the guitar and bass and piano and drums. He clowned laughter from the children in the dark. Kathi and David turned to each other and Peter to share their laughter. During the music they listened intently. Their hands tapped the table. They grinned at Peter and Mary Ann. At intermission Mulligan said he wanted to meet the children. While his group went to the dressing room, he sat on the edge of the bandstand and waved the children forward. Kathi and David talked about going. Each would go if the other would. They took napkins for autographs and, holding hands, walked between tables and joined the children standing around Mulligan. When it was their turn he talked to them, signed their napkins, kissed their foreheads. They hurried back to Peter.

"He's *neat,*" Kathi said.

"What did you talk about?"

"He asked our names," David said.

"And if we liked winter out here."

"And if we played an instrument."

"What kind of music we liked."

"What did you tell him?"

"Jazz like his."

The second set ended at nearly seven; bourbon-high, Peter drove carefully, listening to Mary Ann and the children talking about Mulligan and his music and warmth. Then David and Kathi were gone, running up the sidewalk to tell Norma and show their autographed napkins, and Peter followed Mary Ann's directions to her apartment.

"I've been in the same clothes since last night," she said.

In her apartment, as unkempt as his, they showered together, hurried damp-haired and chilled to her bed.

"This is the happiest day I've had since the marriage ended," he said.

But when he went home and was alone in his bed, he saw his cowardice again. All the warmth of his day left him, and he lay in the dark, knowing that he should have been wily enough to understand that the afternoon's sweetness and ease meant he had escaped: had put together a family for the day. That afternoon Kathi had spilled a Coke; before Peter noticed, Mary Ann was cleaning the table with cocktail napkins, smiling at Kathi, talking to her under the music, lifting a hand to the waitress.

Next night he took Mary Ann to dinner, and as they drove to her apartment, it seemed to him that since the end of his marriage dinner had become disproportionate: alone at home it was a task he forced himself to do, with his children it was a fragile rite, and with old friends who alternately fed him and Norma he felt vaguely criminal. Now he must once again face his failures over a plate of food. He and Mary Ann had slept little the past two nights, and at the restaurant she told him she had worked hard all day, yet she looked fresh and strong, while he was too tired to imagine making love after dinner. With his second martini he said: "I used you yesterday. With my kids."

"There's a better word."

"All right: needed."

"I knew that."

"You did?"

"We had fun."

"I can't do it any more."

"Don't be so hard on yourself. You probably spend more time with them now than when you lived together."

"I do. So does Norma. But that's not it. It's how much I wanted your help, and started hoping for it. Next Sunday. And in summer: the sort of stuff you do, camping and hiking; when we talked about it Saturday night — "

"I knew that too. I thought it was sweet."

He leaned back in his chair, sipped his drink. Tonight he would break his martini rule, have a third before dinner. He loved women who knew and forgave his motives before he knew and confessed them.

But he would not take her with the children again. He was with her often; she wanted a lover, she said, not love, not what it still did to men and women. He did not tell her he thought they were using each other in a way that might have been cynical if it were not so frightening. He simply followed her, became one of those who make love with their friends. But she was his only woman friend, and he did not know how many men shared her. When she told him she would not be home this night or that weekend, he held his questions. He held onto his heart too, and forced himself to make her a part of the times when he was alone. He had married young, and life to him was surrounded by the sounds and touches of a family. Now in this foreign land he felt so vulnerably strange that at times it seemed near-madness as he gave Mary Ann a function in his time, ranking somewhere between his running and his work.

When the children asked about her, he said they were still friends. Once Kathi asked why she never came to Lennie's any more, and he said her work kept her pretty busy and she had other friends she did things with, and he liked being alone with them anyway. But then he was afraid the children thought she had not liked them; so twice a month he brought Mary Ann to Lennie's.

He and the children went every Sunday. And that was how the cold months passed, beginning with the New Year, because Peter and Norma had waited until after Christmas to end the marriage: the movies and sledding, museums and aquarium, the restaurants; always they were on the road, and whenever he looked at his car he thought of the children. How many conversations while looking through the windshield? How many times had the doors slammed shut and they reentered or left his life? Winter ended slowly. April was cold, and in May Peter and the children still wore sweaters or windbreakers, and on two weekends there was rain, and everything they did together was indoors. But when the month ended, Peter thought it was not the weather but the patterns of winter that had kept them driving from place to place.

•

Then it was June and they were out of school and Peter took his vacation. Norma worked, and by nine in the morning he and Kathi and David were driving to the sea. They took a large blanket and tucked its corners into the sand so it wouldn't flap in the wind, and they lay oiled in the sun. On the first day they talked of winter, how they could feel the sun warming their ribs, as they had watched it warming the earth during the long thaw. It was a beach with gentle currents and a gradual slope out to sea, but Peter told them, as he had every summer, about undertow: that if ever they were caught in one, they must not swim against it; they must let it take them out, and then they must swim parallel to the beach 'until the current shifted and they could swim back in with it. He could not imagine his children being calm enough to do that, for he was afraid of water and only enjoyed body-surfing near the beach, but he told them anyway. Then he said it would not happen because he would always test the current first.

In those first two weeks the three of them ran into the water and body-surfed only a few minutes, for it was too cold still, and they had to leave it until their flesh was warm again. They would not be able to stay in long until July. Peter showed them the different colors of summer, told them why on humid days the sky and ocean were paler blue, and on dry days they were darker, more beautiful, and the trees they passed on the roads to the beach were brighter green. He bought a whiffle ball and bat and kept them in the trunk of his car, and they played at the beach. The children dug holes, made castles; Peter watched, slept, and in late morning he ran. From a large thermos they drank lemonade or juice; and they ate lunch all day, the children grazing on fruit and the sandwiches he had made before his breakfast. Then he took them to his apartment for showers, and they helped carry in the ice-chest and thermos and blanket and their knapsack of clothes. Kathi and David still took turns showering first, and they stayed in longer, but now in summer the water was still hot when his turn came. Then he drove them home to Norma, his skin red and pleasantly burning, then tan.

When his vacation ended they spent all sunny weekends at the sea, and even grey days that were warm. The children became braver about the cold, and forced him to go in with them and body-surf. But they could stay longer than he could, and he left to lie on the blanket and watch them, to make sure they stayed in shallow water. He made them promise to wait on the beach while he ran. He went in the water to cool his body from the sun, but mostly he lay on the blanket, reading, and watching the children wading out to the breakers and riding them in. Kathi and David did not always stay together. One left to walk the beach alone. The other played with strangers, or children who were there most days too. One built a castle. The other body-surfed. And often one would come to the blanket and drink and take a sandwich from the ice-chest, would sit eating and drinking beside Peter, offer him a bite, a swallow. And on all those beach days Peter's shyness and apprehension were gone. It's the sea, he said to Mary Ann one night.

And it was: for on that day, a long Saturday at the beach, when he had all day felt peace and father-love and sun and saltwater, he had understood why now in summer he and his children were as he had yearned for them to be in winter: they were no longer confined to car or buildings to remind them why they were there. The long beach and the sea were their lawn, the blanket their home, the ice-chest and thermos their kitchen. They lived as a family again. While he ran and David dug in the sand until he reached water and Kathi looked for pretty shells for her room, the blanket waited for them. It was the place they wandered back to: for food, for drink, for rest, their talk as casual as between children and father arriving, through separate doors, at the kitchen sink for water, the refrigerator for an orange. Then one left for the surf; another slept in the sun, lips stained with grape juice. He had wanted to tell the children about it, but it was too much to tell, and the beach was no place for such talk anyway, and he also guessed they knew. So that afternoon when they were all lying on the blanket, on their backs, the children flanking him, he simply said: "Divorced kids go to the beach more than married ones."

"Why?" Kathi said.

"Because married people do chores and errands on weekends. No kid-days."

"I love the beach," David said.

"So do I," Peter said.

He looked at Kathi.

"You don't like it, huh?"

She took her arm from her eyes and looked at him. His urge was to turn away. She looked at him for a long time; her eyes were too tender, too wise, and he wished she could have learned tenderness and wisdom later, and differently; in her eyes he saw the car in winter, heard its doors closing and closing, their talk and the sounds of heater and engine and tires on the road, and the places the car took them. Then she held his hand, and closed her eyes.

"I wish it was summer all year round," she said.

He watched her face, rosy tan now, lightly freckled; her small scar was already lower. Holding her hand, he reached over for David's, and closed his eyes against the sun. His legs touched theirs. After a while he heard them sleeping. Then he slept.

MAVIS GALLANT

The Assembly

(FROM HARPER'S)

M. ALEXANDRE CAISSE, civil servant, employed at the Ministry of Agriculture, bachelor, thanked the seven persons sitting in his living room for having responded to his mimeographed invitation. Actually, he had set chairs out for fifteen.

General Portoret, ret., widower, said half the tenants of the building had already left for their summer holiday.

Mme. Berthe Fourneau, widow, no profession, said Parisians spent more time on vacation than at work. She could remember when two weeks in Brittany seemed quite enough.

M. Louis Labarrière, author and historian, wife taking the cure at Vichy, said that during the Middle Ages Paris had celebrated 230 religious holidays a year.

M. Alberto Minazzoli, industrialist, wife thought to be living in Rome with an actor, said that in his factories strikes had replaced religious feasts. (All smiled.)

Dr. Edmond Volle, dental surgeon, married, said he had not taken a day off in seven years.

Mme. Volle said she believed a wife should never forsake her husband. As a result, she never had a holiday either.

Mlle. de Renard's aunt said it depended on the husband. Some could be left alone for months on end. Others could not. (No one knew Mlle. de Renard's aunt's name.)

M. Alexandre Caisse said they had all been sorry to hear Mlle. de Renard was not feeling well enough to join them.

Mlle. de Renard's aunt said her niece was at this moment under sedation, in a shuttered room, with cotton stuffed in her ears. The slightest sound made her jump and scream with fright.

General Portoret said he was sure a brave woman like Mlle. de Renard would soon be on her feet again.

Mme. Berthe Fourneau said it was probably not easy to forget after one had been intimately molested by a stranger.

Mlle. de Renard's aunt said her niece had been molested, but not raped. There was an unpleasant story going around.

M. Labarrière had heard screaming, but had supposed it was someone's radio.

M. Minazzoli had heard the man running down five flights of stairs. He thought it was a child playing tag.

Mme. Volle had been the first to arrive on the scene; she had found Mlle. de Renard, collapsed, on the fifth-floor landing, her purse lying beside her. The man had not been after money. The stranger, described by his victim as French, fair, and blue-eyed, had obviously crept in from the street and waited for Mlle. de Renard to come home from vesper service.

General Portoret wondered why Mlle. de Renard had not run away the minute she saw him.

Mlle. de Renard's aunt said her niece had been taken by surprise. The man looked respectable. His expression was sympathetic. She thought he had come to the wrong floor.

Mme. Berthe Fourneau said the man must have known his victim's habits.

Dr. Volle said it was simply the cunning of the insane.

M. Labarrière reminded them that the assault of Mlle. de Renard had been the third in a series: there had been the pots of ivy pilfered from the courtyard, the tramp found asleep in the basement behind the hot-water boiler, and now this.

Mme. Berthe Fourneau said no one was safe.

Mme. Volle had a chain-bolt on her door. She kept a can of insect spray conveniently placed for counteraggression.

M. Alexandre Caisse had a bronze reproduction of *The Dying Gaul* on a table behind the door. He never answered the door without first getting a good grip around the statue's waist.

Mlle. de Renard's aunt said her niece had been too trusting, even as a child.

M. Minazzoli said his door was fully armored. However, the time had come to do something about the door at the entrance to the building. He hoped they would decide, now, once and for all, about putting in an electronic code-lock system.

M. Alexandre Caisse said they were here to discuss, not to decide. The law of July 10, 1965, regulating the administration of cooperatively owned multiple dwellings, was especially strict on the subject of meetings. This was an assembly.

M. Minazzoli said one could arrive at a decision at an assembly as well as at a meeting.

M. Alexandre Caisse said anyone could get the full text of the law from the building manager, now enjoying a photo safari in Kenya. (Having said this, M. Caisse closed his eyes.)

Mlle. de Renard's aunt said she wanted one matter cleared up, and only one: her niece had been molested. She had not been raped.

Mme. Berthe Fourneau wondered how much Mlle. de Renard could actually recall.

Mlle. de Renard's aunt said her niece had given a coherent account from the beginning, an account from which she had never wavered. The man had thrown her against the wall and perpetrated something she called "an embrace." Her handbag had fallen during the struggle. He had run away without stopping to pick it up.

Dr. Volle said it proved the building was open to madmen.

•

M. Alexandre Caisse asked if anyone would like refreshments. He could offer the ladies a choice of tonic water or bottled lemon soda. The gentlemen might like something stronger. (All thanked him, but refused.)

M. Minazzoli supposed everyone knew how the electronic code system worked and what it would cost.

Mme. Berthe Fourneau asked if it would keep peddlers out. The place was infested with them. Some offered exotic soaps, others ivory trinkets. The peddlers had one thing in common — curly black hair.

M. Labarrière said the tide of color was rising in Paris. He wondered if anyone had noticed it in the Métro. Even in the first-class section you could count the white faces on one hand.

Mme. Volle said it showed the kind of money being made, and by whom.

Black, brown, and yellow, said M. Labarrière. He felt like a stranger in his own country.

Dr. Volle said France was now a doormat for the riffraff of five continents.

M. Alexandre Caisse said the first thing foreigners did was find out how much they could get for free. Then they sent for their families.

General Portoret had been told by a nurse that the hospitals were crammed with Africans and Arabs getting free operations. If you had the bad luck to be white and French you could sit in the waiting room while your appendix burst.

M. Minazzoli said he had flown his mother to Paris for a serious operation. He had paid every centime himself. His mother had needed to have all her adrenalin taken out.

Mme. Volle said when something like that happened there was no such thing as French or foreign — there was just grief and expense.

M. Alexandre Caisse said it was unlikely that a relative of M. Minazzoli would burden the taxpaying community. M. Minazzoli probably knew something about paying taxes, when it came to that. (All laughed gently.)

Mlle. de Renard's aunt said all foreigners were not alike.

General Portoret had commanded a regiment of Montagnards forty years before. They had been spunky little chaps, loyal to France.

M. Labarrière could not understand why Mlle. de Renard had said her attacker was blue-eyed and fair. Most molested women spoke of "the Mediterranean type."

General Portoret wondered if his Montagnards had kept up their French culture. They had enjoyed the marching songs, swinging along happily to "Sambre et Meuse."

M. Minazzoli said in case anyone did not understand the code-lock system, it was something like a small oblong keyboard. This keyboard, affixed to the entrance of the building just below the buzzer one pressed in order to release the door catch, contained the house code.

Mme. Berthe Fourneau asked how the postman was supposed to get in.

M. Labarrière knew it was old-fashioned of him, but he thought a house phone would be better. It was somehow more dignified than all these codes and keyboards.

M. Minazzoli said the code system was cheaper and very safe.

The door could not be opened unless the caller knew what the code was, say, J-8264.

Mme. Berthe Fourneau hoped for something easier to remember — something like A-1111.

M. Labarrière said the Montagnards had undoubtedly lost all trace of French culture. French culture was dying everywhere. By 2500 it would be extinct.

M. Minazzoli said the Lycée Chateaubriand was still flourishing in Rome, attended by sons and daughters of the nobility.

Mme. Volle had been told that the Lycée Français in London accepted just anyone now.

Mme. Berthe Fourneau's daughter had spent an anxious au pair season with an English family in the 1950s. They had the curious habit of taking showers together to save hot water.

M. Alexandre Caisse said the hot-water meters in the building needed to be checked. His share of costs last year had been enough to cover all the laundry in Paris.

Mme. Berthe Fourneau said a washing machine just above her living room made a rocking sound.

Mme. Volle never ran the machine before nine or after five.

Mme. Berthe Fourneau had been prevented at nine o'clock at night from hearing the President of the Republic's television interview about the domestic fuel shortage.

M. Minazzoli said he hoped all understood that the security code was not to be mislaid or left around or shared except with a trusted person. No one knew nowadays who might turn out to be a thief. Not one's friends, certainly, but one knew so little about their children.

Mlle. de Renard's aunt wondered if anyone recalled the old days, when the concierge stayed in her quarters night and day like a watchdog. It had been better than a code.

M. Labarrière could remember how when one came in late at night one would call out one's name.

General Portoret, as a young man — a young lieutenant, actually — had given his name as "Jack the Ripper." The concierge had made a droll reply.

M. Alexandre Caisse believed people laughed more easily then.

General Portoret said that the next day the concierge had complained to his mother.

Dr. Volle envied General Portoret's generation. Their pleasures had been of a simple nature. They had not required today's thrills and animation.

M. Labarrière knew he was being old-fashioned, but he did object to the modern inaccurate use of *animation*. Publications from the mayor's office spoke of "animating" the city.

M. Minazzoli could not help asking himself who was paying for these glossy full-color handouts.

Dr. Volle thought the mayor was doing a good job. He particularly enjoyed the fireworks. As he never took a holiday the fireworks were about all he had by way of entertainment.

M. Labarrière could recall when the statue of the lion in the middle of Place Denfert-Rochereau had been painted the wrong shade. Everyone had protested.

Mlle. de Renard's aunt had seen it — brilliant iridescent coppery paint.

M. Labarrière said no, a dull brown.

Dr. Volle said that had been under a different administration.

General Portoret's mother had cried when she was told that he had said "Jack the Ripper."

Mlle. de Renard's aunt did not understand why the cost of the electronic code system was to be shared out equally. Large families were more likely to wear out the buttons than a lady living alone.

•

M. Alexandre Caisse said this was an assembly, not a meeting. They were all waiting for the building manager to return from Kenya. The first thing M. Caisse intended to have taken up was the cost of hot water.

Mlle. de Renard's aunt reminded M. Caisse that it was her grandfather, founder of a large Right Bank department store, who had built this house in 1899.

M. Labarrière said there had been a seventeenth-century convent on the site. Tearing it down in 1899 had been an act of vandalism that would not be tolerated today.

General Portoret's parents had been among the first tenants. When he was a boy there had been a great flood of water in the basement. When the waters abated the graves of nuns were revealed.

Mlle. de Renard's aunt said she often wished she were a nun. Peace was all she wanted. (She looked around threateningly as she said this.)

General Portoret said the bones had been put in large canvas bags and stored in the concierge's kitchen until a hallowed resting place could be found.

M. Labarrière said it was hard not to yearn for the past they were describing. That was because he had no feeling for the future. The final French catastrophe would be about 2080.

General Portoret said he hoped that the last Frenchman to die would not die in vain.

M. Alexandre Caisse looked at his watch and said he imagined no one wanted to miss the film on the Third Channel, an early Fernandel.

General Portoret asked if it was the one where Fernandel was a private who kept doing all the wrong things.

Mme. Volle wondered if her husband's patients would let him get away for a few days this year. There was always someone to break a front tooth at the last moment.

General Portoret was going to Montreux. He had been going to the same pension for twelve years, ever since his wife died.

M. Alexandre Caisse said the film would be starting in six minutes. It was not the one about the army; it was the one where Fernandel played a ladies' hairdresser.

Mlle. de Renard's aunt planned to take her niece on a cruise to Egypt when she felt strong enough.

Mme. Berthe Fourneau and her daughter were traveling to Poland in the footsteps of the Pope.

M. Labarrière knew it was dull and old-fashioned of him, but he loved his country and refused to spend any money outside France.

M. Minazzoli was taking a close friend to Greece and Yugoslavia. He believed in Europe.

M. Alexandre Caisse said sometimes it was hard to get a clear image on the Third Channel. He hoped there would be no interference with the Fernandel, which must be just about starting.

Dr. Volle said he was not likely to see that or any other film. He went to bed every night before ten. He rose every morning before six.

M. Alexandre Caisse said he thought they would all be quite safe if they left, now, together, in a group. (He held the door open.)

Mlle. de Renard's aunt said she thought the assembly had been useful. Her niece would feel reassured.

Mme. Berthe Fourneau said perhaps she would no longer feel impelled to open and close her bedroom shutters the whole time.

Mlle. de Renard's aunt said her niece slept all day.

Mme. Berthe Fourneau said yes, but not all night.

General Portoret said, After you.

M. Labarrière said, Ladies first.

(All said goodbye.)

ELIZABETH HARDWICK

The Bookseller

(FROM THE NEW YORKER)

SATURDAY, NOVEMBER. Winter, thank heaven. Everyone is wearing something new in the fall line. Skirts are shorter and heels are, thereby, lower. Quite old ladies are in schoolgirl sweaters and men far from young are on silent roller skates — curving backward, slowly spinning around to make a deft, brilliant, soundless stop on the sidewalk.

November. People have stopped going to their country places for the weekend, because, it is said, there is too much going on in the city. How true that is. At the opera, machines float swans across the back of the stage and hurl swords through the air; ballet fans are gossiping on the mezzanine; the hardy are standing in fur or in fat jackets of spring-garden pinks and purples in the long lines outside the movie houses. The city people are as strong as athletes and in elevated spiritual condition, too. Happy hours inside the darkened halls, with so many performing up front in a flood of light. Creamy faces on the screen; thin chiffons and heavy velvets on the stage. He leaping, leaping, and she folding her arms in dejection, like the wings of a bird; another reaching so high, up, up, singing of her lover's treachery to the cause of her father. Saturday night, sold out.

The cafés are steaming, and from the restaurant doors garlic floats toward the hoods of cars waiting for the light. The newspaper kiosks have tomorrow's papers stacked outside and, as always, Roger's secondhand bookstore on Columbus Avenue is open for business. The store is called The Pleiade, but Roger likes to refer to it as the "play aid." He says he has learned to watch out for strangers who can pronounce the name properly, because they know what they are doing and are sure to steal him blind. This caution' is not, in fact, Roger's way at all. He approaches theft — the thin volumes hiding in overcoats and the large volumes in shopping bags — with a short cry of pain and a long journey into his imagination, where he finds some poor truant, beaten down by self-awareness like the man in *Notes from Underground,* poring with fevered eyes over his treasure.

It is almost eleven when we stop at the shop. Roger says: The overflow from *The Marriage of Maria Braun* is terrific.

Roger is a large man, with sand-colored skin and hair of a curious tan shade, and he is dressed in a sand-colored corduroy jacket with leather patches on the elbows. The elbow patches and the pipe he sometimes smokes do not give him the air of a professor or of a sportsman. He is too seedy and rumpled and sand-strewn for that. He is just the benign, beaming, outsized owner of The Pleiade, and he and his shop are rooted like cabbages in the mixed sod of Columbus Avenue.

Yes, a lot is going on, but Roger never goes to the opera, never goes to the ballet, seldom goes to the movies. He is stuck in his shop, like a flagpole on the village green. He is a man with a single overwhelming passion out of which his being flows. The modernist classics are his passion. Reverence, the tensions of love, the restlessness of pursuit inflect his utterance of the sacred names. Photographs of Frenchmen, Russians, Americans, Italians, martyrs of inspiration, are in frames on the walls of The Pleiade, and their mostly somber images, caught in the youth of radical invention, are lit like icons by the candle of Roger's beaming eyes. He is haunted by memories. Where, oh where, is his lost copy of *A Barbarian in Asia* with the luck of Michaux's signature circled by cryptic drawings?

Roger and his books. His old friends are aware that he does not *quite* read them and that there is no word accurate for his curious taking in. He flips through the volumes delicately, carefully, and in some agitation of mind and spirit. His classics, with their almost constitutional authority, live under a kind of glass in his admiration. New books, not quite yesterday's or even of the last few years, he receives kindly and with generous hope, and he is quick to sort out those that have about them certain whisperings of futurity, of longevity. But it is not true that Roger has no knowledge of his books. The truth is that he knows them in an intimate, peculiar fashion. He knows well each flavor, each *spécialité*, each domain, and the very quality of the aspiration. In his cheerful heart all the ironies, overturnings, dissonances of modern art ring out their sad notes and fill him with happiness.

If one were to say: Roger, do you admire Bruno Schulz?, he would answer: Oh, yes, oh, yes. And then, reflecting, he might add: But I like *Crocodile Street* better than *Sanatorium*. He has made a judgment, reached into the bibliophile quarry that is his head, and brought to life the elusive pages with their type, their chapter headings, their beginnings and endings, their place-names that sparkle with fresh consonants and vowels. And he knows what there is to know of lives — the terrible struggles of authorship that have undone so many.

At The Pleiade, a thin young woman, with hair cold and shiny like a wet cap, set over large, steady eyes, is drinking coffee at a long table at the back. Lois, Roger says.

Up front, there stands on tiptoe a not unusual bookshop scarecrow in black trousers, frayed jacket, and painful shoes long worn by feet much larger than the feet currently trying to find a grounding in them. This pitiful person is holding a book some distance from his eyes. Crazy, Roger says.

A very large dog, like a huge ball of dust, sleeps in the middle of the shop and must be circled by the customers. So it is, with small variations, seven nights a week at The Pleiade. Now a young couple, whispering, examine the titles on the shelves. Roger's eagerness follows their glances. He is in search of essence, the young couple's essence, to be revealed to him as a hand pulls a volume forward and then slowly pushes it back into place. Roger sees the light of recognition and the blankness of ignorance.

Pound's *ABC*, the young man whispers to the girl. Twenty-five dollars. The expensive jewel lies in the young man's palm for a moment and then is returned to its alphabetical resting place.

Roger watches the unrolling, as it seems to him, of their biography. He is deeply interested, although the couple do not reveal any eccentricity and their passage through poetry, criticism, art, and fiction is unremarkable. But there is a longing, perhaps, a tenderness and wonder, before first American edition and original English edition, before the contemplation of the out-of-print, the signed, and the limited.

At last, the girl buys a paperback for two dollars and fifty cents.

Kafka's Diaries, Volume I. Roger's smile seems to fade a bit, although not in dishonor to Kafka, for whom he feels a love almost criminal. The fading seems to be a disappointment that the young couple had been thus far deprived of the volume.

They go out in their matching ski jackets, jog down the avenue with their blond hair flying behind. Roger collects his decisions about them. Poets, he says. I think they live downtown, but not in the East Village. Something like West Tenth Street. Respectable types, Amherst and Wellesley. Those two are spacing lines on a page.

•

Roger. I can see again his large head bowed, as if in grief, in the Milton seminar at Columbia some years ago. He brought to graduate studies his pen and his notebook and the steady downward tug of his dilatory, procrastinating nature. It was the modernist T. S. Eliot and his resurrection of the metaphysical poets that had led Roger disastrously to the seventeenth century. By the perverse authority of institutions he was brutally dragged by his light curls into the study of Milton, a poet not even very high in the regard of Eliot at the time. Roger endured for a few months. He wrote in the margins of *The Student's Milton:* "Cf. Virgil," after one line; and "See Pliny the Elder," after another; and at the top of a page "Pythagoras was the only one who had heard the spheres' music."

But his head was too big and his eyes were too small for the peering at lines, and he shuffled about in the text like a melancholy sheep in a pen. At last, he gave up and went cheerfully loping off into the meadow of upper Broadway, and came to a stop some years later as the proprietor of The Pleiade. And yet, even now, Roger can sometimes be heard in the doorway of his shop, greeting a friend with "Hail, holy light!" — the only phrase from *Paradise Lost* sequestered in his memory.

Roger knows well a number of regular visitors to The Pleiade and he has friends, themselves a miscellaneous collection, from his Columbia undergraduate days. He knows a French-literature scholar, a Socialist, a Catholic poet, and a lawyer who plays the violin and reads Kleist and Novalis in German.

•

The night is ending and Lois is nodding at the table. Before Lois, Maureen was for some months sitting at the table, sitting there

silent and beautiful and abstracted — very, very much in the Lois
manner.

Where is Maureen?

Gone for a spell to the topless towers, Roger says. Is there regret
in his tone? No, not exactly. It is Roger's way to meet fate with the
sweetest accommodation of the trivial or the violent alteration.
Profound passivity, a little wonder, and a flash of puzzlement here
and there, and the flux of his domestic arrangements serenely
made its way to sea. For this, the troubled people who floated
down on him, as if he were a pier for a sudden anchorage, were
perhaps grateful.

The topless towers was his designation of Maureen's home town,
Troy, New York. And it was there she would go when the peaceful
vacancy of her nature took a little turn to the left or right and she
had to be got back on the road again.

Lois is a friend of Maureen's, Roger explains. She's looking for
work.

Lois nods, and her meditative gaze is so untroubled that it has
the effect of a signal of trouble itself.

From time to time, the iron gates over the front of The Pleiade
remained closed past noon, and some of Roger's commercial
neighbors were taken by curiosity. The cook from the Chinese
restaurant often walked out in his apron and peered through the
gated windows into the impatient jaws of the dog. The fat palmist,
awaiting the evacuation sure to arrive when the landlord, stuck
with the derelict for so many years, could decide to what brilliant,
prosperous use the palmist's street-front broom closet might be
put, glared with deep intention at the locked gates, as if she had at
last accomplished a predicted malediction. There was no cordiality
between Roger and the palmist, because he detested the occult and
the pornographic and, to him, the palmist united the two in her
black coils of hair and in the beseeching, whimpering noises directed at passersby.

But soon there would come Roger in a taxi, and out of the taxi
came shopping bags filled with more books bought from a bank-
rupt hole-in-the-wall competitor. The gates rolled back, the cut-
rate bin was trundled to the pavement, and the luckless, sneering
palmist saw The Pleiade's Mostly Mozart poster return to life. The
slim volumes again dozed in the afternoon light. The large volumes of the *High Renaissance* and *The History of Egyptian Art* listened
once more to the gassy braking of the No. 11 bus. All was well,

except that Roger was undergoing a brief sinking spell because of the new burden of his infatuated buying.

•

Roger does not drink, but he eats quite a lot of apples, pizzas, and hamburgers, and makes many cups of coffee in his electric pot. He lives in the large, decaying building over the shop. He is one of those brought up by well-to-do parents, sent to good schools, to France for a summer — who, on their own, show no more memory of physical comforts than a prairie dog.

Once, in the bookstore, the lawyer friend spoke about a visit to the apartment to look at a violin Roger had bought. Lethal squalor, he kept repeating, lethal squalor. Yet he found in this jumbled, tumbled theatre of belligerent disorder a fine violin, old paintings of curious interest, fine brasses black with tarnish, rare books, carved wood: twenty-five years of desultory buying in junk shops, elephantine carting, and, at last, forgetful dumping. The lawyer observed that Roger would never starve but he might die from stepping on a rusty nail.

Roger has his dog, with its concentrated sleepy look, and his Maureens and Loises with their unconcentrated, dream-heavy eyes. He has his shop, where he spends his waking hours, and when that is over he goes upstairs to rest, like a peasant returning to his hut at sundown. Perhaps he sleeps on a pallet, wrapped in his winter sheepskin in the unthinkable darkness in which one imagines his bright, daylight smile there someplace in the clutter, beaming away like a night lamp. No matter — the patrician in him is not entirely erased and lingers on in an amiable displacement, remaining in his contentment to keep pace with just where he is, to raise prices as the rent rises, to keep out the street winds, to fill the shopping bags with new loot, and to feel a certain discomfort and confusion when he makes a sale. His father left a good deal of money, but Roger does no resentful bookkeeping. Instead, he shows a flare of pride that his mother is in her ninety-sixth year, consuming the real estate, the insurance, the stocks like an admirable, slowly grazing animal.

•

The wind from the river comes up suddenly to disperse the Saturday-night rubbish. Into the air go newspapers, candy wrappers, loose tobacco, and the sluggish waters at the curb stir under the tidal moon. The bookstore empties and Roger sighs in the mixed feelings of the end of another day of his long, long celebration. He

directs Lois to go across the street to the all-night Puerto Rican
grocery store to buy cornflakes. She looks uncertain of this journey
but takes the five-dollar bill, scurries away among the cars, looking
like a small, blackened crossing sweeper of a century ago.

Majored in fine arts, Roger says. And then, looking up into the
sky in which lights from so many rooms flicker like yellow stars,
Roger drifts for a moment into a mesmerized, speculative mode.
In the rooms, he says, he imagines miserable calculations in every
head nodding off to sleep, figures added and subtracted, dreams
of selling the very space that held the bed upon which the sleeper's
head restlessly lay in its blur of arithmetic. On the street, he has
noticed that people keep turning around suddenly, as if future
income taxes were brushing by, grazing coats like a pickpocket.

Lois returns, the gates clang before the darkened window, and
as they start up the stairs of the tenement Roger ends his historical
reverie. Those that are not inside counting up, he says, are outside
making marks in indelible ink on every clean wall. Good night,
good night.

•

Some days after, there is Roger at noon explaining things to the
Hungarian woman who has for twenty-two years managed alone
her dry-cleaning establishment and is now to be evicted in an imaginative glassy renovation which will add its signature to the old
avenue's petition of hope. Roger is saying: Landless peasants, that
is what we are. Till the soil for centuries and then the messenger
comes from St. Petersburg to say the master wants his hectares for
an iron foundry.

The dry-cleaning woman says: Mr. Spiegel does not live in St.
Petersburg but in Bay Ridge.

•

Roger, gregarious as a housefly, is not one asked to dinner at the
home of his friends, although he presents a respectable bohemian
appearance. He has not accumulated anything for social use and
is no more fit for the inside of things than a flowering bush. The
byways of life have captured him, even *captivated* his mind, and it
is possible to think that his contentment comes from never having
to set out the dishes, watch the oven, make drinks, freeze ice, have
coffee cups ready and table chairs assembled. And his curiosity is
disarming — harmless, quickly satisfied, unassuming, wide rather
than deep. It is a sort of credulous, favorable curiosity and sur-
rounds him like heat.

His memory for names is extraordinary. It is names he stores up out of the daily *Times*. Names of painters, names of sopranos, names of leftists and rightists, of murderers, of architects, of film directors, and, above all, the names of writers to go with their titles. These names lie on his brain, smothering it, like the blanketing of the acquisitions in his apartment. His cumulative index of dead and live souls, jangling bits of change with the pennies, nickels, and dimes of celebrity, often has a dampening effect on conversation and, being all-identifying information as it is, the terms of exchange cannot be agreed upon.

Obscure persons, those of some past accomplishment lying under the settled dust, are alarmed by Roger's mysterious recognitions. They start in embarrassment, seeming to fear they have been picked out of the heap by mistake.

Aren't you ——— , author of ——— ? Roger asks with perfect courtesy.

How did you recognize me?

To this Roger can only reply that in truth he does not know. And he is unprepared for the burden his keen eye, his genial salute represented to the modest, the shy, and also to the arrogant.

•

What is the noise in the back of The Pleiade? Like the sound of some smoothly running machine pleased to be doing its part. It is Roger and the great energy of his friendly, healthy, untroubled ways. Unaccountable exertions at the table in the back of the shop. Roger is typing away at an impressive speed, racing along as confidently as an alert stenographer in court. Behind him, stacked in neat black binders, are the thirteen novels he has written on the typewriter. During the slowness just before the dinner hour, there he is, sitting straight and tall for the protection of his back during his labors. Coffee cools beside him, a cheeseburger waits in its wrapping paper. Clang, clang, clang! Loud, joyful clangs from his thick, strong fingers. In goes a sheet of paper to be greeted by the happy rhythmical clatter and soon with a quick, practiced twist out it comes with a very pleasant zing, and another page rolls in. Pure pleasure rattles through Roger's body as the neat, perfectly typed pages pile up. What gladness in numbers: Chapter 7, page 210.

The pages arrive as if telephoned by the stack of index cards on the right, which contain, sketched in Roger's fine script, the characters who are sending the messages.

From an early work: Desmond, thirty-two, in the O.S.S. on the European front, World War II. English by birth but American citizen after marriage to Melissa, proper Bostonian background. These two were to be involved in a tangle of unbelievable but nevertheless predictable complication.

The gathering ledgers — for that is what they appear to be — ledgers with indecipherable figures noting some forgotten transaction, have seen the creation of disaster plots, cancer plots, celebrity-scandal plots, regional plots, international plots. But there is nothing at all in the stacks of black binders of the avant-garde, nothing of the beloved discordance of modernism, that is the pride of the bookshelves, the consolation of the proprietor. The violent, ecstatic typing — so like a fantastic, rejuvenating regime of arcane exercises. The pile of crisp pages sometimes goes out to the world in envelopes, and the return causes no discouragement.

The French scholar, a lonely man and a terrible snob with an almost paranoid resentment of certain French works in current esteem, among them the poetry of Francis Ponge and the essays of Cioran, often says: I do not understand this deranged typing. It is not hope of fame, of money, or even of publication. It is not anything that can be known.

And he tells of seeing Roger once in a mood of despair as he sat ready to attack the keys. A work in the autobiographical mode was planned, but a painful interruption, a stiffening, a paralysis struck Roger after only a dozen or so pages. Mournfully, he appealed to his reliable fingers, the faithful engines, but they could not be urged to move along. At last, he said: The "I" is not for me. The sheet came out, the black leather cover was placed over the typewriter with the solemnity of defeat — a burial.

•

Disquieting events at The Pleiade, in December. Maureen returns suddenly from Troy, looking beautiful, with her tranquil eyes, her short curls, and wearing a graceful skirt of Indian cotton.

Sprung, Roger says.

Now Maureen sits at the back of the shop with Lois, also in her full beauty, if somehow edging into dishevelment, save for a new pair of expensive light-blue leather boots, stitched with patterns of pink roses.

They might be Roger's daughters. And what are they? Mistresses? They and the sulky despot, Jenny, whose reign, before

Maureen, tormented the walls, accused the shelves, menaced with frowns the old New Directions paperbacks and the first hundred titles of Anchor Books, which Roger, knight of perfect faith, had assembled.

Jenny, in her forties, had come to Roger like a message in a bottle, floating from Yugoslavia, where she was born, to London, where she was briefly married to a second cousin of Roger's, and on to New York with the address of The Pleiade in her hand.

Where indeed is Jenny?

New Jersey, Roger says. Relatives. Serbs chanting folktales from the old oral tradition.

Not one of his friends thinks Maureen or Lois is a mistress. It is unimaginable because of the presence of some cheerful absence in Roger, his blameless peculiarity of not seeming to have an interior. For all his curiosity, he is not inclined to analysis and detail, and those about whom he is curious come into his view as traveling objects. It is as if he were to look up and say: That one is blue with yellow stripes and this one is red and black. Except for the tyrannical Jenny. The violinist believes there might have been an affair in that corner.

And why does he think so? Her deprecating ill-humor, for one thing, he answers.

The two girls, Maureen and Lois, were not altogether friendly and took up more room than the shop could bear. They did not make change, did not advise about the existence of a title, never opened the interesting pages of *Books in Print*. Roger himself swept out in the morning, and at night, often the wrong one, took his huge plastic bags of rubbish to the curb for collection. Two girls might have been six girls, and the multiplication sent Roger into a state of mind unusual for him, a state of unhappiness and vexation. The unbalancing scheme seemed to demand something from him, but he was not clear just what that something might be.

It is not as if they were down and out, he would say with a sigh. He repeated this again and again, and although the girls were only a few feet away they did not appear to be listening.

Both girls were indeed cherished by their confused families. They received money and mail, letters filled with encouragement, letters grateful that they were in beguiling, promising New York City in order to get on with their lives. Their hometowns, scenes of disappointment and constriction, were not suitable for advancement. Lois had found early that in her own Pittsburgh there was nothing happening. The two had met in a private sanatorium and each had made her way to therapeutic New York and to the Pleiade hospice. And here they were, in a state of becoming.

The overpopulation left Roger gasping for air, unable to recover his stolen placid breathing. The unmoving freight, stalled, lay in his path, defying all thè tools his accepting nature had at hand. He would find the two silently gazing at the store's landscape and limply he would suggest: Shoo! Take a walk.

We are not twins, Maureen would answer. Let Lois take the walk.

•

The Pleiade is downed by melancholy until Christmas, when Lois is lifted up by holiday sentiment and one morning abandons the bookshop and the apartment for the despised Pittsburgh.

She will not be back, Maureen says. It turns out that Lois's brother walked up and down in front of The Pleiade, entered the challenging stairway of the old tenement, looked in wonder like a detective on a case at Roger, Maureen, the dog, the unkempt and the fashionable customers, and decided that the setting was not promising for Lois's career. With the help of Christmas he led her to take up the trail back home.

The empty chair reassured, space opened up in Roger's heart once more and its steady, comfortable beating returned. The typewriter clanged from four until six in the afternoon. New classics were magically restored after the cruelty of time had spent itself. The tides flowed and Roger swam.

•

It is Christmas at The Pleiade. Roger's days soar as he dispenses, in the spirit of charity baskets, the gifts of the world. Storytellers from Africa, epics from Latin America, painful gutting rituals from Japan, women poets from the Russia of the twenties — the nineteen-twenties, the period of his first passions, now a hallowed battlefield filled with noble headstones. Suicides, early death, transfiguration, words, words, words, in all the tongues of the earth. Roger's head, with its wrinkled sandy waves lapping on the shore of his brow, bobs up and down in time to the sacred music.

On the block, the sepulchre of the old fruit market is now a mausoleum of oak cabinets and kitchen tables from the back porches of the Middle West. Taste itself seems to be laughing in the street.

•

In January, Maureen dimmed and faded away. The dark star of Jenny, with her glimmering scowl, ascended without notice. Remarks burst from her like bullets. He is a toadstool, she would say of Roger in a loud gunfire.

After a pause of shock, Roger found his aim. You see, I am a *cavaliere servente,* he cried out gaily, calling upon page 1 of *The Charterhouse of Parma.*

Jenny gradually displayed a few marks of chastening. An unwholesome strain of choleric domesticity invaded her thoughts, a lesson learned. She had turned a corner, but not the one that led to cooking and housekeeping. She was making her way, as if by a private radar, to the interests of ownership. Swift, proprietary gleamings, a sense of things. Her eyes surveyed the books, the collections, like a guard with his flashlight making the midnight rounds. Stirrings in the blood, storage plans for winter, gathering potatoes in the cellar; she was getting older.

Sometimes one would see her studying a piece of brass or old silver brought down from the apartment. A pawnbroker's stare, cynical smile, and shrug of feigned indifference. Roger did not speak of this alteration in her attention, but found relief in the fact that she stayed upstairs a good deal, pushing objects from one corner to another, making promising groupings, looking for the right screw for a hole, an old curve that would welcome a stray rosette of gold leaf. No mending, no polishing. In her fitful accounting all was equal and she might have been engaged in a nightmare dialogue between buyer and seller. Here is the missing leg, in perfect shape; here is the piece that completes the red tail of the dragon on the green china plate; here is Volume IV. Sorting out, Roger said.

In the middle of March, our lawyer friend who played the violin and read Kleist and Novalis died. The death dug its teeth into Roger's soft heart and he looked backward to remember that the friend had not been in The Pleiade for a few months and had for the past year appeared frail and thin. At the Riverside Chapel, we mourned this death of a hero, with his antique passions, as they seemed, his poets known by heart and whose lives were shorter than his own.

He has gone their way early, Roger said in a throttle of tears.

Nothing in the memorial of all this. Instead, accomplishments unknown to us, the accretion of a short, handsome wife and the production of two tall daughters. They haven't got him right, Roger grieved as the tributes went on with their office jokes, mishaps on the tennis court, charitable contributions, and helping hands for the young.

·

The Pleiade has lost a star and yet, diminished, it faces another spring. Roger himself seems to be adorned with fresh innocence as he watches the begonias and forced gardenias expel the potted chrysanthemums and Jerusalem cherries from the sidewalk outside the florist's. The heavens are clear for a whole week. There is ballet at the State Theatre and yet another at the opera house. Hardly a night passes without an author to be recognized and to receive a murmured approbation, as if a breeze has passed the ear whispering, beloved, here you are at last.

The pleasing winds came one day, drifted away the next, and came once more. The dollar bin at The Pleiade now has a two-dollar sign on it. When the talk turns to unemployment and inflation, Jenny can be heard to say: There is a lot of money in pockets. The Chinese build a glass extension for their restaurant and fill it with smart blue chairs and white tables. In the antique shop a large Art Deco bar of black glass and chrome humbles the lowly, stripped oak.

So the coming of another spring still finds Roger ruling in the heavens like Zeus. And his great stars, Kafka, Beckett, Walter Benjamin, Joyce, Akhmatova, and old men from Japan with their whores in the snow mountains — all of these shine on and on and on.

BOBBIE ANN MASON

Shiloh

(FROM THE NEW YORKER)

LEROY MOFFITT's wife, Norma Jean, is working on her pectorals. She lifts three-pound dumbbells to warm up, then progresses to a twenty-pound barbell. Standing with her legs apart, she reminds Leroy of Wonder Woman.

"I'd give anything if I could just get these muscles to where they're real hard," says Norma Jean. "Feel this arm. It's not as hard as the other one."

"That's 'cause you're right-handed," says Leroy, dodging as she swings the barbell in an arc.

"Do you think so?"

"Sure."

Leroy is a truck driver. He injured his leg in a highway accident four months ago, and his physical therapy, which involves weights and a pulley, prompted Norma Jean to try building herself up. Now she is attending a body-building class. Leroy has been collecting temporary disability since his tractor-trailer jackknifed in Missouri, badly twisting his left leg in its socket. He has a steel pin in his hip. He will probably not be able to drive his rig again. It sits in the back yard, like a gigantic bird that has flown home to roost. Leroy has been home in Kentucky for three months, and his leg is almost healed, but the accident frightened him and he does not want to drive any more long hauls. He is not sure what to do next. In the meantime, he makes things from craft kits. He started by building a miniature log cabin from notched Popsicle sticks. He varnished it and placed it on the TV set, where it remains. It reminds him of a rustic Nativity scene. Then he tried string art (sailing ships on black velvet), a macrame owl kit, a snap-together

B-17 Flying Fortress, and a lamp made out of a model truck with a light fixture screwed in the top of the cab. At first the kits were diversions, something to kill time, but now he is thinking about building a full-scale log house from a kit. It would be considerably cheaper than building a regular house, and besides, Leroy has grown to appreciate how things are put together. He has begun to realize that in all the years he was on the road he never took time to examine anything. He was always flying past scenery.

"They won't let you build a log cabin in any of the new subdivisions," Norma Jean tells him.

"They will if I tell them it's for you," he says, teasing her. Ever since they were married, he has promised Norma Jean he would build her a new home one day. They have always rented, and the house they live in is small and nondescript. It does not even feel like a home, Leroy realizes now.

Norma Jean works at the Rexall drugstore, and she has acquired an amazing amount of information about cosmetics. When she explains to Leroy the three stages of complexion care, involving creams, toners, and moisturizers, he thinks happily of other petroleum products — axle grease, diesel fuel. This is a connection between himself and Norma Jean. Since he has been home, he has felt unusually tender about his wife and guilty over his long absences. But he can't tell what she feels about him. Norma Jean has never complained about his traveling; she has never made hurt remarks, like calling his truck a "widow-maker." He is reasonably certain she has been faithful to him, but he wishes she would celebrate his permanent homecoming more happily. Norma Jean is often startled to find Leroy at home, and he thinks she seems a little disappointed about it. Perhaps he reminds her too much of the early days of their marriage, before he went on the road. They had a child who died as an infant, years ago. They never speak about their memories of Randy, which have almost faded, but now that Leroy is home all the time they sometimes feel awkward around each other, and Leroy wonders if one of them should mention the child. He has the feeling that they are waking up out of a dream together — that they must create a new marriage, start afresh. They are lucky they are still married. Leroy has read that for most people losing a child destroys the marriage — or else he heard this on "Donahue." He can't always remember where he learns things anymore.

At Christmas, Leroy bought an electric organ for Norma Jean.

She used to play the piano when she was in high school. "It don't leave you," she told him once. "It's like riding a bicycle."

The new instrument had so many keys and buttons that she was bewildered by it at first. She touched the keys tentatively, pushed some buttons, then pecked out "Chopsticks." It came out in an amplified foxtrot rhythm, with marimba sounds.

"It's an orchestra!" she cried.

The organ had a pecan-look finish and eighteen pre-set chords, with optional flute, violin, trumpet, clarinet, and banjo accompaniments. Norma Jean mastered the organ almost immediately. At first she played Christmas songs. Then she bought *The Sixties Songbook* and learned every tune in it, adding variations to each with the rows of brightly colored buttons.

"I didn't like these old songs back then," she said. "But I have this crazy feeling I missed something."

"You didn't miss a thing," said Leroy.

Leroy likes to lie on the couch and smoke a joint and listen to Norma Jean play "Can't Take My Eyes Off You" and "I'll Be Back." He is back again. After fifteen years on the road, he is finally settling down with the woman he loves. She is still pretty. Her skin is flawless. Her frosted curls resemble pencil trimmings.

•

Now that Leroy has come home to stay, he notices how much the town has changed. Subdivisions are spreading across western Kentucky like an oil slick. The sign at the edge of town says POP: 10,500 — only seven hundred more than it said twenty years ago. Leroy can't figure out who is living in all the new houses. The farmers who used to gather around the courthouse square on Saturday afternoons to play checkers and spit tobacco juice have gone. It has been years since Leroy has thought about the farmers, and they have disappeared without his noticing.

Leroy meets a kid named Stevie Hamilton in the parking lot at the new shopping center. While they pretend to be strangers meeting over a stalled car, Stevie tosses an ounce of marijuana under the front seat of Leroy's car. Stevie is wearing orange jogging shoes and a T-shirt that says CHATTAHOOCHEE SUPER-RAT. His father is a prominent doctor who lives in one of the expensive subdivisions in a new white-columned brick house that looks like a funeral parlor. In the phone book under his name there is a separate number, with the listing "Teen-agers."

"Where do you get this stuff?" asks Leroy. "From your pappy?"

"That's for me to know and you to find out," Stevie says. He is slit-eyed and skinny.

"What else you got?"

"What you interested in?"

"Nothing special. Just wondered."

Leroy used to take speed on the road. Now he has to go slowly. He needs to be mellow. He leans back against the car and says, "I'm aiming to build me a log house, soon as I get time. My wife, though, I don't think she likes the idea."

"Well, let me know when you want me again," Stevie says. He has a cigarette in his cupped palm, as though sheltering it from the wind. He takes a long drag, then stomps it on the asphalt and slouches away.

Stevie's father was two years ahead of Leroy in high school. Leroy is thirty-four. He married Norma Jean when they were both eighteen, and their child Randy was born a few months later, but he died at the age of four months and three days. He would be about Stevie's age now. Norma Jean and Leroy were at the drive-in, watching a double feature (*Dr. Strangelove* and *Lover Come Back*), and the baby was sleeping in the back seat. When the first movie ended, the baby was dead. It was the sudden-infant-death syndrome. Leroy remembers handing Randy to a nurse at the emergency room, as though he were offering her a large doll as a present. A dead baby feels like a sack of flour. "It just happens sometimes," said the doctor, in what Leroy always recalls as a nonchalant tone. Leroy can hardly remember the child anymore, but he still sees vividly a scene from *Dr. Strangelove* in which the President of the United States was talking in a folksy voice on the hot line to the Soviet Premier about the bombers accidentally headed toward Russia. He was in the War Room, and the world map was lit up. Leroy remembers Norma Jean standing catatonically beside him in the hospital and himself thinking, Who is this strange girl? He had forgotten who she was. Now scientists are saying that crib death is caused by a virus. Nobody knows anything, Leroy thinks. The answers are always changing.

When Leroy gets home from the shopping center, Norma Jean's mother, Mabel Beasley, is there. Until this year, Leroy has not realized how much time she spends with Norma Jean. When she visits, she inspects the closets and then the plants, informing Norma Jean when a plant is droopy or yellow. Mabel calls the plants "flowers," although there are never any blooms. She always notices if Norma Jean's laundry is piling up. Mabel is a short, overweight woman whose tight, brown-dyed curls look more like a wig than the actual wig she sometimes wears. Today she has brought Norma Jean an off-white dust ruffle she made for the bed; Mabel works in a custom-upholstery shop.

"This is the tenth one I made this year," Mabel says. "I got started and couldn't stop."

"It's really pretty," says Norma Jean.

"Now we can hide things under the bed," says Leroy, who gets along with his mother-in-law primarily by joking with her. Mabel has never really forgiven him for disgracing her by getting Norma Jean pregnant. When the baby died, she said that fate was mocking her.

"What's that thing?" Mabel says to Leroy in a loud voice, pointing to a tangle of yarn on a piece of canvas.

Leroy holds it up for Mabel to see. "It's my needlepoint," he explains. "This is a 'Star Trek' pillow cover."

"That's what a woman would do," says Mabel. "Great day in the morning!"

"All the big football players on TV do it," he says.

"Why, Leroy, you're always trying to fool me. I don't believe you for one minute. You don't know what to do with yourself — that's the whole trouble. Sewing!"

"I'm aiming to build us a log house," says Leroy. "Soon as my plans come."

"Like *heck* you are," says Norma Jean. She takes Leroy's needlepoint and shoves it into a drawer. "You have to find a job first. Nobody can afford to build now anyway."

Mabel straightens her girdle and says, "I still think before you get tied down y'all ought to take a little run to Shiloh."

"One of these days, Mama," Norma Jean says impatiently.

Mabel is talking about Shiloh, Tennessee. For the past few years, she has been urging Leroy and Norma Jean to visit the Civil War battleground there. Mabel went there on her honeymoon — the only real trip she ever took. Her husband died of a perforated ulcer when Norma Jean was ten, but Mabel, who was accepted into the United Daughters of the Confederacy in 1975, is still preoccupied with going back to Shiloh.

"I've been to kingdom come and back in that truck out yonder,"

Leroy says to Mabel, "but we never yet set foot in that battle-ground. Ain't that something? How did I miss it?"

"It's not even that far," Mabel says.

After Mabel leaves, Norma Jean reads to Leroy from a list she has made. "Things you could do," she announces. "You could get a job as a guard at Union Carbide, where they'd let you set on a stool. You could get on at the lumberyard. You could do a little carpenter work, if you want to build so bad. You could — "

"I can't do something where I'd have to stand up all day."

"You ought to try standing up all day behind a cosmetics counter. It's amazing that I have strong feet, coming from two parents that never had strong feet at all." At the moment, Norma Jean is holding on to the kitchen counter, raising her knees one at a time as she talks. She is wearing two-pound ankle weights.

"Don't worry," says Leroy. "I'll do something."

"You could truck calves to slaughter for somebody. You wouldn't have to drive any big old truck for that."

"I'm going to build you this house," says Leroy. "I want to make you a real home."

"I don't want to live in any log cabin."

"It's not a cabin. It's a house."

"I don't care. It looks like a cabin."

"You and me together could lift those logs. It's just like lifting weights."

Norma Jean doesn't answer. Under her breath, she is counting. Now she is marching through the kitchen. She is doing goose steps.

•

Before his accident, when Leroy came home he used to stay in the house with Norma Jean, watching TV in bed and playing cards. She would cook fried chicken, picnic ham, chocolate pie — all his favorites. Now he is home alone much of the time. In the mornings, Norma Jean disappears, leaving a cooling place in the bed. She eats a cereal called Body Buddies, and she leaves the bowl on the table, with the soggy tan balls floating in a milk puddle. He sees things about Norma Jean that he never realized before. When she chops onions, she stares off into a corner, as if she can't bear to look. She puts on her house slippers almost precisely at nine o'clock every evening and nudges her jogging shoes under the couch. She saves bread heels for the birds. Leroy watches the birds at the feeder. He notices the peculiar way goldfinches fly past the window. They close their wings, then fall, then spread their wings to catch and lift themselves. He wonders if they close their eyes when they fall. Norma Jean closes her eyes when they are in bed. She wants the lights turned out. Even then, he is sure she closes her eyes.

He goes for long drives around town. He tends to drive a car rather carelessly. Power steering and an automatic shift make a car feel so small and inconsequential that his body is hardly involved in the driving process. His injured leg stretches out comfortably. Once or twice he has almost hit something, but even the prospect of an accident seems minor in a car. He cruises the new subdivisions, feeling like a criminal rehearsing for a robbery. Norma Jean is probably right about a log house being inappropriate here in the new subdivisions. All the houses look grand and complicated. They depress him.

One day when Leroy comes home from a drive he finds Norma Jean in tears. She is in the kitchen making a potato and mushroom-soup casserole, with grated-cheese topping. She is crying because her mother caught her smoking.

"I didn't hear her coming. I was standing here puffing away pretty as you please," Norma Jean says, wiping her eyes.

"I knew it would happen sooner or later," says Leroy, putting his arm around her.

"She don't know the meaning of the work *knock*," says Norma Jean. "It's a wonder she hadn't caught me years ago."

"Think of it this way," Leroy says. "What if she caught me with a joint?"

"You better not let her!" Norma Jean shrieks. "I'm warning you, Leroy Moffitt!"

"I'm just kidding. Here, play me a tune. That'll help you relax."

Norma Jean puts the casserole in the oven and sets the timer. Then she plays a ragtime tune, with horns and banjo, as Leroy lights up a joint and lies on the couch, laughing to himself about Mabel's catching him at it. He thinks of Stevie Hamilton — a doctor's son pushing grass. Everything is funny. The whole town seems crazy and small. He is reminded of Virgil Mathis, a boastful policeman Leroy used to shoot pool with. Virgil recently led a drug bust in a back room at a bowling alley, where he seized ten thousand dollars' worth of marijuana. The newspaper had a picture of him holding up the bags of grass and grinning widely. Right now, Leroy can imagine Virgil breaking down the door and arresting him with a lungful of smoke. Virgil would probably have been alerted to the scene because of all the racket Norma Jean is making. Now she sounds like a hard-rock band. Norma Jean is terrific. When she switches to a Latin-rhythm version of "Sunshine Superman," Leroy hums along. Norma Jean's foot goes up and down, up and down.

"Well, what do you think?" Leroy says, when Norma Jean pauses to search through her music.

"What do I think about what?"

His mind has gone blank. Then he says, "I'll sell my rig and build us a house." That wasn't what he wanted to say. He wanted to know what she thought — what she *really* thought — about them.

"Don't start in on that again," says Norma Jean. She begins playing "Who'll Be the Next in Line?"

Leroy used to tell hitchhikers his whole life story — about his travels, his hometown, the baby. He would end with a question: "Well, what do you think?" It was just a rhetorical question. In time, he had the feeling that he'd been telling the same story over and over to the same hitchhikers. He quit talking to hitchhikers when he realized how his voice sounded — whining and self-pitying, like some teen-age-tragedy song. Now Leroy has the sudden impulse to tell Norma Jean about himself, as if he had just met her. They have known each other so long they have forgotten a lot about each other. They could become reacquainted. But when the oven timer goes off and she runs to the kitchen, he forgets why he wants to do this.

•

The next day, Mabel drops by. It is Saturday and Norma Jean is cleaning. Leroy is studying the plans of his log house, which have finally come in the mail. He has them spread out on the table — big sheets of stiff blue paper, with diagrams and numbers printed in white. While Norma Jean runs the vacuum, Mabel drinks coffee. She sets her coffee cup on a blueprint.

"I'm just waiting for time to pass," she says to Leroy, drumming her fingers on the table.

As soon as Norma Jean switches off the vacuum, Mabel says in a loud voice, "Did you hear about the datsun dog that killed the baby?"

Norma Jean says, "The word is *dachshund*."

"They put the dog on trial. It chewed the baby's legs off. The mother was in the next room all the time." She raises her voice. "They thought it was neglect."

Norma Jean is holding her ears. Leroy manages to open the refrigerator and get some Diet Pepsi to offer Mabel. Mabel still has some coffee and she waves away the Pepsi.

"Datsuns are like that," Mabel says. "They're jealous dogs. They'll tear a place to pieces if you don't keep an eye on them."

"You better watch out what you're saying, Mabel," says Leroy.

"Well, facts is facts."

Leroy looks out the window at his rig. It is like a huge piece of furniture gathering dust in the back yard. Pretty soon it will be an antique. He hears the vacuum cleaner. Norma Jean seems to be cleaning the living-room rug again.

Later, she says to Leroy, "She just said that about the baby because she caught me smoking. She's trying to pay me back."

"What are you talking about?" Leroy says, nervously shuffling blueprints.

"You know good and well," Norma Jean says. She is sitting in a kitchen chair with her feet up and her arms wrapped around her knees. She looks small and helpless. She says, "The very idea, her bringing up a subject like that! Saying it was neglect."

"She didn't mean that," Leroy says.

"She might not have *thought* she meant it. She always says things like that. You don't know how she goes on."

"But she didn't really mean it. She was just talking."

Leroy opens a king-sized bottle of beer and pours it into two glasses, dividing it carefully. He hands a glass to Norma Jean and she takes it from him mechanically. For a long time, they sit by the kitchen window watching the birds at the feeder.

•

Something is happening. Norma Jean is going to night school. She has graduated from her six-week body-building course and now she is taking an adult-education course in composition at Paducah Community College. She spends her evenings outlining paragraphs.

"First you have a topic sentence," she explains to Leroy. "Then you divide it up. Your secondary topic has to be connected to your primary topic."

To Leroy, this sounds intimidating. "I never was any good in English," he says.

"It makes a lot of sense."

"What are you doing this for anyhow?"

She shrugs. "It's something to do." She stands up and lifts her dumbbells a few times.

"Driving a rig, nobody cared about my English."

"I'm not criticizing your English."

Norma Jean used to say, "If I lose ten minutes' sleep, I just drag all day." Now she stays up late, writing compositions. She got a B on her first paper — a how-to theme on soup-based casseroles. Recently Norma Jean has been cooking unusual foods — tacos, lasagna, Bombay duck. She doesn't play the organ anymore, though her second paper was called "Why Music Is Important to Me." She sits at the kitchen table, concentrating on her outlines while Leroy plays with his log-house plans, practicing with a set of Lincoln Logs. The thought of getting a truckload of notched, numbered logs scares him, and he wants to be prepared. As he and Norma Jean work together at the kitchen table, Leroy has the hopeful thought that they are sharing something, but he knows he is a fool to think this. Norma Jean is miles away. He knows he is going to lose her. Like Mabel, he is just waiting for time to pass.

One day Mabel is there before Norma Jean gets home from work, and Leroy finds himself confiding in her. Mabel, he realizes, must know Norma Jean better than he does.

"I don't know what's got into that girl," Mabel says. "She used to go to bed with the chickens. Now you say she's up all hours. Plus her a-smoking. I like to died."

"I want to make her this beautiful home," Leroy says, indicating the Lincoln Logs. "I don't think she even wants it. Maybe she was happier with me gone."

"She don't know what to make of you, coming home like this."

"Is that it?"

Mabel takes the roof off his Lincoln Log cabin. "You couldn't get *me* in a log cabin," she says. "I was raised in one. It's no picnic, let me tell you."

"They're different now," says Leroy.

"I'll tell you what," Mabel says, smiling oddly at Leroy.

"What?"

"Take her on down to Shiloh. Y'all need to get out together, stir a little. Her brain's all balled up over them books."

Leroy can see traces of Norma Jean's features in her mother's face. Mabel's worn face has the texture of crinkled cotton, but suddenly she looks pretty. It occurs to Leroy that Mabel has been hinting all along that she wants them to take her with them to Shiloh.

"Let's all go to Shiloh," he says. "You and me and her. Come Sunday."

Mabel throws up her hands in protest. "Oh, no, not me. Young folks want to be by theirselves."

When Norma Jean comes in with groceries, Leroy says excitedly, "Your mama here's been dying to go to Shiloh for thirty-five years. It's about time we went, don't you think?"

"I'm not going to butt in on anybody's second honeymoon," Mabel says.

"Who's going on a honeymoon, for Christ's sake?" Norma Jean says loudly.

"I never raised no daughter of mine to talk that-a-way," Mabel says.

"You ain't seen nothing yet," says Norma Jean. She starts putting away boxes and cans, slamming cabinet doors.

"There's a log cabin at Shiloh," Mabel says. "It was there during the battle. There's bullet holes in it."

"When are you going to *shut up* about Shiloh, Mama?" asks Norma Jean.

"I always thought Shiloh was the prettiest place, so full of history," Mabel goes on. "I just hoped y'all could see it once before I die, so you could tell me about it." Later she whispers to Leroy, "You do what I said. A little change is what she needs."

•

"Your name means 'the king,'" Norma Jean says to Leroy that evening. He is trying to get her to go to Shiloh, and she is reading a book about another century.

"Well, I reckon I ought to be right proud."

"I guess so."

"Am I still king around here?"

Norma Jean flexes her biceps and feels them for hardness. "I'm not fooling around with anybody, if that's what you mean," she says.

"Would you tell me if you were?"

"I don't know."

"What does *your* name mean?"

"It was Marilyn Monroe's real name."

"No kidding!"

"Norma comes from the Normans. They were invaders," she says. She closes her book and looks hard at Leroy. "I'll go to Shiloh with you if you'll stop staring at me."

•

On Sunday, Norma Jean packs a picnic and they go to Shiloh. To Leroy's relief, Mabel says she does not want to come with them. Norma Jean drives, and Leroy, sitting beside her, feels like some boring hitchhiker she has picked up. He tries some conversation, but she answers him in monosyllables. At Shiloh, she drives aimlessly through the park, past bluffs and trails and steep ravines. Shiloh is an immense place, and Leroy cannot see it as a battle-ground. It is not what he expected. He thought it would look like a golf course. Monuments are everywhere, showing through the thick clusters of trees. Norma Jean passes the log cabin Mabel mentioned. It is surrounded by tourists looking for bullet holes.

"That's not the kind of log house I've got in mind," says Leroy apologetically.

"I know *that*."

"This is a pretty place. Your mama was right."

"It's O.K.," says Norma Jean. "Well, we've seen it. I hope she's satisfied."

They burst out laughing together.

At the park museum, a movie on Shiloh is shown every half hour, but they decide that they don't want to see it. They buy a souvenir Confederate flag for Mabel, and then they find a picnic spot near the cemetery. Norma Jean has brought a picnic cooler, with pimiento sandwiches, soft drinks, and Yodels. Leroy eats a sandwich and then smokes a joint, hiding it behind the picnic cooler. Norma Jean has quit smoking altogether. She is picking cake crumbs from the cellophane wrapper, like a fussy bird.

Leroy says, "So the boys in gray ended up in Corinth. The Union soldiers zapped 'em finally. April 7, 1862."

They both knew that he doesn't know any history; he is just

talking about some of the historical plaques they have read. He feels awkward, like a boy on a date with an older girl. They are still just making conversation.

"Corinth is where Mama eloped to," says Norma Jean.

They sit in silence and stare at the cemetery for the Union dead and, beyond, at a tall cluster of trees. Campers are parked nearby bumper to bumper, and small children in bright clothing are cavorting and squealing. Norma Jean wads up the cake wrapper and squeezes it tightly in her hand. Without looking at Leroy, she says, "I want to leave you."

Leroy takes a bottle of Coke out of the cooler and flips off the cap. He holds the bottle poised near his mouth but cannot remember to take a drink. Finally he says, "No, you don't."

"Yes, I do."

"I won't let you."

"You can't stop me."

"Don't do me that way."

Leroy knows Norma Jean will have her own way. "Didn't I promise to be home from now on?" he says.

"In some ways, a woman prefers a man who wanders," says Norma Jean. "That sounds crazy, I know."

"You're not crazy."

Leroy remembers to drink from his Coke. Then he says, "Yes, you *are* crazy. You and me could start all over again. Right back at the beginning."

"We *have* started all over again," says Norma Jean. "And this is how it turned out."

"What did I do wrong?"

"Nothing."

"Is this one of those women's-lib things?" Leroy asks.

"Don't be funny."

The cemetery, a green slope dotted with white markers, looks like a subdivision site. Leroy is trying to comprehend that his marriage is breaking up, but for some reason he is wondering about white slabs in a graveyard.

"Everything was fine till Mama caught me smoking," says Norma Jean, standing up. "That set something off."

"What are you talking about?"

"*She* won't leave me alone — *you* won't leave me alone." Norma Jean seems to be crying, but she is looking away from him. "I feel eighteen again. I can't face that all over again." She starts walking away. "No, it *wasn't* fine. I don't know what I'm saying. Forget it."

Leroy takes a lungful of smoke and closes his eyes as Norma Jean's words sink in. He tries to focus on the fact that thirty-five hundred soldiers died on the grounds around him. He can only think of that war as a board game with plastic soldiers. Leroy almost smiles, as he compares the Confederates' daring attack on the Union camps and Virgil Mathis's raid on the bowling alley. General Grant, drunk and furious, shoved the Southerners back to Corinth, where Mable and Jet Beasley were married years later, when Mabel was still thin and good-looking. The next day, Mabel and Jet visited the battleground, and then Norma Jean was born, and then she married Leroy and they had a baby, which they lost, and now Leroy and Norma Jean are here at the same battleground. Leroy knows he is leaving out a lot. He is leaving out the insides of history. History was always just names and dates to him. It occurs to him that building a house out of logs is similarly empty — too simple. And the real inner workings of a marriage, like most of history, have escaped him. Now he sees that building a log house is the dumbest idea he could have had. It was clumsy of him to think Norma Jean would want a log house. It was a crazy idea. He'll have to think of something else, quickly. He will wad the blueprints into tight balls and fling them into the lake. Then he'll get moving again. He opens his eyes. Norma Jean has moved away and is walking through the cemetery, following a serpentine brick path.

Leroy gets up to follow his wife, but his good leg is asleep and his bad leg still hurts him. Norma Jean is far away, walking rapidly toward the bluff by the river, and he tries to hobble toward her. Some children run past him, screaming noisily. Norma Jean has reached the bluff, and she is looking out over the Tennessee River. Now she turns toward Leroy and waves her arms. Is she beckoning to him? She seems to be doing an exercise for her chest muscles. The sky is unusually pale — the color of the dust ruffle Mabel made for their bed.

JOSEPH McELROY

The Future

(FROM THE NEW YORKER)

AFTER THE EVENT he will have his story and she will have hers. The event will amount to little more than a brief, unwelcome scare. They're the same people before and after the event, the mother and her twelve-year-old son, her "twelve-year-old." They are still there. They won't go away. But he will have his story and she will have hers. After all, they never were the same. There they are at the end of the day, at seven-thirty, quarter to eight, when she swung open the front door and he was waiting for her and tonight not on the phone but right there in front of her, standing in the entrance to their living room. He was sort of smiling, as if he had seen her coming. He was wearing the pale-orange collarless shirt she'd decided he didn't like, and his new, expensive sneakers. He had combed his hair wetly, having apparently taken a shower. Waiting for her there between living room and front hall, he made her think of times she had come home from the office thinking, What if he isn't there? — aged ten, aged eleven. It was his sneakers that made her think of those times. And she knew now, in the instant before he said, "Can we go out to dinner?," that, getting in ahead of his mother, he was going to say what she was about to say. Her keys in one hand, in the other her shopping bag from the fruit-and-vegetable market, she went and kissed him and seemed to walk around him and into the apartment. "Shall we?" she said. She put the two pink grapefruit and the beautiful bluish-green broccoli and the watercress in the refrigerator and the bananas in the wooden salad bowl on the kitchen table. Had she really been about to say, "Let's go out to dinner"? She remembered the large, unripe avocado in her leather shoulder bag on the chair, and she removed it and put it with the bananas, laid it within the curve. She had not paid for the avocado.

•

In the small, narrow restaurant are two rows of tables against either wall. At one end, the kitchen; at the other, the street window, maybe fifteen feet from their table. Tonight she was facing the street.

There was the door to the street, to the vestibule, actually, and between the door and the first table, across the aisle from where she and her son sat, was a nook for the cash register. This was an ornate, old-fashioned thing that, if you looked at it, maybe didn't go with the fresh, elegant plainness of the place. It was a French restaurant, but it was cheap. A black man who she was sure wasn't French worked in the kitchen, and the owner, a tall, gray-haired, gently tense man who looked as if he had been in another profession for years, did much of the cooking. They served mainly crêpes and quiches. The tables were set with green-rimmed butter plates and a flower in a cheap glass vase. All around was a composed look of care and economy. Her son usually faced the street window and she faced the rear of the room, which gave her a view of all the tables. Tonight he put his hand on her elbow as they entered, and she went first; so she was sitting with her back to the kitchen and to most of the restaurant.

She would see her son and herself before and after the event. The event itself will be in question, come and gone along the greater event of their life together, which is also in question, and she will know that she could have predicted this — she had the power, the experience; for a long time she let her power be.

They are quite content together. On several other visits here, they never once found this table occupied; it was their regular table. When she and Davey sat down together here at the end of a long day, she didn't care about anything, not even — but in a good sense — the questions she asked him about his day, his friends Michael and Alex and the others, homework, the cleaning woman, a thank-you letter he was supposed to write. These questions he answered. Actually, tonight he had been talking since they left the apartment about his weekend arrangements. She always wanted him to tell her what he was feeling when she came home at night. It was important.

The waitress, a young Frenchwoman, who wore a white blouse and a black skirt, brought a glass of white wine and a Coke and the menus. The wine, like a lens, held a pale-saffron transparency, and for a minute it stood untouched between the butter plate and the flower in the vase while Davey drank his Coke and, changing the subject, told his mother about a new record. He had only three dollars left from his allowance. She smiled with skeptical indulgence. She liked reading the menu, which never changed.

Davey had it all planned. He laid out the whole weekend and she listened. She sipped her wine and thought about a cigarette. He would take his suitcase to school in the morning and he and his friend Alex would be picked up in the car by Alex's mother. Alex's father came out by train in the early evening. They were going horseback riding and deep-sea fishing, and Alex's parents had a tennis court and a pool. The pool was empty until next month. The weekend was a *fait accompli*, Davey's mother was going to point out to him, for she had not been consulted.

"I see we're getting something for the money we're shelling out on your tuition," she said.

"Yeah, Ann, you've got the weekend off," he said.

She liked him. He was surprising. "Yeah, Dave, I'm glad for you," she returned.

"For me?"

"For both of us."

"Are you going out?" he asked.

"Haven't been asked," she said.

"You poor thing," he said.

"But I don't need to be," she said.

"But you've got stuff to do around the house, right?"

"Don't I ever surprise you?" she said.

The waitress came, and Davey had what he always had, cannelloni with meat sauce — not exactly French. His mother decided to have marinated celery roots first, and then a vegetable crêpe. Davey asked the waitress if they had avocado. The waitress smiled and shook her head. He had developed a taste for avocado.

The waitress came back with the julienned celery roots. Ann tasted some; she held it in her mouth like wine, and her stomach seemed to contract. The taste swelled in three or four distinct waves.

Two couples came in together but sat at separate tables. The place was quiet and private. Davey asked his mother if that stuff was any good. She nodded. He broke off a hunk of bread.

She was feeling O.K., she thought. She let the marinade dilute along her tongue before she drank off her wine.

She told Davey he could have asked her before arranging his weekend. Call them, he said. She certainly would, she said; he would need money for the horseback riding. No, he said, the horses belonged to Alex's aunt, who was in the hospital with arthritis. You don't go to the hospital for arthritis, she said, and wondered if that was true. Alex's aunt had to go, said Davey; she was having an operation. One horse was a palomino.

Davey looked at the bread he was nibbling, and kept an eye on the kitchen. His mother offered him the last forkful of the celery roots, but he pulled in his chin, shaking his head. The waitress paused to see if Ann was through and discreetly crossed to the cash register and wrote something down. She came back and took Ann's plate.

"So Alex's aunt has galloping arthritis."

"My God, that's sick," said Davey, shaking his head and sort of smiling.

"You, my dear," said his mother, "mentioned the operation and the palomino in one casual breath."

"It's what Alex said."

"It's what you said."

"Well, 'galloping arthritis' is what *you* said."

"That's true."

"You just don't want me to go," her son concluded.

This wasn't true, but she didn't say so. For a moment they looked over each other's shoulders.

The waitress came with Ann's vegetable crêpe and Davey's cannelloni. She held her tray and with a napkin put Davey's dish in front of him; it was an ovenproof dish with raised edges. "It's hot," his mother and the waitress said.

A year of weekends, a future of learning the deep seas and the American trails. A back flip so slow above the blank tiles of an empty April pool that the diver holds virtually still among all his dreams of action within unlimited time, and before he finds the pool below him it has been filled.

She raised her empty glass and caught the waitress's eye.

"They have a diving board," said Davey. "I told Alex you were a champion diver."

"That's not true, dear," she said, startled.

"Well, you did it in college."

"For a while I did."

"We're going to a drive-in movie Saturday night," said Davey. "They've got a drive-in right near this golf course, Alex said."

She's already there, but it's somewhere else, and she imagines a couple passing on an adjacent highway, and the giant heads of the two romantic leads stand high to the left at an angle like that of a door ajar. And she has arranged for this night highway to run in the opposite direction at a speed of fifty-five miles an hour, so that the couple can keep driving and still see their movie from that tall and curious angle all the way to the end.

"If I give you money for the movie, you won't spend it on that record, will you?" said Ann.

"I was thinking of giving the record to Alex," said Davey. "You know, as a present. I know he wants it."

"Why don't you give his mother something; she's picking you up and driving you out there."

"I don't know what she'd like," said Davey.

Ann did not care any more than he did. They were enjoying the advantage of the menu's variety, as they would not be able to do at home, where an avocado was slowly ripening and watercress didn't need to be bought for tomorrow night's salad. Her hand dropped to feel her shoulder bag hanging from the back of her chair by its strap. She had enough money to fly to Boston and leave Davey in front of the TV set watching the game; the Yankees were on the road in a different time zone. She'd fly to a city that was part Boston, part San Francisco, and fly back before the game was over, as if Davey couldn't put himself to bed. But, once begun, the picture would not stop, and something stirred in the kitchen of her dark apartment and she heard him get out of bed and go see what it was. She kept forgetting what it was that was in Boston and San Francisco, and she kept falling asleep when she knew he was in the kitchen alone with that sound that didn't stop. It was the avocado sprouting from its pit — hard to believe but easy to hear — and he was having an educational experience in the middle of the night watching it, but she couldn't keep awake she was so mad.

"I'll give you fifteen dollars and that will be your allowance, and you can pay for your movie and you can buy them all ice cream Saturday night," she said.

"O.K., Mom, thanks. How's your crêpe?"

Her vegetable crêpe was better than his cannelloni, she was sure. While she listened to him volunteer a progress report on what was going on in science — which he almost never did, the avocado pit kept shedding light by means of the tree that grew out of it. She was sure. The light opened up the apartment house and flattened it and spread it out to become something like land, but it was more like time, and time that there was no way anymore of measuring. And the answer was that this new variety of avocado could either ripen or at its heart be totally and with unprecedented richness a pit, all pit — hence the tree, hence the light, and the apartment house turning into a land of new time. Picture all that, she thought.

She thought he was being nice to her, telling her what they were doing in science class. Yes, she knew about genes and she had heard of Mendel, but she had forgotten that it was pea plants he studied. It was about inheriting traits, and it was all about dominant and recessive. She thought of chins, she thought of personalities. Davey talked fast, looking over her shoulder, and she told him she thought he had it just slightly mixed up but she couldn't remember for sure. He said that was how Mr. Skull had explained it.

Mr. Skull?

Mr. Skull.

She hadn't heard of Mr. Skull. Maybe they presented it differently now, she said.

Well, according to Mr. Skull, Mendel was a monk and a schoolteacher, and wasn't known during his own lifetime, and eventually his eyesight started to go; but what mattered was that he took the next step. Nowadays, they knew that Mendel didn't have the whole truth; there was a lot of stuff he hadn't gotten up to.

"But you will," she said.

"But it won't necessarily be true," said Davey, and as his mother reached in her bag for her cigarettes he opened a book of matches that had been lying in the ashtray, but she put her cigarette pack on the table and shook her head.

"True?" she said, remembering words. "Truth is just what two people are willing to agree on."

"It must be more than that," said Davey.

"Nope," she said.

"Who said?"

"Actually, your father. He said that."

"He did?"

"Yes, he did. I can assure you he said that."

She didn't like her tone. Alone with her son, Ann had gotten used to being very alert, yet she lived also with this single-minded sense of hers that she wasn't seeing everything. Yet she knew she was a good mother.

•

She hadn't seen the door to the small vestibule open. She was mopping the last of the oil off her salad plate with the last crust of their bread. Then she saw the young man in the white doorway. He wore bluejeans and a leather jacket. He paused, she felt, to give a person he'd come to see time to see him. He was looking toward the far end of the restaurant, where the kitchen was — the far end of what was really just a room.

The young man passed their table, and she said, "*He* didn't come here to eat."

"How do *you* know?" said her son. "He probably works here."

"Either he's the dishwasher or his girlfriend works here," she said.

"Well, he's talking to the waitress," said her son. "She's sitting at the last table and he said something to her."

"You see?" she said, observing Davey, and chewing her bread and holding and gently tilting her wineglass. She knew that the man in jeans wasn't the young French waitress's boyfriend.

"She's pointing," said her son, and his mother raised her finger to her lips in case they could hear Davey back there. "He's going to the phone. There's a phone on the wall right by the entrance to the kitchen."

"Well, that's what he came in for," she said. "He's not the waitress's boyfriend."

"Isn't he a little young for her?" said her son.

"I wouldn't be surprised," she said. The young man had long ginger hair, lank but carefully combed, and eyes like those of some animal so rarely seen that its ordinariness is what is most striking during a brief moment of exposure; his short, light-brown leather jacket looked as if it had traveled, and there was a touch of color about him she didn't identify at the moment. She looked into her son's face and was tired for the first time today.

"That was a pretty quick phone call," he said. "That was a quickie."

"Maybe he was calling his girlfriend," she said.

"He just disappeared, if you want to know," said her son. "He must have gone to the bathroom."

"I bet that's why he really came in here."

"But he asked the waitress for the phone."

"That was what he was thinking of when he first came in."

"Hey," her son remarked, looking toward the far end of the room, "that was quick. He came right out." Davey stared intimately or absently into her eyes, so she knew the man was approaching. She felt the vibrations in her feet and her chair.

As the young man in the leather jacket passed and she smelled a smell she couldn't quite place, her son looked around over his shoulder and watched the man leave after pausing once more, as if the brass doorknob in his hand had made him remember something.

"Did he get through to the person he was calling?" she asked.

"I don't think so," said her son, as the waitress came to their table and the man left.

The waitress told them what there was for dessert. The boy turned around in his chair to look at the table by the window, where there were some fruit tarts on two plates. His mother knew he would have mousse. The owner was standing by the cash register, and the waitress excused herself and turned to him. The owner raised his hand and pointed with a finger that seemed to have just pressed a cash-register key, and she went back toward another table. She returned with a twenty-dollar bill and a check.

Music got turned on and off. Ann knew Davey was aware of her mood; otherwise he'd have forgotten their little discussion about the weekend except as part of a general mulling-over that he probably didn't spell out.

They were going to have chocolate mousse and apricot — no, strawberry — tart. The waitress went to the kitchen, the owner right behind her.

"Alex's mother swam the English Channel," said Davey.

"She did not," said Ann. "That just isn't true."

"All but two miles, coming from France; if she'd been swimming the other way, she would have made it."

"Where did you hear that?"

"Alex said so," said Davey.

"Well, I doubt it," his mother remarked.

Behind him, she thought, was her dessert, on a table; behind her was his dessert, in a refrigerator in the kitchen. The two of them might be having the littlest of fights; no outsider would be able to tell. The young man with ginger hair appeared again in the doorway and entered the restaurant.

"Here he is again," said Ann softly, looking Davey in the eye so that he turned around and stared at the man, who looked at Ann, who, when her son turned back and put his elbows on the table facing her, said to him as if she were talking about anything but the young man, "Maybe he's suddenly developed an interest in the waitress."

"Mom," said Davey softly, embarrassed.

The young man was waiting for something to happen, she was sure, but it wasn't clear what.

"Can I have a taste of your mousse?" she said.

"If it ever comes," said Davey.

The young man strode past them toward the rear of the restaurant.

"What's he doing?" said Ann.

"He's got his hand on the phone and the owner's telling him not to keep coming in here using the phone."

"How do you know?"

"I can tell."

"Well, what's he going to do about it?"

"It's a free country," said Davey. "I'd call the police."

Ann laughed and for a moment found she couldn't stop — it was all over her face and in spasms in her abdomen. Davey smiled with grudging modesty at his remark, keeping an eye on the far end of the room. Ann started up again and stopped. She drank some water as if she already had the hiccups. "You're good for a laugh, kid," she said. Her impulse to laugh had passed.

"He's talking to the waitress," said Davey.

"What is *le patron* doing?"

"You mean the owner?" said Davey. "He's talking to the black guy in the kitchen."

"Where is our waitress?"

"She's talking to the guy who came in. Or he's talking to her. She smiled. At least, I think she did."

"She what?"

"She doesn't have my chocolate mousse."

Ann felt the treads coming along the carpeted floor, and the waitress and the young man in bluejeans passed, and the waitress went to the cash register.

"You see?" said Ann, and Davey turned to look. "She *is* his girl." For the man, who had his back to them, had put his hand lightly on the waitress's shoulder. The waitress wasn't doing anything.

"You might just be right," said Davey, glancing back at them and seeing what his mother meant. He shrugged.

"Or his sister, maybe?" said Ann, who turned instinctively to see the owner, at the back of the restaurant, step out of the kitchen.

The ginger-haired man now brought his other hand up and gripped the waitress's right arm just above the elbow, and she jerked her head around to the right, as if the street door were opening.

"No, I'm wrong," said Ann, and Davey, hearing her voice, turned to look and half rose in his chair as the man standing behind the waitress at the cash register drew her back and pivoted her away from the register and around to face back down the length of the restaurant, as if, breaking the restaurant's privacy, she were going to announce that there was a call for someone — or not, that there was a fire, no problem, or something had been lost, or the place was being closed down and the money would be refunded. And as he spoke, sharply and low behind her, there was a close moment not of ventriloquism so much as intimate agreement, when his command seemed jointly to be hers: they were about the same height, he was the roughly dressed brother or consort, and the composed life of this pleasing place derived from his behind-the-scenes industry.

His information that they were to go into the bathroom was as clear as the angle Davey's half-risen body cast in relation to his mother facing him and to the close pair on his right, three or four feet behind him.

She said, "Sit down" — was it that he was trying to be brave? — but the man, having spoken, looked away from the rest of the restaurant at the two of them and particularly at Davey, as if he could do more than speak. Ann felt the chill. And Davey was not sitting down. He had pushed his chair back and was standing up, turned to the waitress and the holdup man.

His mother had, she felt, received for them both the news that they were all going to the rear of the restaurant, into the bathroom, which was the place where you waited out this mandatory drill, which was to see how well it could be done. There must have been words; why they were so low she did not know, but what was happening was clear enough. Davey stepped away from the table and stood contemplating the young man and woman up against each other, the one somewhat hurried and scanning the room, the other rigid, and Ann for a moment didn't reach for Davey, in case the man did something. The man was saying, Hurry, with his eyes.

In one movement she rose and stepped around the table, hearing others behind her moving — she couldn't look back quite yet — and she got Davey by the elbow, his arm firm but not muscular, and drew him with her away from the waitress and the man. The man's hand, his left hand, was definitely up against the waitress's spine, and his forearm had seemed turned, as if a knife handle was gripped in his palm.

Ann had her leather bag on her shoulder. She was startled not to remember taking it. She had her arm around Davey's shoulder. The five or six customers ahead of them moving politely, as if there had been a power failure to be patient about, were people she'd hardly noticed when she'd come in — when they'd come in. Now, following them, she found them even less real to her — all except a blond woman in her fifties with a lacquered bouffant — less real to her than they had obscurely been in the privacy of her dinner with her son. Tonight Davey had had the view.

She remembered nothing and prophesied little, but she had seen finality in the alert glance the young man had given Davey. It didn't matter who Davey was — he was a person who happened to be there there and then, from out of a field of chances. And a sudden killing in self-defense followed their backs as, the last customers to file to the rear and turn right and crowd into the bathroom, she and Davey were followed in by the owner, who shook his head gently at her and the others and raised his palm — as if any of them were going to do anything.

The little bathroom was unexpectedly long. Davey's hair was up against her nose and she put her arm around in front of him across his stomach, and she turned to look into the eyes of a short, bald man, who instantly frowned and turned away from her toward the toilet end, where there was a small, half-open window. "Where does that lead to?" he asked importantly, but the owner, whom he did not look back at, continued to shake his head. The bald man said, "Excuse me," and edged between the others and reached around them to the toilet, leaning over it. "Anyone else want to leave your wallet behind the toilet?"

A dark woman in a dark turtleneck sweater, whose shoulder was against a dark man, also in a dark turtleneck, with such firm tightness that you knew if you followed their arms downward you would find them holding hands, said, "What if he wants your wallet — what are you going to give him?"

"I got ten bucks in my pocket," the man said.

"Ten bucks," said the woman. "Are you kidding?"

The waitress had not appeared. The owner was shaking his head, but now to himself. They were close together in the narrow, longish lavatory, yet exposed by the peculiarly high ceiling. Ann didn't count how many were crowded in here. Davey whispered huskily, so the others heard, "There are ten people in here."

The dark man in the dark turtleneck looked a bit scared. The blond woman, whose lacquered bouffant seemed to be in the wrong restaurant, had pursed her lips but she bent around and gave the bald man a kiss that just missed his mouth. The black man at the door turned on the basin faucet and turned it off. The two young men who were at the rear by the toilet and the window had given way for the bald man to stash his wallet. One of them now said, "Are your lunch receipts in that register?"

The owner hestitated. He seemed to have a clear sense of what was outside the room where they were. "There's always a first time," he said, and his accent gave a poignance to his words. "Well, it's too bad," said the other young man by the toilet. "It really is." His friend said, "My spinach quiche is getting colder by the minute," and the other said, "Remember Greece — they said you should never eat food piping hot."

Davey leaned the back of his head against his mother's shoulder and growled softly, "Where's my mousse?" He said to the owner, "Somebody ought to see what's happened to the waitress."

The owner opened the door and seemed to hear something and slipped out.

Ann hugged Davey. Her arm came around his stomach. "Did he say, 'Everyone into the bathroom'?" she asked, and she looked down at her bag, its flap covering the top but not fastened down through its leather loop.

"No," Davey said, "he said, 'Everyone get into the back into the bathroom' — that's what he said."

"I guess he doesn't want us," said the woman in the dark turtleneck.

"Beware of pickpockets," growled Davey in his mother's ear.

A terrific sadness descended upon her. The black man eased himself out the door.

"I don't think I want my mousse," said Davey.

"We'll ask for the check," Ann said. She put both hands on Davey's shoulders. *When this is all over,* she meant.

"Do you want your strawberry tart?" he asked.

The owner appeared and said the man had gone.

The man who had hidden his wallet asked one of the young men to pass it to him.

•

The restaurant, when they came out, seemed especially empty, because the waitress was at the far end by the window, sitting beside the pastry desserts, huddled in the chair, and the black man was comforting her. She was quietly hysterical; she was not quite sobbing. She looked as if she were waiting for someone. There were half-empty wineglasses and salad plates with forks across them and chairs pushed back. Someone said, "I wonder if he helped himself."

It had been over so soon that Ann couldn't think, except that with a pistol the young man could have made them go with him. Or killed someone just like that, so the person wouldn't be around to go through mug shots at the local precinct. She didn't know the address of the local precinct or what number precinct it was.

The waitress sat in the window crying. People were sitting down again. Ann told the owner she would have her coffee later. This sounded as if they were having hot dogs and beans in a diner. The check included the chocolate mousse and the strawberry tart. The owner subtracted the desserts.

The waitress stood up and smiled. Now it was the waitress Ann was paying; the owner was outside in the street. Davey looked up into the waitress's face. He didn't say anything.

"Are you all right?" said Ann as the waitress put down on the table the change from a twenty. "Have you ever been in a holdup before?"

The woman shook her head. She had shining blue eyes and rather curly brown hair, and she was tall and had delicate shoulders.

Davey said, "Our money is all that's in the cash register."

Ann, being a genial, alert parent in the waitress's presence, said, "Then where did she get the change from?"

"That's a good question."

"Have you seen him before?" Ann asked the waitress.

The waitress shook her head. "I hardly looked at him."

"I'd never forget him," said Davey.

Ann heard herself say, "He was wearing a turquoise belt buckle."

The waitress excused herself. Ann left two dollars and as they got up to leave Davey asked what percentage that was.

"Something over fifteen percent."

It was the very same restaurant, except that the owner, like a neighborhood Parisian, was standing out front, looking contemplatively down the street. A cab turned into the street and came very slowly by with a passenger looking out the window.

"Do you think he was dangerous?" Ann asked.

"Mom," said Davey, embarrassed.

"I think so," said the gray-haired man, his eyebrows raised.

"How much did he get?" asked Davey.

The man looked down at Davey and smiled and shook his head, but it didn't mean he didn't know.

"Are the police coming?" said Davey.

The owner gestured toward the street. "That's what they said."

When Ann and Davey said good night to the owner, the holdup was all his. At the next corner Ann looked back and he was gone. Some people seemed to be looking at the menu in the window.

"Why did you shush me when I asked if the man was dangerous?" Ann asked.

"Because of course he was dangerous. He had a gun."

"I think it was a knife."

"No, it was definitely a gun. I saw it."

"I don't see how."

"I was even closer than you."

"But they were still behind you, and when he pulled her out into the aisle his arm, his forearm, was turned around the way it would be if he had a knife handle in his palm."

"I know·I saw the metal of a gun."

"I'm sure you're wrong."

"I saw it."

"You saw something."

They crossed another avenue as the light changed in the middle. Ann took Davey's arm. He didn't crook it at the elbow.

"It's going to be a good weekend," said Ann.

They walked in silence.

"I got to call Michael and Alex," said Davey.

"You're going to see Alex tomorrow."

"I'm going to see them both tomorrow. I've got to tell them about the holdup."

"Listen, it was real, Davey, it was serious."

"You're not kidding it was serious," said her son. "We could have gotten killed."

"Well, I doubt that," she said, "but I was afraid he might reach for you, Davey, and he might have if the police had arrived." But it wasn't delayed-reaction fear that seemed now to be overtaking her.

"How could the police have arrived?" said Davey. "No one called them till after it was over."

"You know what I mean."

"This was my first holdup. I want to tell Michael and Alex about it, O.K.?"

"We're not even sure what happened."

"I know what I saw."

"In the bathroom?"

"In the restaurant."

"But before and after the holdup."

"*And* during."

"But we can't even agree whether it was a knife or a gun."

"*You* can't agree."

"Look, let's go back and ask the waitress."

"*Mom.*"

"Why don't we phone them when we get home?"

"That's fine with me. I don't know why you don't want me to phone my friends."

"It was *my* first holdup, too," she said, taking his hand and squeezing it.

But as soon as they got home she went and ran herself a bath. It was what she should have done in the first place this evening when she came home from work. She was so tired it had to be in her head. She stepped outside the bathroom and closed the door. The water pouring into the tub seemed larger at a distance.

She listened for a moment and went to the bedroom door. She knew Davey; she pictured him. She heard him open the refrigerator, and she was sure she heard the freezer door unstick. She did not hear the refrigerator door close, but she heard a plate rattle in the closet and a kitchen drawer open. He was looking for a spoon. She heard the voice of a baseball commentator come on, and a moment later she heard Davey's voice, talking fast and excited.

She was sitting in the tub, leaning forward to turn off the water. The door was open a little, so she heard the voices in the living room.

Davey called. She called back that she was in the bathtub.

The voices continued.

Then it was only the baseball commentator's voice, rising and falling. She let it stay where it was. Somewhere in the silence around that voice, an icepick was being hammered into a stolen, rock-hard avocado. The hot water was almost too hot to dream in. She'd had the money for that avocado but would rather shuttle herself by astral projection to Boston/San Francisco — not that anyone was there anymore.

She heard Davey's voice again; it didn't sound the same. It sounded as if he were phoning the movies for the times, but the call went on longer.

Then there was only the TV again, then a knock on the bathroom door, which moved, but Davey didn't come in. "You were wrong," he said. "It was a gun."

"Well what do you know," she said quietly from the still tub.

"No, I'm only kidding, Mom; they wouldn't tell me."

"You spoke to the waitress?"

"No, he wouldn't let me, and he said they weren't discussing the matter."

"O.K.," she said very quietly.

"Hey, don't go to sleep in there."

She thought she heard steps cross the carpet. In a moment she heard Davey on the phone again. Which friend would he have phoned first? The picture wasn't clear. He was closer to Michael; their lives had some big similarities, like his father not living with him.

The bath seemed to become deeper and deeper. Her legs came up in a revolving jackknife and she did a two and a half, a three and a half, an unheard-of four and a half, the way she would do slow-motion somersaults underwater at the deep end of a pool in the summer while Davey would hold his nose and do underwater somersaults with her, though he couldn't really stay down.

She didn't want to go to sleep in the bath, but she was damn well going to. If she'd taken a bath when she'd gotten home from the office, they would never have had a holdup. They would have had broccoli and melted cheese, and green noodles, with garlic (which Davey now liked). And strawberry ice cream, which he had just been eating anyway.

She might have been asleep when she heard Davey call from the middle distance, "Are you asleep in there, Mom? Are you O.K.?" But she felt she had had her eyes open. She didn't want to talk about the holdup, didn't want to think about it. She closed her eyes. The water didn't have quite the hot fixity it had when she first stepped cautiously in. But it was good to her and she let the questions called to her go unanswered. Her eyes were closed, but she wasn't sleeping. She heard Davey come across the carpet, and though she heard the door move, she didn't think he was looking at her. She felt the water stir subtly about her; she had willed it to move for her benefit. She knew he had gone away. She massaged her dry face, and her knees broke the surface.

She listened for a while. The TV was still on. She heard Davey's voice, its quality of inquiring esteem for the other person, its habit of waiting humor. For a second she thought of her son's, any kid's, inspired account of a brush with violence — *And then you know what happened?* — and she smelled in her soap, melting somewhere near her leg, a sweeter apricot smell of freesias. (They had tried to charge her six-fifty for a small bunch last week at the supposedly wholesale flower market.) Within the scent of freesias there was a hidden, earlier, heavier vein of sweetness that she now identified as after-shave but didn't want to think about. For some moments Davey hadn't been speaking, or not so she could hear, but the TV was still on, so he hadn't gone to bed. And yet the silence beyond the TV wasn't quite silence. He would be getting away from all the city noise this weekend. A lot *he* cared about the noise.

She got herself out of the tub, and against the wash of the bath-water listened again. She ran her arms damply into the sleeves of her terry-cloth robe. She pulled open the door and put her wet foot down on her bedroom carpet.

Have a nice evening, lady, the flower man had said. Have a nice life, he said. The pale-apricot-colored freesias were doing pretty well on her bureau. The man had let her have them for six dollars.

Halfway to the door leading to the living room, she was on the point of calling to Davey that it was time for bed, when she heard his voice. "I don't know whether I can," he was saying, and then there was a pause. "Maybe I'll ask her." Then, "I will ask her; I definitely will." Then, "She's O.K." Then, "Fifteen dollars, includ-ing my allowance." Then, "Yeah, I love you too." Ann knew the voice on the other end of the line without hearing it; but she owed Davey his privacy even after he said goodbye and hung up. The commercial between innings ended, and the deep-voiced, happy commentator was back on.

She stood in the living-room doorway. Davey was sitting over near the entrance to the front hall beside the phone. He could see the game only at the narrowest angle; he could hardly see the screen.

Ann went to the set and turned it off. "Time for bed," she said. Davey just sat there by the phone. They had divided the evening between them.

She had to give them both a break, so she said. "You didn't need to call collect." They both knew what she meant.

"How did you know I called collect?" Davey asked.

"I've known for a long time, but you really don't have to."

"Thanks," he said, and stayed where he was, still dressed for the restaurant.

She didn't tell him not to thank her. "You're welcome," she said.

"So are you," he said.

"So are you," she said.

ELIZABETH McGRATH

Fogbound in Avalon

(FROM THE NEW YORKER)

NEITHER LAUREL NOR I will ever be certifiable, I imagine, though, having put in, between us, going on a hundred years in this world, we have inevitably had a brush or two with the darker side of things. So this will not be a story of alienation. And to put your mind at rest, right from the beginning, we have never been in love with each other, in spite of having been reared in the most repressive of girls' schools from the ages of five to eighteen.

Laurel and I, middle-aged, neurotic, still thin, still suffering, still fascinated by the world and ourselves in it, are friends. We were born on this rock, Newfoundland, and are fixed in the cracks of it, through and beyond the sparse topsoil, in a way that makes us neither want to nor be able to free ourselves, ever. Laurel, except for holidays in Europe and the Caribbean and occasional forays into New York, has been here all her life. I, Anne-Marie, onetime academic — Presentation Convent, Collège Sophie-Barat, Memorial, Oxford — am another kettle of fish.

For about twenty years we circled each other, meeting once a year when I came back from wherever I had been, tentative, polite, mildly admiring of each other, gradually spilling a bean here and a bean there until so many beans had been spilled that there was no going back from it. And we found ourselves, not unhappily, in that giggling communion characteristic of the passionate friendships of thirteen and a half. What we don't know about each other now you could put in your eye. What is more, what she and I don't know about the others on this rock isn't worth knowing. When we put our heads together, and we frequently do, we can pool enough of everyone's tatty little secrets to blackmail all the professions,

including the oldest, the civil service, the clergy, and every House
of Assembly back to 1855.

Just about everybody here is related by blood, marriage, or sheer
tomfoolery to everybody else, and we all know our cousins to the
third and fourth degree. At the rate we reproduce, emigrate, wander the world, and keep in touch, there is no secret service that
can approach us. What may be called ESP elsewhere can be nailed
down here by genealogy, and we are all expert. Yesterday morning
Laurel was telling me that when they were five she and her twin
brother took the diapers off the minister's daughter to get a look
at what was so carefully concealed. In the afternoon I called her
and said, "Hey, remember Daphne Green?" "Remember her?"
said Laurel. "She's the one Leonard and I took the diapers off.
What in God's name made you ask about her?" "I've been hearing
little baby voices all day," I said, "whispering to me, '*Daphne Green,
Daphne Green.*'"

The truth is, I'd been warming a bench at Canada Manpower
most of the afternoon with one of the other rock-born overedu-
cated, bilingual unemployed and Daphne's name came up, the way
names do, because I'd asked who his wife was. All you need in this
town to get a reputation for extraordinary powers is a large acquaintance, a few elementary research skills, and coincidence.
Laurel, of course, being a thoroughgoing romantic, wants to believe in the spookies and so she does. I don't, but I like to cater to
her. My own reluctant rationalism is one of the things that keep
me from going mad, but I do break out from time to time.

Fern, Laurel's husband — surgeon, reliable backbencher, utterly devoted to her (christened, unfortunately, Ferdinand, because his mother was a great reader of the lesser works of Lord
Beaconsfield) — is the only one of us who can pass muster as a
healthy, well-integrated, well-adjusted dealer with life. If he
weren't there to remind us unremittingly of health, sanity, hard
work, and the old-fashioned values of the Church of England in
Canada, I don't know where we'd be. He and Laurel have lived
amid her storms and his calms for twenty years, and their daughters, both at college on the mainland, are beautiful and bright and
loving and a credit to them. Actually, all our children are pretty
good.

Though the men on this island are great talkers — never shutting up, as the rest of the country has cause to know — they don't

talk much about themselves to women. If they do talk to each other of how they feel, they certainly don't let on about it. As a charter member of the Status of Women Council I should, I suppose, hack away at that, but I don't and won't. I am concerned with what people do. What they think in the inner recesses of their own beings is their own damned business. Unless they are moved to tell me, I will never know, and it is better not to ask. It wasn't very long ago that my children's father, Con O'Neill, told me what was in his head, at my request. It took him four and a half days, at the end of which I prevailed upon him to buy me four plane tickets from Vancouver to St. John's. I then resigned from the only really good job I have ever had and launched myself back to the rock, the Public Service Commission, Canada Manpower, the vagaries of Memorial University, and a dilapidated three-story frame dwelling fifty yards from where I had been born forty-two years before.

•

Not five hours out of Vancouver, coincidence and further disaster overtook me in the person of Hugh Forbes, run into at Halifax Airport as I shepherded three dazed and baffled kids off one flight and onto another. Hugh, asking loudly, "Jesus, Annie, what have you got there, a traveling circus?" Hugh, whom I hadn't seen since the winter I was twenty-one, changed almost beyond recall but merging into himself, Cape Shore voice and all, as we talked on the two-seat side of the DC-9 and the kids slept, across the aisle, on the three-seat side.

I had braced myself for what had appeared to be only the first of many awkward but insignificant encounters with my past. After the usual stylized exchanges, I realized I had miscalculated.

"Going home on holiday, Annie?" asked Hugh.

"Not exactly," I said.

The feeling of being at a disadvantage with Hugh was familiar. Even the setting was eerily appropriate — Hugh and I, side by side in some vehicle, each wondering who would be the first to break the silence. I plunged in. "As a matter of fact, I am right this moment *leaving* home. I'm a bit punchy, so don't expect me to make too much sense."

"Annie, I don't remember your ever making too much sense. But I think I get the message. You blew it."

Lack of directness had never been one of Hugh's failings. I must have looked stricken, for he was immediately contrite and slightly embarrassed.

"Annie, I'm sorry. I didn't mean to be quite so blunt."

"It's all right," I said, making a face at him. "I find it reassuring that you haven't changed all that much."

He still looked embarrassed.

"Perhaps I'd better go sit somewhere else." He started to un-buckle his seat belt. "You'd probably rather not be bothered with me right now."

"Hugh, no," I said. "I'd like to talk. Please."

I looked at him. He seemed solid and friendly and, in spite of being annoyed with himself for his blunder, amused and curious. So I gave him fifteen minutes of the story of my life.

He listened without interrupting. As I talked, I watched his hands rebuckling the seat belt, unbuttoning his jacket, adjusting the tray, reaching for coffee from the stewardess, scratching his head, using a handkerchief, twisting his ring. Guilt and nostalgia flooded over me.

"Your hands," I said, "your arms, they're all right!"

He turned his palms upward, flexed his fingers, stretched his arms. "Yes," he said. "Good enough."

"How did you do it?"

"On hate, mostly."

There was a long silence. Nineteen fifty-nine had been the year of the last St. John's polio epidemic. Hugh, home from McGill, engineer's iron ring on his finger, job offer in his pocket, had found himself one August morning, after a weekend of pain and fever, flat on his back in the Fever Hospital with both arms immov-able.

"September," he said quietly, looking at me with a face devoid of expression. "All September I spent two hours a day watching my girl Annie making a public spectacle of herself on bloody tele-vision. I told myself that I was going to get my hand and arms back, if only to wring your neck. I hated and Ma prayed. It worked like a charm. By Christmas I was going to dances. My arms were in slings, but the fingers were good. By spring I had the slings off. After eighteen months I was able to work. After two years I was ready to pick a fight with Con O'Neill and break his jaw. After that I packed my bags and lit out for Ontario, all cured."

"None of it had anything to do with Con," I said.

"As I perceived it, it had a great deal to do with Con. And apart from everything else I was disgusted with your whole carry on."

"I was afraid of you," I said. "You scared me to death. All I could see was you beating around while I minded youngsters and forgot how to read and write."

"It wouldn't have been like that."

"Don't tell me," I said. "Anyway, what about my neck?"

"What?" He was momentarily puzzled.

"Do you want to wring it?"

"Hell, no, girl. I never wring ladies' necks when they're down and out. I kiss them instead. Better for everybody."

He leaned across and kissed me. The tears stung in my eyes.

"Oh my God, Annie, you're not still at that!"

"I always get tears in my eyes when in the grip of strong feeling," I said in my lecture-room voice.

He looked at me in amazed disbelief, then looked again and exploded into laughter. I could feel the hot blush climbing to my hairline.

"Dear Lord above! Every time I'd put my arm around you, you'd start to bawl. I though you were afraid for your virtue. Well, I'm damned."

I blinked, sniffed, and smiled at him. "Well, now you know," I said. "Better late than never."

Hugh smiled back. "Thanks, Annie."

Sweetest Mother, I thought, I love him. "Hugh," I said quietly, "I think we scuttled the ship."

"Yes," he said. "We sure as hell did."

He turned to look out the window, then adjusted his seat to the horizontal and closed his eyes.

"My son Gerald," he said. "My wife Clare."

Again there was silence. He readjusted his seat to the vertical and turned back to face me. "Gerald died one night when he was six months old. Crib death, they called it; no explanation, no one's guilt, they said. Still, Clare took to the bottle and after three years of it I took to the girls. And there we are. But we're still married and we're going to stay married. Make no mistake."

I said nothing. Hugh's forthrightness had left me stunned.

"One thing more, Annie. If you and I are going to be friends, you will never refer to any of it again. But I want you to keep it in mind."

He pointed a thumb across the aisle at the sleeping children. "What about them? Were you good at it?"

"Yes," I said, clutching at a subject I could at least talk about. "Like falling off a log. It's in the blood."

He looked at me speculatively. "I should have stuffed you full of babies and stuck you down with Mom on Cape St. Mary's. She'd have learned you the five sorrowful mysteries all right."

"I learned," I said,

"I don't know. Seems to me you could still use some toughening up."

He took my hand, called the stewardess, ordered a bottle of champagne, and told her we had just got engaged.

"Forbes," she said, "if you get engaged on my flight one more time, I will personally drown you in champagne."

The landing was the worst I have ever had, even in Torbay fog. Passengers I recognized as old hands showed in the rigid set of their shoulders what I myself felt — too much airspeed, the runway overshot, and a violent touchdown with too many rebounds off the tarmac. I was trying to remember if the runway ended at a cliff, a hill, or the woods, when we came to a shuddering stop. There was absolute quiet and then the captain's voice: "Ladies and gentlemen, as you may have noticed, we have just landed at St. John's."

A ripple of laughter ran through the aircraft and an audible communal sigh of relief. Hugh stood up, collected his briefcase and raincoat, and touched my shoulder with his free hand. "That time, Annie, it almost ended happily ever after." He smiled bleakly. "I'll call you."

I watched him as he headed up the aisle, and then I busied myself with the children. My sister Catherine met me in the crowded terminal. We went to Mother's, put the still groggy children to bed, took care of half a bottle of Captain Morgan, and turned in ourselves. The next morning I was going to have to turf my tenants out of my house on St. Columb's Street and start job hunting.

•

What happens when you bolt after sixteen years, four universities, three kids, the whole of Eng. Lit. read together, Paris, Florence, London, Oxford, Toronto, Lisbon, Washington, Vancouver, and hundreds of friends held in common? What I did was stash my books in Vancouver and go back home. I went because I wanted to do nothing else. I didn't want to face another city, another group of strangers. My ears hungered for the accents of the island. I wanted the smells and sights and sounds of St. John's Harbor, my father's grave, my mother's tenacious grip on life, old people I had known when they were young, middle-aged people I had known when they were children. I wanted my house on St. Columb's Street, groceries from Belbin's, gas from Fred and Eric Adams, vitamins from Stowe's Pharmacy, understanding from Laurel and Fern, and the children of my friends for my children. I wanted to terrify myself climbing up Barter's Hill in the sleet, to drive to Corner Brook and back in a night and a day, seeing if I could still evade the Mounties and not kill myself, to lie on the grass listening to the blessed silence in St. Mary's, and to breathe on the embers of old friendships and see if the flames would light my way out of the dark.

In spite of the encounter with Hugh, I was in good shape when I arrived. "Am I not the very picture of the wronged wife?" I said to Fern, and he laughed and hugged me and we all had a drink to celebrate. Five months later I had lost twenty-five pounds I could ill afford losing, my temper was unreliable, and I was still unemployed, but my children were happy and my house was looking less like a slum.

St. Columb's Street used to be solidly middle-class, occupied by people associated with the ships and stores of the port. My own house once belonged to a ship's chandler. Some of the others were built by captains and shipowners who lived here because of the incomparable view of the town and the harbor — every ship that comes and goes can be seen from my kitchen window. Now many of the bigger houses have become "multiple-family dwellings," the pretty, decrepit terraces are occupied by the poor, and some foreign entrepreneur has put up a yellow brick apartment house directly opposite me. The roadway is potholed, the sidewalks crumbling and cracked. Rough-looking teen-agers skylark and cat-call outside the corner stores, speaking a dialect that suggests a lengthy inheritance of infected adenoids and bad teeth.

But at the top of the street is the hospital where I was born; farther down is St. Columb's Church, which my grandmother's grandfather helped build; and beside it is St. Columb's Convent, which houses an elderly nun who taught me to read and write and made me, over six years, memorize the whole of Butler's *Catechism* and MacLaren and Campbell's *Grammar*. These are the things I think about on the days when I struggle with the idea that I do not really belong here. And, try as I may, I cannot see myself old, with my grandchildren visiting, in this house on St. Columb's Street. It makes me unbearably, unutterably, sad. The Heritage Foundation is interested in us now and determined to improve us. I am afraid I may have to move, along with the other poor, since I cannot afford to be improved any further. Sooner or later someone with the money to repair the roof flashings and the rotting window frames and the exterior paint and the leaking laundry room will make me an offer and I will have to accept it.

The house — my house for the moment — is a narrow, plain three-story with bow windows and a peaked roof. It must have been intended for a large family with no servants, for the kitchen is the biggest room and there is only one bathroom and no back stairs. Built the year that I was born, it just misses being good, even of its kind. I suppose the ship's chandler ran out of money, too. The house has that look. The exterior walls and the floors are sound and strong and draftproof; the fireplaces are pleasant thirties neoclassical; the doors are paneled and the windows big and generously framed. But the walls are surfaced with painted or papered fiberboard instead of plaster, and the wainscoting and the additions made over the years are ill-conceived and cheap, running to plywood and wood-grained Arborite and acoustic tile.

How I acquired the house at all is an earnest of the emotional myopia with which I am afflicted. My marriage to Con had gone through one of its intermittent crises following a move from Toronto to Vancouver. Con suggested that since we hadn't much capital, certainly not enough to buy a house in expensive Vancouver, it would be sensible to invest in a house in an older part of St. John's, live in it for a summer, and then rent it. Our children would then have a base of operations, a home that would exist in their minds wherever they happened to be in actuality. To me the proposal made perfect sense. I had never seen myself as an emigrant, merely a traveler. The idea of a home on the island appealed to me and I liked the implicit promise that we would eventually all return. When the break came, the house was there, with boxes of old toys and baby clothes in the attic, discarded prams and pushchairs in the cellar, clothes hooks with the children's names on them in the bathroom, and odds and ends of furniture from my own childhood home in the bedrooms and living room.

By then responsibility for the house, for keeping it insured and tenanted, had gradually devolved on me. I was mildly mystified but not displeased. I saw the process as being one with the independence I was gaining as the children grew older and I settled, once again, into a full-time job at the university. The years during which I had been, uncomfortably and resentfully, a financial dependent faded away and I assumed, along with the house on St. Columb's Street, responsibility for paying for almost everything to do with myself and the children, except keeping the Vancouver roof over our heads. Food, clothing, dentistry, toys, Christmas, birthdays came out of my income from my job. We had been setting the stage for years. When the curtain went up, I said my lines and made my moves. We all did, even the children. "We knew it was a matter of time," my daughter said. "We just didn't know when. We thought it wouldn't be so soon." Nor did I.

•

My first morning in St. John's, Laurel met me at Mother's and came with me to look at the house. All my tenants had been university students, so I assumed that not much housekeeping had been done. They had rented rooms to one another in a complex set of permutations that I had never tried to keep track of as long as they paid the rent punctually. Time and the salt air had worked their will on the exterior paint of the house, but it had been fairly shabby to begin with. When I opened the door, Laurel went rigid with shock. An effluvium of Victorian dimensions assaulted us. The hall was crammed with old boots and dust-laden cartons of empty beer bottles. The windows were opaque with dirt, and where the panes had been broken, on either side of the door, pieces of plastic had been stretched over them and secured with bits of rough lath nailed into the moldings. The walls and floors had not been washed since I had left. The carpets were stained and felted with dog hair. Filthy and half furnished, without curtains or pictures, with its paint scabby, its wallpaper peeling, and its plastic tile discolored, the house was tawdry. "You cannot propose to live in this," Laurel said flatly. But I could and I did.

The children, when I moved them in, wept over their shattered fantasies. I attacked what I could with bucket and mop, Glass Wax and cloth, crowbar and paintbrush. The children, after their initial distress, channeled their energies and their disappointment into working with me. They took apart the broken fences and cut them into kindling. They lugged out sheets of wallboard and plywood and eight-foot two-by-fours as my crowbar did its work. They carried mattresses and bedsteads down from the attic and up from the cellar. I had not realized how strong ten- and twelve-year-olds can be when they have a job they want to do. When a semblance of normality had been achieved, they just quit and concentrated once again on their private concerns — school, games, hobbies, squabbling, television, and eating.

They were puzzled by my evident lack of pleasure in just being alive, in having a house to live in and enough to eat and wear and them to love me. I overheard one saying, "Why is she unhappy?" and another answering, "Life gave her a raw deal." I felt ashamed of not being happier and tried to smile more, but they asked me why I had that funny look on my face. I opted for the truth, which they found odd but uninteresting.

The process of recovering the house was alternately uplifting and depressing. "I refuse to lie here and watch you seesaw," said my mother, but she did it nonetheless. When I had got one room fit for human habitation I persuaded her to stop for lunch on her way back from a visit to her doctor. "This is perfectly respectable," she said, on looking around my sitting room. "I fail to see what you are making such a fuss about." At that point, I found myself wanting not even to think about another tin of paint. I let the brushes dry and the children revert to their usual slovenly practices. I began, in spite of myself, to think of what it was going to mean to be on my own with no one to bitch at, no one to protect the kids from my habitual anxieties, no one to lean on, no one to sleep with, and, above all, no one to tell me, perhaps for the rest of my life, that I was essential to his breathing and being. Hugh? It was two months before Hugh turned up.

I was hammering palings into the front fence when a Land-Rover stopped at the curb and Hugh got out. I wanted to put my arms around him, but he had a very don't-touch-me look about him, so I just said it was good to see him and held on to my hammer for security. He said that he had just swung by to see how I was getting on and that I should write or call if there was anything he could do to help. I replied dryly that there were more accessible sources of help than his sweet self but that I would be glad to see him any time he got tired of doing whatever it was he did. He gave me his card, said he'd be back to share a dinner the following weekend, got into his Land-Rover, saluted, and drove off. I looked at the card and put it in my pocket. It had a Toronto address, and I thought how for seven years we had probably lived no more than fifteen blocks from each other in Don Mills.

I threw down the hammer and went into the house to make tea. I drank it too fast, burned my tongue, and fired the mug viciously against the fireplace, smashing it and splattering tea over the newly scrubbed hearthrug. The mug had had a motto painted on the side. Later, I fitted the bits together, and read, "A house is made of bricks and stone but a home is made of love alone." I put the pieces on the hearth and bashed them to powder with the poker.

Hugh then appeared out of nowhere every two or three weeks, only to disappear into nowhere again. It seemed he did something with fish and oil and airplanes for the federal government. That made for a connection with Fern and Laurel. Sometimes he arrived on my doorstep monumentally plastered, mirthful and bawdy, two quintals and a fathom of black-hearted, cod-fed bayman. Sometimes, rarely, he was sober and subtle, all civil servant and about as friendly as a cobra. I would hear his acquired Toronto accent overpowering the dental *t*'s and fog-soft vowels of the Cape Shore, and it served to remind me of what I would have preferred to forget.

I didn't ask questions of Hugh. He was there or he wasn't. He was sober or he wasn't. He loved me or he didn't. When he was drunk, I told him how beautiful he was and how I adored him. When he was sober, we talked politics and oil and mutual friends; I was careful not to show temper, and we tacitly avoided discussing how we felt. Either way, I was put into a state of elevation that sometimes lasted for days. The rest of my life the cats could have. But what was there to do? Making things happen was not my line. I watched, I listened, I cared. Nothing else was possible for me. I was through with moral imperatives: I care, therefore I am. I think, therefore I will make mistakes.

Though jobless, I was neither idle nor solitary. There was, if anything, too much to do, too many obligations, hordes of visiting children, and endless chores. I was ruthless about protecting my privacy, however, and my three hours of peace after the children were in bed and before midnight had overtaken me. I did not, except on very rare occasions, turn on television or stereo or take to drink. Except for smoking, I tried to do myself as little physical or spiritual harm as possible. Sometimes I even went to mass at St. Columb's, just in case. But I did, all the same, spend many days and nights in domestic squalor and intellectual tedium. I would go as much as six or eight weeks without balancing my checkbook, reading nothing but old copies of the *Atlantic* and the *Saturday Review*, washing the children's clothes in the bathwater and hanging them to dry on the bannister rails because I couldn't be bothered calling the repairman to fix the washer and dryer. I was sick to death of being bullied by ambition, concepts of efficiency, the demands of an academic conscience, fear at being out of work, or even my own convenience.

Laurel held Hugh responsible for my otherwise unaccountable behavior. I was a veteran of unrequited love, though, and surely familiar with its symptoms. I diagnosed, rather, some unease of the soul. Muddled and grubby, I read third-rate fiction and fourth-rate biography, thought fifth-rate thoughts, and felt sixth-rate emotions. And I was not at home on St. Columb's Street. I was, instead, like a bird on a bush, waiting for whatever would happen next so that I would know what to do.

I talked a lot to Laurel. We were on the phone for at least thirty minutes a day. She visited me only rarely, for both the house and the neighborhood were in a world she did not care to inhabit and they made her uneasy. More frequently I visited her, early in the morning after I left the children off at school. I entered her world more easily than she did mine. We would sit in her ordered living room (oh, the relief of it!), me in jeans and sweater, with untidy hair, she combed and brushed and tidily made up but in an ugly green fuzzy dressing gown, hands shaking from insomnia and cigarettes and not following the diet required by her mild diabetes. We would ask each other if we were, as people told us, eccentric or simply mad as hares. We considered our acquaintances and determined that by and large they were even more appalling than ourselves, apart from the few saints who were out of our league and therefore irrelevant to the discussion. We concluded that we did not want to be other than who we were. What we were was another question. We spent a scandalous amount of time talking it out. I talked about my past, my emotions, unemployment, the current state of my house, my mind, or my bank account. She talked about her depression, the causes of which had never emerged. I talked about my rages, the causes of which had been only too evident. We compared childhoods, holiday trips, attitudes, fantasies. I suggested that she got depressed because of hunger, perversity, boredom, and the indulgence of an excess of sensibility. She suggested that my malaise could be cured by Hugh. I told her that it was just as likely to be cured by the Atlantic Loto, the Riding of Placentia-St. Mary's, or the Henrietta Harvey Professorship. Even as I said it, I thought it was probably not true. But if I had lived my life as Hugh said I should have done, I should now be like Laurel and be hankering after the kind of life I had had and botched.

Laurel knows that everyone assumes that she is lazy and self-indulgent and ought to have a job to do. But I am aware of how scared she is and how her mind and energy are drained by fear, so that she stays in bed for days and weeks at a time. Her concern for Fern makes her come awake long enough to straighten the house and get the meals, and she always seems to deal with any emergencies, including the most trivial social ones. Her usual waking time, though, is between three and eight in the morning, when she reads, makes notes, writes letters and poems in her head that never see the light of day, thinks of killing herself, and tries to stop the shakes by force of will. Her will power is irresistible, and sooner or later anyone who has much to do with her will be made to dance to her tune. Though she has had virtually every psychogenic symptom known to medicine, she succeeds always in looking as healthy as a chestnut in blossom.

Once Laurel actually did swallow sleeping pills and then, in her wayward fashion, followed them with a tin of anchovies and was sick all over the kitchen. She cleaned up while Fern continued to sleep the sleep of the just. As she tells it, he had one of his rare fits of furious exasperation when she refused to get up and prepare his breakfast. There is no questioning that in Laurel's life the farcical element continually intrudes.

All the same, her headlong emotionalism may be one of the things that make Laurel a superb political wife. She and Fern attract a variegated tribe of friends, because he is true blue and she is beautiful and amusing and enormously sympathetic. Some of her enthusiasms have led to dinner parties that could bring the government down, and Fern has learned to keep a covert eye on their guest list. Because Laurel takes everyone at face value, she is the repository of a multitude of confidences, which frequently inspire her to quixotic action. One Saturday, early on, she dropped in at my house without calling first and encountered Hugh. Hugh will inflict his adventures on anyone he can pin down, but even when well oiled he tends to keep himself to himself. Laurel got more out of him in ten minutes than I had done in as many weeks.

After she had left, he turned to me indignantly and said, "Why do I tell Laurel all that stuff? I must be cracked."

"People do," I said, and shrugged. "They spend five minutes with her or get her when they've dialed a wrong number and she has their life stories, just like that."

"I suppose she knows enough of both of us now to write the book."

"No," I said. "But she has eyes in her head. And she loves me. She may try to help things along. I can't stop her, you know."

He made a particularly vulgar comment.

•

When Laurel gets upset and concerned about someone, she has the gall of a robber's horse. Last February, I had an especially trying couple of weeks, with frozen water pipes, an ill-functioning furnace, kids home from school with the flu, and three job interviews at which I had been told I was overqualified. I was tense and miserable and jumpy. I had been expecting Hugh and looking forward to seeing him, but he hadn't turned up. Laurel called to say that she and Fern had met Hugh at a government function the previous night and that he had been in great form. One of the crosses I was having to bear was being unable to prevent Laurel from reporting on Hugh's whereabouts. I heard her out and then I ventilated for an hour and used some fairly extravagant language, including a reference to slitting my wrists Roman style so that I wouldn't leave too much mess behind.

That evening Hugh was at my door. I had temporarily dismissed him from my mind and had been attempting to concentrate on sick, crotchety children and on the dirt and snow and oily handprints left by furnace men and plumbers. I needed a bath and was red-eyed and sleepless from nights of keeping coal fires going in the bedroom grates and was in no mood for dealing with Hugh's usual attitude of detached amusement at my ridiculous plight.

"Come in," I said. "If you can get in." A gust of icy wind accompanied him — and more snow. "Don't bother taking off your boots. The mess is past the point where I even care about it."

"You're all right, though?" he asked, looking at me warily.

"Sure," I said. "Dandy." I jammed my coal-blackened hands into the pockets of my jeans and leaned against the newel post.

"You look done in," he said.

"Beat to a rag. Want some coffee?"

"No, thanks. I just took a notion to stop by. I've got a meeting to get back to. You're sure you're all right?"

"Perfectly fine." I tried what I hoped was a cheerful grin. "I'm cold, I'm tired, I'm unemployed, and the house is falling down. Don't expect Pollyanna in this climate."

"Kids O.K.?"

"Sick as pigs," I said. "And crooked as sin."

"Anything I can do? You've only to ask."

"I know," I said, "I know. But there isn't anything, truly. I just need some sleep and a change in the weather."

"Don't overdo it, Annie." He put his hand under my chin and made me look at him. "Anything on your mind? You're sure you're all right?"

This sort of solicitude was unheard of from Hugh, who would normally only inquire about my state of being if he found me with my head under my arm like the ghost of Anne Boleyn. I had a sudden shattering glimmer of understanding.

"Have you seen Fern lately?" I hazarded.

"Not this trip," he replied blandly. "Too busy." He looked at his watch. "I'd better get back. Take care, Annie."

"Sure," I said. "Pray for a thaw."

As soon as I'd closed the door on Hugh, I called Laurel.

"What did you tell him, Laurel?" I said. "That I was about to hang myself in my garters because he done me wrong?"

"An-nie, you puz-zle me," she said in her most nervous and distinct Bishop Spencer College accents.

"And you are a damned liar," I said.

"You know I ne-ver tell an untruth, An-nie."

"Laurel," I said, "I can tell when you're lying within five syllables. I'll see you in the morning if I don't die of shame first." I hung up.

After another night of sleeplessness, half a bottle of Irish whis-

key, and a packet of lethal American cigarettes from our all-night
pizza parlor, I went to Laurel's to tell her to get off my case. It
wasn't easy. In twenty years we had never had a serious difference.
With the help of a couple of pints of Strongbow, I managed to
enlighten her on the enormity of what she had done. By lunch-
time, when Fern got home, I was wandering the house barefoot,
hugging the cider mug and humming a dirty song that I'd learned
from Hugh when I was a freshman. Fern patted me on the head,
said it must be great to have nothing to do, and went back to the
hospital to see someone whose legs were in traction. Laurel took
her telling-off far better than I dealt it out, and promised never to
interfere again.

Then she asked me how my life was going and how I thought it
would all work out. I turned the question back to her, and she said
she should never have thrown up the pills. I said that perhaps she
and Hugh would be killed in a car crash when they wickedly, and
in heedless contravention of all the ground rules of friendship,
slipped off to Clarenville for a weekend, leaving me and Fern,
given a decent interval of mourning, to console each other. Her
eyes widened and she laughed with delight.

"An-nie, you are naugh-ty," she said. "How per-fect!" And I
knew I had not been all that far from the truth.

"It won't work," I said. "It's a horrible cliché."

"No, no," she said, and laughed again. "I can't wait to tell Fern."

What actually did occur was one night in early spring, having
read myself into a stupor, fully clothed in my bed, along with dirty
ashtrays, my accounts and calculator, carbons of job applications,
the phone, an alarm clock, unanswered letters, unsent Christmas
cards, *The Oxford Book of Oxford,* unread, *The Pauper's Cook Book,*
and an illustrated essay on the paintings of Edvard Munch, I fell
asleep smoking a cigarette and woke at dawn to find that I had
burned a hole through two carbons, a book bill from Blackwell's,
and my only pair of sheets.

For some minutes I stared at the burn without moving, then I
headed for the bathroom. My hands were shaking and my eyes
were large and dark and frightened. My impulse was to wrap
myself in a blanket, crawl back into bed, and go to sleep — deeply,
deeply to sleep — when one of the children knocked at the door
and asked the time. I snapped to attention, cleaned out the sink,
called the others, and went downstairs. I made an unusually big

breakfast and insisted that it be eaten. After I had taken the children to school, I returned home, washed the dishes, then gathered up all the loose papers I could find — the year's small collection of books and the 1669 Donne I had brought in my pocket from Vancouver. I put them in the ashcan, and carried it out to the sidewalk. I washed my hair, had a bath, and dressed in a silk shirt and a suit. I called my mother's cleaning woman and arranged for three days of her time. As I left the house again, the phone rang, and while I stood in the doorway, not answering it, I saw that the ashmen had been and gone. I got into the car and drove slowly down St. Columb's Street.

The fog was coming in through the Narrows, but the sun was still shining and the town and the harbor were brilliant with color and beautiful beyond the reaches of fantasy. My throat hurt and I could hardly see. I thought about my grandmother's grandfather leaning out over the unfinished walls of St. Columb's, watching the arrival of the White Fleet. I thought about Sister Columba in her convent and about the day I was born in the hospital at the top of the street. I thought about Hugh and Laurel and Fern and the Heritage Foundation. My heart was breaking, for I knew inescapably that I had already, once again, set out on my travels.

AMELIA MOSELEY

The Mountains
Where Cithaeron Is

(FROM THE MASSACHUSETTS REVIEW)

Of the women who plan to have children, 10% said they plan to give birth to a girl. Of those, 23% said they plan to give birth to more than one.
— New York Times, *September 1982*

Before this, in dreams too, as well as oracles, many a man has lain with his own mother. But he to whom such things are nothing bears his life most easily. — Sophocles, *c. 425 B.C.*

I CAN'T BELIEVE Dion is dead though I saw him buried three days ago. An impossible accident — his legs and arms mangled, his beautiful chest crushed — it could not have happened. Yet I am beginning to believe it. Only a moment ago I thought to tell him about something terrible that happened to us, and he is not here. So I opened this book, this empty farmer's diary for the year we were married (fifteen years ago; is it possible?), a duplicate wedding present. Doubly hideous. Blank paper instead of Dion.

Of my husbands, he is the one I could talk to, and that is what I will miss most. But I will not stop to cry. He is with his last Mother now and someday . . . Phooey, I'll leave that to the preachers.

It is not that I loved him most. A mother can love all equally, and I have. But he was the first, and that counts for something. And the oldest, which is why, I suppose, we could talk almost as friends. But it should not have happened! A mother should be spared this. He should have outlived me. He should have.

I whine like a child. Yes, it's bad luck, but I've had good luck too. How few are chosen to have a daughter, yet I was. And for my first natural child. I can thank God I have a healthy daughter in school, studying to learn the care of a family of her own. I should think forward to next winter when I can go and visit her and see my old friends and teachers and hear someone call me by my name instead of mama, mama all the time.

I maunder. The wind has come up early this afternoon, the summer wind come early. I'll walk through the vines, then work in the garden a while. And I can do it alone. This is the first time in how many years I can say that? Is it unmaternal of me to say I should enjoy it while I have the chance? God knows when it will happen again.

Mahon was even more upset than I, and left after the burial. I could not comfort him. Even when he wasn't blubbering, he couldn't speak. Ah, he's always been a crybaby. I can see him looking at me across the grave with tears in his eyes, almost as if he blamed me for Dion's death. But men are foolish. They think because we are the source of life, we are also the source of death.

Still, Mahon is a good boy. Both times when I couldn't bear to take the little ones out of my body to their real mothers (It was very stupid of me, I admit) he went with them instead, and saw them settled and came back and told me everything. Well, he's always liked to travel; but, unlike Yakos, he's always back for the First of the Month.

And what of Yakos? We haven't heard from him since he left after harvest. Yet I have the feeling he will come home before this harvest. I do long to get my arms around him and to hear his stories. But not now. Right now, all I want is a couple of weeks to myself.

I had closed this book, but open it again to say one more thing. Though my spirits are low, by the laws of the perversity of fate, my health has not been so good in weeks. Just when I would expect to lie awake tossing and turning, I find myself sleeping like a well-fed baby. The indigestion, the racing heart, have been gone for two nights.

•

I have indulged my grief like a pig rolling in the dust. But finally, what I hated a week ago — the smooth hills beginning to show

their tan, the new shoots poking bravely from the stick that will be
vines — these begin to give me comfort.

And my strength, despite me, is improving daily. Yesterday at
sunset, after a full day on the Combination, I walked the entire
circumference of my land. It reminded me of the year I moved
here, bringing Dion from the Valley because he hated the heat so
much. I was pregnant with Maria and we walked every evening.
He was still shorter than I then, with only a few soft hairs on his
lip.

Later that year, before Maria was born, I took Mahon from his
natural mother, and the three of us would take walks. Mahon
would dawdle and complain, then suddenly dart ahead and run
up the hill and run back. He ended by going the whole distance
twice.

In my memory, every evening that year was like last night —
warm, still, the pale orange and pink of the sunset covering the
sky, seeming to last forever, making us lose awareness of everything else. How self-satisfied I felt, only three years out of school
and surveying my own land. (It's a good thing I didn't know then
what I know now of mortgages.)

•

I've had my two weeks and more, and now I'm beginning to get
restless. I dream about Dion. Too much. But I want Mahon. I
want my child's arms around me and it is Mahon I want. And since
he is not here, I begin to imagine horrible things happening to
him, like Dion.

There is yet another thing I don't want to think about. Even
when Yakos comes back, I can't run this place with only the two of
them. And — horrible words — it will take two to replace Dion.
Well, I will think about that when Mahon comes home, and talk
about it then. It may be he knows of someone. It is always better if
they are friends.

These dreams about Dion, they're not right. That is, they don't
come out right. Last night I dreamt of our first summer, in the
Valley when it was just the two of us and I was learning to be a
farmer. We had an apprentice's cabin, a tiny one-room beehive, in
the middle of the fields. Every day I would go out and drive the
tractor. The children there worked in the fields, but it was early in
the season and Dion didn't have enough to do. I remember he
used to get bored.

Every night I came home tired and hot, but bursting with this new theory or that news. Dion always had something good ready to eat, and we would eat and talk and make each other comfortable and go to sleep. At least Dion would go to sleep. Usually I would stay up and make a few notes in my new almanac, make plans about having a place of my own, and wonder whether I would be better off with grain or livestock or what.

In the dream I came home as usual and we ate and went to bed. We looked very young, which I suppose we were. But I looked younger than I have ever imagined looking and, in the course of the dream, Dion grew older, older then he was a month ago. And the atmosphere of the hut was different, smaller than it ever seemed in real life and darker, very closed. And instead of Dion's going to sleep and my staying awake, I fell asleep and he got up and walked around the room, paced it and began nervously handling the forks and spoons, picking them up and putting them down again. I could see him, almost transparent but with clear outlines, through my sleep, and I wanted to tell him to stop, but I couldn't wake up. By this time he was a large, pot-bellied, sinister-looking old man, such as I have never seen. When I finally managed, after great struggle, to wake up, I woke up really.

All of the dreams, at least the ones I remember, are like this. They begin from something pleasant, then go off, not to terror, but to something bad tasting.

I need to go to town to buy supplies. We're out of rice, and low on beans and flour. It wouldn't hurt me to have some company either. But I don't want to be gone in case Mahon arrives. It always upsets them to come home to an empty house.

•

Mahon came home around noon today, just as I was coming in from the north circle. How strange he looked at me! All at once I noticed changes in him that probably took place years ago, how thick his chest has become, how his neck is no longer too long for his body. And he had his hair cut, which I think he did just to spite me because he knows I love it long.

We flew to each other and, wrapping ourselves around each other, we laughed and fell to the ground in front of the house. And, being Mahon, his eyes filled with tears even as he was unbuttoning my shirt. Why does he cry? Joy at being home? Sorrow at Dion's death? Misery at this place reminding him of Dion? Probably it's all mixed up in him. Well, it's good for men to cry. I kissed his tears and did what you do to stop them.

Afterwards, I brushed the back of his head above the neck with my fingers. His hair is so soft and thick, it feels only a little prickly, like fur, even cropped.

"Your hair looks terrible."

"*My* hair?" He was very indignant. "Look at yourself." He ran his fingers through my hair, which I admit had a few tangles. "You haven't combed it since I left."

"What difference does it make?"

"When I was in The City, there were mothers wearing their hair down to here." He placed the edge of his hand in the small of my back.

"Huh. Rich ones with children who have nothing to do but brush their hair."

"Do you think we could spare the time to brush it once a month?"

He got up to get the hairbrush and came to the door again in a few minutes. "Where's the hairbrush? It's not in your bedroom."

For a moment we were both reminded that Dion wasn't here to pick up after us, then I went in to help look for it. It turned up, for some reason, in the living room, under Mahon's mattress, which neither of us had bothered to put away. Dion's is still rolled up and tied neatly against the wall, just as he left it.

We sat quietly on the mattress while he concentrated on getting out the worst tangles. He made the part, and then I felt a little prick. He hooted and dangled a white hair in front of my face.

"My mother is becoming venerable."

"Twit! I'm venerable no matter what the color of my hair."

He kept brushing and, I have to admit, it was very soothing.

"Why don't you let your hair grow?" he said. "Dion adored it long. Do it for him."

I turned and spoke, too sharply perhaps. "Dion is with another mother now. I don't have to worry about him any more."

He turned his face away, but I took his chin and turned it back so he couldn't avoid my eye. More gently, I hope, I said, "But if you want me to grow my hair, I will."

For an instant his eyes showed . . . what? Disbelief, fear, pain. Only for an instant, because I pinched his nose and said, "Providing, of course, you let yours grow."

He smiled. "Agreed." But the smile faded in a moment. "He's gone, then."

"Yes. We loved him and he's dead."

But still he looks troubled. He's not free of it yet, not free as I am, and I was his mother.

•

We had our First of the Month, just the two of us. It was very strange and quiet. No little ones looking on, no Yakos, no Dion. We drank less than usual (a benefit, no headache the next day), but we omitted nothing, shortened nothing, and made each other happy.

I let him sleep in my bed with me. With just the two of us, it seems silly not to. We are both still having bad dreams and it's good when you wake up to grab a body instead of a shadow. His dreams are worse and more frequent than mine, but fade faster; I've become so used to his moaning I no longer wake up. In the morning I can tell he's wakened when I find his arms around me and his lips against my breast. As for me, I'm not so kind. I wake him up, but in a way he does not mind.

During the day he's doing well enough, except for using every excuse not to do any tractor work. It finally came to me that he's avoiding the Combination, so I haven't made an issue of it.

As for the rest, little by little I get the news from his trip. What do I care what they're wearing in The City or about so-and-so's new tractor? His first news, about the little ones out of my body, was the best. He went all the way around the Bay and saw them each at their real mother's. They are well. I knew they would be; their mothers are good. I would not have let them go to any other kind. Still I can't help thinking about them.

Mahon says, "You think about them too much because there's no one here to replace them." I know that too, but I was not willing to say so, not so soon. But he has stopped being subtle.

We're working too hard and the work is getting ahead of us anyway. We had to take our dinner to the far circle today because we couldn't take time to come to the house at noon.

"When are you going to get me a brother?" Mahon asked, chewing his beans, "Preferably one who can cook. These beans are awful."

"What's wrong with them? I think they're delicious." (They were awful, but he cooked them. What could I say?)

"You're avoiding the issue," he said sternly, shaking his spoon at me like a mother. He made me smile, imitating me without realizing it. "We could use two more around here, three if they are very young."

"Huh. You just want some friends to play with on the mattresses."

"Mama, that is very cheap. Tell me, who wouldn't rather have his mother all to himself? Do I say this for my own good? No, for yours. Two can't work a farm. Two is no family."

And, to tell the truth, two get bored with each other. Well, he is right. This is my plan: I will go to the County Council and get one of the motherless ones there, a grown-up widower. No more straight from their natural mother! I have taken Dion, Mahon, and Yakos and they are paid for with the three from my body. That's enough. No more little ones for me. I couldn't bear it. And besides they would be of no use with the harvest.

·

A month has passed since I recorded that excellent plan and every day I find myself with an excuse not to go. Yesterday I promised myself (and Mahon) I would do it before the First of the Month.

·

In two days it will be the First of the Month. I have delayed as long as I can. Tomorrow is the last day I can keep my promise and I'm as ready as I'll ever be. After supper we checked and cleaned the car and Mahon washed my hair. I'm leaving him at home to clean house. With luck, I'll get my business done early, do some shopping, and be home by midafternoon in time to show the new one around before supper.

·

Dear God, where do I begin? What can I say? One has only to make a firm resolution to have it instantly thwarted by fate.

I got a good early start in the morning, with the result that I had to stand around for God knows how long until the office opened. When they finally let me in, it was into a huge room, completely carpeted, impossibly clean, with no furniture but a long table in the far corner where the councillor sat. I went and lowered myself across from her at the table. The carpet under us was a deep maroon, springy, and soft as Mahon's hair after a cut.

The councillor was a pudgy woman wearing a green, figured silk kimono rather like the red one Mahon brought me from The

City. Her hair was as neat as her desk. She took one look at my work clothes — she had no reason to be snitty, they were perfectly clean — and said good morning rather coolly. I resisted the urge to answer good afternoon, and simply stated my business.

As I spoke, her expression went from cool to interested to warm, and by the time I finished, she was in an ecstasy. She clasped her hands and looked to heaven, in this case an immaculately white plaster ceiling.

"Oh, Our Mother provides for Her own. I knew I would have them in their new home by the next First of the Month."

Then she shifted her gaze to me. "You are in luck. I have three perfectly lovely children. Orphans. Their real mother died nearly two months ago and they've been languishing, absolutely languishing here, ever since."

"Good. I'll take the oldest and be on my way."

"Oh my dear, they couldn't possibly be separated. Not after the shock they've had. The oldest," she put her hand up to forestall me, "who would have been much too old for you in any case, is already gone. And the third oldest," she paused and looked out into the distance, "met with an unfortunate accident."

She lowered her voice and spoke behind her hand. "Mangled to death in the fields by one of those new Combination Tractor-Harvesters."

For a moment I didn't take in what she said, it was only more of her chatter. Then all I wanted was to get out of there. Can anyone imagine how I felt? To think that his death was the fault of the equipment.

I started to get up and said as casually as I was able, "Well, if they're little ones, they won't do for me."

"No, no." She made as if to push me back. "They're fully grown." Then honesty got the better of her. "Well, the youngest is a little little."

Next, taking advantage of my mental immobility, she got up and went to the wall, which turned out to be a bank of files. She wrapped her sleeves out of the way, soon found my records, and looked them over. She then eyed me with surprise that turned to accusation.

"You have only two at home now." I didn't bother to tell her Yakos was away. "You can easily handle three more. Look at me, I have twelve. And you know very well, that for every one . . ."

Why go on? The upshot is that I went to see her orphans and brought them back to the office to register the marriages. All of us except the councillor were in shock. She exceeded herself in ecstasy and rained kisses and blessings on us all until I said I'd like to get home before dark.

"Well, well, I suppose so. There are just a few more details."

I sent the two older ones to get their things together and kept the little one with me while I attended to the few more details.

The councillor licked her fingers and started shuffling through papers, shaking her head.

"My dear, you have six husbands now and only two children out of yourself. You're in arrears by four, plus you, that's five. And you're thirty-five. You've got to get busy."

"Wait a minute. In the first place, I have three out of myself; one's a girl."

She looked at me with new respect that lasted only a second. She continued to shuffle through the papers. Daughters, it seems, are recorded on another sheet. She confirmed it, then looked up.

"Well, still . . ."

I interrupted. "In the second place, the three I took today are already paid for by their first real mother."

She reached for more files, handy on the table, and started shuffling some more. "Hm. The two older ones are, but not the little one, Shuzo."

To make a long story short, she wanted me to hand in my pills and I began to get angry. Before long, she was shouting.

"Look," I said, a little loudly perhaps, "first you force this baby on me, then you want me to have another to pay for him."

"He is not a baby." She slapped the papers in front of her. "He's been away from his natural mother for four years."

"Really! Then she must have thrown him out of his cradle." I flung my arm around toward the little one, who was sitting against the wall with his knees up to his chest. "He's been there for hours. Have you seen him take his thumb out of his mouth yet?"

When we turned to look, he rolled his brown eyes towards us, looking over his thumb. We suddenly realized he'd overheard everything and turned back chagrined.

"He does seem small for his age," she mumbled. "Maybe you should wait until New Year."

"New Year!" I whispered back hoarsely. "I'm a farmer, not a sow. It'll take me four years to get this one on his feet."

"That's absurd!"

To make a long story short, I managed to get a full year from her, and then I can renegotiate.

It was nearly suppertime when we got out of there and the children still hadn't had any dinner. So we had to eat, then shop for supplies, then get some pants for the little one because he's outgrown his, even though it seems impossible he was ever any smaller.

And the little one would wander away. Not far, but out of sight so we worried and had to look for him. They call him Shu-shu-shu-shu-shu, the way you call the cat.

I must say the two older ones were helpful, especially the oldest, Claire. I liked him right away. He's older than Dion was, though younger than I, and already has a bald patch in his black hair. He's thin, the kind you can't fatten up, and wears glasses. His habitual expression looks worried because he has frown lines above his nose.

He doesn't say much, but what he says is pleasant and to the point. And if something funny happens or Florio says something especially good, he smiles at me very sweetly and doesn't mind catching my eye. Then his whole face relaxes and you realize how pretty a blue his eyes are.

Florio is the other one. He is Mahon's age and a witty one. I don't know if what he says is so funny, but he has a dry way of talking that makes anything he says sound humorous. You would probably laugh if he came and told you the house was burning down.

He is shorter than Mahon, but still taller than I, well built on a small scale. He has curly hair that he frequently arranges, not because it ever needs it, but as punctuation to his stories. Like Mahon he is up on the styles, but unlike Mahon he seems to remain tidy with no effort. His shirt stays tucked in, his pants don't wrinkle, and even though he's wearing the same sort of things as his brothers, he seems more expensively dressed.

He took an intelligent interest in Shuzo's new pants, turned them inside out, looked appalled at what he saw, snorted at the child behind the counter, and talked me into buying two pairs of the ones that finally satisfied him. When I thought to buy three,

he advised against it, saying there were two pairs in their boxes
that could be cut off for shorts, and by fall he would need larger
and heavier ones.

But when he is tense or tired he begins to babble. At the Council
he filled every silence with a smart remark, and when we drove
home in the dark he sat forward in the back seat, surrounded by
boxes and bundles, and delivered a monologue.

From all his talk I gathered that his mother suffered a long, slow
illness, poor woman, and died around the same time as Dion. Her
third — the one who was killed by the Combination — died shortly
after. She was that Flora whose farthest circles just touched mine
for a short arc at the north boundary. Our children evidently knew
each other because Florio asked after Mahon and had a few cheerful words to say about Dion. The subject of how he died was
somehow avoided.

All this time, Claire sat in front by the window with his arm
around the sleeping Shuzo between us. Every time I slowed down,
he craned his neck forward and tilted his head up to peer through
the bottom of his glasses and through the windshield, hoping, I
suppose, by his vigilance, to keep me from running off the road.
Each time he leaned forward he half-wakened Shuzo who would
squeeze his eyes tighter, put his thumb in his mouth, and try to
make himself comfortable on his brother's swaying chest. The
emergency over, Claire would lean back again and the little one
fall deeper into sleep, letting his thumb slip out of his mouth.
Then Claire would smile at me sideways, shyly, and add a word or
two to Florio's narrative.

I attended to all this with part of my mind; with another part I
drove and worried about Mahon, wondered if he'd had the sense
to go ahead and eat, wondered how they would get along, and on,
and on. I got more and more tired and began to imagine, trance-
like, I was doomed forever to drive on a dark country road in a
car with a broken heater, always pushing something hateful to the
back of my mind having to do with faulty machinery and mangled
children.

When we finally got to the house, I honked to break the spell.
Immediately the front light went on; Florio and Claire jumped out
of the car and started collecting boxes to take in. I left them to it
and guided the little one in. His face looked pale and sickly and he
was still asleep though his eyes were wide open.

Mahon and Florio recognized each other, but avoided meeting

each other's eyes. This was but an instant's play, for everything was suddenly confusion, with the older ones running in and out with boxes and groceries and unpacking without knowing where things should be put. Claire won my immediate approval by quietly putting the kitchen things away without asking about every single item.

We were all sick with fatigue, stumbling, and barely coherent. Finally I told them to finish the rest in the morning. I introduced them properly, had them kiss each other, and sent them to bed. Then I, exhausted, had a cup of tea, went to my room, and closed the door.

This morning, of course, we slept late. Then they had to finish unpacking and I showed them around. Between that and knocking off at noon for the First of the Month, we've done no work at all today. Still, after tonight there should be less awkwardness among us.

All in all I am optimistic. The older ones, at least, are strong and healthy and used to farm work. And the little one is not really sickly, just dazed from all that's happened in the last two months. He is older than he looks, about the same age as Dion when I took him. In the sunlight you can see fair hairs sticking out from his face and for all I know — he's said next to nothing to me — his voice is breaking.

Right now, I'm at my desk. Through the bedroom door I can see him and Florio on a mat in the living room. Florio is on his knees combing the little one's hair for tonight. The little one sits with his legs sprawled in front of him, his back rounded, one hand supporting the elbow of the arm whose thumb is in his mouth. Without removing the thumb he sputters complaints about the job done on his hair. If I were Florio I would have shaved the little snit's head by now. But Florio, I think, takes a disinterested, aesthetic pleasure in that hair. I'm glad he does. The little one is very sweet-looking with his fair ringlets all around his head like a halo.

Florio confines himself to whacking him on the head from time to time with the comb. It's hard to blame him, but I don't like to see it. I'm afraid they've spoiled him while their mother was ill and I'll have a great deal to undo. For now, I say nothing. I'll wait until after tonight.

No bad dreams last night.

•

232 The Mountains Where Cithaeron Is

Our First of the Month went better than I expected, with little awkwardness. Shuzo came to me first; I got him to take his thumb out of his mouth to kiss me and he even smiled. The excitement and wine sent him to sleep early. The other three conspired to make me (as well as themselves) drunk and happy and very comfortable.

That was six days ago and I haven't been troubled by bad dreams since. I wish I could say the same for Mahon and Florio. Mahon, I think, is still upset about Dion, but it's hard to tell exactly what's bothering him. What he says in his sleep is incomprehensible. Florio occasionally moans the names of his mother Flora and someone called Mento, presumably his dead brother Clement.

I must say my sympathy is running out. At different times during the night they each come crawling into bed with me, never failing to wake me. Sometimes one has the consideration to leave, which also wakes me up. Two night ago I got so disgusted I kicked them and threw them both out. Last night even that failed. They were so fast asleep I ended by giving up and sleeping the rest of the night on the floor. Still their sleep is badly broken and they are both edgy from it.

Shuzo and Claire, thank God, sleep like well-fed babies. And Claire, the sweet one, turns out to be a model child. He's a good worker on the hills, but his heart is in the living room with the stove, the pots and pans, orderly cupboards, and meals served on time. In the same way Florio babbles when there is unease, and Mahon weeps, Claire turns to tidying the drawers, scrubbing the table, and concocting ever more elaborate breads and stews. I have never eaten better in my life. It's a pity it's at the cost of Claire's peace of mind.

For there is unease in this house. And Shuzo is at the heart of it. In the space of five days, he's turned into an impossible brat. This morning he woke everyone before dawn by whooping and screaming into my bedroom and jumping on the bed. He ripped the blankets off the huddled Mahon and Florio, and then fell off the bed and onto me. When I pushed him away, he ran back to Claire, who was still groping for his glasses, and started to pummel him.

Once he had us all up, stumbling into each other and cursing him, he went back to his own mat, stuck his thumb into his mouth, covered his head with blankets, and refused to budge even when Claire called him for breakfast.

When we were ready to go out — Mahon and Claire had washed

up and Florio was out getting things together — he finally decided to get up. Knocking over everything in his path, he fixed himself some jelly and bread, and ran outside, not neglecting to leave out the knife, bread, crumbs, and jelly smeared around. I didn't ask what he did outdoors, but it must have been very bad, for the next thing we knew, he came running back into the house chased by Florio, who was shouting, "I'm going to break the little shit's head!"

In a moment they were all shouting at him, including Claire whom he was trying to hide behind. At that, I got very angry. I told them all to leave the house and followed them out, leaving Shuzo to stamp and cry by himself.

Honestly, I don't know which of them is more exasperating, the little one or the older ones who egg him on. Mahon, I flatter myself, has not acted as badly as the other two. Their mother must have been a very poor disciplinarian. Well, it's hard to blame her, poor woman, she was ill for so long.

I all but pushed them out the door to where we couldn't hear Shuzo.

"You are spoiling him by yelling and whacking and I won't have it!"

Shower of protestations and complaints. I cut the air with my hand to stop it.

"I don't care. If he irritates you, walk away from him. If it's very bad, come to me and I'll deal with it."

Oh, he always does this, he always does that, he always does the other. As if I didn't know. Still, if I tell them to come to me with their complaints, presumably I have to listen to them. I listened as long as I could, then sent them to work, promising to keep Shuzo out of their hair for the morning. Poor children. No wonder they were grumpy. It was still dark.

I stayed away from the house and went around to work in the garden. When I went in, a few hours later, Shuzo had cleaned up the jelly and bread, and was rolling up his mat. He ignored me while I fixed myself a cup of tea and watched him. When he finished the job, I went to him and told him how happy it made me, and took off both our shirts and gave him a big hug. At first he accepted it, then he pulled away and socked me in the stomach. Fairly calmly, I walked away to my room, saying nothing, and closed the door (avoiding, I hope, the twin dangers of laughing or appearing hurt).

Since then I've been sitting here writing, mostly catching up with the records.

He's still in the living room muttering to himself and kicking things. When he stops I'll go out and lie down with him for a while. The poor child doesn't trust me yet. Does he imagine I'm going to die on him too? Or does he see her cold body still and resent it that I'm warm and moving? I must win him or, in a year or so, one of his punches may truly hurt me, and then one of his brothers really will break his head. Well, little by little.

I don't remember ever having this trouble with the others. Ah, maybe a little with Dion and Mahon. With Dion it was understandable. His natural mother kept him too long and spoiled him. Mahon was easier because I took him very young.

But Yakos, Yakos was always an angel. Last night, while I was asleep on the floor, I dreamt I was lying with him. I suppose that means I want him and he is thinking of coming home. God knows I do want him, but at the same time I pray he doesn't come back until we are more settled here.

•

It's just as well we got an early start this morning. It was so hot by noon, I had them stay in after dinner and nap. We went out afterwards and worked till dark. Right now they're in there giggling and playing cards. From what I can tell, Claire has won all their money and is now acquiring credits in the form of chores.

As for me, I've been sitting here at my desk trying to decide what to do about the Combination. I've checked it from end to end and I can find absolutely nothing wrong with it. If it weren't that the same horrible accident happened twice, I would assume it was a fluke. As it is, I don't dare let the children use it, and if I make a move toward using it myself, they get very upset. There's a flaw in the design somewhere, but it's certainly not obvious.

I have a good case for a full refund. But where am I going to find another harvester at this time of year? Damn! I wish now I'd kept the old one instead of trading it in. Even if I have it repaired, it will take weeks, not to mention the time getting it there and back. The damned thing is impossible on the road. Getting them to come here will take even longer. And I still need the tractor.

I may be exaggerating the difficulties. After all, I have a couple of months until the table grapes start coming in and, if worst comes to worst, we can pick those by hand. And we've been doing

well enough with the small tillers. By next week I should be able to
get away for a few days. I suppose I can leave the others in charge
and take Shuzo with me.

I have just reread what I wrote this morning. It seems to me I
was wrong when I said Shuzo is at the heart of our unease. I think
rather that Shuzo is responding to it with mischief, in the same
way the others do in their own ways. It is easy to lay it to lack of
sleep and it seems like looking for trouble to pursue it further now
when they're playing so happily in there. But it is the deaths that
still bother them, and for some reason I can't put my finger on.

•

I've been too busy to write these six weeks. Between the new plant-
ings Dion and I made last winter, the season's routine, and Shuzo,
I've scarcely had time to draw a deep breath. Somehow the subject
of the harvester got buried in the press of work. And now, every
time I bring up the subject, there's uproar. Mahon and Florio lose
what few brains they have. *Don't leave us. It will be too expensive. We'll
lose too much time. Can't we all come? How come only Shuzo gets to go?*

Claire is the only one with any sense. He advises just what I
would do if only I didn't have to face taking an uncivilized creature
on a week's trip. I wish I could send Claire. The only trouble is,
you send a child and they don't take him seriously. I'm so disgusted with the whole mess, I'm tempted to use the bloody machine and hope for the best.

This Claire has unexpected talents. While the others nap in the
heat of the afternoon, he and I potter around the house, he usually in the kitchen and I at my desk. (A benefit of middle age: you
no longer need to waste so much time in sleep.) A couple of weeks
ago he came to my door.

"Are you *very* busy?"

I was, but didn't say so.

"I have something in my eye."

We went to the bed where the light was better. It didn't take me
long to discover what was really on his mind. But imagine his
taking so much trouble to lead up to it! When the others are
around he hangs back; even on First of the Month he's hesitant.
But alone, he doesn't waste any time. And he's not a bit like his
lazy brothers, who expect me to do everything.

So nearly every afternoon we spend some time together in bed.
Afterwards I rest my head on his shoulder while he discusses his

favorite project, the pros and cons of adding a separate new kitchen as opposed to enlarging the present living room.

Just as I'm dozing off, Florio usually bangs the door and comes in like a dorm mother, snapping up the shade and clapping his hands.

"Come on, you two, time to work. To the worker goes the fruit of his labor. Tsk, tsk, Claire, your beans lie alone and drying up in your absence."

Claire never takes offense, but rolls over, carefully puts on his glasses, and slowly gets up, smiling as if puzzled.

"Come, come, Mother Worm, the afternoon breezes beckon."

Florio and Mahon have taken to calling me Mother Worm from the lectures they've overheard me giving Shuzo on how a mother's love is infinitely divisible like the living earthworm.

•

I've set the date to go to town with the Combination. I've decided to leave them all at home. I cannot face taking Shuzo with me, he's become so obnoxious. I can't trust him not to embarrass me. I only hope he's not crippled or otherwise maimed by the time I get back.

•

There is nothing wrong with the harvester. And that is the only good thing I learned this evening. Tonight for the first time Mahon and Florio sleep like well-fed babies, and I lie awake, afraid of my dreams.

Where to begin? How did it come out? Not because I was perceptive, but because Mahon and Florio could no longer keep it in. We were sitting on the mats after supper, too tired to make the effort to go to bed. I think I was being more than usually tiresome on the subject of the Combination: the expense, the time, the bungling fools that made the machine, their poor service, and so on.

Obviously bored with the subject, Florio said petulantly, almost by the way, "There's nothing wrong with the damned Combination."

Even then, I would have noticed nothing, simply redoubled my tirade, if it hadn't been for Mahon.

"Shut up!" This he directed to Florio with a look that would kill.

Suddenly Florio went pale and Mahon looked away and I asked, without thinking, "How do you know?"

Then all at once, again without thinking, I knew how.

"Claire!" I must have spoken very urgently, for without my having to turn my head, he understood, grabbed Shuzo by the neck, and took him outdoors.

"So. How do you know?" I asked Florio because he looked the more capable of speech, belligerent and guilty like a little one who has disobeyed but is going to brazen it out. Mahon's face was hidden in his arm.

"Well," he said lightly, arranging his hair, "the last time I drove it, it was all right."

Numbness crept over me and I was not even shaking when I asked, "And when was that? Not since I've taken you."

He ran his fingers through his hair again, but with less bravado. He was nearly in tears. But Mahon raised his head. He was not weeping; instead he looked straight at me and spoke.

"One day last spring we traded jobs."

Still he could not bring himself to say what they had done.

"You mean," I said, "the day your brother Dion was killed."

He looked away, but his voice remained steady. "Yes, the very day Clement was killed."

"You ran down and mangled to death your brothers? Why, in God's name?"

"Haven't you ever heard of jealousy, Mother Worm?"

"I have, but among ten-year-olds, not you. You loved him as much as me."

He looked aside with his chin in the air, as if he would say no more. But Florio, in tears, managed to speak.

"Tell her. Why should she hate us instead of Dion?"

From Mahon, in the same voice as before, "Shut up!"

"No!" Florio was sobbing. "They poisoned my mother Flora and they were poisoning you." And having said that, his sobbing ceased and he looked through his tears at me with some of his former bravado. "With foxglove. They were lovers and they had a plot."

"What lovers? Who isn't a lover? And what did they need with a plot?"

"Because they were crazy. They liked only each other."

"And who was preventing them? Why didn't they go away? They could have gone on a trip, like Yakos, and not bothered to come back."

"They didn't want to go away. They wanted to kill the mothers and set fire to the county council."

And like a child who has finally stopped acting, he put his hand on his forehead. "Well, it made sense when they talked about it." He squeezed his eyes shut as if to black out a vision. "But they made my mother so dead." He was entirely dry-eyed by now and despondent, "and so sick for so long before that."

"And you watched them do it."

"Yes. I don't know." He seemed genuinely confused about his motives. "I didn't really believe it. It was a game until I saw her."

"The idiots! Did they think they would burn down the world and everyone would sit by and watch?"

And suddenly I became angry with Mahon. "You too? You knew and you didn't tell me?"

His face was still turned away, expressionless, eyes closed. I lost my temper.

"What did you think, that I loved him so much I couldn't bear to find out he wanted to kill me? You nitwit!"

"Who do you think you are kidding, Mama?"

"Oh, Mahon, you exasperate me! I loved him, yes. Terribly, yes, but not more than my life. If you had told me we could have done something. Now what am I supposed to do? Now I have two more murderers on my hands."

As much as I have studied children, in school and in my family, and as long as I have taken care of them, I will never truly understand them. What I said, and my rage, should have sent them into a panic or, at the very least, into dejection. Instead, their spirits seemed to lift and I could almost feel their relaxation.

"You both disgust me." I could not keep anger in my voice, though I tried. A great empty calm was stealing into my stomach that is with me still. They had been afraid I would fall to pieces and I did not. Our first lesson in school: children can stand anything but their mothers' falling to pieces. So the worst was over for them. Each looked down at his hands, not daring to catch the other's eye, and pursed his lips to hide his relief.

"Yes," Mahon finally said, "we were very bad, but as you said, we could not stand by while they burned down the whole world."

"Someone had to do it; it was us."

"And what good is a child that can't protect his mother?"

"Come, Mama," Florio said, "don't be too hard on us. You know how much we have suffered."

Truly, at that moment, they did disgust me. "All right, all right.

Enough. Go get Claire and bring in the little one. They're freezing out there. I'm going to bed. Don't anyone come in. Tell the others."

Indeed, what can I do with them? Nothing. The truth is I could not bear to lose them. And they did it for my sake.

I accuse myself, first, of self-deception. Then, of every crime against Dion that he should have turned out as he did. Then, defending myself, I say it was because his natural mother kept him too long, giving him a bad start, spoiling him. Then, heavier in my stomach, the feeling that the same thing might happen to Shuzo. But I mustn't ask for trouble. Shuzo is not the same child. I still have time with him.

My dreams were nothing to be afraid of; they've disappeared for a while. We are in the midst of a hot spell which takes most of our energy and is bringing on the table grapes sooner than we had any right to expect. I only pray it continues.

I explained everything to Claire. His frown deepened and has not gone away, but he is a great comfort to me. I had him tell Shuzo, who crept under his covers and stayed there with his thumb in his mouth for a couple of days. He emerged his old mischievous self. It seems to me he is a little subdued. Perhaps it's because there are no more mysteries.

Mahon and Florio do their best to draw no attention to themselves. Florio goes about his work silently. And wisely, they stay away from my bed. I suspect that when they're out of sight, they're perfectly cheerful.

The First of the Month is only two weeks off and I can't imagine how we'll be able to face it. Still, I take it as a good sign that I'm able to write at all. And there is so much to do, I am burying myself in work. With so many mouths to feed, I'm expanding the garden for the fall planting. And the truth is — no farmer likes to say this out loud — the harvest looks to be the best yet. Claire might get his kitchen sooner than he expects. I'm struggling not to let my hopes get too high.

After so many years, that Dion should not be here to see it.

•

I knew Yakos would come home in time for harvest! And in time for the First of the Month, too. What a festival we held, celebrating the end of our gloom! We made Shuzo's eyes pop. And the stories he tells! Between him and Florio, it's non-stop talking. Whoever speaks doesn't dare draw a breath for fear someone else will take over.

How easy it is to idealize a child when he's away. Really, he's the same young rascal he always was.

•

The hot spell continues and the harvest has begun. This morning I was able to take the time, with Shuzo, to work in the garden. We took out a mountain of dried corn stalks, but there's plenty of the late crop still ripening. God willing, we'll have tomatoes and peppers for two more months this year.

We set out rows and rows of broccoli, cabbages, and cauliflower. He worked so well at this, so cheerfully and without complaining, that I let him plant the carrot seeds. The job usually falls to me because the others are too clumsy for the tiny seeds. And I detest it myself; I'm too impatient.

But Shuzo kneels over the rows with such concentration his tongue sticks out and he doesn't notice the sweat collecting on his face. I was so pleased with him, instead of going straight in at noon, I undressed and lay down in the cool furrow between the corn stalks and told him to come and have what he wanted of me. I think it's the first time he hasn't preferred the breast. In the past, anything else he's done was because his brothers would make fun of him if he didn't.

It's such a great pleasure for a mother to see a boy become a man, to feel under her hand his trembling, bony shoulder and the long muscles under the smooth skin where he never gets tan. Afterwards, sitting straddling my waist, he bent forward and noticed the tears spilling from my eyes. Curious, he traced them with his finger to my hairline.

"Why are you crying?"

"Oof. I'm not crying. The sun's in my eyes. Get up, you're getting too heavy."

And right away, he jumped up and ran toward the house.

"Come back here and get your shirt," I had to shout, "and help me carry some of this junk."

Well, he's still a good child.

ALICE MUNRO

Wood

(FROM THE NEW YORKER)

ROY FOWLER has a business in Logan, Ontario. He is a sign painter, the only one in this part of the country, and he gets more business than he can handle. He doesn't want so much business. If he hires anybody to work for him, it means he has to go through a lot of red tape, and he doesn't want that. He is a very good sign painter; he can do any kind of lettering, and a picture if required. Often the farmers want a picture to hang beside their gates; they want a picture of a pig or a turkey or a Hereford or a Black Angus or a Charolais. They always want a background of rolling green farm-land and blue summer sky, even though the pigs and turkeys are raised by modern methods in specially designed and equipped barns, where they never see daylight, and the cattle are often fat-tened in feedlots.

Roy does his painting in a shed behind the house. It is heated by a small wood stove and smells strongly of paint, turpentine, linseed oil, and lumber. Getting the fuel for the stove led him to his other interest, which is private but not secret; that is, everybody knows about it but nobody knows how much he thinks about it or how important it has become to him: woodcutting. He has a four-wheel-drive truck and a chain saw and an eight-pound splitting axe. He spends more and more time in the bush cutting firewood — not just for himself but to sell. His wife, Lila, suspects that he is more interested in cutting wood than in painting signs; she worries about his letting his business go and about his going into the bush alone. He is aware of this, though they never discuss the subject. If he is going out to the bush, he waits till she has gone to work. She works in the office of the new dentist — a good thing for her, because she is friendly and talkative and needs company, as well as some extra money; and a very good thing for the dentist, because he is building up his practice and if he gets all Lila's relatives that is a sizable block of patients.

These relatives, the Voles and the Pooles and the Devlins, are a close-knit clan. They don't always enjoy each other's company but they make sure they get a lot of it. At Christmas and Thanksgiving they squeeze into a house thirty or forty people, counting children. On ordinary Sundays they manage a dozen or so, watching television, talking, cooking and eating a big meal. Roy says he likes to watch television or talk — either one but not both at the same time. Sometimes on a Sunday, with the living room full of his wife's relatives, he gets up and goes out to the shed and builds up a fire of either ironwood or apple wood; both burn with a pleasant smell. On the shelf with his paint he has a bottle of rye, and he will take a drink by himself, but he doesn't drink very much: seldom when he's working on a sign and never when he's going into the bush — just on these Sundays full of visitors. It doesn't cause trouble. The relatives don't feel slighted — they are too busy visiting — and Lila doesn't reproach him or apologize for him. She is an easygoing person most of the time, and her family has a limited interest in people like Roy, who have just married into it, not been born in it, and haven't even contributed any children. As a rule, they don't take much notice of people who aren't like themselves. They are large, spread-out, talkative; Roy is short, compact, quiet.

Sometimes Roy finds a bush that the sawmill people have logged out, leaving the tops on the ground, and sometimes he finds out where the forest-management people have gone in and girdled the trees they think should come out because they are diseased or crooked or no good for lumber. Ironwood, for instance, is no good for lumber, and neither is hawthorn or blue beech, though blue beech is seldom worth cutting for firewood, either. When he spots a bush like this he goes and bargains with the farmer or whoever owns it, and if the payment is agreed on he goes in to get the wood. A lot of this activity goes on in late fall — in November or early December — both because that is the time for selling firewood and because it is a good time to get the truck into the bush. Farmers nowadays don't always have good lanes going back to the bush, as they did when they cut and hauled wood themselves.

Often you have to drive in across the fields, and this is possible at only two times during the year: when the crop is just coming up, and you can drive between the rows, or after the crop is off.

This fall the demand for wood was greater than ever, and Roy was going out two or three times in a week. Most people recognize trees by their leaves or by their general shape and size, but Roy, walking in the leafless deep bush, knows them by their bark. Ironwood, that heavy and reliable firewood, has a shaggy brown bark on its stocky trunk, but its limbs are smooth at their tips and decidedly reddish. Cherry is the blackest tree in the bush, and the bark lies in neat scales. Most people would be surprised at how high the cherry trees grow in the bush; they are nothing like orchard trees there. Apple trees are not so tall, or so dark, or so definitely scaled, but their wood burns for a long time and smells sweet. Ash is a soldierly tree — straight, corduroy-ribbed columns. Maple has a gray bark with irregular roughness, the shadows making black streaks; there is some comfortable carelessness about these streaks and shadows — which meet sometimes in rough rectangles, sometimes not — that is suitable to the maple, which is homely and familiar and what everybody thinks of when they think of a tree. Beech trees and oak are another matter; there is something notable and dramatic about them, though neither is so lovely in shape as the elm trees, which are gone. Beech has the smooth gray bark that is usually chosen for the carving of initials. These carvings widen with the years, the decades, from the knife's slim groove to blotches that make the letters wider than long. Beech will grow a hundred feet high in the bush. In the open they spread out — they are as wide as high — but in the bush they shoot up, and then the limbs at the top will take radical turns; they look like stag horns. But this arrogant-looking tree can have a weakness of twisted grain, which can be detected by ripples in the bark. That is a sign that it may break, or go down in a high wind. As for oak trees, they are not common in this country, not so common as beech, and always easy to spot. Just as maple trees always look like the common, necessary tree in the back yard, so oak trees look like trees in storybooks, as if in all the stories that begin "Once upon a time on the edge of the woods," the woods were full of oak trees. Their dark, shiny, elaborately indented leaves contribute to this look, but they are just as remarkable when the leaves are off and they show their thick corky bark, with its gray-black color and intricate surface, and the elaborate twisting and curling of their branches.

Roy thinks that there is very little danger in going tree cutting alone if you know what you are doing. When you are going to cut down a tree, the first thing is to assess its center of gravity, then cut a seventy-degree wedge, so that the center of gravity is just over it. The side the wedge is on, of course, determines the direction in which the tree will fall. You make a falling cut, from the opposite side, not to connect with the wedge cut but in line with its high point. The idea is to cut through the tree, leaving at the end a hinge of wood which is the very center of the tree's weight and from which it must fall. It is best to make it fall clear of all other branches, but sometimes there is no way this can happen. If a tree is leaning into the branches of other trees, and you can't get a truck into position to haul it out with a chain, you cut the trunk in sections from beneath, till the upper part drops free and falls. When you've dropped a tree and it's resting on its branches, you get the trunk to the ground by cutting through the limb wood until you find the limbs that are holding it up. These limbs are under pressure — they may be bent like a bow — and the trick is to cut so that the trunk will roll away from you and the limbs won't whack you. When it is safely down, you cut the trunk into stove lengths, and split the stove lengths with the axe. Sometimes there's a surpise. Some squirrelly wood blocks can't be split with the axe; they have to be laid on their sides and ripped with a chain saw; the sawdust cut this way, with the grain, is ripped away in long shreds. Also, some beech or maple has to be sidesplit, the great round chunk cut along the growth rings on all sides until it is almost square and can be more easily attacked. Sometimes there's dozy wood, in which a fungus has grown inside, between the rings. But in general the toughness of the blocks is as you'd expect: greater in the body wood than in the limb wood, and greater in the broad trunks that have grown up in the open than in the tall, slim ones that have pushed up in the middle of the bush.

Roy's thoughts about wood are covetous and nearly obsessive, though he has never been a greedy man in any other way. He can lie awake nights thinking of a splendid beech he wants to get at. He thinks of all the woodlots in the country that he has never even seen, because they are hidden at the back of farms. If he is driving along a road that goes through a bush, he swings his head from

side to side, afraid of missing something. Even what is worthless
for his purposes will interest him; for instance, a stand of blue
beech, too delicate, too weedy to bother with. He sees the dark,
vertical ribs slanting down the paler trunks; he remembers where
they are. He would like to map every bush he sees, get it in his
mind, know what is there.

In the bush it isn't good to let your mind wander or your worries
intrude. Roy is not a worrier anyway. He doesn't think about the
signs he hasn't finished or about the number of relatives who will
be invading his house next Sunday. Sometimes he does think, not
exactly with worry but with bewilderment and sadness, of his niece
Karen — his wife's niece, really. They had her with them from the
time she was eight until she was seventeen, when she quit school to
marry a truck driver they didn't even know she knew. She had a
talent for drawing, and she loved lettering, including the Old English style. She called those the twitchy letters. When she was helping him in the shop, people naturally thought that she was Roy's
daughter and had inherited her talent from him. She had a round
face like his, and a neat, strong body, but she was not quiet; before
she had the door of the shop halfway open she was into everything
that had happened at school and every joke she had heard. He
used to wonder how any child who went around in such high gear
could be patient enough to do lettering.

Now she is the mother of five children and has lost most of her
back teeth. When she smiles, as she still does readily, you can see
that. She has got thick and shapeless, as the women tend to do in
that family, and Roy has seen her on the street in an old torn ski
jacket, with her hair held back with a bit of elastic. Her husband
doesn't work steadily, so she took a job in a highway tavern, where
the noise was so loud it damaged her hearing. Now at least she is
out of that — she works as a chambermaid at the River Inn.

Lila never seems to think that anything much has gone wrong
with this girl's life, though of course she would like to see them
living in a better house and taking in a bit more money. It is Roy
who thinks Karen has wasted herself, and wishes there were something he could do for her. If her husband would get a wood stove
Roy could keep them in fuel, but they burn oil.

•

A day or so after the first snow Roy was out in the bush looking at
some girdled trees. At the edge of the bush, by the road, was an

illegal dump. People had been throwing their trash in this lonely spot rather than taking it to the township dump, which was open only at certain hours, and Roy saw something moving there. He thought it was a dog, but when the figure straightened up he saw that it was a man in a ragged brown coat. When he got a little closer he saw that it was Percy Marshall, poking through the dump to see what he could find. Sometimes you used to be able to find valuable old jars and bottles, or even a copper boiler, at these places, but that is not likely anymore. Percy was not a knowledge-able scavenger anyway — he would just be on the lookout for something he could use, though it was hard to see what that might be in this pile of torn plastic bags, detergent bottles, mattresses with the stuffing popping out.

Percy lives alone in a room at the back of an empty, boarded-up store at a crossroads a few miles from here. He walks everywhere, talking to himself, poking about. His life of malnutrition, dirt, and solitude is his own choice. He has tried the comforts of the County Home, but he couldn't stand being shut up with a lot of other old people, so he left. Starting out with a fairly good farm, Percy has worked his way down — through bootlegging, odd jobs, penury, brief spells in jail — and in the last ten years worked his way up again, maintained by the Old Age Pension, getting his picture and a writeup in the paper. He was described as the last of a breed of colorful, independent, self-reliant men. Under his picture it said, "A Genuine Local Character."

"You going to be taking them trees out?" Percy said when he saw Roy.

"I might," said Roy, who thought Percy could be after a donation of firewood.

"You better hurry up."

"Why's that?"

"This bush is all supposed to be going under contract."

Roy could not help asking what this contract was. Percy was a gossip but not a liar. He was constantly interested in deals, sales, inheritances, insurance, money matters, to the surprise of people who expected him to be all wrapped up in memories of olden times. It is a mistake to think that people who never managed to get any money aren't interested in it.

"There's this fellow from Goderich is under contract to the River Inn to get them all the wood they need for the winter. He's got to get them a cord a day. They burn a cord a day."

"I never heard about that," Roy said.

"I was into Goderich the day before yesterday and that's where I heard it."

"Where in Goderich?"

"Wasn't in the beer parlor," said Percy. "It was on the Square. Fellows talking."

"Did you hear who it was then?"

"No. I didn't hear the name. If I did, it didn't mean nothing to me, so I forgot it. I did hear what he does. I think it was carpentering. No. Painting or maybe paperhanging. Some work like that."

"Does he work for Coombs Decorating?"

"I don't know who he works for."

"He's going into this bush?"

"This and across the road as well. See, this is a big bush."

"Well, I don't know," said Roy. "I was just looking around." He had actually spoken to the farmer last week and got a price on these trees.

"They got them big fireplaces. They don't heat with it — they just burn it for the looks. They burn a cord a day."

"Lot of wood."

"It is."

"I never heard that any fellow from Goderich was interested."

"If I could think of his name, I'd tell you."

"Maybe a housepainter — he wouldn't be getting work in the wintertime."

"I guess he wouldn't."

"Well, it's no difference to me. I got all the woodcutting I can handle."

"That's right. You got all you can handle."

Roy thought all the way home about this story. He himself had sold some wood to the River Inn, but they must have decided to get it all from one supplier, which meant he wouldn't have any more sales. They did burn a lot of wood, though he didn't know if they would go through a cord a day. He thought about the problems of getting that much wood out now, when the snow had already started. The only thing to do would be to pull the logs out into the open field, before the real winter got under way. You'd have to get them out as quickly as possible, make a big pile of them there, saw them, and chop them up later. And to get them out you'd need to use a bulldozer or a big tractor. You'd have to make a road in, pull the logs out with chains. You'd need a crew of men working; there was no way this could be a one- or two-man operation. It would have to be done on a big scale. It didn't sound like any housepainter's off-season project. Maybe the outfit's name was Painter, or Paynter. He thought he knew of a construction business of that name, but they were from Stratford. It could easily be somebody from out of the country altogether. The farmer Roy had talked to had not said anything about such a scheme, but then it might all have been arranged since Roy had seen him. No money had changed hands, nothing was put in writing. It was quite possible that the farmer had reconsidered, got a better offer, decided to forget the agreement with Roy and let the bulldozer go in. During the evening Roy thought of phoning him to ask what was going on. But then he thought that if the farmer had indeed changed his mind there was nothing to be done about it. A spoken agreement was nothing to hold to. The farmer could just tell Roy to clear out. The best thing to do, really, was to act as if he had never heard anything about the other fellow — just go in and take what trees he could as quickly as he could, before the bulldozer got there.

It occurred to him, of course, that Percy might be mistaken, not only about the woodcutter's occupation and where he was from but about the whole story — he could have got it badly twisted. But the more Roy thought about it the more he lost sight of this possibility. He could see in his mind the bulldozer and the train of chained logs, the great log piles in the field, the men with chain saws, and soon it was as if he had got the report first hand. Partly this was because he disliked the River Inn and distrusted the people there and expected some sort of high-handed pillage to be connected with them.

The River Inn was a resort hotel built on the ruins of an old mill not far from the crossroads where Percy Marshall lived. In fact, the Inn owned the land and the building that Percy lived in and had been going to tear it down, but it turned out that the guests, having nothing much to do, liked to walk over and take pictures of the derelict building and the old harrow and upturned wagon and useless pump. Sometimes Percy allowed himself to be photographed and talked to as well. Some guests did sketches. The overnight guests came from as far away as Montreal and Ottawa, and no doubt thought themselves in the real backwoods. Local people went to the Inn for lunch or dinner. Lila had gone once. Roy would not go. He said he wasn't going to pay an arm and a leg to eat a meal.

He didn't really know what he had against the Inn. He was not against the idea of people spending money to enjoy themselves or against the idea of other people making money out of the people who wanted to spend it. It is true they got their signs made elsewhere, but if they had come to him he would probably have said he had too much work to do already. When Karen first applied for a job there, she applied to be a waitress, because that was what she had done before. They turned her down. "I'm afraid you're a bit overweight," the woman said to her. Karen told that — she made a joke of it. "They only want skinnies." And she got the job as a chambermaid, so she did not care. Nevertheless, Roy thinks of the owners as grabbers, and the management as snobs. They own the land along both riverbanks, they are putting up a new building, and they are rumored to be planning chalets and an old-time store and an old-time opera house. They burn wood for show. A cord a day. Now some operator with a bulldozer will be cutting down the bush as if it were a cornfield. Easy for him.

•

The next morning Roy works on a sign for a while. About eleven o'clock he decides he has caught up enough for that day. He is cleaning brushes when he hears a car door slam. He looks out and sees Karen's badly rusted old Buick, a car they couldn't afford when they bought it and can't afford to run now.

Karen opens the work-shed door and says, "Howdy."

"Howdy."

"So. What are you up to today?"

"Just a little of this and a little of that."

She is every bit as fat and as sloppily dressed as when he has seen her on the street. Nevertheless, it cheers him up a bit to see her.

"You're cleaning up. You must be going out to the bush."

"I thought I might take a run out."

"Aunt Lila meanwhile thinking you're hard at work."

Roy sees her looking around to see what he's working on and he says, "Offer you a job?"

"I got one. Changing sheets and mucking out bathrooms. Listen. That's why I came. I gotta take the car in today, and tomorrow I have to be at work early. I thought I had a ride, but it fell through."

"You want to borrow the truck?"

"Well, I hate to ask, but I don't see how I can get to work otherwise."

"That's O.K."

"You sure? You staying home tomorrow?"

"I can stay home any day. I got enough to do."

"I can't not show up. We're getting ready for the weekend. Well, that's a load off."

He had been thinking of how to ask her about the wood, or perhaps of just telling her what the Inn is up to. In his mind, he hears himself starting: "You know, something's happened that makes me mad." He doesn't get a chance to say it out loud, because she's out the door and heading for the car.

"I gotta have it in by noon and before that get the groceries and pick up Tiger at the vet's. Did I tell you he got his ear chewed? Can I come and get the truck tonight? I'll put some gas in."

Tiger at the vet's. That would cost them something. He'll fill the tank this afternoon.

As soon as she's gone he gets into the truck and drives out to where he was the day before. He thinks about stopping by and questioning Percy further, but knows it wouldn't be any use. Such a show of interest might just get Percy inventing things. He thinks again about talking to the farmer but decides against it for the same reasons he had last night.

He parks the truck on the trail that leads into the bush. This trail soon peters out, and even before it does Roy has left it. He is walking around looking at the trees, which look just the same as yesterday and don't give a sign of being party to any grand hostile scheme. He feels as if he has to hurry. He has the chain saw and the axe with him. If anybody else drives in here, if anybody challenges him, he will tell them that he has permission from the farmer and that he never heard of any other deal. He will say that furthermore he intends to go ahead and cut unless the farmer personally comes and tells him to get out. He catches himself muttering this answer out loud. "Nobody else has got any authority to put me out." He is talking out loud to himself, like Percy Marshall.

The floor of any bush is usually rougher than the surface of the surrounding land. Roy has always thought that this was caused by

trees falling, pulling up the earth with their roots and just lying
and rotting. Where they rotted there would be a mound; where
their roots tore out the earth there would be hollows. But he read
somewhere — not too long ago, and he wishes he could remember
where it was — that there is a theory that all this happened long
ago, just after the Ice Age, when ice formed between layers of
earth and pushed it into odd humps, just as it does today somewhere in the Arctic. Where the land has not been cleared or
worked the humps remain.

What happens now is the most ordinary and yet the most unbelievable thing. It is what might happen to the most stupid day-
dreamer walking in the bush — a guest from the River Inn,
somebody who thought the bush was a kind of park to stroll in and
wore light shoes instead of boots and didn't watch the ground. It
has never before happened to Roy in thousands of times of walking in the bush, or come near happening. A light snow is falling,
making the earth and dead leaves slippery. One of his feet skids
and twists, and then the other plunges through a cover of snowy
brush to the ground, which is farther down than he expected.
That is, he steps carelessly — is thrown, almost — into the sort of
spot where you always step testingly, carefully, and not at all if you
can see a better place. Even so, what happens? It is not as if he has
stumbled in a groundhog hole. He is thrown off balance, falls
disbelievingly; he is down, the skidding foot caught somehow
under the other leg. He holds the saw out from himself as he goes
down in slow motion, and flings the axe clear. But not clear
enough; the axe handle hits him hard against the knee of his
twisted leg. The saw has pulled him over in its direction but he
hasn't fallen against it. He went down slowly, thoughtfully, inevitably; he could have broken a rib, but he didn't. And the axe
handle could have flown up and hit him in the face, but it didn't.
He could have gashed his leg. He thinks of all these possibilities
not with relief but as if he still can't be sure they haven't happened.
Everything he did — the way he skidded, and stepped into the
brush, and fell — was stupid, awkward, unbelievable.

He starts to pull himself up. Both knees hurt. One came down
hard on the ground, and the other was hit by the axe handle. He
gets hold of the trunk of a young cherry tree and pulls himself up
gradually, puts weight on both feet, and bends to pick up the saw
and nearly buckles again. A pain shoots up from the ground and

doesn't stop till it reaches his chest. He straightens, not sure where the pain came from, but instinctively keeps from putting weight on the foot that skidded and twisted underneath him. That is where the pain is. Not in the foot but in the ankle. He straightens out that leg, considering it, and very cautiously lets a little weight down. He can't believe in the pain. He can't believe that it could continue so, could continue to stop him. The ankle must be more than twisted — it must be sprained. What is the difference? He knows he will just have to test the pain and bear it; he will have to get used to it, and after a while it may not seem so bad. He keeps trying but he doesn't make any progress. He can't put his weight on it. Is it broken then? A broken ankle — even that seems a minor injury, the sort of thing old ladies get when they slip on the ice. He has to see himself as lucky when he thinks of what might have happened. A broken ankle, a minor injury. Nevertheless, he can't take a step. He can't walk.

What he understands, finally, is that in order to get back to the truck he's going to have to abandon his axe and his chain saw and get down on his hands and knees and crawl. He lets himself down and hauls himself onto the track of his bootprints, now filling with snow. He thinks to check the pocket where his keys are, making sure it's zipped. He shakes off his cap and lets it lie; the peak interferes with his vision. Now the snow is falling on his bare, partly bald head. Once he accepts crawling as a method of loco-motion it's not so bad — at least, it's not impossible, though it hurts his knees. He's careful enough now, dragging himself over the brush and through the saplings, over the hummocky ground. Even if he gets a little slope to roll down, he doesn't dare— he has to guard his leg. He's glad he didn't go through any boggy places, and he's glad he didn't wait any longer before starting back; the snow is getting heavier and his prints are almost blotted out. With-out that track to follow, it would be hard to know, at ground level, whether he was going the right way.

The situation, which seemed at first so unreal to him, is getting to feel more natural. Going along on hands and knees, close to the ground, testing a log for rot, then pulling himself over it on his stomach, getting his hands full of rotten leaves and dirt and snow — he can't keep his gloves on, can't get the proper hold and feel of things on the bush floor unless his hands are bare — he is no longer surprised at himself. He doesn't think anymore about his axe and saw left back there, though at the beginning he could scarcely pull himself away from them. He hardly thinks back to the accident itself. It happened, never mind how. He has stopped believing in an order of things in which it couldn't happen. He has a fairly steep bank to get up. When he reaches it he is relieved to have come so far, and daunted to see what hard terrain he must now take on. He stops and warms his hands by turn inside his jacket. For some reason he thinks of Karen in her red ski jacket and thinks that Lila is right: there is no use worrying about people. He starts up the bank, digging in his elbows where he can. If they had had kids of their own he might have worried too much. Lila, who doesn't believe in worrying, does worry about him, though that is mixed up with worrying about the business. These thoughts go through his mind as if they were going to link up somewhere, but they don't. He keeps going, he grabs at anything that will hold, he pushes his sore knees into the earth. A couple of times he slides back but stops himself. Nobody knows what anybody else is thinking about or how anybody else is feeling, he thinks. Nobody knows how others see themselves.

He pulls himself onto level ground and raises his head and sees the truck. The sight of level, trodden ground raises his expectations of himself again and he lifts himself to his knees, gets shakily up on his good leg, dragging the other. He tries a hop. No good. He would never get anywhere that way — he'd fall over. He tries the bad leg just a little, gently, and realizes that the pain could make him black out. He goes back on his hands and knees and starts to crawl in a businesslike way toward the truck. He crawls along on the hard frozen mud, splintering the ice in the dry puddle holes. It's cruel punishment for his knees, but otherwise so much easier than his journey through the bush that he begins to feel almost light-headed. Some sort of song line is going through his mind.

> *Crawlin' down the road,*
> *Crawlin' down the road . . .*

He'll be able to drive. He'll drive along to that old fraud Percy's. Percy at least has a telephone. Beyond this thought lie a lot of vexing questions: What will his wife say; who will go and get the saw and the axe for him; how can he direct anyone to where these things are; how soon will the snow cover them up; when will he be able to walk? But he pushes all that away. He lifts his head to get another encouraging look at the truck. He hopes old Percy will be at home, or, at any rate, have left his door open.

He stops again to rest and warm his hands. He could put his gloves on now, but why ruin them? A large bird rises out of the bush beyond the truck. He thinks it's a hawk, but it could be a buzzard. If it's a buzzard it will have its eye on him, but he'll have it fooled. He is still thinking about Percy, and while he watches to see the bird again, to tell what it is by its manner of flight and its wings, he sees something else quite plainly: the truth of Percy's story.

The truth is that the paperhanger, the decorator, the house-painter doesn't exist. The contractor, the operator, the man from Goderich doesn't exist. It is Roy himself. Not a housepainter — a sign painter. And not from Goderich — from Logan. Not so long ago, he sold that wood to the River Inn. And he has a contract, you might say, to clear out this bush. That's all it needs to start some kind of story. The next thing you know, it's a hundred cords a day. Everything connected with the River Inn turns into some big fable. Everything that involves money, in this country, gets talked up, distorted. Around here any set of facts gets turned into a story.

The bulldozer isn't coming, the men with chain saws are not converging. The ash, the maple, the beech, the ironwood, the cherry, the hawthorn are safe for him. Nobody but himself and the forest management has taken note of them.

Roy's mind operates very economically at this moment — perhaps more selectively than ever before. It manages to turn everything to good account. It no longer dwells on the foolishness of the accident but triumphs in the long, successful crawl and the approach to the truck. (He is on his way again.) It cancels out any embarrassment at his having been so mistaken; it pushes out any troubling detection of waste and calamity; it ushers in a decent sense of victory. Safe.

JOYCE CAROL OATES

Presque Isle

(FROM THE AGNI REVIEW)

AT ABOUT THE TIME the gulls' crazy shrieking woke Jean-Marie, her mother Eunice was halfway to Skye Harbor in the little red Fiat. But then the Fiat caught fire: Eunice happened to glance in the rearview mirror and saw clouds of angry white-gray smoke. Oh my God, she said, not again . . . Her first instinct was to brake to a stop, right on the road. But the road was narrow. And the shoulder sloped away to a deep sandy ditch. So she drove, at five miles an hour, to Jake's Service on the outskirts of Skye Harbor.

Where the owner, Jake, who knew Eunice's former husband, James, and knew all about the wealthy Scudders, hid his contempt, and said he would do what he could on the car — but that make, he said, was a pile of junk. Eunice blinked tears angrily out of her eyes. She had to fight the impulse to weep in front of strangers; there was never any temptation to weep at home. Yes, all right, I know, Eunice said, this is the second time it has happened, can you fix it? — that's all I want to know. Jake was charmingly unkempt, and his bib-overalls were stiff with grease. That make of car, he said, was a pile of junk. He didn't know what he could do with it. He couldn't be responsible.

Eunice decided to forget about the groceries, no doubt someone else would be driving in, wasn't Kim planning on a luncheon for a dozen or more people? — and went to the liquor store instead, where she spent $67 in ten minutes. She used the telephone there to call the lodge but no one answered. She hung up, and dialed again, because her hands were shaking slightly and she might have misdialed . . . that happened sometimes. But no one answered.

It was almost 11:00. Too early for her guests to be out on the beach (and the air was uncomfortably chilly — the sky was one of those hammered-tin skies), but late for them to be sleeping. Though maybe not. Eunice thought, staring at her watch, because everyone had been up late the night before. How late, she didn't know. She had fallen onto her bed, half-dressed, around 2:30. She really couldn't remember.

Something odd had happened the night before, something un-pleasant and unexpected, but she couldn't remember. She sup-posed she would remember, in time. That usually happened.

The taxi driver helped her with the liquor — the bottles had been placed, for convenience, in a cardboard carton — and drove her the seven miles out to the tip of Presque Isle, to the Scudder camp. It was easiest simply to call it that, since everyone on Presque Isle knew where it was, the Scudder camp, though Eunice detested the name Scudder, and was contemplating a name change — maybe the resumption of her maiden name (Pemberton — a nice enough name, though somewhat prim), or a new name entirely (Maas, Hugo, Woolf, Lorraine — and there was still the possibility of Kleiboldt, if she and Reed did get married after all). The Scud-der camp was really a compound. Fifty acres, a ten-foot chain-link fence (which needed repairs, Eunice knew, but *she* wasn't going to bother), no-trespassing signs every forty feet. The Scudders had owned it for generations, though in recent years, with everyone dying off, and James's trips to Brazil, it was rarely used and would probably have to be sold. But then it was an investment — it was real estate — palpable, as James's accountant would say. Eunice didn't know. She tried not to care. In this phase of her life a sense of fatality overcame her, or was it perhaps a sense of destiny ("des-tiny" had a nobler ring), and she found it halfway pleasant. I have been active, I have been *scrambling*, she thought, for too many years.

The taxi driver commented, as everyone did, on the beautiful view of the ocean — the handsome "cottages" — the stand of tall, perfectly straight Scots pine. It was impressive, yes. Eunice remem-bered how impressed she had been, twenty-five years ago, and intimidated, which had been part of James's design, certainly. Or his mother's. She wondered if Reed had been impressed, last week. He had said nothing except, What's all the way across there — Spain, Portugal? — Morocco? Eunice said she didn't know exactly, she thought it might be France.

Oh yes, Reed had said something more — were the people around the camp, Presque Isle people, in James's hire? (By "people" Reed meant "servants" though he couldn't bring himself to use the word, and by "hire" he meant were they spies for Eunice's former husband.)

But they were safe, Eunice explained. They were safe now. James had turned 180 degrees (if that was the correct expression) and was now going to be very liberal and tolerant, even sympathetic; there would be no more detectives; no more grubby nonsense. You're grown up now, Eunice, he said, chuckling sadly, you're a big girl now, and though he had disappointed her in the past by lying he had never lied in quite *that* style. So they had the camp for the entire month of August and it was only August 8.

As Eunice paid the driver, her sharp eye darted everywhere — to the little cottage by the sea-cliff path called Windy Dells, to Sunny Haven, the Pines, and the main lodge — but no one seemed to be around.

She walked in the kitchen door, struggling with the carton of bottles, and had the surprise of her life — there was Jean-Marie — leaning against the kitchen sink, smoking a cigarette, obviously waiting for her. She saw me carrying this box, Eunice thought, and didn't even —

What are you doing here! she heard herself cry out.

What? said Jean-Marie.

I mean — did you say — what about music camp? — Eunice stammered.

I *told* you last night about music camp, Jean-Marie said.

You did? You told me? Last night — ?

Mother, I explained it all last night, don't you remember? Jean-Marie said with that hateful quizzical little smile of hers. I got here last night, don't you remember? . . . These guys were driving to Quebec, I ran into them at Polly's new place, in the Village, I told you about it last night, you seemed to be listening.

Well, you shouldn't scare me like that, Eunice said.

She began putting bottles away, noisily. — You know what my nerves are like, she said.

She could feel her face growing warm. And red. Oh yes — it would be blotched with red! Though why *she* should be embarrassed she didn't know. After all, Reed and Jean-Marie had already met. In June, in the city. Lunch at a pub on Third Avenue, a visit to the Metropolitan, where, in the Egyptian wing, Reed had made them giggle by warning a group of black boys, junior-high-aged, that there was an ancient mummy's curse on anyone who fooled around in the presence of the dead. (The boys had slipped away from their teacher and were acting a bit rowdy.) Jean-Marie had been *very* amused.

It was erroneous to think, as Eunice sometimes did when she wasn't thinking clearly, that Reed was young enough to be her son. He wasn't: he was twenty-seven. And Jean-Marie was only sixteen. Her sixteenth birthday had been back in May. — Did James bring you here? Is he in town? Eunice heard herself asking.

For God's sake, Mother, Jean-Marie said, exhaling smoke from her nostrils in a harsh dramatic gesture (picked up, Eunice supposed, from one of James's "model" friends), I *told* you about last night.

Are you in contact with James?

Well — not exactly — but he knows about the music school — he knows it wasn't working out.

And what about the tuition? Eunice asked. She opened the refrigerator and looked inside but couldn't remember what she wanted.

Jean-Marie shrugged her shoulders.

Your father isn't going to like it, Eunice said nervously.

He already *knows*, Jean-Marie said.

I'm just so shaky, the car broke down and I should call the garage, but the man there is so rude. Eunice said, shutting the refrigerator door with a thud, and everything is so . . . You aren't supposed to hitchhike, Jean-Marie. You know that.

I didn't hitchhike. It was a *ride*.

And they drove you all the way to Skye Harbor — ?

They let me out at the exit. By Plainsboro.

And then you hitchhiked!

Mother, it's only fifteen miles.

But then how did you get out here?

What do you mean — out here?

Out here. To the camp.

I said — I got a ride.

To Skye Harbor, and then — ?

To Skye Harbor, yes, and then he was nice enough to drive me out here, Jean-Marie said patiently.

But this was another person, wasn't it! Eunice said.

Oh Mother, for God's sake, it's only fifteen miles from the Plainsboro exit, Jean-Marie said, flicking ashes into the sink. Anyway I told you last night. I told Reed last night, she said with a queer little smile.

Reed? When did you see Reed?

Down on the beach! — you were all down on the beach when I got here, Jean-Marie said.

Eunice remembered, now. And her face grew hotter.

Well — you shouldn't sneak up on me and scare me, she said, yanking open a drawer, you know what my nerves are like — you didn't give me any warning — just walked away from that camp — and you said, you promised, you'd stay there! — you said how beautiful it was in Virginia and you never wanted to leave and the city air is foul, you were never coming home again —

She crouched down to open a cupboard door. Her knees bent fatly.

Mother, Jean-Marie said, with that faint air of incredulity, of polite astonishment, that so exasperated both her parents — she had come back from St. Ann's with it, at the age of fourteen — Mother, what the hell are you looking for?

The telephone book! I am looking for the telephone book! Eunice shouted.

It wasn't in the kitchen, so mother and daughter searched in the other room — a long high-ceilinged room with a dozen windows, screened, and a large fieldstone fireplace, and wicker furniture with yellow-and-green striped cushions, now rather faded. Jean-Marie found the telephone book in one of the window seats. He should have given you a card or something, at the garage, she said. She flicked through the telephone book. Some of the pages are missing, she said.

Well he didn't *give* me any card, Eunice said angrily.

Here's my old guitar, Jean-Marie said, I didn't know I left it out here. She laughed and wiped at her nose with her fingers. — So this is where it is.

She began plucking away at the strings energetically. Eunice looked through the telephone book, in the yellow pages, trying to remember the name of the garage — it was a man's name, a very simple name.

The exhaust was on fire, Eunice said. And that disgusting little man said the car was a pile of junk . . .

Jean-Marie strummed away, faster and faster. In a high thin

voice she sang, O Shenandoah, I love your daughter . . . O Shenandoah, I'm bound to leave you . . .

In the kitchen, Eunice poured herself a tall glass of tomato juice
and added a touch of vodka. And lemon. Her hands were shaking
badly because too much was going on: the car breaking down,
Jean-Marie showing up unannounced, everyone sleeping late.
(Though she heard — she *thought* she heard — heavy footsteps
overhead. Someone going barefoot down the hall, to the bathroom. Did the footsteps come from her room, hers and Reed's? Or
Kim's? Or maybe it was that girl from Ireland, what was her
name . . .)

Jean-Marie slouched in the doorway, picking at the guitar, at
single strings. Her fingers were quick and impatient, as if she
halfway wanted to break the strings. There's something called
Jake's Garage, she said.

Jake's — ! Yes, that's it, Eunice said, closing the telephone book;
but in the next moment she snatched it up again, to look for the
number. Oh God, I just can't send your father another bill, she
said. You know I had that awful root canal work last winter . . .

Jean-Marie strummed and sang, John Henry he had a little
woman, woman dressed in green, she used to come to the . . . used
to come to the mountain every day, just to hear John Henry's
hammer ring, Oh God, just to hear John Henry's hammer ring
. . . She said, in a flat, low voice: Reed didn't seem very friendly
last night. In fact he seemed a little unfriendly.

Well—

I don't think he remembered me, actually.

Of course he remembered you! Eunice said, turning the pages
nervously. It's just that . . . he . . . he's sometimes . . . he's sometimes moody . . . And you came unannounced . . . And there's
some tension between him and that boy Kim . . . you know . . . did
you meet Kim . . . the photographer . . .

Oh yes: Kim! Jean-Marie said, laughing.

Eunice swallowed a large mouthful of her drink. Someone was
running upstairs, along the corridor.

It sounds as if your guests are up, at least, Jean-Marie said.

Well — it's our vacation, Eunice said weakly.

Did Reed go to Arizona, after all?

Arizona? Why Arizona?

Wasn't there some film or something? — Tucson? — he was saying, in June, he might get a grant from the film institute or whatever it's called —

I don't think that came through, Eunice said.

He had the script mostly written, didn't he?

Jean-Marie, I don't know, why don't you ask him yourself . . .

Eunice had found the number and was about to dial. Her fingers *were* shaking. — Niall Sullivan, that was her name. That charming pug-nosed girl from Ireland.

Reed was distinctly unfriendly last night, Jean-Marie said, running her fingernails sharply across the strings. And Kim too. Oh yes, Kim! And what's-her-name — Sandra.

Honey, you took us by surprise, Eunice said. You know how Reed feels about James.

What's that got to do with me? Jean-Marie asked, opening her eyes wide, as if such a thought had never occurred to her.

I've got to telephone that awful man . . . You wouldn't like to do it for me, Jean-Marie, would you?

Look — you invited me here, Jean-Marie said. *You invited me.*

Of course I invited you, honey, you're always welcome, but we had agreed — you seemed so enthusiastic — the music camp, the mountains —

You're just worried about the fucking tuition, aren't you, Jean-Marie said.

Jean-Marie, Eunice said sharply, I don't *want* you to use that kind of language, I've told you a dozen times . . .

There was a pounding on the stairs, and Kim ran into the kitchen in his bathing trunks, barefoot — short tanned bustling Kim, said to be half Greek and half Spanish, a handsome smiling boy in his early thirties. His dark hair was graying, there were sharp laugh lines around his mouth, but he looked extremely young. He was a quite successful photographer in New York. Eunice was always meeting people who knew him, since she had become acquainted with him — but wasn't that always the way — everyone knew everyone else. Ah, Eunice, he said, blinking, hello Eunice, good morning Eunice! — and Jean-Marie — it *is* Jean-Marie? — yes? Good morning, but is it a *good* morning, the sky looks disappointing again, and I have these people due in an hour and a half for lunch, and I haven't even *begun* thinking — ! He shivered, hugging himself. Eunice noted, sipping at her drink, that there were goose pimples on his arms and shoulders, and that his fingernails were turning mauve. She liked Kim very much. He was so high-spirited, so good-natured. And talented as well. She was not in the slightest jealous of Kim. — What's that you have, Eunice, he asked, sniffing, may I join you? — may I help myself? It's so wretched, waking up, he laughed, baring his splendid white teeth at Eunice and Jean-Marie, it becomes more of an effort every *morning*.

He splashed vodka into a tall blue glass and added a few inches of tomato juice, humming loudly. Eunice saw, but discounted, the odd white strained look on her daughter's face.

Fourteen people are driving out from the city, Kim said, taking a swallow, half-closing his eyes, and I can't begin to *think* about them . . . I intended to make a perfectly delicious curry dish, chicken with diced celery and cucumbers and apples, and slivered almonds, and pineapple, of course, fresh pineapple . . . and as a first course a soup of my own invention . . . and fruit with rum for dessert, maybe a little yogurt . . . plain sugarless astringent yogurt . . . But I couldn't force myself out of bed, and the morning is practically gone, and I'm just going to ask them to turn right around again and I'll take them to lunch at . . . what is that place . . . the lighthouse . . . Reed hates it but I think it's perfectly adequate . . . the lighthouse, he said, snapping his fingers, what is it . . . !

Just The Lighthouse, Jean-Marie said. That's its name.

I should make that call, Eunice said apathetically. She lifted up the receiver and listened to the dial tone. So that I *know* what is going on . . .

One of my guests, Kim said, drawing in his breath luxuriously, is an epileptic.

An epileptic? Eunice said. But —

Oh, he's perfectly safe, Kim said, I doubt that he'll have a fit in front of us, they control these things with pills now, you know. One can lead a normal life, an *almost* normal life, he said, winking at Jean-Marie who was staring stonily at him, the way things are today . . . medical technology . . . that sort of thing. He had colored slightly, perhaps at Jean-Marie's rude stare. His thick eyelashes fluttered. — Oh there was this boy, this pathetic boy, in my high school geometry class, and he choked and fell out of his seat in the aisle and had a fit, right there in the class, a terrible convulsive fit, just like that, his nose was bleeding and blood splashed on

the floor and the desks and the girls' skirts . . . and I almost
fainted, myself . . . I'm such a coward . . . And you know it just
goes on and on: he flopped around like a huge fish.

Did he choke? Jean-Marie asked.

Well — the teacher fortunately had her wits about her, and put
something under his tongue, Kim said, giggling, I think it was,
actually, an emery board — you know, for filing your fingers. So
he didn't die, and he said afterward he didn't remember a thing!
But they just go on and on, you know. Those fits.

That must have been terrible, Eunice said.

She was staring at the tile floor and seeing star-splashes of red
against the simulated slate.

They go on and on, it seems for hours — ! Kim said, shivering.

What happened to him then? Jean-Marie asked.

What do you mean? They came in to get him, he was carried
out, taken to a hospital, Kim said.

Jean-Marie strummed the guitar. The chords were harsh and
flat.

I mean, the rest of his life, she said, what happened to him the
rest of his life . . .

Kim stared at her, sipping at his tall drink, as if he had never
heard of such a peculiar question. Well, he said finally, with a small
laugh and a glance at Eunice, I really don't *know* about the rest of
his life.

Eunice looked from Jean-Marie to Kim, and from Kim to Jean-
Marie again. Her hands were shaking and it terrified her that her
head might begin to shake too. (James's mother, in her dotage, the
skinny neck trembling, the soft hairless dewlaps quivering. As if
with feeling. Anger. Intensity of some sort. But not at all, not at
all — she wasn't the slightest bit of trouble, the nurses bragged,
she could just sit by herself for hours and hours and never complained if the television went on the blink! — she was one of their
pets at the Home.) So she put the receiver down carefully.

It was rude, Jean-Marie's cold pinched stare. The girl had a long
pale horsey face, and her forehead had broken out again, which
was why she had combed bangs down practically to her eyebrows.
She *might* have been pretty, anyway attractive, with her urgent
gray stare that was like James's, and her cute snubbed nose like
Eunice's, if only her skin would clear up. (She refused to go back
to the dermatologist. And probably failed to take her antibiotic

pills every morning.) She might have been very pretty, Eunice used to say, if only she wouldn't *think* so hard that the skin between her eyebrows puckered.

Many years ago, Jean-Marie had slipped away in one of those child-sized sailboats, no more than five feet long, and by the time they missed her she was carried out to sea . . . no, into the Bay . . . they were at the Martzes' place in North Carolina . . . and the Coast Guard rescued her. There was a regular Coast Guard boat, and a helicopter too. Eunice had been terrified, but of course her little girl was perfectly all right, just a bit sunburned, and her photograph was in the paper (the Martzes sent them several copies, for fun) above the caption ADVENTUROUS LITTLE MISS RESCUED BY COAST GUARD. Jean-Marie had been nine at the time.

Out here, at Presque Isle, a helicopter sometimes appeared, making a terrific din. Another Coast Guard helicopter, patrolling the beach. James had made such a fuss, one August, that the officers in Skye Harbor told their men to avoid the Scudder compound; James had threatened to get an injunction against them, or sue them for disturbing the peace. He was a friend of the lieutenant governor's at the time — he had designed a controversial but very striking house for him, in the hills near the state capitol. The house had received a great deal of publicity, not all of it favorable, but Skye Harbor did not want any trouble with James Scudder in any case. His family had once owned half of Presque Isle.

The telephone rang. Eunice knew it was James — she had jinxed herself, thinking of him.

Mother, aren't you going to answer it, Jean-Marie giggled, it's right under your *hand.*

There were footsteps overhead, and on the stairs, and Eunice caught sight of Reed on his way out — swimming trunks, coral sweatshirt, thick coarse wiry dark hair. Behind him, Niall Sullivan, carrying towels and manila folders. (They were working on a project together — authentic folk songs from the West Coast of Ireland — Niall was a Dublin girl, actually — though she had recently received a Ph.D. degree in Anglo-Irish studies at Yale.) Evidently they were not hungry for breakfast.

Eunice picked up the phone and of course it was James.

Kim hurried after Reed and Niall, and Jean-Marie chose that very moment to let her guitar fall, and go rummage through the

refrigerator. Suddenly she was hungry. She hadn't eaten for eighteen hours or more.

Of course it was James, and Eunice had no choice but to talk
with him. He sounded distant and formal, inquiring about tax
records — boxes of tax records — going back to 1974 — in their
apartment in the city. At first Eunice thought he was blaming her
because something was lost, then she thought, gripping the receiver and staring down at her open-toed Italian shoes, at her gay
brave pink-bronze painted toenails (now beginning to chip —
Reed had painted them himself, for fun, one sunny afternoon on
the beach when they had all been in excellent spirits), he's lost a
box of receipts and he will be furious with me because I had the
cleaning woman throw them out, and she had even begun to apologize when it became clear that the material wasn't lost at all and
James was not blaming her: he was only asking permission to enter
the apartment.

Eunice was distracted by her daughter's behavior. Jean-Marie
was squatting before the refrigerator, picking and sampling, poking her finger in the liver paté (which should have been wrapped
up, it was dismayingly expensive and would last another five days),
scooping up a quavering pinkish paste Eunice couldn't identify at
first — oh yes, it was caviar: but it had not been especially good —
making faces, sniffing, wriggling her eyebrows. The eyebrows
were too thick to be attractive: like James's: growing hard and
blunt and dark over the staring gray eyes. What on earth *was* the
girl doing . . . She had opened a can of Tab and was drinking it
thirstily, her head flung back, the tendons in her neck working. A
hungry creature, ravenously hungry, like something that had crept
in from outdoors driven by a ferocious hunger it could not control
. . . Outside someone was yelling, it sounded like Reed.

James was asking: could she call home, tell the doorman to let
him in, have the key ready for him, he'd like to bring the records
to Lou (Lou was James's tax lawyer) this afternoon . . . Eunice,
distracted, had to ask James to repeat himself. Which always annoyed him.

What was Reed yelling about? One of the girls — Sandra Rei-
nert — yelled an answer. The keys to her car? (She drove a
Renault station wagon, a charming little vehicle.) Towels? Eunice
wanted to cup her hand over the receiver and call out that there
were plenty of towels in the downstairs closet, the girl had done a

load of laundry yesterday afternoon. But she didn't want to confuse James.

Jean-Marie was gnawing at a hunk of cheese, still squatting in front of the refrigerator. Close the door, you're wasting energy, Eunice whispered, but she didn't hear. She was eating Stilton cheese, Eunice winced to see her, wasn't it awfully strong like that . . . ? Eunice reached over to poke Jean-Marie on the shoulder. Make yourself a real breakfast, she said. Jean-Marie wiped her fingers on her soiled white bell-bottoms and pulled open one of the bottom drawers, and discovered the heel of a loaf of French bread, which she began to nibble at immediately, though it must have been stale — it was days old.

Odd, how Jean-Marie didn't glance at her mother, or make signals, asking her to say hello to James, or not to let him know she was here: at one time she had been an impish little monkey if anyone was on the phone. Tell Daddy hello, tell Daddy come back here right away, tell Daddy to land by parachute . . . I hear you, James, Eunice said, sipping carefully at her drink (for if he heard the ice cubes clink he would know at once — he always did), you needn't speak as if I'm deaf.

Jean-Marie opened another can of Tab, and shut the refrigerator door with her foot, rather hard. She bounced up, her breasts wobbling inside that shapeless, unbecoming mustard-yellow jersey; Eunice could not help but think that the girl's body was as sullen and antagonistic as her face.

Jean-Marie? What about Jean-Marie? Eunice said cautiously.

Mother and daughter now exchanged a glance — razor-quick, alarmed.

Well, Eunice said faintly, as far as I know . . . *I* don't know . . . instruction in the flute, I remember that . . . and something like music theory . . . harmonics . . . it's written down somewhere but . . . Yes it's said to be a lovely place. Mountains, and . . .

A call came in on James's other phone, and he asked Eunice to wait. She poured herself another inch or two of vodka. Jean–Marie finished the second can of Tab, drinking like a truck driver, as if she were violently thirsty. Her hard little nipples showed through the jersey blouse and Eunice could not help but stare at them, blinking.

You know it makes me nervous, someone eavesdropping, she said to Jean-Marie.

I'm not eavesdropping, for Christ's sake! Jean-Marie laughed. As if I gave a shit what you two talk about.

Jean-Marie! Eunice hissed.

Oh fuck Jean-Marie, Jean-Marie laughed.

Eunice swiped at her with the flat of her hand, and caught her on the side of the head; but not hard; Jean-Marie only giggled.

You don't love me, you don't love any of us, Eunice whispered, her hand pressed over the receiver, I just don't *know* why you came here . . .

Polly threw me out, 's why, Jean-Marie said.

James? Eunice said shakily. James? Are you there?

He was still on the other line, making her wait. That was exactly like him, that rudeness: but she hadn't the strength to hang up.

Outside, Reed and Kim and Niall were headed for the beach. Reed and Kim wore sunglasses though the sky was still gunmetal-gray. Eunice watched them through the screen. What was Kim carrying? A guitar?

Hello James? Eunice said anxiously. I'm afraid I will have to hang up here — I've got to make an emergency call. James?

The line crackled emptily.

Eunice stared at her slow wriggling toes and thought, How vulnerable, how exposed, do they belong to me, and suddenly she was seeing again the Fine Arts building of her undergraduate days, she was on the third floor landing peering up to the fourth floor where the Architecture Department was housed, and where brilliant ambitious young men like James Scudder were working for graduate degrees . . . Eunice was studying interior design, she liked to say, in recent years, that she had had a career "in interior design," but of course that wasn't true: her grades were all C's, she had managed only a single B- and that was a gift from a sympathetic woman teacher who liked to encourage women students: Eunice hadn't any talent at all, and not much enthusiasm for a career. She had been vastly relieved as well as happy when James Scudder asked her to marry him . . . Relieved too when she was finally pregnant, after three years of trying. Now I have done it, she thought, gloating. *Now.*

Jean-Marie, her daughter, now sixteen years old, pirouetting about the kitchen as if she both wanted, and did not want, Eunice to tell James about her. Let me talk to Daddy! Put me on the phone! Daddy, Daddy! When are you coming back! Did you get me a present! . . . An enormous doll from Rio de Janeiro, three feet tall, with a prettily blank porcelain face and rosebud lips: but it was too *big*, it stared too bluntly at Jean-Marie who burst into tears at the sight of it. I hate it! Take it away Mommy! I *hate* it!

Eunice stared at her daughter and remembered suddenly that Jean-Marie was the one who had helped her to bed the night before. Jean-Marie, sniffing and wiping at her nose. But why? Crying. Puffy-eyed. But why?

On the beach, the icy-cold surf stinging her toes. Reed and Niall singing at the top of their lungs: With a down, derry-derry-derry down, down!

Reed gripped her tight. His steel-hard arms closed about her, tight, tight. Laughing, protesting, she was whirled around and around and around . . . Hey nonny, nonny-nonny! Hey nonny nonny-no! The others clapped their hands. The transistor radio was turned up as high as it would go, but the station was distant, the rock music marred by static. Someone appeared at the top of the sea-cliff path, a girl in white bell-bottoms, and no one knew who she was, until she came slipping and scrambling down the path . . .

Later, much later, Jean-Marie had helped Eunice up to the lodge, and up to the room. Where Reed's things were tossed about: jeans, sports shirts, underwear, a handsome linen sports coat with a cuff button missing. Eunice had collapsed onto the bed and Jean-Marie, sobbing, had pulled off her sandals, and loosened her clothing, and wiped the vomit from her mouth . . . The white cashmere sweater from Scotland, someone's Christmas gift from years ago, had been folded with desperate neatness and laid on the ladder-back chair by the window.

Jean-Marie pirouetted again, and did an awkward split. (She had once studied "modern dance" for several months, at St. Ann's.) She said, giggling, You know, Mother, I saw something strange last night. *I saw something strange.* Can you guess what it was?

Eunice shook her head impatiently, indicating the telephone. But James was still on the other line.

Jean-Marie said, First I was going to sleep in Windy Dells, but I changed my mind, I thought maybe I should be closer to you, if you needed me, so I slept down the hall in my old room. There wasn't any linen on the bed but I didn't mind, I slept on top of the bedspread. The rest of them stayed down on the beach for a long time, I fell asleep listening to them, then I woke up and it was quiet and very dark and I didn't know where I was at first, until I heard the surf . . . Mother? Are you listening?

I'm trying to talk to your father! Eunice hissed.

I got up to go to the bathroom, Jean-Marie said in her quick flat voice, and when I opened the door there was Reed and what's-his-name with the curly graying hair . . . Reed had only a shirt on, nothing but a shirt on, and the other one, Curlylocks, Kim, baby-faced Kim, was kneeling on the floor in front of him, and they were really going at it . . . I mean Reed had hold of Kim's head with both hands and he wasn't about to let go, no sir . . . I ran back to my room and pulled the bedspread up over my head, I said *I didn't see right, I didn't see anything,* and all the while, Mother you were snoring your head off — poor Mother!

James returned to the line with an abrupt click. He began speaking rapidly and earnestly about a client from White Plains, a meeting scheduled for later that afternoon, so could Eunice please telephone the doorman and leave instructions *immediately* . . .

I don't want you in that apartment any more! Eunice cried. I don't want you pawing through my things!

James protested — he *certainly* didn't want to paw through her things.

We've been through this, Eunice said wildly, I've begged you to stop harassing me — interfering with my private life —

James shouted something. Eunice began to sob. She held the receiver out to Jean-Marie. I can't tolerate this, Eunice said, twenty-five years — it's your turn — you will have to help me —

Jean-Marie, frightened, began to back away.

You and your filthy mouth, miss, Eunice whispered, shaking the receiver at her. Filthy, lying . . . Malicious . . .

I saw what I saw! Jean-Marie said.

Filthy, lying . . . If your father ever knew . . .

I saw you — all of you! I won't forget! Jean-Marie shouted.

She ran out of the kitchen. Eunice shouted something incoherent after her. She was so upset her entire body shook, her teeth were chattering, a terrible weight pressed against her chest. You liar! Filthy-mouthed liar! she shouted. But the doorway was empty.

Two fat angry tears rolled down her cheeks, immense as rocks on a hillside. Something whined like a mosquito, a tiny voice, and Eunice realized that James was still talking to her, the fool didn't know a thing that was going on, wasn't that just like him — ! Eunice said hotly and harshly: Your daughter is sick! She has an imagination filthy and sick as a schizophrenic's! And *ugly* — you don't know how ugly!

James tried to speak but Eunice interrupted. You don't know! You're only the father! *What do you know!*

She slammed the receiver down, trembling.

She strode into the other room.

Jean-Marie? Where are you?

She retrieved her drink, and took a large swallow. It was tepid, it had no taste. She pressed the glass against her warm forehead but it did little good.

The room smelled faintly of ashes though no fire had been lit in the fireplace for many months. Jean-Marie was nowhere around. The lid of the window-seat was raised. What had they been looking for? The telephone book? Oh Jesus, Eunice thought, the pressure increasing in her chest, I have to telephone the *garage* . . .

She stood at the foot of the stairs, gripping the railing for support. Jean-Marie! she called. Come back down here at once!

She wondered why she had insisted upon giving her baby daughter such a pretentious name — she wondered why James had not dissuaded her.

Jean-Marie! she shouted.

But Jean-Marie did not reply, of course, and Eunice hadn't the strength for the stairs, not at the moment. She studied her watch. Five minutes to twelve. Unless the watch had stopped. A Saturday in early August, and the sky was beginning to clear, and they had several weeks at Presque Isle . . . Reed would regain his good spirits once the sun came out: simple things pleased him. And James had not been angry, he had not accused her of anything.

Eunice stood at the foot of the stairs for some time, until her breathing returned to normal. Finally Jean-Marie appeared above, looking disheveled and puffy-eyed. Mother and daughter stared at each other in silence. Well — ! Eunice said, after a long moment. Jean-Marie stared at her. Her face was long and pale, her skin looked coarse. The downward cast of her mouth was sullen, but contrite as well. Still, she was silent: stubborn and silent: not a word of apology.

You can call that awful man at the garage, Eunice said.

Jean-Marie did not acquiesce. But she did not refuse either.

CYNTHIA OZICK

The Shawl

(FROM THE NEW YORKER)

STELLA, cold, cold, the coldness of hell. How they walked on the roads together, Rosa with Magda curled up between sore breasts, Magda wound up in the shawl. Sometimes Stella carried Magda. But she was jealous of Magda. A thin girl of fourteen, too small, with thin breasts of her own, Stella wanted to be wrapped in a shawl, hidden away, alseep, rocked by the march, a baby, a round infant in arms. Magda took Rosa's nipple, and Rosa never stopped walking, a walking cradle. There was not enough milk; sometimes Magda sucked air; then she screamed. Stella was ravenous. Her knees were tumors on sticks, her elbows chicken bones.

Rosa did not feel hunger; she felt light, not like someone walking but like someone in a faint, in trance, arrested in a fit, someone who is already a floating angel, alert and seeing everything, but in the air, not there, not touching the road. As if teetering on the tips of her fingernails. She looked into Magda's face through a gap in the shawl: a squirrel in a nest, safe, no one could reach her inside the little house of the shawl's windings. The face, very round, a pocket mirror of a face: but it was not Rosa's bleak complexion, dark like cholera, it was another kind of face altogether, eyes blue as air, smooth feathers of hair nearly as yellow as the Star sewn into Rosa's coat. You could think she was one of *their* babies.

Rosa, floating, dreamed of giving Magda away in one of the villages. She could leave the line for a minute and push Magda into the hands of any woman on the side of the road. But if she moved out of line they might shoot. And even if she fled the line for half a second and pushed the shawl-bundle at a stranger, would the woman take it? She might be surprised, or afraid; she might drop the shawl, and Magda would fall out and strike her head and die. The little round head. Such a good child, she gave up screaming, and sucked now only for the taste of the drying nipple itself. The neat grip of the tiny gums. One mite of a tooth tip sticking up in the bottom gum, how shining, an elfin tombstone of white marble gleaming there. Without complaining, Magda relinquished Rosa's teats, first the left, then the right; both were cracked, not a sniff of milk. The duct-crevice extinct, a dead volcano, blind eye, chill hole, so Magda took the corner of the shawl and milked it instead. She sucked and sucked, flooding the threads with wetness. The shawl's good flavor, milk of linen.

It was a magic shawl, it could nourish an infant for three days and three nights. Magda did not die, she stayed alive, although very quiet. A peculiar smell, of cinnamon and almonds, lifted out of her mouth. She held her eyes open every moment, forgetting how to blink or nap, and Rosa and sometimes Stella studied their blueness. On the road they raised one burden of a leg after another and studied Magda's face. "Aryan," Stella said, in a voice grown as thin as a string; and Rosa thought how Stella gazed at Magda like a young cannibal. And the time that Stella said "Aryan," it sounded to Rosa as if Stella had really said "Let us devour her."

But Magda lived to walk. She lived that long, but she did not walk very well, partly because she was only fifteen months old, and partly because the spindles of her legs could not hold up her fat belly. It was fat with air, full and round. Rosa gave almost all her food to Magda, Stella gave nothing; Stella was ravenous, a growing child herself, but not growing much. Stella did not menstruate. Rosa did not menstruate. Rosa was ravenous, but also not; she learned from Magda how to drink the taste of a finger in one's mouth. They were in a place without pity, all pity was annihilated in Rosa, she looked at Stella's bones without pity. She was sure that Stella was waiting for Magda to die so she could put her teeth into the little thighs.

Rosa knew Magda was going to die very soon; she should have been dead already, but she had been buried away deep inside the magic shawl, mistaken there for the shivering mound of Rosa's breasts; Rosa clung to the shawl as if it covered only herself. No one took it away from her. Magda was mute. She never cried. Rosa hid her in the barracks, under the shawl, but she knew that one day someone would inform; or one day someone, not even Stella, would steal Magda to eat her. When Magda began to walk, Rosa knew that Magda was going to die very soon, something would happen. She was afraid to fall asleep; she slept with the weight of her thigh on Magda's body; she was afraid she would smother Magda under her thigh. The weight of Rosa was becoming less and less; Rosa and Stella were slowly turning into air.

Magda was quiet, but her eyes were horribly alive, like blue tigers. She watched. Sometimes she laughed — it seemed a laugh, but how could it be? Magda had never seen anyone laugh. Still, Magda laughed at her shawl when the wind blew its corners, the bad wind with pieces of black in it, that made Stella's and Rosa's eyes tear. Magda's eyes were always clear and tearless. She watched like a tiger. She guarded her shawl. No one could touch it; only Rosa could touch it. Stella was not allowed. The shawl was Magda's own baby, her pet, her little sister. She tangled herself up in it and sucked on one of the corners when she wanted to be very still.

Then Stella took the shawl away and made Magda die.

Afterward Stella said: "I was cold."

And afterward she was always cold, always. The cold went into her heart: Rosa saw that Stella's heart was cold. Magda flopped onward with her little pencil legs scribbling this way and that, in search of the shawl; the pencils faltered at the barracks opening, where the light began. Rosa saw and pursued. But already Magda was in the square outside the barracks, in the jolly light. It was the roll-call arena. Every morning Rosa had to conceal Magda under the shawl against a wall of the barracks and go out and stand in the arena with Stella and hundreds of others, sometimes for hours, and Magda, deserted, was quiet under the shawl, sucking on her corner. Every day Magda was silent, and so she did not die. Rosa saw that today Magda was going to die, and at the same time a fearful joy ran in Rosa's two palms, her fingers were on fire, she was astonished, febrile: Magda, in the sunlight, swaying on her pencil legs, was howling. Ever since the drying up of Rosa's nipples, ever since Magda's last scream on the road, Magda had been devoid of any syllable; Magda was a mute. Rosa believed that something had gone wrong with her vocal cords, with her windpipe, with the cave of her larynx; Magda was defective, without a voice; perhaps she was deaf; there might be something amiss with her intelligence; Magda was dumb. Even the laugh that came when the ash-stippled wind made a clown out of Magda's shawl was only the air-blown showing of her teeth. Even when the lice, head lice and body lice, crazed her so that she became as wild as one of the big rats that plundered the barracks at daybreak looking for carrion, she rubbed and scratched and kicked and bit and rolled without a whimper. But now Magda's mouth was spilling a long viscous rope of clamor.

"Maaaa —"

It was the first noise Magda had ever sent out from her throat since the drying up of Rosa's nipples.

"Maaaa . . . aaa!"

Again! Magda was wavering in the perilous sunlight of the arena, scribbling on such pitiful little bent shins. Rosa saw. She saw that Magda was grieving for the loss of her shawl, she saw that Magda was going to die. A tide of commands hammered in Rosa's nipples: Fetch, get, bring! But she did not know which to go after first, Magda or the shawl. If she jumped out into the arena to snatch Magda up, the howling would not stop, because Magda would still not have the shawl; but if she ran back into the barracks to find the shawl, and if she found it, and if she came after Magda holding it and shaking it, then she would get Magda back, Magda would put the shawl in her mouth and turn dumb again.

Rosa entered the dark. It was easy to discover the shawl. Stella was heaped under it, asleep in her thin bones. Rosa tore the shawl free and flew — she could fly, she was only air — into the arena. The sunheat murmured of another life, of butterflies in summer. The light was placid, mellow. On the other side of the steel fence, far away, there were green meadows speckled with dandelions and deep-colored violets; beyond them, even farther, innocent tiger lilies, tall, lifting their orange bonnets. In the barracks they spoke of "flowers," of "rain": excrement, thick turd-braids, and the slow stinking maroon waterfall that slunk down from the upper bunks, the stink mixed with a bitter fatty floating smoke that greased Rosa's skin. She stood for an instant at the margin of the arena. Sometimes the electricity inside the fence would seem to hum; even Stella said it was only an imagining, but Rosa heard real sounds in the wire: grainy sad voices. The farther she was from the fence, the more clearly the voices crowded at her. The lamenting voices strummed so convincingly, so passionately, it was impossible to suspect them of being phantoms. The voices told her to hold up the shawl, high; the voices told her to shake it, to whip with it, to unfurl it like a flag. Rosa lifted, shook, whipped, unfurled. Far off, very far, Magda leaned across her air-fed belly, reaching out with the rods of her arms. She was high up, elevated, riding someone's shoulder. But the shoulder that carried Magda was not coming toward Rosa and the shawl, it was drifting away, the speck of Magda was moving more and more into the smoky distance. Above the shoulder a helmet glinted. The light tapped the helmet and sparkled it into a goblet. Below the helmet a black body like a domino and a pair of black boots hurled themselves in the direction of the electrified fence. The electric voices began to chatter wildly. "Maamaa, maaamaaa," they all hummed together. How far Magda was from Rosa now, across the whole square, past a dozen barracks, all the way on the other side! She was no bigger than a moth.

All at once Magda was swimming through the air. The whole of Magda traveled through loftiness. She looked like a butterfly touching a silver vine. And the moment Magda's feathered round head and her pencil legs and balloonish belly and zigzag arms splashed against the fence, the steel voices went mad in their growling, urging Rosa to run and run to the spot where Magda had fallen from her flight against the electrified fence; but of course Rosa did not obey them. She only stood, because if she ran they would shoot, and if she tried to pick up the sticks of Magda's body they would shoot, and if she let the wolf's screech ascending now through the ladder of her skeleton break out, they would shoot; so she took Magda's shawl and filled her own mouth with it, stuffed it in and stuffed it in, until she was swallowing up the wolf's screech and tasting the cinnamon and almond depth of Magda's saliva; and Rosa drank Magda's shawl until it dried.

LOUIS D. RUBIN, JR.

The St. Anthony Chorale

(FROM THE SOUTHERN REVIEW)

WHEN I WENT TO STAUNTON to work on the newspaper there I had
the feeling, which I never afterwards quite lost, that I was moving
to a far-off place, remote and different from what I had known. It
is quite possible that if I had first gone there in any other season
than wintertime it might not have seemed that way. As it happened, though, when the bus from Lynchburg turned off the
highway east of the mountains to begin its climb over the Blue
Ridge it was soon traveling along a steeply graded road with ice
and snow everywhere about, and I had the sense that I was engaged in traversing a high wall, a barrier that shut off the Valley
of Virginia from the rest of the world. But it was not only the
mountains and the winter; I saw later that it was also the way that
I was at the time.

I was twenty-three years old then, and this was little more than
a year after the war ended. I had gone for a job interview in
Lynchburg, and from there I took the bus for another interview
in Staunton — pronounced, I reminded myself so as to be sure not
to make a mistake, as if it were spelled Stanton, with no *u* in it.
Once the bus left the main highway and turned westward the
ascent was steady, and soon there came hairpin turns and sharp
climbs. From the window I could look down along the slopes of
mountains and down ravines for long distances, and see only
snowy hillsides and snow-covered trees.

It was a gray day and the clouds were low and heavy, a grayish
white against the sky, so that it was difficult at a distance to tell just
where the horizon ended and the clouds began. I wondered
whether the deserts of Africa were any more desolate in appear-

ance. The bus was a long time making its way over the summit and descending the western slope of the mountains, and even after it reached the floor of the valley and turned toward Lexington and Staunton there were mountains in sight east and west, and snow in every direction.

The impression of the city of Staunton that I took that day was that it was a raw, windy place, somewhat as I imagined towns might be like in the Far West. The wind was blowing very sharply, and though by then it was no longer snowing, fine grains of powdered snow from the mounds heaped along the sidewalks were flying about in the air. The sky had cleared a little, so that there were patches of blue. The buildings and stores of the city seemed old, as if built before the turn of the century or earlier. I saw very few trees along the street. Everything appeared open and exposed to the wind from off the mountains.

The newspaper office, which I found without difficulty, was the kind of old wooden building that I thought of as belonging to Civil War times. It had a show window, just like a store, with the words *Staunton News-Leader — Staunton Evening Leader* in black-shaded gold script on the plate glass, and above the second story a false front with scrolled woodwork and cornices. By comparison with the newspaper that I had worked on in New Jersey, and with others of my acquaintance, it was a very small plant, with business office, newsroom, composing room, pressroom all located on the ground floor.

Even so, I accepted the job when the publisher offered it to me. I had not been told whether or not there would be an opening for me in Lynchburg as a reporter on the considerably larger newspaper there. The job in Staunton was as city editor, with a $50 weekly salary — $12 more than I had been earning in New Jersey before my engagement had been broken and I had quit and come back home. To be made a city editor, after no more than six months of full-time newspaper work, was an elevation in status. True, there was only a single reporter on the staff, and the city editor handled all the telegraph, local, and sports news, made up the pages, and even edited the church news. Nonetheless it could be considered a promotion, and after all that had happened I was in no condition of mind to pass up anything that might enhance my estimate of my own worth.

The Sunday before I left New Jersey for the South I had gone

up to Newburgh to see my uncle. He was my father's older brother
and originally from South Carolina, too. He lived by himself in a
hotel room, and had a collection of phonograph records. He had
begun his career as a newspaper reporter and now wrote radio
scripts. He lived in a place like Newburgh, he said, because he
detested living in New York City but had to be near enough to it
to confer with the network on his script writing. Each morning,
before beginning the day's stint at the typewriter, he would play
music on his phonograph for an hour. In particular he liked the
symphonies of Johannes Brahms.

What we usually did when I went up to visit him was to talk and
listen to music. He had never met my fiancée, and did not offer an
opinion about whether the cancellation of our plans to be married
was a good thing or not. He merely listened. Talking to him about
what happened made me feel less panicky, even though I was
unable to bring myself to speak of the humiliation I felt. I made
out as if the breaking of the engagement had been a mutual decision, but I think he suspected what had happened. When it was
time for me to return to New Jersey he rode the ferryboat with me
across the river to Poughkeepsie, and we walked out along the
station platform to await my train. When the train had pulled into
the station, and I was stepping aboard the coach, he said, "Don't
worry, bud, it'll all come out in the wash."

After I agreed to take the job in Staunton I went back to Richmond on the bus to collect my belongings. My parents were
pleased. They had understood why I had given up my job in the
North, but would have preferred that I move directly from it to
another. As for myself, I too had begun dreading the possibility
that I might have to ask them for help, as if I were still a child.
When I had gone up to work in New Jersey I had felt that at last I
was going to be earning my own living and otherwise becoming,
for the first time in my life, a successful young man, practical and
self-sufficient, able to make my own way. And for almost six
months, despite my small salary, I had been able to convince myself that it was so — until my plans had collapsed and I had lost
any reason for being up there.

The next morning I departed for Staunton, not on the bus but
riding on a train, in a comfortable coach with a reclining seat. I
had lunch in the dining car. Up ahead the locomotive whistled
musically for the crossings. As I watched the piedmont Virginia
countryside pass by the window, I thought that it was a consider-

able improvement over the previous train trip I had made, when I had come home to Richmond from New Jersey. The train that night had been late in leaving Washington and then had been delayed for several hours because of a wreck on the line just south of Fredericksburg. I had to sit for a long time at night in an old, overheated coach with uncomfortable, hard plush seats, trying to read but more often staring out into the darkness, thinking how I was going back to where I came from, and not even able to return there without trouble. My hopes for success as a newspaper reporter in New Jersey and then, as I had confidently expected, in New York City itself were gone. So, too, the notion that I might quickly be able to emulate my uncle and move from newspaper writing into, if not radio scripts, perhaps plays, or, as seemed more appropriate to my interests, poems and stories. Instead I was back in the South, far away from where plays were produced and books published, and I had accomplished nothing. It had been after three in the morning before the train finally arrived in Richmond, and I had taken a taxi home and then had to beat on the front door for a long time before my father at last heard me and came down to let me in. "Well," he had said.

But now, en route to Staunton — pronounced without the *u*, I kept reminding myself — the immediate future at least seemed no longer so uncertain, for I was riding aboard a fast train westward to the mountains, to be the city editor of a daily newspaper, however small.

In Staunton, the place I found to stay was on the top floor of an old three-story house which had been divided up into rooms for rent. The room was large, with windows on two sides, a double bed, a desk, an easy chair, and a wash basin. Compared with the tiny room I had rented in New Jersey for the same price, it was far more satisfactory. It was located just at the eastern edge of the business district, a block south of the campus of a women's college, and about five blocks from the newspaper office, up a steep hill. The city of Staunton was very hilly and had considerably more trees along the streets than I had thought when I first saw it. The snow had melted a little when I arrived to stay, but it was still along the sidewalks and on the lawns and the rooftops. The people at the newspaper said that we would be likely to get several more heavy snows, for it was only February and the weather did not customarily break until about the first week in March.

However, in my new job the weather would be of comparatively little importance to me, for from the time I began work, in the late afternoon, until I left the office after 1 A.M., almost the only time I ventured outside the building was when I went out to eat dinner. I came to work about 4 P.M., checked the night Associated Press budget to see what was expected over the teletype that evening, learned from the woman who was the paper's only reporter what she would have in the way of local news, then began laying out the front page and editing copy. As the evening's news from the outside world began arriving on the teletype, I edited it up and wrote headlines. The teletype copy was in all capital letters, and it was necessary to mark it for capital and lower case for setting on the linotype. About six o'clock I went out to dinner. On the way I usually stopped at a newsstand to buy a magazine or a paperback book to read at dinner. An hour later I was back at work, editing copy steadily. Sometimes I took news over the telephone from a correspondent, and sometimes the reporter had an evening City Council meeting or another such late story, but usually everything was on hand by ten o'clock, except for breaking news on the AP teletype. If I had a story to send out over the AP, I scheduled it on the wire, and when the bells rang to signal me to begin sending, I punched it out on the teletype keyboard.

When most of the copy had been set into type and I had edited and placed headlines on all the news that was to go into the paper, I went into the composing room and saw to the page layout, making cuts and changing about type to fit. There were only two or three pages of fresh type, which was all that the plant's four linotype machines could handle in an evening. Much of the type we carried was picked up from the afternoon paper, with the headlines reset into the morning paper's typographical style and the time references changed. By midnight we were usually ready to pull a proof of the front page, and after I checked it over for errors I went to work editing up some of the assortment of copy that was mailed in by rural correspondents in outlying areas, which would be set into type early the next day. The edition came off the press about one o'clock in the morning, and I was free to leave once I had finished editing up all the correspondents' copy and a few filler stories.

Several blocks away, not far from the railroad station, there was an all-night restaurant, and when I finished work I went there for what in effect was my supper. Since I knew no one, I sat by myself at the counter, reading the paper or a magazine while I waited for my order to be filled. After eating I walked up the long hill to my room. By then it was close to 2 A.M., but I was far from feeling sleepy yet, so I read for a while and listened to the radio. Because of the altitude I could pick up stations in the Midwest much more clearly than those to the east or the south. From two to three in the morning I listened as I read to a classical music program on a Chicago station called the Starlight Concert. By three o'clock I was usually sleepy enough to turn off my reading lamp and go to sleep.

•

The truth is that during all of this time, from the very night I had come back to Richmond from the North, throughout the several weeks of job hunting, and now in the first weeks of my new job, I was waiting for a letter. Exactly what its contents were to be I should have been unable to say, even though I wrote drafts of it to myself in my mind from time to time. It was from the girl to whom I had been engaged to be married, and what it was supposed to announce was that everything was not irrevocably over between us.

It was not that I did not possess all the proof to the contrary that should have been needed to convince me. During the weeks after I left New Jersey I had come to realize in retrospect that the breaking of the engagement had not been a sudden decision, but planned out well in advance. I saw too that her parents, both of whom I had liked very much, had undoubtedly been in on the secret, and the three of them had plotted how and when it was to be done. In my naïveté I had failed to read signs that were being flashed to me. No doubt her parents, who I was sure liked me, had been chagrined at my inability to realize what was taking place. The thought of that was so humiliating that I could not bear to think about it.

Yet despite the fact that such realization was intermittently coming to me, I was managing to keep from dwelling upon it most of the time, shoving it back into the periphery of my consciousness, as it were, by assuring myself that it did not matter, that one day soon the letter would arrive that would change everything. There need not be an outright confession of error and remorse, a plea to resume as before, to have the ring returned to her, to plan the wedding. What would suffice was a letter which took up as if nothing had happened, implicitly assumed a continuing relationship,

expressed pleasure and interest in my new job, even hinted perhaps of a desire to come for a visit sometime to see me in my new
surroundings.

Because of the late hours I was now working, when I woke up in
the morning it was seldom earlier than eleven o'clock. I went out
to a restaurant to get my breakfast while others were eating lunch.
Then I stopped in at the newspaper office to see whether there
was any mail for me. Afterwards there were three hours or so
remaining before time to begin work. Usually I went back to my
room, since there was no place else for me to go. I hoped that
there would be mail, for then I could answer it. If not, usually I
read until time to begin work. The city library was located near my
room, and several days a week I stopped in there to find new
books, usually taking three and four at a time to my room. What I
liked most were archaeology and Civil War history. The library
was housed in the former residence of Stonewall Jackson's cartog-
rapher, the famous Jed Hotchkiss, and there were many books
about the war.

During my first few weeks in the new job I was busy learning
what was involved in getting out the newspaper. Not even in the
afternoon, in my room, did I often think to feel bored or lonely.
My first Sunday in town, when there was no paper to get out that
evening, I had felt the time hanging heavy for a little while, but I
wrote letters. I rather liked being there by myself in my room,
listening to the New York Philharmonic concert on the radio, with
the snow falling steadily beyond the windowpane. I could hear the
truck traffic on the Valley Pike, which ran just below my window,
laboring up the hill, and the road maintenance crews scraping the
snow and spreading sand and salt on the icy grade. Later on I
heard the westbound Chesapeake and Ohio train whistling on its
way through town. After dinner I wrote a letter to my uncle. He
had responded to my account of my new job with the observation
that it would be good training, though his guess was that after a
time I would find it tiresome to be doing only a routine of desk
work each day. I told him that while he might well be right, for
now at least I found the editing quite interesting. I did not add
that what I liked most of all was just that routine, and that the
more hours a day it demanded of me, the more grateful I was for
it.

The day when the letter arrived was at the very end of February.
It came in response to one that I had finally written, on a pretext

having to do with the return of a book I had borrowed from a library some time ago and left behind me in New Jersey. It was one of several letters waiting in my mailbox at the office, and my first, reflexive response was to shove it quickly to the bottom of the stack of envelopes I was holding, as if by postponing the reading of it, even for a few minutes, I might also postpone its meaning as well. For at that instant I was quite certain of what it would say, and I realized too that I had known all along. After a moment I tore open the envelope and hastily scanned the words, written in the familiar penmanship, on a double sheet of notepaper.

What was said was little more than a repetition of what had been said to my face a month earlier, together with the comment that my own letter had seemed to be written in anger, and that she was happy to see that I was indeed angry, which I had every right to be, she said. "The little bitch!" I said aloud, and looked around me to assure myself that no one had heard me speak. "The little bitch," I repeated under my breath. For not only had I not written in anger, but I saw that by pretending that I had been angry she was assuaging any feelings of guilt she might have had at having hurt me. What I had accomplished by writing was to provide her with an opportunity to enjoy feeling distressed at having to decline my love. I thrust the letter into my pocket and left the office. "The damn spoiled little bitch!" I said aloud as I walked up Coalter Street, after first looking to see that no one was within hearing distance. "Now I really *am* mad. Mad as hell!"

Yet as I was saying these things, I knew I was deceiving myself not at all. The truth was that I should have liked to be angry, to resent the way I had been put aside, as one might put aside a novel when one finished enjoying it, or, more appropriately, I thought, as a child might put aside a set of finger paints once the novelty of being able to make pretty configurations with one's fingers had worn off. But I could not make myself feel anger — only a sense of humiliation.

I felt grateful that the barrier of the mountains existed, protecting me from further involvement. The condition to which I should aspire, I felt, was an emotional and moral numbness, a complete freezing of emotional engagement, so as to make myself impervious. If I could cultivate an attitude of unconcern and indifference to my present circumstance, then ultimately I might be able to bring my memory to a similar invulnerability.

And for a while it seemed to be working. I found that if I went to the office a little earlier than usual, and if I worked a little later after the paper had gone to press, I could stretch my working hours so that they filled most of my waking hours, leaving only a brief period between the time I arose in the very late morning and went out to get breakfast, and the time I began the night's work, when my thoughts were not occupied by the requirements of my job. And after I had put the paper to bed and gone by for a sandwich at the all-night restaurant, I was sufficiently tired that when I went to my room I could read about the Civil War or the exploration of the Upper Nile and listen to music on the radio until almost dawn without feeling restless and lonely. After a few days I came to know something close to actual contentment at the way I was managing. I even decided that there would be no need for me to go home to Richmond on weekends. I would simply stay in my room and read. For the first time since I had come back South, I felt that I was close to being master of my emotions. I did not require anyone else's company.

•

How long I might have continued in this way if the winter had held on, I cannot say. But there came a day when the ice and snow were gone, the streets and lawns were wet from the melting, and the temperature was suddenly up in the sixties. Almost overnight the Valley changed from a stronghold of frozen rock into a swiftly thawing garden. Everything around me now began turning toward color and warmth. To the west of my room, and visible from my window, was a low mountain called Sally Grey, which had loomed over the little winter city in barren woods and stark granite. So perfectly had it seemed to match the frame of mind to which I aspired that I would sit and look at it for long intervals, as if through focusing my thoughts upon it I might acquire its hardness. But now the bare crest was giving way to a faint but unmistakable green, and the trees along the slopes, which had seemed so sterile and rigid, were fringing into a blurred growth that softened and obscured the harsh outlines of the hillside. And late at night, when I finished my work and went by the all-night restaurant, I discovered to my dismay that the darkness, which had seemed so chilled and barren that I was glad to retreat to my room where I could read and listen to music, had now acquired a depth and resonance that I found threatening to my feeling of immunity.

Yet the night proved to be as much my ally as my enemy. For it was, after all, very late when I finished at the newspaper and had eaten my supper; I had been at work for ten hours and more, so that I was not obligated to reflect that under more fortunate circumstances I should have been enjoying the company of a girl — if I had a girl. Rather, by the time I was done with work it was an hour when I could only have expected to be alone anyway, so that I did not need to be ashamed at my solitary condition or believe that if only I were more attractive and desirable than I was I would not be left to myself.

Thus on a Saturday night in March, after the paper had been printed and I had stopped by the restaurant, I found the night so warm and inviting that instead of proceeding home to my room I decided to walk down to the railroad station two blocks away. It was, after all, no longer Saturday night at all but very early on Sunday morning, so that I need not feel, as I had so often done, that there was something wrong because I did not have a date.

The station was deserted except for a clerk in the ticket office of the lighted but unoccupied waiting room. I walked out along the platform to the west of the station, where the rock cliff that lay just beyond the double track slanted off. To the west I could hear a train whistle blowing. It must be a freight train, I decided. I would wait and watch it come through town before I went back to my room. I took up a seat on an empty baggage cart. Except for the whistle of the train, the town was still; I could hear an occasional automobile go by along Beverley Street three blocks away, but that was all.

Listening to the train drawing nearer, until eventually I could begin to hear the iron wheels reverberating along the rails, I felt a note of satisfaction in my solitariness that made the night seem not merely amiable but even harmonious, as if I were a part of it. To be seated there by myself in the darkness, past two in the morning, with no one else nearby and very few of the inhabitants of the community that lay around me even awake, seemed entirely appropriate. I felt a measure of pride in my separateness, a sense of resolution in being as I was, alone in the nighttime in a mountain town where I knew almost nobody and was known to few. The road that had brought me there, I thought, had been deceptive and erratic. It had not been remotely what I had imagined or intended for myself. Yet here I was, on a faintly warm night in the very early spring (or the tail end of winter, according to the calendar), with the city asleep around me and the C&O freight train blowing for the crossings as it neared town.

Finally the night freight came banging into the city, the locomotive headlight probing through the darkness like a baton, until as it drew close the light thrust into view, in swift counterpoint, objects I had not hitherto made out: a row of boxcars on a siding, semaphores, telegraph poles, switch blocks, a warehouse alongside the tracks. It played upon the jagged rock wall of the cliffside across the way, breaking it into a mosaic of planes and recesses. The locomotives — there were two of them, their drive wheels performing in unison — rolled powerfully up and past, and I could see for a moment the firemen and engineers in their cabs, high above the tracks, illuminated by the red glow of the open firebox doors. Then a freight car, and another, and another; one after the other clanged past, chains rattling and the flanged wheels singing as they cruised along, their song punctuated with a chorus of creaks and bangs and bumps as the cars held to the rails, in cadenced processional, a hundred cars and more, until at last the sound lightened and the caboose swung past.

As I turned to watch it go I saw a trainman standing on the rear platform, lantern in hand, with the red and green lamps above him. He waved to me and I waved back, and I watched as the caboose receded rapidly past the columns of the station platform and into the darkness, the signal lights solemnly glowing, and then around the bend of the rock cliff and out of sight. And all I could hear was the movement of the wheels in the distance, growing fainter as the train cleared the city limits and headed eastward. Further and further away, off to the east, the whistle sounded ever more distantly for the crossings. I sat on in the darkness, all by myself again, in no hurry to leave, listening pleasantly.

"The sleeping city," I said to myself, half aloud. I might write a poem entitled that. And only myself awake to listen. Lyrical whistle of the freight train, miles to the east and receding eastward. But then I heard another and, as it seemed, answering whistle, dirge-like and much fainter. The freight train could not possibly have moved so far away so rapidly. It must be the westbound passenger train, which came through the city each morning at about three o'clock. I looked at my watch in the darkness. It was indeed after three. If I waited for the passenger train to come and go, it would be almost four before I got back to my room and to bed. And what of that? What was to hinder my staying here for as long as I wished, till broad daylight if I chose? Tomorrow I could sleep even later than usual. Besides, tomorrow was Sunday — more properly, it had now been Sunday for more than three hours. I might do whatever I wanted; there was no one to object. Since I worked when others slept, the night was fairly my own.

I could now hear two trains whistling; there was no doubt of it. They were both far away, but one was coming toward Staunton. There was a noise behind me, not far from where I sat. I turned and saw a man engaged in loading some sacks of outbound mail onto a cart. When he was done he began pulling it up the concrete station platform. The train whistle was closer now, and presently I could hear the monotone of the wheels on the rails. Far down the platform, almost past the station, a man and a woman were standing, with suitcases alongside. That was where the pullmans would be stopping.

Now the passenger train came gliding into the station, the headlamp abruptly materializing from around the rocky bend. The locomotive moved up and past me, immense and stern, its high drive wheels performing their revolutions very slowly. It pulled to a stop a hundred yards ahead. Opposite me on the rails was a darkened coach. I watched down the track as the porters swung down with their yellow footstools. Even at that hour there were some passengers debarking. The man and woman I had seen waiting now stepped aboard, with the pullman porter following them, carrying their luggage; the arriving travelers walked off toward the station.

The train did not stay long. After only a few minutes I heard the conductor calling "All aboard!" and saw him signaling with his flashlight to the engineer up ahead. The air brakes went off with a hot iron hiss. The locomotive coughed twice in staccato explosion, and the train began easing forward into a slow, sustained rolling. I watched as the day coaches went by, then the dining car, cold and dark and the windows fogged, each to a swifter rhythm than its predecessor. Then the pullmans: City of Ashland, Collis P. Huntington, Balcony Falls, Gauley Bridge. The last pullman swept past in clattering haste. The red and green lamps receded westward. I listened until they were well out of sight. Soon the locomotive was blowing for grade crossings to the west of town. It would not be long before the train would have cleared the valley and begun climbing into the Alleghenies. As for the freight train, it was out of earshot now, and doubtless thundering along the grades of the Blue Ridge, bound for Charlottesville and the Northeast.

I walked home in the dark, feeling tired now and quite pleased with myself. It was well on toward four o'clock in the morning, I had seen two trains arrive and depart, and now I was all alone again on the deserted streets of the mountain town. I felt that I had accomplished something, had asserted my sensibility. I was persuaded, too, that whatever my present inconsequence, I was inevitable. On just what grounds this assurance was to be based, and for what, I could not have said. Yet the certainty, as I thought it, made me walk faster and breathe hard as I climbed up the hill toward my rented room, all by myself, at four in the morning, acting out a silent melodrama of prideful fulfillment.

•

The next day, however, after I had gone out almost at noon to eat breakfast at the hotel restaurant, I felt no such assurance. My confidence, my optimism of the evening before now seemed not merely misplaced but pathetically absurd. For in the light of a warmish Sunday in mid-March I saw myself in a different perspective, as a self-important young man with neither talent nor assurance, who had thus far failed at everything he had ever undertaken to do. I worked at a nighttime job that made it almost impossible to meet other people and make friends and have dates with girls. And what was worse, I had been glad of it, because it enabled me to hide from myself the knowledge of my ineptitude and unattractiveness. Now, because it was Sunday and I possessed no such refuge for the ten or twelve hours before I could fall asleep again, I felt trapped and in panic.

I remembered how, the previous evening when the freight train had been calling in the night as if to me alone, I had fancied that I was going to write a poem about the sleeping city. What vanity! For I knew very well that on all occasions when I had attempted to write anything, I had been quite unable to produce three lines that were not empty, pompous, and flat. Whenever I actually sat down before my typewriter and tried to begin anything other than a routine newspaper article, all my confidence, and all the ideas I had in mind, swiftly went stale.

I read the Sunday *New York Times* in my room, then tried reading a book for a while, but could not escape my gloom. I decided to go out for a walk. Perhaps the spring weather would divert me. On Sundays only there was an eastbound local passenger train that came through town about two o'clock. I would go down to the station and watch it.

As I headed eastward on Beverley Street I saw several couples, my age or younger, strolling along, looking at the displays in the store windows, chatting happily. There were two couples who were holding hands. Students from the local women's college and their dates, I decided. A year ago and I had done as much.

I passed the Stonewall Jackson Hotel. Would I end up like my uncle, living in a hotel room somewhere? He didn't seem to mind. I envied him his spartan invulnerability, his hermit-like ability to live by himself and not care about anything except his work.

I walked on toward the depot. Waiting near the tracks were a young man and several girls who seemed to be a little older than college age; they did not look like students. I walked past them, near enough to be able to hear what they were saying. They were talking with each other in French, and laughing at each other's pronunciation. They must be teachers at the college, I thought.

I should have liked very much to get to know people like that. I would have delighted in using my French, as they were doing. But I had no excuse for venturing into their conversation. As if waiting for the train, I stood not too far distant, observing them from the corner of my eye. If only I had some reason, some plausible excuse, for joining them. I knew that someone more sure of himself, more sophisticated and less self-conscious, would need no occasion but would simply go up to where they waited and strike up a conversation.

The train came drifting into the station. I had been so preoccupied that I had paid it no heed. One of the girls was apparently going away on a trip, or else returning somewhere after a visit to the others; the man was carrying her suitcase. I watched them as they said good-bye. Then after the girl who was leaving had gone inside the coach and found a seat by a window overlooking the platform, they were waving. *"Bon voyage!,"* one of the girls on the platform kept calling, mouthing her words very deliberately so that her friend on the train might read her lips.

If I were to go aboard, I thought, I might take the seat next to the girl and strike up a conversation. And why should I not do so?

I might ride as far as Charlottesville and then take the evening train back to Staunton. I was free; I had nothing to prevent me from getting aboard and going along on the journey eastward. The thought frightened me, and instead I merely looked on as the railroad conductor signaled to the engineer, the vestibule doors slammed shut, the airbrakes went off, and the train moved from the station.

The young man and the two remaining girls who had escorted the traveler to the station waved good-bye, then walked off toward town. As they went by, one of the girls glanced at me for an instant. Hastily I averted my eyes, and so as not to seem to be following them, I walked a block eastward along the station platform and then took a side street back toward my rented room.

When I reached my room I turned on the radio. The New York Philharmonic Sunday concert was just beginning. Dmitri Mitropoulos was conducting the *Symphonie Pathétique,* which I disliked. Yet I did not switch it off. As if to torture myself, to make my afternoon complete, I lay on my bed, face downward, and listened to the oh-so-melancholy music.

They had been conversing in French. How very cultured, how very toney! And I, eavesdropping, watching them from a few yards away, had been standing there like a gawky fool and wanting to join them. The sensitive soul indeed. How very Romantic! The lonely young man in the mountains! The thought of my pathetic posturing made me wince.

A few months ago on a Sunday afternoon, and her father and I would probably have been playing chess and listening to this self-same concert. That *he* had been in on the plan! I writhed at the thought. During all that time, for at least a month and very probably two or three, she had her mind made up to send me packing, and had only been awaiting the Proper Moment. But in my invincible vanity I had proved so obtuse as not to see what should have been plain. So there had been the need to make it obvious, overt. And in discussing it, they had pitied me! The poor, naïve young man from down South . . .

"Damn!" I said aloud, over the melancholy music. "Damn!" Who in hell was she, who were they, to pity me?

It was true. Who *were* they? For while it was undeniable that I was lonely and missed very much having a girl, it need not be *her.* I could see that now.

I leaped up from the bed and walked across the room to the east window. The Sunday afternoon traffic was moving along Route 11. I thought, by God, I will write her a letter and tell her exactly what I think of her spoiled, stinking self. I went over to my typewriter, placed a sheet of paper in the machine. I stared at it a minute, then ripped it out. Hold on now, I told myself, just because you see daylight you are not out of the woods just yet. It would be exactly what she would want — another sequel to the little game of Falling Out of Love. I had had all I wanted of games. I crumpled the sheet of paper into a ball, threw it across the room at the wastepaper basket. It hit the wall, bounced in.

It must have been the people at the train station. I thought of how I should enjoy cramming their French conversation and their silly chatter down their cultivated throats. But that was not what I was angry about, was it? No, I had wanted to join them. My anger was for myself. Yet how could I expect to be other than what I was?

I lay in bed, and gradually became aware that the *Symphonie Pathétique* was concluded, and the commentator, Deems Taylor, was talking about the next number to be played by the orchestra. His mellifluous, too urbane voice droned on. Johannes Brahms had long put off writing a fully symphonic work, and it was not until he was forty-three years old that he completed his first symphony. The *Variations on a Theme by Haydn,* though originally composed for two pianos, was really a trial run, so to speak, whereby Brahms had for the first time used the full resources of an orchestra to develop an extended symphonic creation. The theme he had chosen, said Deems Taylor, was a choral work by Haydn, the *St. Anthony Chorale.*

Then, without warning, all unprepared as I was to meet it, there came the most cadenced, masterfully gentle music, calm and reassuring, that I had ever heard. In unhurried progression, tranquil and controlled, yet by no means without strength or resonance, the theme spoke out confidently, sustained and borne alone by the horns and violins. I had always liked Brahms, but this composition possessed a sweetness and harmoniousness that seemed to soften and transform everything around me — the air, the room, the time of day. The music formed itself into an assertion, an acknowledgment of purpose, but without either panic or desperation. It climbed steadily forward, building to a more urgent reiteration, but only enough to make its point, without any clamor or abandonment of its dignity and congruence. It closed on three drawn-out, unhurried chords. ST. ANTHONY, I thought, as if punching out the letters on a teletype keyboard, STANTON. Without the *u* in it.

The variations that Johannes Brahms had made on the theme by Haydn continued, and I listened on. But because I was young and had almost until that moment been in love, as I lay on my bed and the music played I did not think to wonder why it was that the pleasure I drew from the music was so like that which I took from the trains. Neither did it occur to me, being neither traveler nor musician but only a newspaperman temporarily resident in a mountain town in Virginia, to consider the odd coincidence in names, or even to ask who St. Anthony was. That truth, if such it proved to be, would come. For now, for Sunday afternoon, I was content to lie and listen to the music.

RICHARD STERN

Wissler Remembers

(FROM THE ATLANTIC MONTHLY)

MISS FENNIG. Mr. Quincy. Mr. Parcannis. Miss Shimbel. Ms. Bainbridge. (Antique, silver-glassed, turn-of-the-century Rebecca West
face, at twenty-two.) Miss Vibsayana, who speaks so beautifully.
(You cannot relinquish a sentence, the act of speech such honey in
your throat. I can neither bear nor stop it.) Miss Glennie. Mr.
Waldemeister. All of you.

Do you know what it is for me to see you here? To have you in
this room three hours a week? Can you guess how I've grown to
love you? How hard it is for me to lose you?

Never again will you be a group. (Odds against, trillions to one.)
We've been together thirty hours, here in this room whose gaseous
cylinders amend the erratic window light. Those spritzes of autumn the neo-Venetian neo-Gothic windows admit. We have spoken in this room of Abbot Suger, minister of state, inventor of
Gothic, have cited his "dull minds ascend through material
things." (Not you, never yours.) But did I tell you that I took a
trolley to his church, Saint-Denis, sitting next to a Croatian lady
who trembled when I told her that just a week before I'd talked
with the little salesman Peter who'd been, who was, her king?
There's been so much to tell you, woven by my peripatetic memory
to our subject.

The thing is I want to tell you everything.

Though I will see some of you again, will write many of you
letters of recommendation — for years to come — may even, God
knows, teach your children (if you have them soon), may, someday, in Tulsa or West Hartford, see you when your present beauty
is long gone, I know that what counts for us is over. When you

come up to me in Oklahoma or Connecticut and ask if I remember you: "I took your Studies in Narrative course nine years ago" — or twenty-five — I will not remember. If you remind me that you wrote a paper on Wolfram's *Parzival,* that you were in class with the beautiful Indian girl, Miss was-it-Bisayana? and Mr. Parcannis, the boy who leashed his beagle to his bicycle, perhaps I will make out through the coarsened augmentation and subtraction of the years both you and that beautiful whole that was the class of Autumn '77, Winter '62. But what counts is gone.

Teaching.

I have been teaching classes for thirty years. Age twenty-one, I had a Fulbright Grant to teach fifteen hours a week at the Collège Jules Ferry in Versailles. The boys, *in*-and-*externes,* ages ten to nineteen, prepared for the baccalaureate exam. Four days a week, I walked the block and a half from the Pension Marie Antoinette and did my poor stuff. I was so ignorant of French, I had addressed the director as *"Directoire."* ("I thought you were trying to get to a government bureau.") When I entered the classroom, the boys rose. A thrill and an embarrassment to an awkward fellow not born a prince of the blood. "Good morning, boys." "Good morning, Meestair Weeslair." Much sweetly wicked *ritardandi* of those long syllables. "Today we will do an American poem. I'll supply the French translation, you translate into English. Anyone who gets within twelve words of the original gets a present." Five of the twenty-five understand; they whisper explanations to the others. Blue, black, brown, gray, green eyes intensify and shimmer with competitive greed. (Every student is numbered by class standing and introduces himself accordingly: "I am LeQuillec, sixteenth of twenty-five.") "Here's the poem. Forgive my pronunciation.

> *"A qui sont les bois, je crois le savoir,*
> *Il a sa maison au village.*
> *Et si je m'arrête, il ne peut me voir,*
> *Guettant ses bois qu'emplit la neige."*

The next day I collect the English versions.

> *To whom are that wood, I believe to know it.*
> *It have its house at the village.*
> *And if I arrest, it is not able to see me,*
> *Staring its woods who fills the snow.*

"Not first rate, LeQuillec. *Pas fort bien.*" I read them the original. "*Ça vous plaît?*" "*Ah ouiiii, M. Weeslairrre. Beau-coup!*"

I see LeQuillec's dark pout, the freckles of Strethmann, the begloved, elegant what's-his-name? — Persec? Parsec? — who wrote me the next year in Heidelberg: "Dear Mr. Wissler. How are you? I am well. You shall be happy to know I am fourteen of thirty-one this trimestre. How do you find Germany?"

Très bien, Persec. I am teaching at the university here. In the *Anglistikabteilung.* Two classes. For the *Öhrgeld,* four hundred marks — a hundred dollars — a semester. Not a great fortune, so I work for the Department of the Army decoding cables at the Staff Message Control. I have Top Secret clearance, which enables me to forward the reports of suspected Russian breakthroughs at the Fulda Gap the coming Christmas Day. One week I work from six P.M. to two A.M., the next a normal daytime shift. My classes adjust to this schedule. *The American Literary Experience.* 1: *Prose.* 2: *Poetry.* The first assignment, James's *The Ambassadors.* American libraries all over West Germany send me their copies of the book. I give the class a week to read it. The class shrinks from forty to seven. I don't understand; they rapped on their desks for two minutes after Lecture One. Still, even students who apologize for dropping "because of schedule conflicts" come to me on the street, doff caps, shake hands. A girl runs up the Hauptstrasse to me, asks if I will sign a petition. "For Helgoland, Professor." "Fräulein . . . ?" "Hochhusen, Professor." She is nearly as tall as I, has hair a little like Ms. Bainbridge's, heart-rending, popped blue eyes, hypnotic lips. "Forgive me, Fräulein, I don't think I can sign political petitions when I work for the American Army." Unlike students later on, she says, "I understand, Professor." What a smile. "Excuse me for troubling you." "No trouble, Fräulein. It's a pleasure to see you. I love you." (I do not say the last three words aloud.)

•

I teach the sons and daughters of soldiers whose bones have been left in the Ukraine and the Ardennes. I teach those who themselves fired guns, were prisoners, received lessons on such scum as I. We read Emily Dickinson, Thoreau, *Benito Cereno,* Hawthorne (some of whose nastier views run parallel to their old ones). I talk of the power of blackness and try and connect it to the rubble of Mannheim, Ludwigshafen, Frankfurt.

The first poems we do are German: Goethe, Trakl, Heine. To show them what close reading can do for poems. They take to such naked delights like literary sailors ashore after months. *Sie sassen und tranken am Teetisch, Und sprachen von Liebe viel.*

American soldiers fill the Heidelberg streets, eat in special restaurants with special money. I live in a special hotel, buy food in the American Commissary. *The ambassadors.*

Fräulein Hochhusen helps me with my first German poem. "Will you check this for me, please, Fräulein? I just felt like writing it. I don't trust my German."

Wir waren einmal ganz neu.
Solange die Stellen brennen,
brennen wir Heu.

Once we were utterly new.
So long as places burn
we burn [make?] hay.

"It is not exactly correct, Professor, but very — how shall I say? *Eindrucksvoll. Original.* Original. And your German is beautiful, Professor."

No, Fräulein, berry-cheeked Fräulein with the burnt-hay hair, it's you who are beautiful. Give me the petition, darling Fräulein. Tell me about Helgoland. Will they test bombs there? And who owns it? Germany? Denmark? I want to know everything. Is my poem true German? Is it a poem? Do you love me as I love you? "You're much too generous, Fräulein. I feel so bad about the petition."

Herr Doppelgut, stooped, paper-white, dog-eyed, had walked three hundred kilometers, "black across the border," yet manages to get whitely back to see his mother and bring me dirt-cheap books from East Berlin. When I go there at Christmastime, with my visa stamped by all four occupying powers, I walk through thirty ex-blocks of ex-houses and ex-stores. Ash, stone dreck, half an arch, a pot, a toilet seat, a bicycle wheel, grimacing iron struts. Insane survivals. In front of the Russian memorial tank, a young guard holds a machine gun. From my new language text, I ask, *"Vy govoritny russki?"* Silence. *"Nyet?"* I think I see the muzzle waver. "Robot," I say, yards off. Gray ladies in beaten slippers fill carts with rubble and push them on tracks across the street where other aged ladies unload them. I go back to Thoreau's beans, to the white whale, to intoxicated bees and Alfred Prufrock, to Herr Doppelgut and Fräulein Hochhusen, to close readings of poems. Of breasts.

Yes, I cannot omit something important. In every class, there is another system of love at work. The necks, the ears, the breasts, the cropped hair of Ms. Bainbridge, the go-ahead green eyes of Miss Fennig, the laughter. There are more parts of love than a city has sections, theaters, parks, residences, businesses, Skid Row.

I move to Frankfurt. To take a higher paying job teaching illiterate American soldiers. A tedium relieved only by new acquaintance with the bewildered backside of American life: ex-coal miners, fired truck drivers, rattled welterweights, disgraced messengers, sharecroppers, fugitives, the human rubbish conscripted to fill a quota, shoved now into school for the glory of the Army. I have the most beautiful single class of my life with them. End of Grade Four. There is a poem in our soldiers' textbook, "A Psalm of Life." *Tell me not in mournful numbers, Life is but an empty dream, For the soul is dead that slumbers, And things are not what they seem.* We go over every word, every line. How they begin to understand, how deeply they know these truths. Sergeant Carmody, whose boy is dead in the new Korean War. Gray-haired Private Grady, who writes his mother the first letter of his life: "I am in Grad To, mother. I work hard every day but mother I think it is to late for me now." Pfc. Coolidge, mouth a fortune of gold teeth, a little black man who joined up after being injured on the job (the Human Missile in Bell and Brothers' Circus) and whom I summon to VD clinic every Monday afternoon. "Dese froolines lak me, Perfesser." Carmody, Coolidge, Grady, Dunham, Leake, Barboeuf. The class ends on your breathlessness, your tears, your beautiful silence.

•

Back home, then, to Iowa, to Connecticut, and then here, in the great Gothic hive of instruction and research. Hundreds of classes, hundreds and hundreds of students. Themselves now writing books, teaching classes, building bridges (over rivers, in mouths), editing papers, running bureaus, shops, factories. Or dead in wars, half alive in madhouses. *"Dear Mr. Wissler. I am in a bad way. No one to write to. There is nothing for me. Help, help, he . . . ,"* the *"lp"* dropped off the postcard (mailed without return address from Pittsburgh). *"Dear Professor Wissler. Do you remember Joan Marie*

Rabb, who wrote the paper on Julien and Bonaparte in 1964?" I do remember. For it was a paper so gorgeously phrased and so profoundly opaque that I called in the dull, potato-faced Miss Rabb to explain it. And with explanation — missed connections filled in, metaphors yoked to amazing logic — the potato opened into a terrible beauty. *"I married, Professor. A ruffian, a churl. Children have come. Four, under six. I could not sustain the hurts."* "Miss Rabb, if you can ever put down on paper what you've told me in the office, you will write a work of genius. But for now, you see why I must give you a C." *"You liked the paper, thought it, thought I, had promise. What I have done, with great laboriousness, is to transmute it into the enclosed poem. Will you see if the promise is herewith fulfilled? Have I a work which has at least merchandisable power?"* Fifteen penciled pages, barely legible, and when read, wild, opaque, dull. "Dear Mrs. MacIllheny. I look forward to reading your poem when the pressure of the term is over. Meanwhile, I hope you regain your health. With good wishes from your old professor, Charles Wissler."

At times — very few, thank God — there have been students who've rubbed me the wrong way. (How many have I antagonized? Surely many more, but the standards of courtesy are so powerful, only the rudest and angriest breach them.) "I have never, never, never, never, never in my life had a C before. Is it your intention, Mr. Wissler, that I not go to law school? Do you delight in ruining my *entire academic record?"* Terrifying calm from the plump, parent-treasured, parent-driven face. "One C does not a bad record make, Ms. Glypher. Admissions officers know that anyone can have a bad class, an imperceptive instructor." "Lovely philosophy, sir, but that does not change the C. It does not get me into LAW SCHOOL." (May I never be cross-examined by Sophia Glypher.) "What can I do, Ms. Glypher? Can I change the grading system to accommodate your ambition?" A wicked stare from the not unbeautiful gray eyes. Since you are so clearly intelligent, Ms. Glypher, why is it that you don't see that my standards curve around sweetness, beauty, charm?

"I'll write an extra paper. Retake the exam."

"There are two worlds rotating around each other here, Ms. Glypher. One is the world of papers, exams, grades, degrees, applications, careers. It is a fairly rigid world." Or unfairly. "It is as strictly ruled as chess. Break the rules, you break the world. This is the world that's supposed to count. In the other world, there are no grades. In that world you're not a C student. I don't know what you are. Or what I am." Ms. Glypher rumbles here on the verge of a discourtesy which might draw us into open combat. As it is, there is struggle. (Unequal.) "That world's one without end. I see my job more in that world than in the one in which I grade you C." Even as I oppose her, wrestle within her magnetic hatred, I believe this. "In that world, we're equal. To some degree partners. Your accomplishment there becomes mine, mine yours. It's the world that counts."

"But not for law school, Mr. Wissler. I don't object to poetry, but I'm talking reality."

"Ms. Glypher, the whole point is that you aren't. You are so attached to the one world that you don't even see it clearly. The admissions officers, happily, do. They will recognize your talent even through what you think of as this stain on your record. If you like, I will put a letter in your dossier explaining my belief in your talent along with the reasons I graded you as I did."

"I don't think I'll trouble you to do that," says Ms. Glypher in her finest moment. One which tempts me to the drawer where the change-of-grade slips are kept.

Before, within, and after classes, the stuff of articles, books, lectures — San Diego, Tuscaloosa, Cambridge — East and West — Lawrence, Kansas, Iowa City, Columbia, South Carolina, Columbia, 116th Street, New York, Kyoto, Bologna, Sydney, Buenos Aires, Hull, Nanterre, Leiden. Everywhere wonderful faces, the alert, the genial, the courteous (the bored, the contemptuous, the infuriated — but few). And everywhere, love, with the sexuality displaced (except in the instance that became Wife Number Three). That has been priestly excruciation.

Then pulling toward, docking at, and taking off from fifty, I became conscious of the love that has been under all the others. I love individuals, yes, and I stay aware of clothes, bodies, gestures, voices, minds, but it is the class itself I love. The humanscape. The growth of the unique molecule of apprehension and transmission. From the first, tense, scattered day through the interplay, the engagements, the drama of collective discourse, to the intimate sadness of the last class. How complicated the history, the anatomy, the poetry of such a body.

Miss Fennig. Mr. Quincy. Mr. Parcannis. Miss Vibsayana. Except

for your colors, your noses, your inflections, your wristwatches, I
can tell very little about your status. (You are from a warrior caste
in Bengal, Miss Vibsayana. You wrote it in a paper. Miss Glennie,
you were the brilliant, solitary black girl in the Harrisburg paro-
chial school. You gave me hints of it in office hours.) But I know
you inside out, would like to give you all A's. (Won't.) All that part
is clear, though Mr. Laroche won't know that the extra paragraph
he tacked on his paper lowered his grade from B-plus to B; nor
Mrs. Linsky that if she'd not spoken so beautifully about Stavrogin,
she would not have passed.

                                    •

December. The last class. There is amorous ether in the room.
(Isn't it what alumni organizations try to bottle?) Don't we all sense
it this last time?

   "There's a fine book by the French scholar Marrou on the history of education in antiquity. I recommend it generally, but mention it in this windup class because in that book I first encountered
the idea that there are strikingly different notions of individuality.
One sees this also in the first volume of Mann's Joseph series.
People hardly know where their ancestors leave off and they
begin. That might be straining a bit. Marrou speaks of family
identity. So certain Roman families were known for certain sorts
of generosity, others for sacrifice. That's certainly still true. Think
of American families associated with philanthropy or public service. Even if an individual in the family feels it goes against his
grain to go public — as it were" — smiles from Miss Fennig, Mr.
Waldemeister — "he is still conscious of the possibility of public
life. I don't say that makes it harder or easier for him."

   Miss Fennig's slim face is alight, her eyes floatingly green under
her large spectacles. She runs her hand through her long hair, in,
up, out, back. Mr. Quincy's urchin face is stippled — such pain for
him — with hormone frenzy. He tries to sit where he can see Miss
Fennig. The brilliant, troubled Miss Shimbel is about to speak. I
wait. She shakes her head. How she understands, speaking only
on demand, resigned from so much, but — who knows? — perhaps already launched on some intricate enterprise.

   I talk more. I watch. Mr. Parcannis questions. Miss Vibsayana
responds, endlessly, softly, the thousand bees of her throat dis-
charging their nectar into syllables.

   "Forgive me, Miss Vibsayana, what you say is beautiful, but I'm
afraid we must finish off."

Wonderful inclination of eyes, head. "Excuse me, Professor."

"Not at all. You know how much I enjoy your notions. How much I enjoy all your notions. It has been a splendid class. For me. There is almost no future I think should be denied you. What world wouldn't be better led by you?"

I don't say that. Instead: "I will have office hours next week. If you have questions about your papers, the course, anything at all, please come see me. And come whenever you like next quarter. We haven't gotten as far as I'd like, but you've helped get us quite far. Good-bye and good luck to all of you."

We have no tradition of farewell — applause, rapping, waving. Still, the faces compose a fine comprehension of our bond. There is the sweetness of a farewell between those who have done well by each other. (It does not exclude some relief. On my part as well.)

In the hall, Miss Vibsayana approaches. "May I — I don't quite know how to put it, Professor — but I feel privileged that you permitted me to take this course."

"I'm grateful to you for contributing so much to it. Thank you."

•

Outside, darkness falling into the white lawns. The paths are mottled with perilous clots of ice. The Gothic buildings shine beautifully under the iron filigree lamps. A half-moon hangs off the bell tower.

People, thickened bundles of cloth and fur, walk home. Hellos, good nights, goodbyes. Talk of exams, of Christmas plans. Streaks of snow like hardened meringue. The fierce winter looms. And whoops, heart gripped, I'm heading down, gloved hands cushioning, but a jar.

"Oh, Mr. Wissler. Are you hurt?" Miss Fennig. What an embarrassment.

"No, no, not at all." She bends, gives me her bare hand. I hold it and get pulled while I push up. "Thanks so much. My first fall of the year."

"I took two awful ones yesterday," she lies.

"I wish I'd been there to pull you up. Thank you again."

"Are you sure you're all right?" Her fine green eyes, unspectacled, shimmer with tenderness.

"I'm just fine, thank you. I think it's wonderful that our last day should see me being pulled out of the snow by you. I wish you were around whenever I took a tumble."

"I'll try to be. It almost makes me hope you'll fall again."

"I will, Miss Fennig. And I'll look for you. Good night now."

"Good night, Mr. Wissler. Take care."

You too, Miss Fennig. You too, dear Miss Vibsayana. Mr. Parcannis. And LeQuillec, wherever you are. *Gute nacht,* Fräulein Hochhusen. So long, Sergeant Carmody. You too, Ms. Glypher. So long. Take care. Good night, my darlings. All of you, good night.

ELIZABETH TALLENT

Ice

(FROM THE NEW YORKER)

THE ABYSSINIAN CAT will not bear kittens; at some point during her pregnancies she aborts them. The veterinarian who sees her refers to these as spontaneous abortions. After the abortions the cat eats roses — yellow roses, tea roses, Seashell roses, white roses on thornless stems. My mother knows she will then find the cat, emptied of her litter, crouched on the highest shelf of the linen closet. My mother always keeps roses in her house. She is adamant about the value of certain things: old Persian rugs, McGredy's Ivory roses, Abyssinian cats. Sometimes I have seen her watch the cat doubtfully, stroking her — not with her fingertips but with her knuckles, her hand curved like a boxer's fist when his manager is lacing the gloves, at once relaxed and expectant — down the nape of the neck to a point between the shoulder blades, where her knuckles rest, having found the cat's center of gravity. The cat stares through the window. Her shoulder blades seem thinner than the bones in my mother's hands. I have seen my mother, when she thinks she is alone, examining her breasts in a mirror.

Whenever I call, she tells me first about the cat, whose nuances of behavior must be studied and reflected upon in the way that Eskimos analyze falling snow.

"Perhaps her pelvis is too narrow," my mother said the last time we talked. "Mine nearly was."

"I didn't know that," I said.

"No?"

"No."

"You don't need to worry," my mother said. "Yours isn't."

•

My grandmother hated cats. She is supposed to have thrown one of the earlier Abyssinians out of the window of a second-story apartment; the cat landed lightly on the roof of a cream-colored Mercedes-Benz. It was the eve of my mother's wedding when this happened. Her eyes, the next morning, were painfully red behind her veil, which my father forgot to lift before he kissed her. My grandmother was said to have given them an enormous sum of money; she wanted them to buy an island. Islands were the only way you could be sure of what was yours. In the end, she doubted everyone around her — the priest, the neurosurgeons, my mother. I remember her as an old woman who could not sleep. Once, when I went into her room to kiss her good night, she took my hand and held it to her throat, asking me whether I could feel the pulse. Her skin felt like a series of damp veils, like the wet paper you fold over the wires when you are making papier-mâché animals; it was cool against the tips of my fingers. I could smell her Chanel No. 22. "I feel it," I told her, though I wasn't sure. She was angry and thrust my hand away.

I think my mother envisioned oxygen tents and sudden intimacies, but my grandmother broke her neck falling down a flight of icy steps one evening in 1979. She had rested for a time at the bottom of the steps, one gloved hand below her cheek, the other hand (mysteriously ungloved) outstretched before her in the snow. When they lifted her, one of the ambulance men blew the snow from the deep creases in her knuckles. My mother called the undertaker to inquire about the use of perfume. "She has always, always, worn Chanel No. 22," my mother told them. Worn it, treading delicately down the centers of the icy steps, on the inside of her wrists, above the collarbones that curved like gull's wings against the cloth of her little black dress, and (for all anyone knew) in the blue-veined hollows of her skinny thighs. Before the funeral, my mother daubed Chanel behind my grandmother's ears. Her head was posed oddly on the pillow, her neck craned into a rigid, chin-upward position, the way someone will suddenly stare if you say, "Look, skywriting!" Afterward, immediately before they closed the casket, one of the neurosurgeons who had been attending my grandmother since her first stroke touched my mother lightly on the arm. "You know, she wasn't in any pain," he said. "Your mother probably never even knew what hit her."

My mother made a barely perceptible movement with her left

shoulder, upon which the neurosurgeon's hand rested. No one, not even someone who was watching closely, could have called that movement a shrug.

All of this, my mother insists, was probably for the best. "In all seriousness, I don't know whether she could have endured another year," she says. The old woman sometimes forgot the names of the cats, the various species of roses; she confused the names of composers with those of television anchormen. In the last few weeks she is supposed to have taken to hiding food in her bedroom, eating it furtively at night.

•

And now my grandmother does not have to endure, as my mother does, the spectacle of her grandchild as a figure skater. According to my mother, skating in the Traveling Ice Adventures is only one or two extremely narrow social notches above working in an actual circus. She came to see me once, in a brand-new city amphitheater so luminous and silent that the sounds of our skates hissed back at us from the curving walls. The streets around the amphitheater had been plastered for weeks with posters advertising our coming. I could tell that my mother was shocked by my face on those billboards, two stories high.

When we spoke of the show later, over dinner, she was diplomatic. "Those lights do make your skin look odd, don't they, darling," she said. It is the lights — streaking the ice in gaudy purples, watermelon reds, deep indigo — that most people remember, not the skating. She speared a scallop with the tines of her fork, scrubbing it vigorously in the sauce. "But I did like it when you went into those pirouettes," she said. "If I squinted, I didn't really have to see the ice. I only saw you, and it looked as if you were dancing by yourself instead of with that bear."

"There's nothing wrong with the bear," I said.

"No, darling, I didn't say there was," she said. "He was very amusing."

"Whenever you unsquinted your eyes."

"I dislike glaring lights."

"It is a show. For little kids. Who *like* glaring lights."

"Of course," she said.

The bear's face is painted in an amicable grin. When we waltz, he looks out over my shoulder, grinning and nodding. The photographer used to like to photograph the bear like that, catching the line of my bare back beneath the bear's sloping jaw. For a while I was sleeping with the photographer, who traveled with us doing publicity stills for local television spots. He was a very good photographer, and he left to work for Japan Air Lines. He called me one evening from Los Angeles, where he has been taking pictures of Japanese stewardesses. They are all beautiful, he says, although he is not used to their eyes; he can't seem to bring out any reflections in them. They arrive at his studio with truckloads of kimonos; they pose with their hands in their sashes, and their skin is powdered to the color of the insides of almonds.

After dinner my mother kissed me good night; I had to catch a taxi to the airport. After the kiss she paused, her hand still cupping my cheek. I could feel her wedding ring, round and cool against the knuckle. "Roses have become my whole life," she told me. "I wish you could find something that would suit you, something you could put your whole heart into." She paused. "Don't think you know everything," she said finally. "It could happen to you. You could end up alone."

•

"I don't like to see you taking chances," my partner says. He is already half dressed, wearing the bear mask, which rests against his chest. His body always seems incredibly slender before he puts on the rest of his shaggy bear's outfit. Half man, half bear; I rather like him in his hybrid condition. He watches me put on my makeup, blinking at the light in my streaked blond hair. My hair wasn't always blond, but it seems that the promoters of the show cannot envision a dark-haired woman dancing with a bear — only a blond one. He lifts a human hand and strokes his dark bear's cheek softly.

"You could lose your job," he says. "They don't mind canning the women. They can't come by male skaters anymore, so they're careful, but women skaters are a dime a dozen. You've seen those girls following Harry around, trying to catch his eye."

"Harry doesn't *know* skating," I say. I choose my lipstick judiciously. If you take very good care of your lipsticks, you trim the tips with a razor blade so that they give you the cleanest line. My lipsticks are always blunt — I used some of them for years — and sometimes my mouth seems pouting and smeared. I unscrew the lipstick from its gold cylinder, I shape my mouth into a firm oval. The mirror blazes with the reflections of small blue-white bulbs; I can see the bear watching curiously over my shoulder. I am not good with the makeup tonight, and my partner notices.

"It's not whether he knows skating, it's whether you want to keep your job." He is disturbed, because, last week, I fled from him in earnest. I skated fast and hard, eluding his rough bear paws until the last possible moment, when our record was running out. When he caught me I could feel the heat of his breath on my face. The lines we had cut stretched behind us in the glossy ice. My ankles were trembling. He held me softly. No one laughed or applauded. It will not happen again.

"Of course I want to keep my job," I say. "Nobody wants to lose their job. Sometimes I antagonize Harry, sometimes he antagonizes me. That's the way it goes." I fold a Kleenex into an origami swan, which makes me think of the photographer. In L.A. there must be swans. When I was a child I made origami birds, horses, strange fish in many-colored translucent papers. My mother urged me to take up oil painting. "You're so artistic," she would say. "You should make things that will *last*." It was true — the origami animals did not last. I lost them, or the Abyssinians tore them apart, or they blew out of windows into the street. I blot my lipstick with one of the wings of the origami swan. The bear watches me closely.

"How did you do that with just Kleenex?" he asks.

"Sometime I'll show you."

"I don't want to lose you," he says carefully. "You're a good partner; you really take it seriously. We understand each other."

"You're not going to lose me. You're stuck with me for a long while yet."

"If you could just watch it on the artistic stuff. You know how Harry feels when you get artistic. You raise his blood pressure a couple of points. He likes nice balance, accuracy, definition. You go off into a world of your own, you're lost to the rest of us, you botch the rhythms. That's what Harry sees. We try to cover for you, but he sees."

"It hasn't been that often," I say. "I've been sticking pretty close to the program, and you know you like it when I change things. You know you like it."

"All right, I *like* it," he says. "It gets so damn boring out there — all those little girls in pink birthday dresses, all the mothers in common-sense-care Dacron pantsuits. Sometimes I think they're bringing the same people in to every show — they just haven't told us. I think I recognize some of the faces. I've seen them in Toronto, in Tallahassee, in Sioux Falls. One of these days I'll just start waving at them and I won't be able to stop. The dancing bear always gets a laugh when he does anything human. That's the point. Not that he's a bear but that he's a clumsy, aborted, blotchy human being, puttering around on his ice skates with a blond woman in his arms. I can't skate without music, you know? Even in my head, when I dream about skating I hear this terrible tinny music in the background. I have to hear it before I can face the ice."

The bear's theme is played on trumpets and cymbals. He dances out into the light, he spins into a series of figure eights with his paws arching above his head, he cocks his head at the audience. He told me right away, as soon as we started working together, that he was gay, that he had once wanted to be a welder. Hundreds of little girls wave at him. He is bathed in a pink spotlight that follows him across the ice, veering and pausing skittishly.

"I know," I say. "It can get to you."

"You can't fight it," he says. He shakes his head. "Harry sees you. He's not dumb. He knows you're trying to sabotage the routines, bring the artistic stuff in. You can't go off on your own like that; the spot men don't know what you're doing. You have to stay with me, in my arms."

"I'll stay with you," I tell him. I want the bear to calm down; he seems badly shaken. His huge furry mittens lie side by side on the dressing table, like companionable Scottish terriers. I choose the small jar of plum-colored cheek highlighter. I have always had good cheekbones. The bear pulls on his arms, and then his legs. He has to fight to get his skates on; the massive bear-middle has made him unwieldy. I watch him in the mirror. The bear will court me with wit and elegance while I skate in carefully circumscribed arcs, the light shining in my blond hair. The meaning of this is not lost on the small girls who watch so intently from the bleachers.

He finishes with his skates, and although he is thinking it, he does not say "Come on." I choose an eye pencil and remove its cap. Thoughtfully, taking great pains, I lean forward toward my reflection in the mirror and fill in the colored shadows around my eyes.

•

Harry watches me from the entrance ramp, keeping his hands in his pockets. Over his shoulder, the no-smoking sign glimmers purple. The narrow-hipped ballerinas sidle meekly past him, emerging one by one from the darkness into the brilliant light of the rink. I have seen Harry interview the ballerinas; he leans forward confidentially across the width of his marble-topped desk, his hands resting palm upward, beseechingly. He wriggles his fingers; it is somehow an extremely intimate gesture. His office is filled with cigarette smoke and old posters of Traveling Ice Adventures. He stares intently into the ballerina's eyes until she looks down, or away. "Are you on the pill?" he asks finally. His fingers tremble.

Now, as the ballerinas move across the ice, the beam falls through the translucent petals of their tutus. Their bare arms, held rigidly above their heads, are goosepimpled in the sudden cold. They hold their heads down shyly, watching one another from the corners of their eyes, and flutter across the ice on their skates.

"Swan Lake again," the bear says. "I hope to dance to Swan Lake at Harry's funeral."

In the darkness near us, children eat popcorn from oil-stained white paper bags, staring at the rink in a kind of ecstasy, their faces tense. Beside me the bear fidgets with one of his knees, which is loose. I have never really got used to the darkness; you skate from the shadows into the light so fast that there are always a few moments when the nerves in the retina of your eye cannot adjust, when you are skating purely by instinct.

•

When my mother called me this afternoon, she said that the cat had lost another litter, had vomited the petals of a Kordes' Perfecta all across the Persian rug. "I might as well give up on her," my mother said. "She will never have the temperament for it. The vet has prescribed a series of mild tranquilizers. He says it may be something in the environment which disturbs her, it may be purely psychological. But I really thought she was going to keep them this time. I just had a feeling."

"You couldn't know," I said.

"I shouldn't have forced her," my mother said sadly. "You should see how frightened she is of the toms. She just looks at them with her eyes squeezed almost shut, and then she flattens her whole body against the floor. But her face is so beautifully marked;

everyone notices the shadings in the gray around her eyes. I think to myself that if she could only have kittens she would feel tranquil, that she'd adjust to them once they were born. It changes you, you know. I've never seen another like her. Now I have no choice."

"You couldn't have known," I said again. "You've been patient with her, haven't you?"

My mother paused, and I could hear the static in the background rising and falling. It sounded as if someone, not my mother, was breathing, listening impatiently to the awkward silence that had fallen between us. "Did I ever tell you that on the day your grandmother died she was running away from home?" she said softly. "The neurosurgeons had recommended confinement. It wasn't that she was dangerous, but she was badly in need of counseling, absolute quiet and rest. Somehow she overheard a conversation, and she climbed out of the window of her room."

There was a sudden fumbling at her end of the line, and a silence. "Here," she said suddenly. "I'm holding kitty up to the phone so that she can hear you. Whisper something in her ear, just between the two of you, won't you? Whisper something."

·

"I had a letter from Ben this morning," the bear says suddenly. "Ben is doing fine, isn't he?" Ben is my lover, the photographer.

"If you had a letter from him, then you should know how he is," I say.

"As far as I can tell, he's O.K.," the bear says. "But there is this odd tone to the letter — a disjointedness, as if he can't really make the connections, he just knows where they should be. I'm used to Ben, you know; I've worked with him for months. That's not the way he talks." He pauses, looking away from me into the brilliantly lit rink. The ballerinas skitter and regroup. They cling to one another, glittering, their bodies transparent beads fitted together on the slenderest stems.

"I don't think that anything's really gone wrong," I tell him. "It might just be L.A. — some kind of culture shock."

I can see the profile of the bear, dark and thoughtful. He strokes his cheek, clumsily now that he has his paw on. The paw has no claws — only black rubber hooks that curve down over the broad fur toes. "I don't know," he says. He is thinking hard. "He said he pulled some pictures of you from the developing fluid, and there you were. He said it occurred to him then that he was sorry he'd left."

"Why are you telling me this? Wasn't it supposed to be confidential?"

"I'm not sure about that, either," says the bear. We both hear the cymbals at the same moment, and the bear readies himself. He skates out, gliding alone onto the glaring ice, his head tilted back so that his eyes gaze upward into the crowd. There is an expectant ripple of applause. The bear bows. He moves with a dainty, shaving noise across the ice. Ballerinas file past me in the darkness, on the way back to their dressing rooms. "Damn!" one of them says. "I lost an earring. Everybody look for a small pearl earring." The ice itself is vast, the bear is a solitary misshapen figure gliding in a circle of light. He does his figure eights, and I close my eyes, following his movements on the inside of my mind. I have seen him so many times, and he always uses the same inflections, the same half-humorous, half-mocking gestures. I wait for my cue, then I appear at the entrance to the ramp. The yellow light filters through my hair, it slides in a pale aura across the ice where I am to skate, it falls from a tiny window high in the darkness above us. It brushes the ice soundlessly, colliding playfully with the bear's spot, me in my colored circle, he in his. He stares at me, pretending to be startled. The children laugh. He holds out his arms, he wags his head. My bones will show through my skin, this light is so brilliant. It is very cold. We dance, keeping the slight distance between us, me skating backward, him forward. The blades of our skates cut small curved channels in the mirroring ice, a fine powder clings to the white suede of my skates. The bear rocks forward; he catches me on one of my shy, evasive sprints, and we close and dance together, woman and bear, my blond hair against the massive darkness of his chest. His chin rests lightly on the crown of my head as he stares past me into the crowd. Suddenly, astonishing both of us, I find myself weeping in the circle of his shaggy arms.

The bear tilts his head and whispers, "You know, don't you, that you are not yourself?"

JOHN UPDIKE

Still of Some Use

(FROM THE NEW YORKER)

WHEN FOSTER helped his ex-wife clean out the attic of the house where they had once lived and which she was now selling, they came across dozens of forgotten, broken games. Parcheesi, Monopoly, Lotto; games aping the strategies of the stock market, of crime detection, of real-estate speculation, of international diplomacy and war; games with spinners, dice, lettered tiles, cardboard spacemen, and plastic battleships; games bought in five-and-tens and department stores feverish and musical with Christmas expectations; games enjoyed on the afternoon of a birthday and for a few afternoons thereafter and then allowed, shy of one or two pieces, to drift into closets and toward the attic. Yet, discovered in their bright flat boxes between trunks of outgrown clothes and defunct appliances, the games presented a forceful semblance of value: the springs of their miniature launchers still reacted, the logic of their instructions would still generate suspense, given a chance. "What shall we do with all these games?" Foster shouted, in a kind of agony, to his scattered family as they moved up and down the attic stairs.

"Trash 'em," his younger son, a strapping nineteen, urged.

"Would the Goodwill want them?" asked his ex-wife, still wife enough to think that all of his questions deserved answers. "You used to be able to give things like that to orphanages. But they don't call them orphanages anymore, do they?"

"They call them normal American homes," Foster said.

His older son, now twenty-two, with a cinnamon-colored beard, offered, "They wouldn't work anyhow; they all have something missing. That's how they got to the attic."

"Well, why didn't we throw them away at the time?" Foster asked, and had to answer himself. Cowardice, the answer was. Inertia. Clinging to the past.

His sons, with a shadow of old obedience, came and looked over his shoulder at the sad wealth of abandoned playthings, silently groping with him for the particular happy day connected to this and that pattern of coded squares and colored arrows. Their lives had touched these tokens and counters once; excitement had flowed along the paths of these stylized landscapes. But the day was gone, and scarcely a memory remained.

"Toss 'em," the younger decreed, in his manly voice. For these days of cleaning out, the boy had borrowed a pickup truck from a friend and parked it on the lawn beneath the attic window, so the smaller items of discard could be tossed directly into it. The bigger items were lugged down the stairs and through the front hall and out; already the truck was loaded with old mattresses, broken clock-radios, obsolete skis and boots. It was a game of sorts to hit the truck bed with objects dropped from the height of the house. Foster flipped game after game at the target two stories below. When the boxes hit, they exploded, throwing a spray of dice, tokens, counters, and cards into the air and across the lawn. A box called Mousetrap, its lid showing laughing children gathered around a Rube Goldberg device, drifted sideways, struck one side wall of the truck, and spilled its plastic components into a flower bed. As a set of something called Drag Race! floated gently as a snowflake before coming to rest, much diminished, on a stained mattress, Foster saw in the depth of downward space the cause of his melancholy: he had not played enough with these games. Now no one wanted to play.

•

Had he and his wife avoided divorce, of course, these boxes would have continued to gather dust in an undisturbed attic, their sorrow unexposed. The toys of his own childhood still rested in his mother's attic. At his last visit, he had wound the spring of a tin Donald Duck that had responded with an angry clack of its bill and a few stiff strokes on its drum. A tin shield with concentric grooves for marbles still waited in a bushel basket with his alphabet blocks and lead airplanes — waited for his childhood to return.

His ex-wife paused where he squatted at the attic window and asked him, "What's the matter?"

"Nothing. These games weren't used much."

"I know. It happens fast. You better stop now; it's making you too sad."

Behind him, his family had cleaned out the attic; the slant-ceilinged rooms stood empty, with drooping insulation. "How can you bear it?" he asked her, of the emptiness.

"Oh, it's fun, once you get into it. Off with the old, on with the new. The new people seem nice. They have little children."

He looked at her and wondered if she was being brave or truly hard-hearted. The attic trembled slightly. "That's Ted," she said.

She had acquired a boyfriend, a big athletic banker fleeing from domestic embarrassments in a neighboring town. When Ted slammed the kitchen door two stories below, the glass shade of a kerosene lamp that, though long unused, Foster hadn't had the heart to throw out of the window vibrated in its copper clips, emitting a thin note like a trapped wasp's song. Time to go. Foster's dusty knees creaked when he stood. His ex-wife's eager steps raced ahead of him down through the emptied house. He followed, carrying the lamp, and set it finally on the bare top of a bookcase he had once built, on the first-floor landing. He remembered screwing the top board, a prize piece of knot-free pine, into place from underneath, so not a nailhead marred its smoothness.

After all the vacant rooms and halls, the kitchen seemed indecently full of heat and life. "Dad, want a beer?" the red-bearded son asked. "Ted brought some." The back of the boy's hand, holding forth the dewy can, blazed with fine ginger hairs. His girlfriend, wearing gypsy earrings and a "No Nukes" sweatshirt, leaned against the disconnected stove, her hair in a bandanna and a black smirch becomingly placed on one temple. From the kind way she smiled at Foster, he felt this party was making room for him.

"No, I better go."

Ted shook Foster's hand, as he always did. He had a thin pink skin and silver hair whose fluffy waves seemed mechanically induced. Foster could look him in the eye no longer than he could gaze at the sun. He wondered how such a radiant brute had got into such a tame line of work. Ted had not helped with the attic today because he had been off in his old town, visiting his teen-age twins. "I hear you did a splendid job today," he announced.

"They did," Foster said. "I wasn't much use. I just sat there stunned. All those things I had forgotten buying."

"Some were presents," his son reminded him. He passed the can his father had snubbed to his mother, who took it and tore up the tab with that defiant-sounding *pssff*. She had never liked beer, yet tipped the can to her mouth.

"Give me one sip," Foster begged, and took the can from her and drank a long swallow. When he opened his eyes, Ted's big hand was cupped under Mrs. Foster's chin while his thumb rubbed away a smudge of dirt along her jaw which Foster had not noticed. This protective gesture made her face look small, pouty, frail, and somehow parched. Ted, Foster noticed now, was dressed with a certain comical perfection in a banker's Saturday outfit — softened bluejeans, crisp tennis sneakers, lumberjack shirt with cuffs folded back. The youthful outfit accented his age, his hypertensive flush. Foster saw them suddenly as a touching, aging couple, and this perception seemed permission to go.

He handed back the can.

"Thanks for your help," his former wife said.

"Yes, we do thank you," Ted said.

"Talk to Tommy," she unexpectedly added. She was still sending out trip wires to slow his departures. "This is harder on him than he shows."

Ted looked at his watch, a fat, black-faced thing he could swim underwater with. "I said to him coming in, 'Don't dawdle till the dump closes.' "

"He loafed all day," his brother complained, "mooning over old stuff, and now he's going to screw up getting to the dump."

"He's very sensi-tive," the visiting gypsy said, with a strange chiming brightness, as if repeating something she had heard.

•

Outside, the boy was picking up litter that had fallen wide of the truck. Foster helped him. In the grass there were dozens of tokens and dice. Some were engraved with curious little faces — Olive Oyl, Snuffy Smith, Dagwood — and others with hieroglyphs — numbers, diamonds, spades, hexagons — whose code was lost. He held out a handful for Tommy to see. "Can you remember what these were for?"

"Comic-Strip Lotto," the boy said without hesitation. "And a game called Gambling Fools there was a kind of slot machine for."

The light of old chances and payoffs flickered in his eyes as he gazed down at the rubble in his father's hand. Though Foster was taller, the boy was broader in the shoulders, and growing. "Want to ride with me to the dump?" Tommy asked.

"I would, but I better go." He, too, had a new life to lead. By being on this forsaken property at all, Foster was in a sense on the wrong square, if not *en prise*. Once, he had begun to teach this boy chess, but in the sadness of watching him lose — the little bowed head frowning above his trapped king — the lessons had stopped.

Foster tossed the tokens into the truck; they rattled to rest on the metal. "This depress you?" he asked his son.

"Naa." The boy amended, "Kind of."

"You'll feel great," Foster promised him, "coming back with a clean truck. I used to love it at the dump, all that old happiness heaped up, and the seagulls."

"It's changed since you left. They have all these new rules. The lady there yelled at me last time, for putting stuff in the wrong place."

"She did?"

"Yeah. It was scary." Seeing his father waver, he added, "It'll only take twenty minutes." Though broad of build, Tommy had beardless cheeks and, between thickening eyebrows, a trace of that rounded, faintly baffled blankness babies have, that wrinkles before they cry.

"O.K.," Foster said, greatly lightened. "I'll protect you."

LARRY WOIWODE

Change

(FROM THE NEW YORKER)

THE DOORKNOB now glows. I've cleaned the paint spots and spatters off its surface and dug the paint and grime out of its ornate grooves at last, after being bothered by it for several months; it took a pointed tool and emery cloth, to begin with, and then steel wool and Brasso. Now, with the door swung in against the left end of this table, as I like it, walling me in somewhat on the one open side, the knob shines above the edge of my vision like a miniature burnished sun. First, the spattered radiator in the corner — spattered in the way that fixtures and hardware in a ramshackle, citified (this is Chicago), wood-frame apartment house get spattered with the near-yearly hasty paintings — wasn't to be borne anymore, so I offered my daughter, who's eight, two dollars to repaint it, and since the day she finished, stepping back in the smock she wears when she paints at her easel (or was it one of my work shirts?), the haze of the multicolored knob has hovered on and off to my left as if in reproach. That was April, and now cold is rising in the night air again: fall.

I'm transcribing a work that at times I believe will be an indisputable proof of the existence of God, at least for me. I say "transcribing," pulling down the word with the closest bearing on this into the slot, because I'm arranging and recopying notes and notebooks and files of pages and scenes I've got down over a period of thirteen years, attempting to deal in a literal way with exact events from my past, and I find now that I've had different opinions or interpretations of their meaning during different recastings of them that I'd like to get rid of, leaving the events, which were almost wholly not of my making, as free of any subjective coloring as on the days they brought me down. This relief from that might be, as I see it, then, a stock-taking interim.

Lightning has struck here twice. Each time, it's knocked out the power lines to our house. Our kitchen is on the ground floor, at the back of the house, facing east, and a recently installed window above the sink looks out on our small fenced-in yard to the black-topped parking lot for our building; directly across this small lot is a triple garage, of rock-faced cement block, once a carriage house, or a small barn, perhaps (there's a big central gable with a door that opens on a mow), since this was a rural area not so many years ago — anyway, a perfect cupped reflector, all complete, to amplify the effects of such a blast. The power lines swag past the garage and across the alley up to transformers on a pole.

Even before the first bolt hit, I'd been sensitized; I'd gone to the Driver's Services Department to renew my many-months-expired license, and had passed the written exam and was on the last of the mechanical tests, gazing into one of those machines where miniature road signs and rows of letters are cranked up for you to read, when its interior went black and my knees gave with the pressure of an impact that seemed to bring in the glass wall behind. The lights were out. Most of the state employees, perhaps war veterans, were stoical but wore looks of being at the ready, and the applicants were scrambling around to hide behind counters or find a way out.

A maintenance man in gray twills came running in and cried, "That big baby damn near took my head off! I just stepped out when he hit and he got that pole right outside the door there! You seek them sparks come down? They just missed!"

Later, I was at the table facing the kitchen window, shakily guilty about not being at the work I'd set for myself that day — the tightly bunched kind of guilt, as of a hangover (indeed, I was probably trying to quit drinking, again, with every day a hangover of sorts) — reading a piece in a magazine whose glossy pages pooled white headaches of light, about guerrilla warfare in Palestine, including accounts of bystanders being injured by bombs, which sharpened the guilt in bright obliquenesses I didn't wish to examine, when the first bolt hit.

I was underneath the table, and the impact of the report going back at the sky, a force I felt would pull me out the window, before I consciously heard it. Reflex of expecting the worst. The lights were out, and I could hear fizzing and a sound like a whip being cracked out by the barn-garage. The transformers were smoldering, and men arrived in slickers, in the rain that the lightning had released, to fix the lines.

It was a matter of months before the next one struck, tearing off the upper limbs of our oak and knocking the lines out into the street, which the police had to cordon off until the men in slickers again arrived, and a week or two later there was a cartoon in that same magazine which pictured a pair of angels on a cloud, looking over its edge, one of them with a bunch of jagged cartoon thunderbolts under an arm, and had a caption that went something like "Get him again!"

In the space between then and the present, my wife has given birth to a son, our first, here in this house, in the ground-floor apartment where we mostly live (when, before, I said "our house," I meant that we rent the entire ground floor and three rooms upstairs, and have been given by our absentee landlord a shoplike room in the basement, in acknowledgment of the maintenance and repairs that I do; sometime I hope to be able to talk about the other two tenants), and he's already rising from that indrawn center of internal listening — his eyes an unplumbable cobalt blue — that is every infant's retreat, on and off, until about three months, from the depths of which those around must seem incarnate aspects of gratification that he's at last getting under control, so that he's more free, finally, to be his own self. He's beginning to grasp and grab at objects held up; he's three and a half months.

Unplumbable cobalt blue. Which is their essential impact, as if opening onto quirky, inky regions of the brain, back to its primitive origins, the moment of being called into matter, a place too appalling to retreat to once common sense has invaded the breathing body around (mostly through its contact with our encircling hands), but for him, for now, basking easily within that state, at peace with his source, the only natural place to look up out at his frightened elders from.

This evening, I did "Rock-a-bye-baby" with him for the first time, and, pretending to drop him in a shaky way, brought out his laugh — three or four hearty, open-throated bleats that always seem to take him by surprise, with a gasping intake, at the end, of absolute delight.

He first laughed that way when I threw him to the ceiling at about two months — a daily game until my wife walked in on us and cried out in alarm. After that, he was dubious, and clasped his hands as if in prayer as he went up, not daring to look down on me in exhilaration as he once had, and one time started to cry. The end of that.

The next big bursts of laughter came in the bathroom, where all four of us got wedged once (a room, not counting the inset for the tub, that's three feet wide where fixtures don't protrude, and whose shredding ceiling I have yet to fix), as such things happen in a house with an infant, and especially one who's been waited and prayed for, at large. I was running a tub for his bath and my wife held him up to the medicine-chest mirror, drawing my daughter and me around, our heads close together; he wobbled his own from side to side, realizing he could see us on either hand, and then looked straight into the mirror, where our faces also were, looking out, and then our daughter, who was so far forward that the top of her head was just beneath his feet, lunged farther in and said *"Boo!"*

His response, several ringing tones from his belly, with that gasp at the end, was electric. I wouldn't have thought that a child of mine could laugh with such seizures of freedom if our daughter didn't. And then, immediately serious, he was staring into the mirror again, and then again she did it, with the same response. We were at this until I felt he was tired of it, as I was, and couldn't take any more; it was time to stop, I said.

He's never cried very much, but he has a vociferous cry that lets you know it's time he was attended to, and he's fed on demand, no matter the inconvenience of place or mood or hour, at breasts no longer so accessible to me (a matter that even Frued, rooter among sexual arcana, seems reluctant to bring up).

The expression on his face is dependent upon the position he's in — lying, propped, sitting, resting over a shoulder — and in each position is an entirely different one, perhaps because of his face's fleshy mobility (though his lip and cheek muscles are strong), which widening awareness and the encounter with making choices will temper and change. But it might also have to do with the rearrangements (in different bodily positions) of his delicate but crowded internal organs and their interconnected systems of exchange — a correlative of this family that he's held within and of how one or another of us expresses at different times the tensions and the value of his presence among us.

His babbling is taking on more of the consonants, and he's trying harder to reproduce at least shades of what I say, watching my eyes and mouth with an open, sombre look as I talk, and then leaping in with a sudden smile, curling his upper lip as he goes on at length, still observing out of his own pleasure, but now with a look to determine how much pleasure he might be giving me. Though this isn't entirely so recent and has been going on, in shorter spells without so many convolutions, from the time he was six weeks, when, usually just before dinner, I'd get drawn down in front of where he was lying, or sitting, on one of those chairs that enable an infant to sit, and have what I called "one of our talks," the sight of which caused our daughter to shriek with embarrassed hilarity; she's at that age, talking and laughing with her whole body, as if to discover, at the least, the limits of its effects.

She's again in a phase of wearing my wife's and my clothes, which comes in regular cycles, at crises in her development, as though, while in them, she has to put on parts of us in appropriate ways to help her through the time to her next plateau. Until, eventually, we'll be abandoned in the way that the clothes are — seldom picked up, left lying where they've been discarded — or so I think when I'm able to hold down my anger at this habit of hers, and realize that the day indeed will come when she'll be gone.

For the first month after he was born, she'd slump in a chair in a sulk if she couldn't change his diaper to begin her day (her waking for her long ride to school generally coinciding with his, at six), and had to be allotted a certain amount of time besides that with him, alone, to hold him and talk. She's closer to his state than we are, of course, and the only jealousy I've been able to detect, if it is that, is a certain careful, detached, and wholly silent observing of him at times, as though each were in an isolated room, and especially after school; and lately she's said, and not wistfully, either, "I wish I could be his age again, Mom."

"Whatever for?"

"It's so much fun. There's nothing to do!"

My wife reached up with one large-boned hand to her own yellow-brown hair and caught it in a tail behind, in a way that glances against me as especially Scandinavian, and then threw it over her back as she laughed with the freedom our children have. She's the one whose feet are mostly down firm from these clouds I weave.

She drives our daughter to the early pickup for school, picks her

up again at night, cooks so many of the meals there's no need to
mention the few times I stir up some eggs, or whatever, and no
longer has help in the house, as she did last year; she handles our
accounts, shops, generally sees to taking care of the car, hauls
home jugs of water from a well in a city park, so we can drink and
cook from an untainted source, does our laundry and the diapers,
and hangs them out, sometimes in frosty weather, on the lines I've
strung across our back yard like a large antenna, but of rope.
There's no use attracting trouble that appears attracted to you.

I can afford to read when I should be working to collate these
pages from those thirteen years to advance my proof, I was wise
enough to say aloud once, but we can't afford a clothes dryer. The
excuse is energy, I said, in these days when everybody seems to be
cutting down, and she said you sound like President Carter. She
also keeps up on politics, does some of our correspondence and
the correspondence for our church, and on the nights when we
can persuade our pastor to stay after a Bible lesson, she sweeps
placemats and plates and silverware and a couple of the pieces of
pottery and silver that she's been able to preserve through our
many moves (six geographical states within our daughter's first
seven years) down on the shining grain of the oak table I've refin-
ished, and a common meal takes on the contours, within candle-
light, of a tasteful, Old World fête.

But I was talking about my daughter's jealousy, or lack of it, and
trying to avoid *this:* just recently, coming from her morning bath
before her terribly early-hour departure for school, she found me,
usually alseep then, in my bathrobe, sprawled across her bed with
him, the baby, the newly loved one — what thoughtlessness! or
worse — and there was a pained and ferocious evasiveness in her
look that reminded me of the boys next door.

•

So here now I write this with night on and all of them asleep
below. "The boys" was our usual, all-inclusive name for them,
these neighbors, three brothers ranging in age from about twelve
to eight, who had their hair clipped close to their skulls in burr
cuts, as we used to call them, an anomaly from the fifties here at
the seventies' end. They threw eggs and tomatoes at our windows
and across the windshields of cars in the parking lot (with a vehemence that remains so present it seems they're still at it), threw
clods of dirt and rocks at our daughter and other neighborhood

LARRY WOIWODE   323

children, broke windows in our basement and their own garage,
set fire to ants on the outside of their house with lighter fluid, set
a wall of their garage on fire, tore down part of the rococo stone-
work of the Italian neighbor across the alley, and beat on one
another with a round-the-clock vehemence that sometimes awakened us at 2 A.M. (their bedroom window was exactly across from
ours, ten feet away, and all three slept in the same room), that
drew blood and knocked the youngest one out, and that for a
while kept me in a kind of constant fear for their lives, and, in a
way, for mine and my family's too. The unendingness of violence.

Their house is a rickety one-story affair, with a room and then
another and then a closed-in porch scabbed on to its back at different transitional stages, each a bit more temporary than the one
before, at least in looks, and all covered with that composition
sheeting that simulates brick, but is gray-black. The tail end of it
nearly rubbed the branches of the oak in our yard. It was owned,
as it turned out, by the casket-vault company across the street that
the boys' father works for; this was once the far edge of the city,
the last stop of the trolley-car line, and cemeteries spread out in
silence from us for blocks and blocks.

This father was a huge, unsmiling man, with a woman's wide
hips and a truculent loser's look in his unsteady eyes, and an air of
gloom that seemed to settle somehow around his G.I. flattop, so
that I wanted to ask him how Korea was: an impulse from the
same source that causes me to wonder, whenever I walk the street,
how many of these man I'm passing — when you consider the First
and Second World Wars, Korea, Vietnam, and other holding and
"police" actions — have been trained to kill.

He worked outside nearly every night, a can of beer close at
hand, polishing again his brand-new van with bluely translucent
windows, or adding a frill to it, or, with barking commands at the
boys, wielding a variety of implements in the family's endless ef-
forts to keep the lawn around their fraily deteriorating house in
the meticulous condition of golf green.

When he was confronted with something his sons had done, or
might have had a hand in, he'd say, "Ah, come on, now, you got
the wrong guy," with a measuring look off over your shoulder,
and turn away. He didn't beat them, as I first thought, hearing the
noise, but his wife, who was home all day, did, or tried to, and she
also screamed. Seen through their side windows, most of which

matched one or another of ours, she was magnificently overweight, usually treading around in a shaking bathrobe of an anonymous color, and I never noticed her out of the house more than once, and then at night, as though she went only by stealth.

You stop listening closely and then you stop listening at all, unless you're forced to, in order to live. Or so you say to yourself in the city; there seem enough troubles in your own attempts to cope with existence hour by hour. We seemed a cove facing away from the sea of chaos battering us at that side. We became close as a family in ways we'd never been before. We continued to study with the pastor, a former missionary to Ethiopia, who claims that Chicago is harder to crack than darkest Africa (always with a look at me, I feel), and attended a Reformed and Presbyterian chapel that he preached at; and with his firm grasp of the Bible informing my shaky one, and the birth of our son, and my work on the transcription continuing in force (every incident, once down clean, clustering and accreting around other ones that became increasingly linked and rooted as Scripture was revealed to me), my election and calling became sure.

We made public profession of our faith in Christ, were received into the pastor's church, and had our son baptized the same day.

We prayed for the boys, and their family in general, and then began to ignore them more and more, not relishing any further confrontations, and suddenly the three of them became friendly; they talked to our daughter now and then across the fence in a way that made me bristle at their youthful innuendos, and would come up to me and say hello with such an open, searching look — spanning that generational superiority I often find myself caught in, even with my daughter — that I'd stop in my tracks and stand perplexed, considering what I could say.

We tried to be more "Christianly neighborly," as I put it, and took them cake and ice cream on our daughter's birthday, tried to talk with them when they came up as they did, retrieved for them the balls and toys of theirs that ended up in our yard, and I tried not to imagine what mischief they'd been up to when I saw them come tearing, breathless, from the alley up into their back porch, or when I saw the police, as I once did, at their front door.

Shortly after this, our phone rang one night at 1 A.M.

"Is this the guy next door?" It was a breathless, girlish, somehow teasing voice, perhaps involved in a prank, I thought, as I tried to place it.

"You there?"

"Yes, I — Who — ?"

"Did you hear that window go?"

"Which window? Where?"

"Between our houses here."

"Who is this?"

"Your neighbor."

"Across the street?" There was a woman I'd talked with there about her cat.

"No, no. Right next door here." She gave the address, not her name, but I couldn't quite believe her, or connect this voice to the massive, moving presence that filled our window frames.

"You didn't hear it go?"

"I'm not sure I — "

"It's probably one of those kids in your house there."

"Not mine."

"No, no. Those that've been throwing crap on the windows and busting stuff in the neighborhood up." Did she laugh? Gasp? "I hear them down in that basement of yours a lot. A couple weeks ago, they were making such a racket down there at one in the morning I had to scream my lungs out at them out the window to get them to shut up, the creeps. The light's on down there now. Will you go see what they're up to?"

I was about to say that there were three tenants here but only two children, ours, and one an infant, and that the noise she'd shouted about that night was me down in the basement, in the workshop I've set up there, sanding a tabletop. Which I'd meant to apologize about at the time, and now, feeling the heat of a blush, prepared to, but then heard incoherent sounds, as if the call had become a prank again, or she was noisily crying.

"My husband can't sleep with all this noise? This racket going on! He works odd shifts and has to sleep when he can! You didn't hear a window crash?"

"I haven't heard a thing and I've been sitting right here." At the table; reading again.

"It sounded like it fell from high up. It woke me up. I'm alone."

"Maybe it was from across the street." There's a three-story glass-walled apartment building there.

"Will you go check, please. Check between the buildings here. I'm awful afraid. I can't sleep. And then check and see what those kids are up to down in that basement of yours. The light's still on."

She hung up.

I took a flashlight and went outside, shining it along both houses, and saw that the only broken window was the one to our furnace room, which the boys had broken out some time before and I'd put off replacing until the winter, when it would be needed, and less likely to be broken again, and then, beyond some shrubs, the glowing gold square, greasily dim in the flashlight beam, of the window to the part of the basement where I usually work.

I must have absent-mindedly left the light on. I sensed more than saw the gray shape of her move backward into darkness from the window behind me and felt physically silenced with the strangeness of this night, and the implications of it, closing around my guilt.

I went into the basement and turned off the light.

Anyone with the least bit of good sense, and especially one who'd presume to have the crushing sort of prescience that's permitted me to undertake the grandiose project I'm now working on, not to mention similar troubles I myself have had, would recognize that something other than confusion or simple night anxiety was up, and get at what it was.

I went to bed feeling drugged.

•

Her husband left soon after that, or had left by then, and a week or two later one of the boys, the middle one, was at our door; I couldn't remember any of them ringing our bell, and was taken aback to see him standing in our porch. "I'm David," he said. "From next door."

"Sure."

"Mom wants to know if you'll come help move this refrigerator from down our basement back upstairs. She'll pay you. She's got her own account now. See, our dad left and is getting a divorce, so all our things is being dispossessed. Except this refrigerator is paid for."

"Yeah, and it works just as good as a new one," another voice said, and I looked around and saw the oldest at the bottom of the steps to the outside door.

Another neighbor was already waiting there — one I'd noticed at times across the alley, with the build and comportment of a city policeman, smiling under his mustache. He pulled open the rickety side door. "You know Bob?" he asked.

"No."

"I've known him and Betty here for twelve years. I guess he's finally had it with her."

We started down to the basement to her fluttery cries above of paying us, down a crook in the stairs, through a hanging curtain, into what appeared to be the business end of a demolished bowling alley, possibly because the ceiling was so low, and I'd worked in one in another city when I was the age of the boys. There were benches and boxes of tools and parts and paint cans, plus piles of wood like shattered pins, lying and sitting around in a way that was like the back of one of the worst alleys I'd worked, where children and lofters were sent, but all in a dimness that seemed to call down damp, and without the shining, lighted lanes opening out onto the bowler's side of the world. It was the kind of clutter you don't want to observe too closely, for fear of becoming involved in it in a way that might carry over into your own life — that threatening and dense to my self-regarding eye.

One of the boys leaped up on the top of a rusting old refrigerator, scrambling below the web-woven joists close above, and, lying there on his stomach, reached down inside the refrigerator's swung-open door and pulled down the door of its freezing compartment.

"See, we defrosted it all," he said. "So it won't be so hard to carry up. We used to keep all our storage stuff in here. Well, mostly ice cream."

"Yeah, till you put that damn dead mouse in there," another said.

"He was live when I put him in!"

The other fellow was staring at a pile of dismantled bicycles. "Did your dad ever get any of these fixed?" he asked.

"Just that one we got upstairs."

"Yeah, but that one ran before."

The man stood for a while and then shook his head.

It took the two of us, with help from all of the boys, and a piece of pipe as a pry, about twenty minutes to get the refrigerator up the switchback stairs. She would call down encouragement, or cry "He's left me!" and cover her face with a heaving sound, and when we got it into the kitchen where she wanted it, beside a tall tin cupboard like one we once had, but with the door torn off, she said she'd give us checks because he'd taken all her cash. We kept backing away and insisting no, and in the movement, the floor

creaking under us, I got a glimpse into the boys' bedroom and saw
that the blue curtains that faced us, printed with Snow White and
the Seven Dwarfs, were tattered and discolored, trailing whitish
threads along their frayed bottoms. A tangle of beds and covers I
didn't care to take in.

And then she ran shaking into the living room and came out
with a hand-carved leather purse and tried to give us that. Finally,
the other man took it, for his wife, he said, and as we stepped out,
my sweat lifting away in the bright air, a young woman in her suit
as blond and impeccable as her hairdo came up: a social worker,
he said, though in the afternoon light, after that, she seemed an
angel.

"Am I too late?" she asked, looking dazed and troubled in the
brightness that affected even her, it seemed, as if she expected the
worst, and the policeman neighbor crushed the purse up under
one arm. "No," he said. "Betty's still there."

A few nights later, her husband came home to visit, to settle
some matters, it was said, urged by the social worker and also the
police (or so we heard), whom she was calling nearly every night,
and while he was there she shoved her hands through a window,
or so we heard, and raked them downward, trying to cut her
wrists, fulfilling her plea and warning to me.

•

They're gone now. When she was taken to the hospital, her husband came back to live with the boys. It seemed a more settled
relationship than before, though his voice would sometimes come
thundering down, and they all carried articles and boxes and cans
and boards back to the alley by the garbage cans nearly every
evening: cleaning house, we thought. And then one day a circular
was stuffed into our mailbox about a village meeting in which a
vote would be held to decide if the neighborhood would allow the
casket-vault company to demolish the house and put in a parking
lot. I couldn't attend the meeting, because of my work, but my wife
did, and said that everybody was so vocal for the change, on account of the boys, and the blight of the house, as it was put, that
she was embarrassed she'd been worried about a parking lot. Our
son.

I tried to visit the woman in the hospital where she was taken,
near this neighborhood, but was told I'd need special permission
from her psychiatrist to see her, and couldn't, in my imaginary

conversation with him, quite come up with the credentials for that. So I went to the boys instead, and gave them Mrs. E. Norton's paper edition of the Gospel of John I'd intended to give her, saying to them that I'd been in the same place once, and this had helped me out; and they said, Yes, they'd give it to her when they saw her, thanks, making me draw back in — unable to mention, as I'd intended, the gift of Christ and the grace of God — at the unplumbable look like my son's in them all, but not his basking one.

•

The day before yesterday, I lay wide awake, with the bed shaking under me as one had shaken and given way only once before, during a California earthquake, and then a great crash of noise resounded off the house. A low-throated motor, with a diesel's flat assurance, throttled up, backing away from our place, it seemed, and with the clanking sound that came of metal treads, I knew the bulldozer had arrived.

I looked through the curtains and saw our daughter at the back of the yard with her box camera, taking pictures before her trip to school. I needn't have worried about how all of this would interfere with my work or our lives here; the house was leveled to the ground, and the scraps and timbers of it — along with that old refrigerator, which went tumbling back down into darkness — were mashed into the basement, and packed there, in less than an hour.

Some hauling was done by dump trucks yesterday, a bit more was done today, and now the lot, skinned of sod from sidewalk to alley, is covered with six inches (I almost wrote "feet") of packed, crushed rock. Only a great scattering of glass is left from it, lying over our strip of lawn — not from the window she broke, but where the wall of the boys' bedroom collapsed.

The chill of late night is on now, a cold that comes from both above and below this season, not just the ground, as in the spring, and since the last cold spell here came and then left, our thermostat has never been set back up, as it needs to be, at this hour — discounting, even, the feel of emptiness where their house once was, and that white array of packed, crushed rock at my back. But the thermostat is on the ground floor, where we mostly live, as I've said, and once I sit down here I feel I must not move until a certain amount of work is fixed in my files for good.

The doorknob above intrudes, pulses, and glows in its distract-
ing watch, mirroring me, I see, as I look up — a meditative king-
bolt: Which side do you open a door from if the door's never really
closed, but more a wall that holds you more inward? From spring
to fall. Six months.

The knob is clean even of any fingerprints.

Biographical Notes

Other Distinguished
*   Short Stories of 1980*

Editorial Addresses

Biographical Notes

WALTER ABISH received the PEN/Faulkner Award for his novel *How German Is It* (1980). He is the author of four additional books, and has published extensively in literary magazines including *The Paris Review, TriQuarterly,* and *Transatlantic.* At present he is completing a self-portrait. In 1977 he received an Ingram Merrill Fellowship, in 1979 a National Endowment for the Arts, and in 1981 he was awarded a CAPS grant and a Guggenheim. He teaches writing at Columbia University and lives in New York City.

MAX APPLE, who was born in Michigan, has lived in Texas for the last eight years. Mr. Apple is the editor of *Southwest Fiction* (1981) and the author of *The Oranging of America and Other Stories* (1976), *Zip* (a novel, 1978), the screenplay "Smokey Bites the Dust," and numerous short stories published in many literary magazines.

ANN BEATTIE is the author of two collections of short stories — *Distortions* and *Secrets and Surprises.* Her first novel, *Chilly Scenes of Winter,* has been made into a motion picture, *Head Over Heels;* her second, *Falling In Place,* was published in 1980. Miss Beattie is a recent recipient of an award in literature from the American Academy and Institute of Arts and Letters.

ROBERT COOVER is the author of the novels *The Origin of the Brunists* (1966), *The Universal Baseball Association, J. Henry Waugh, Prop.* (1968), *The Public Burning* (1977), and *A Political Fable* (1980), and of collections of both short fiction and plays. He has published, but not collected, numerous other stories, poems, radio plays, film scripts, and essays. Mr. Coover was born in Iowa in 1932 and is at present teaching a writing course on "narrative movement and the camera eye" at Brown University.

VINCENT G. DETHIER was born in Boston and educated at Harvard University. He has taught biology at Johns Hopkins University, the University of Pennsylvania, and Princeton University. He has published twelve books including a novel, children's stories, popular natural history, and technical works. His book *Fairweather Duck* was a Literary Guild alternate choice. His short stories have appeared in *The Texas Quarterly, Era, Kenyon Review,* and *Catholic World.* The story "Haboob" was anthologized in *Gallery of Modern Fiction: Stories from the Kenyon Review 1966.* He presently lives in Amherst, Massachusetts.

ANDRE DUBUS was born in 1936 in Lake Charles, Louisiana, and now teaches at Bradford College in Massachusetts. He has published a novel, *The Lieutenant,* and three collections of stories: *Separate Flights, Adultery and Other Choices,* and *Finding a Girl in America.*

MAVIS GALLANT is the author of five collections of short stories and two novels. Most of her short fiction has appeared in *The New Yorker,* to which she has been a contributor since 1950. Her most recent book, *From the Fifteenth District,* a collection of short fiction, was published in 1979. Mrs. Gallant is at present completing a long study of the Dreyfus Affair. She lives and writes in Paris.

ELIZABETH HARDWICK's most recent books are *Seduction and Betrayal,* essays on women in literature, and *Sleepless Nights,* a novel. Miss Hardwick was born and educated in Kentucky. She has lived in New York City for many years and is a contributor of essays and fiction to many magazines, most notably *The New York Review of Books,* of which she was one of the founders. One of Miss Hardwick's first published stories appeared in *The Best American Short Stories 1947.*

BOBBIE ANN MASON grew up in Mayfield, Kentucky. After graduating from the University of Kentucky, she wrote for a fan magazine in New York, then received a Ph.D. in English from the

University of Connecticut. *Nabokov's Garden,* her doctoral disser-
tation on Vladimir Nabokov's novel *Ada,* was published by Ardis
in 1974. She wrote *The Girl Sleuth,* a critical survey of children's
mystery series books, for the Feminist Press in 1976. Her fiction
has appeared in *The New Yorker* and *The Atlantic Monthly,* and she
is a frequent contributor to "Talk of the Town" in *The New
Yorker.* She is currently working on a collection of short stories
for Harper & Row.

JOSEPH MCELROY is the author of five novels — *A Smuggler's Bible,
Hind's Kidnap, Ancient History, Lookout Cartridge,* and *Plus.* He is
currently at work on a new novel, which will be published in
1982.

ELIZABETH MCGRATH was born and lives in St. John's, Newfoundland. She was educated at Presentation, Mercy, and Sacred
Heart convents, Memorial University, the Sorbonne, and
Somerville College, Oxford. "Fogbound in Avalon" is her first
published story.

AMELIA MOSELEY was raised in Pasadena, California, and now lives
in the San Francisco Bay Area. "The Mountains Where Cithaeron Is" is her first short story. She is at present editing an anthology of Bay Area women writers to be published in the fall of
1981, and is finishing her first novel, *Amongst the Trees a Solitary
Baboon.*

ALICE MUNRO was born in Wingham, Ontario, and attended the
University of Western Ontario. She received the Governor General's Award not only for her most recent book, *The Beggar Maid*
(published in Canada under the title *Who Do You Think You Are*),
but also for her first book, *Dance of the Happy Shades.* She is also
the author of *Something I've Been Meaning to Tell You* and *Lives of
Girls and Women.* Her stories have appeared in *The New Yorker,
Redbook, Grand Street,* and other magazines. Miss Munro has
three daughters. She and her husband live in Clinton, Ontario.

JOYCE CAROL OATES has published, since 1958, approximately 300
short stories. She is, in addition, the author of numerous novels
and collections of stories, criticism, and poetry. Her most recently published books are *Contraries* (a collection of critical essays) and *Three Plays.* She is currently at work on a new collection

of stories set mainly in eastern Europe, and her newest novel, *Angel of Light,* is to be published this fall.

CYNTHIA OZICK is the author of *Trust,* a novel, *The Pagan Rabbi and Other Stories,* and *Bloodshed and Three Novellas.* She has also published essays, poetry, criticism, reviews, and translations in numerous periodicals and anthologies, and has been the recipient of several prizes, including two O. Henry First Prizes in Fiction and an Award for Literature of the American Academy of Arts and Letters.

LOUIS D. RUBIN, JR., grew up in Charleston, South Carolina, and now lives in Chapel Hill, North Carolina, where he is University Distinguished Professor of English at the University of North Carolina. A new novel, *Surfaces of a Diamond,* will appear in the fall of 1981.

RICHARD STERN'S most recent novel is *Natural Shocks* (1978), and his most recent collection of stories is *Packages* (Coward, McCann & Geohegan, 1980). His 1962 novel, *In Any Case,* has been reissued under the title *The Chaleur Network* (1981), and his second "orderly miscellany," *The Invention of the Real,* is to be published in 1982.

ELIZABETH TALLENT was born in Washington, D.C., in 1954. She now lives in Eaton, Colorado. Other of her stories have appeared in *The New Yorker,* and her work has also been included in the *Pushcart Prize* of 1981.

JOHN UPDIKE was born in Shillington, Pennsylvania, in 1932. After attending the public schools of that town, he attended Harvard College and the Ruskin School of Drawing and Fine Art in Oxford, England. After two years on the staff of *The New Yorker* magazine, he moved to Massachusetts, where he has resided ever since. He is the author of some twenty-three books, including ten novels and six collections of short stories. This is his sixth appearance in *The Best American Short Stories.*

LARRY WOIWODE was born in North Dakota in 1941 and presently lives in the southwestern corner of that state with his wife and three children. He has been a contributor to *The New Yorker* since 1964. His prose and poetry have also appeared in *The Atlantic Monthly, Esquire, Harper's, Partisan Review,* and others. His first novel, *What I'm Going To Do, I Think,* was the recipient of the William Faulkner Foundation Award for 1969, and *Beyond the Bedroom Wall* was a nominee for the National Book Award and the Critics Circle Book Award.

100 Other Distinguished Short Stories of the Year 1980

SELECTED BY SHANNON RAVENEL

ARDIZZONE, TONY
Ritual. Chariton Review, Spring.
ATTHOWE, JEAN FAUSETT
A Measure of Spindrift. San Jose
Studies, May.

BARTHELME, DONALD
Heroes. The New Yorker, May 5.
BAUMBACH, JONATHAN
The Conference. The North Ameri-
can Review, March.
A Story for All Seasons. Plum, No. 3
BLAISE, CLARK
Man and His World. Fiction Interna-
tional.
BONNIE, FRED
Widening the Road. Confrontation,
No. 19.
BOSWORTH, DAVID
Anti-War Story. The Agni Review,
No. 13.
BOWLES, PAUL
The Dismissal. Antaeus, Spring.
The Husband. Michigan Quarterly
Review, Winter.
BRUBAKER, BILL
The Country Singer. Cimarron Re-
view, April.
BYRD, LEE MERRILL
Sour Cream. Quarry West, No. 12.

CALLAGHAN, BARRY
The Black Queen. The Ontario Re-
view, Fall-Winter.
CAMOIN, FRANÇOIS
Diehl: The Wandering Years. West-
ern Humanities Review, Winter.
CLEARMAN, MARY
Forby and the Mayan Maidens. The
Georgia Review, Spring.
COOK, MARSHALL
Le Gran Naranja. Ascent, Vol. 6,
No. 1.
COSTELLO, MARK
The Soybean Capital of the World.
Story Quarterly, 10, 11.
COVINO, MICHAEL
The Lament of the Salesman. Caro-
lina Quarterly, Fall.
COX, ELIZABETH
Land of Goshen. Fiction Interna-
tional.
CRONE, MOIRA
The Kudzu. The Ohio Review,
No. 24.
CURLEY, DANIEL
Reflections in the Ice. Story Quar-
terly, 10.

DAVIS, OLIVIA
The Ingrate. Western Humanities
Review, Summer.

Running Away to Warsaw. The Virginia Quarterly Review, Autumn.

DEW, ROBB FORMAN
A Satisfactory Life. The Virginia Quarterly Review, Spring.

ENGBERG, SUSAN
Trio. The Massachusetts Review, Winter.

GARDINER, JOHN ROLFE
Hunter Out of Season. The New Yorker, July 7.

GOLD, HERBERT
Stages. TriQuarterly, 47, Winter.

GOLDSTEIN, SANFORD
Japanese Rotarian. Arizona Quarterly, Summer.

GOULD, TERRY
The Payment of Little Debts. The Malahat Review, No. 56, October.

GRAVES, WALLACE
Bread and the American Dream. Western Humanities Review, Summer.

GRIMSLEY, JAMES
City and Park. Carolina Quarterly, Fall.

GROSS, CHARLES M.
Golda Rifka. The Agni Review, 12.

HALLEY, ANNE
A Berlin Story. Fiction, Vol. 6, No. 2.
A Modern Instance: Molly and Anita. New England Review, Vol. 3, No. 1.

HEINEMANN, LARRY
Good Morning to You, Lieutenant. Harper's, June.

HELPRIN, MARK
A Vermont Tale. The New Yorker, March 10.
Ellis Island. The New Yorker, December 8.

HENDERSON, ROBERT
Mizpah. The New Yorker, June 23.

HUDDLE, DAVID
The Wedding Storm. Prairie Schooner, Winter.

JACOBSEN, JOSEPHINE
The Squirrels of Summer. New Letters, Fall.

KAPLAN, JAMES
Climbing. Esquire, February.

KELLYTHORNE, WALT
The Last Long Summer. Grain, Vol. 8, No. 1.

KINGERY, MARGARET
In Dulci Jubilo. Prairie Schooner, Fall.

KITTREDGE, WILLIAM
Performing Arts. TriQuarterly, 48, Spring.

KLOEFKORN, WILLIAM
Sweetness and Light. The South Dakota Review, Summer.

L'HEUREUX, JOHN
Witness. The Atlantic Monthly, April.

LOESER, KATINKA
Company Manners. The New Yorker, October 13.
Taking Care. The New Yorker, March 24.

MADDEN, DAVID
Putting an Act Together. The Southern Review, Winter.

MAKUCK, PETER
Breaking and Entering. Sewanee Review, Summer.

MARTONE, MICHAEL
Nein. Northwest Review, Vol. 18, No. 3.

MASON, BOBBIE ANN
Offerings. The New Yorker, February 18.

MASON, HERBERT
Gilpin's Point. Sewanee Review, Fall.

MATTHEWS, JACK
Trophy for an Earnest Boy. Western Humanities Review, Autumn.

McGUANE, THOMAS
Nobody's Angel, TriQuarterly, 48, Spring.

MEHTA, JAYA
A Good Wife. Bennington Reivew, April.

MITTER, SARA S.
In the Land of the Gold Rush. Redbook, April.

MONK, ELIZABETH GRAHAM
Is Eating Necessary? The Virginia Quarterly Review, Winter.

MOORE, HALL
Where Is the Ladybug Going? Western Humanities Review, Autumn.

MURRAY, WENDELL CARL
Lela. Yale Review, Spring.

MYERS, LES
Potpourri. Ascent, Vol. 5, No. 3.

NICHOLS, DON
My Grandmother's Rhetorician. The Yale Review, Autumn.

OATES, JOYCE CAROL
Mutilated Woman. Michigan Quarterly Review, Spring.

OHLE, DAVID
The Flocculus. The Paris Review, No. 77, Winter-Spring.

O'NEILL, KEVIN
Plymouth: 1939. The New Yorker, October 27.

PESETSKY, BETTE
Three Girls on Holiday: A Play. Canto, May.

PETESCH, NATALIE L. M.
A Journal for the New Year (Resolutions, Memos, Whimsies). The Georgia Review, Summer.

PETT, STEPHEN
The Face of the Waters. Quarterly West, No. 11.

PFEIL, FRED
The Idiocy of Rural Life. The Georgia Review, Spring.

PODHORETZ, JOHN
The Piano Recital. Harper's, November.

RICHARD, MARK
Twenty-one Days Back. Shenandoah, 31/1.

RICHLER, MORDECAI
Seymour. Playboy, June.

ROBERTSON, MARY ELSIE
Vision. The Seattle Review, Fall.

ROCHLIN, DORIS
Duxelles. Confrontation, No. 19.

ROSS, GARY
Blueberries. Saturday Night, November.

SADOFF, IRA
Raphael's Madonnas. The Seattle Review, Fall.

SATRAN, KAREN
The Scent of Lime Trees. The New Yorker, January 21.

SAWADA, NORIKO
Papa Takes a Bride. Harper's, December.

SEGAL, LORE
Burglars in the Flesh. The New Yorker, June 16.

SELIG, ROBERT L.
Borowska and Golden. Ascent, Vol. 5, No. 2.

SMILEY, JANE
Sex. Mademoiselle, July.

SMITH, LEE
Between the Lines. Carolina Quarterly, Winter.

SVENDSEN, LINDA
Who He Slept By. The Atlantic Monthly, July.

TARGAN, BARRY
Father and I and the Movies. Ascent, Vol. 6, No. 1.

TAYLOR, L. A.
In the Dream State. Carolina Quarterly, Spring/Summer.

TEVIS, WALTER
The Apotheosis of Myra. Playboy, July.

THACKER, JULIA
In Glory Land. Antaeus, 37, Spring.
THACKERY, JOSEPH C.
A Lover. New Letters, Winter.
THOMAS, ANNABEL
The Phototropic Woman. Wind/Literary Review, Vol. 10, No. 36.
THOMAS, LISA
So Narrow the Bridge and Deep the Water. Michigan Quarterly Review, Summer.
THOMPSON, KENT
Green Things. The Tamarack Review, Spring.
THOMPSON, ROBERT
Briefing: New Clues to Saint Beatrice's Early Years. The Kenyon Review, Summer.
THRAPP, DANIEL
Bird Killers. Quarterly West, No. 10.

VANDERHAEGHE, GUY
The Watcher. Canadian Fiction Magazine, No. 34/35.

WEAVER, GORDON
Ah Art! Oh Life! Bennington Review, September.
WEBB, FRANCES
The Memoir Man. The Antioch Review, Spring.
WETHERELL, W. D.
The Watchman. The South Carolina Review, Fall.
WHITTIER, GAYLE
Lost Time Accident. The Massachusetts Review, Fall.
WOLFF, TOBIAS
The Liar. The Atlantic Monthly, February.
WOOD, ANNE HILLSMAN
Rhythms. Cimarron Review, January.

Editorial Addresses of American and Canadian Magazines Publishing Short Stories

Adena, Kentuckiana Metroversity, Garden Court, Alta Vista Road, Louisville, Kentucky 40205

Agni Review, P.O. Box 349, Cambridge, Massachusetts 02138

American Poetry Review, Temple University City Center, 1616 Walnut Street, Room 405, Philadelphia, Pennsylvania 19103

Ann Arbor Review, Washtenaw Community College, Ann Arbor, Michigan 48106

Antaeus, 1 West 30th Street, New York, New York 10001

Antioch Review, P.O. Box 148, Yellow Springs, Ohio 45387

Apalachee Quarterly, P.O. Box 20106, Tallahassee, Florida 32304

Aphra, RFD, Box 355, Springtown, Pennsylvania 18081

Ararat, 628 Second Avenue, New York, New York 10016

Arizona Quarterly, University of Arizona, Tucson, Arizona 85721

Ark River Review, English Department, Wichita State University, Wichita, Kansas 67208

Ascent, English Department, University of Illinois, Urbana, Illinois 61801

Aspen Anthology, The Aspen Leaves Literary Foundation, Box 3185, Aspen, Colorado 81611

Atlantic Monthly, 8 Arlington Street, Boston, Massachusetts 02116

Bachy, 11317 Santa Monica Boulevard, Los Angeles, California 90025

Back Bay View, 52 East Border Road, Malden, Massachusetts 02148

Ball State Forum, Ball State University, Muncie, Indiana 47306

Bennington Review, Bennington College, Bennington, Vermont 05201

Blood Root, P.O. Box 891, Grand Forks, North Dakota 58201

California Quarterly, 100 Sproul Hall, University of California, Davis, California 95616

Canadian Fiction, Box 46422, Station G, Vancouver, British Columbia V6R 4G7, Canada

Canto, Canto, Inc., 9 Bartlet Street, Andover, Massachusetts 01810

Capilano Review, Capilano College, 2055 Purcell Way, North Vancouver, British Columbia, Canada

Carleton Miscellany, Carleton College, Northfield, Minnesota 55057

Carolina Quarterly, Greenlaw Hall 066A, University of North Carolina, Chapel Hill, North Carolina 27514

Chariton Review, Division of Language & Literature, Northeast Missouri State University, Kirksville, Missouri 63501

Chelsea, P.O. Box 5880, Grand Central Station, New York, New York 10017

Chicago, 500 North Michigan Avenue, Chicago, Illinois 60611

Chicago Review, 5700 South Ingleside, Box C, University of Chicago, Chicago, Illinois 60637

Cimarron Review, 208 Life Sciences East, Oklahoma State University, Stillwater, Oklahoma 74074

Colorado Quarterly, Hellems 134, University of Colorado, Boulder, Colorado 80309

Commentary, 165 East 56th Street, New York, New York 10022

Confrontation, English Department, Brooklyn Center for Long Island University, Brooklyn, New York 11201

Cosmopolitan, 224 West 57th Street, New York, New York 10019

Creative Pittsburgh, P.O. Box 7346, Pittsburgh, Pennsylvania 15213

Cumberlands (formerly Twigs), Pikeville College Press, Pikeville College, Pikeville, New York 41501

Cutbank, Department of English, University of Montana, Bainville, Montana 59812

Dark Horse, c/o Barnes, 47A Dana Street, Cambridge, Massachusetts 02138

Denver Quarterly, University of Denver, Denver, Colorado 80210

Descant, P.O. Box 314, Station P, Toronto, Ontario M5S 2S5, Canada

descant, Department of English, Texas Christian University Station, Fort Worth, Texas 76129

Ellery Queen's Mystery Magazine, 380 Lexington Avenue, New York, New York 10017

Esquire, 2 Park Avenue, New York, New York 10016

Event, Douglas College, P.O. Box 2503, New Westminster, British Columbia V3L 5B2, Canada

Fiction, c/o Department of English, The City College of New York, New York, New York 10031

Fiction International, Department of English, Saint Lawrence University, Canton, New York 13617

Fiction-Texas, College of the Mainland, Texas City, Texas 77590

Fiddlehead, The Observatory, University of New Brunswick, Fredericton, New Brunswick E3B 5A3, Canada

Four Quarters, La Salle College, 20th and Olney Avenues, Philadelphia, Pennsylvania 19141

Georgia Review, University of Georgia, Athens, Georgia 30602

Good Housekeeping, 959 Eighth Avenue, New York, New York 10019

Grain, Box 1885, Saskatoon, Saskatchewan S7K 3S2, Canada

Great River Review, 59 Seymour Avenue, S.E., Minneapolis, Minnesota 55987

Greensboro Review, Department of English, University of North Carolina at Greensboro, Greensboro, North Carolina 27412

Harper's Magazine, 2 Park Avenue, New York, New York 10016

Hawaii Review, University of Hawaii, Department of English, 1733 Donaghho Road, Honolulu, Hawaii 96822

Helicon Nine, 6 Petticoat Lane, Kansas City, Missouri 64106

Hudson Review, 65 East 55th Street, New York, New York 10022

Indiana Writes, 110 Morgan Hall, Indiana University, Bloomington, Indiana 47401

Iowa Review, EPB 321, University of Iowa, Iowa City, Iowa 52242

Jewish Dialog, JD Publishing Company, 1498 Yonge Street, Suite 7, Toronto, Ontario M4T 1Z6, Canada

Kansas Quarterly, Department of English, Denison Hall, Kansas State University, Manhattan, Kansas 66506

Kenyon Review, Kenyon College, Gambier, Ohio 43022

Ladies' Home Journal, 641 Lexington Avenue, New York, New York 10022

Lilith, The Jewish Women's Magazine, 250 West 57th Street, New York, New York 10019

Literary Review, Fairleigh Dickinson University, Madison, New Jersey 07940

Louisville Review, University of Louisville, Louisville, Kentucky 40208

Mademoiselle, 350 Madison Avenue, New York, New York 10017

Malahat Review, University of Victoria, Box 1700, Victoria, British Columbia, Canada

Massachusetts Review, Memorial Hall, University of Massachusetts, Amherst, Massachusetts 01002

McCall's, 230 Park Avenue, New York, New York 10017

Michigan Quarterly Review, 3032 Rackham Building, University of Michigan, Ann Arbor, Michigan 48109

Midstream, 515 Park Avenue, New York, New York 10022

Mississippi Review, Department of English, Box 37, Southern Station, University of Southern Mississippi, Hattiesburg, Mississippi 39401

Missouri Review, Department of English 231 A & S, University of Missouri, Columbia, Missouri 65211

Mother Jones, 607 Market Street, San Francisco, California 94105

Ms., 370 Lexington Avenue, New York, New York 10017

Nantucket Review, P.O. Box 1234, Nantucket, Massachusetts 02554

National Jewish Monthly, 1640 Rhode Island Avenue, N.W., Washington, D.C. 20036

New England Review, Box 170, Hanover, New Hampshire 03755

New Letters, University of Missouri at Kansas City, 5346 Charlotte, Kansas City, Missouri 64110

New Mexico Humanities Review, Box A, New Mexico Tech, Socorro, New Mexico 87801

New Orleans Review, Loyola University, New Orleans, Louisiana 70118

New Renaissance, 9 Heath Road, Arlington, Massachusetts 02174

New Yorker, 25 West 43rd Street, New York, New York 10036

North American Review, University of Northern Iowa, Cedar Falls, Iowa 50613

Northwest Review, University of Oregon, Eugene, Oregon 97403

Ohio Journal, Department of English, Ohio State University, 164 West 17th Avenue, Columbus, Ohio 43210

Ohio Review, Ellis Hall, Ohio University, Athens, Ohio 45701

Old Hickory Review, P.O. Box 1178, Jackson, Tennessee 38301

Only Prose, 54 East 7th Street, New York, New York 10003

Ontario Review, 9 Honey Brook, Princeton, New Jersey 08540

Paris Review, 45–39 171 Place, Flushing, New York 11358

Partisan Review, 128 Bay State Road, Boston, Massachusetts 02215

Pequod, P.O. Box 491, Forest Knolls, California 94933

Phantasm, Heidelberg Graphic, P.O. Box 3606, Chico, California 95927

Playboy, 919 North Michigan Avenue, Chicago, Illinois 60611

Ploughshares, P.O. Box 529, Cambridge, Massachusetts 02139

Plum, 549 W. 113th Street, #1D, New York, New York 10025

Prairie Schooner, 201 Andrews Hall, University of Nebraska, Lincoln, Nebraska 68588

Present Tense, 165 East 56th Street, New York, New York 10022

Primavera, Ida Noyes Hall, University of Chicago, 1212 East 59th Street, Chicago, Illinois 60637

Prism International, University of British Columbia, Vancouver, British Columbia, Canada

Quarry West, College V, University of California, Santa Cruz, California 95060

Quarterly West, 312 Olpin Union, University of Utah, Salt Lake City, Utah 84112

Queen's Quarterly, Queens University, Kingston, Ontario, Canada

RE:AL, Stephen F. Austin State University, Nacogdoches, Texas 75962

Redbook, 230 Park Avenue, New York, New York 10017

Richmond Quarterly, P.O. Box 12263, Richmond, Virginia 23241

St. Andrews Review, St. Andrews Presbyterian College, Laurinburg, North Carolina 28352

Salmagundi Magazine, Skidmore College, Saratoga Springs, New York 12866

San Jose Studies, San Jose State University, San Jose, California 95192

Sands, 7170 Briar Cove, Dallas, Texas 75240

Sandscript, Box 333, Cummaquid, Massachusetts 02637

Saturday Night, 69 Front Street East, Toronto, Ontario M5E 1R3, Canada

Seattle Review, Padelford Hall GN-30, University of Washington, Seattle, Washington 98195

Seneca Review, Box 115, Hobart and William Smith College, Geneva, New York 14456

Seventeen, 850 Third Avenue, New York, New York 10022

Sewanee Review, University of the South, Sewanee, Tennessee 37375

Shadows, Creighton University, 2500 California Street, Omaha, Nebraska 68178

Shenandoah, Box 722, Lexington, Virginia 24450

Shout in the Street, Queen's College of the City University of New York, 63–30 Kissena Boulevard, Flushing, New York 11367

South Carolina Review, Department of English, Clemson University, Clemson, South Carolina 29631

South Dakota Review, University of South Dakota, Vermillion, South Dakota 57069

Southern Review, Drawer D, University Station, Baton Rouge, Louisiana 70893

Southwest Review, Southern Methodist University, Dallas, Texas 75275

Sou'wester, Department of English, Southern Illinois University, Edwardsville, Illinois 62026

Steelhead, Knife River Press, 2501 Branch Street, Duluth, Minnesota 55812

Story Quarterly, 820 Ridge Road, Highland Park, Illinois 60035

Sun and Moon, 433 Hartwick Road, College Park, Maryland 20740

Swift River, Box 264, Leverett, Massachusetts 01054

Tamarack Review, Box 159, Station K, Toronto, Ontario M4P 2G5, Canada

Texas Review, English Department, Sam Houston State University, Huntsville, Texas 77341

TriQuarterly, Northwestern University, 1735 Benson Avenue, Evanston, Illinois 60201

U.S. Catholic, 221 West Madison Street, Chicago, Illinois 60606

University of Windsor Review, Department of English, University of Windsor, Windsor, Ontario N9B 3P4, Canada

Vanderbilt Review, 911 West Vanderbilt Street, Stephenville, Texas 76401

Virginia Quarterly Review, 1 West Range, Charlottesville, Virginia 22903

Vision, 3000 Harry Hines Boulevard, Dallas, Texas 75201

Wascana Review, Wascana Parkway, Regina, Saskatchewan, Canada

Waves, 79 Denham Drive, Thornhill, Ontario L4J 1P2, Canada

Webster Review, Webster College, Webster Groves, Missouri 63119

West Branch, Department of English, Bucknell University, Lewisburg, Pennsylvania 17837

Western Humanities Review, University of Utah, Salt Lake City, Utah 84112

William and Mary Review, College of William and Mary, Williamsburg, Virginia 23185

Wind/Literary Review, RFD Route #1, Box 809K, Pikeville, Kentucky 41501

Wittenberg Review, Box 1, Recitation Hall, Wittenberg University, Springfield, Ohio 45501

Yale Review, 250 Church Street, 1902A Yale Station, New Haven, Connecticut 06520

Yankee, Yankee, Inc., Dublin, New Hampshire 03444